# *the* GIRL *& her* REN

NEW YORK TIMES BESTSELLING AUTHOR

# PEPPER WINTERS

# The Girl
# &
# Her Ren

by

*New York Times Bestseller*
## Pepper Winters

## The Girl & Her Ren
## Copyright © 2018 Pepper Winters
## Published by Pepper Winters

**Published:** Pepper Winters 2018 **pepperwinters@gmail.com**
**Cover Design:** Ari @ Cover it! Designs
**Editing by**: Editing-4-Indies (Jenny Sims)
**Proofreading by:** Landers Editorial Services (Tiffany Landers)

www.pepperwinters.com

# OTHER BOOKS AVAILABLE FROM PEPPER WINTERS

## Ribbon Duet
*The Boy & His Ribbon*
*The Girl & Her Ren*

## Dollar Series
*Pennies*
*Dollars*
*Hundreds*
*Thousands*
*Millions*

## Truth & Lies Duet
*Crown of Lies*
*Throne of Truth*

## Pure Corruption Duet
*Ruin & Rule*
*Sin & Suffer*

## Indebted Series
*Debt Inheritance*
*First Debt*
*Second Debt*
*Third Debt*
*Fourth Debt*
*Final Debt*
*Indebted Epilogue*

## Monsters in the Dark Trilogy
*Tears of Tess*
*Quintessentially Q*
*Twisted Together*
*Je Suis a Toi*

## Standalones
*Destroyed*
*Unseen Messages*
*Can't Touch This*

# *Prologue*

## DELLA

## 2032

*FIRST, I WANT to say thank you.*

*Thank you for falling in love with Ren just as much as me. Thank you for allowing me to share our journey. Thank you for forgiving my youth, my jealousy, my possessiveness; but most of all, thank you for understanding what our story has always been about.*

*It wasn't about two children falling for each other.*

*It wasn't about sex or hunger or selfishness or want.*

*It was about love.*

*True love.*

*Love that spans decades, infects souls, and turns you immortal because, when you love that deeply, nothing can ever die.*

*It transcends time, space, distance, universes.*

*A love like this isn't confined to pages or photos or memories—it's forever alive and wild and free.*

*Love.*

*That is what our story is about.*

*Romance comes and goes, lust flickers and smoulders, trials appear and test, life gets in the way and educates, pain can derail happiness, joy can delete sadness, togetherness is more than just a fairy-tale…it's a choice.*

*A choice to love, cherish, honour, trust, and adore.*

*A choice to be there when arguments occur, and agony arrives, and fate seems determined to rip you apart.*

*A choice to* choose *love, all the while knowing it has the power to break you.*

*A choice, dear friend, to give someone your entire heart.*

*It's not easy.*

*No one ever said it was.*

---

*Some days, you want it back, and others, you wish you had more than just one heart to give.*

*Love is the hardest thing we'll ever have to do because love, as miraculous and wonderful as it is, is also cursed and soul-breaking.*

*Because of love, life is a war of moments and time and bargaining for more of everything.*

*But in the end, love is what life is about.*

*And love is the purpose of everything.*

*So, thank you.*

*Thank you for sharing our love.*

*Thank you for living, for choosing, for being brave enough to fall.*

# *Chapter One*

## REN

## 2018

WHEN I RAN from the Mclary's, took a baby that wasn't mine, and chose to keep her against all odds, I never stopped to wonder...how.

*How* did we survive all those years?

*How* did I keep myself alive, let alone baby Della?

*How* did one choice change my entire world—not only giving me a family of my own, but teaching me, before it was too late, that not everyone was evil.

Della Mclary successfully stopped me from going down a very dark and lonely path by forcing me to know the opposite of hate. I supposed, if someone were to judge the kid I was against the man I became, they'd say she saved me.

They'd say, without her, I would be a very different person.

Probably one a lot less forgiving, understanding, and most likely violent, angry, and dangerous.

They'd be right.

Those tendencies were still there, born from being abused and unwanted, forever a part of me whether I wanted to admit it or not. But I was also so much more, and those parts, the *better* parts, were stronger.

I chose kindness over cruelty, honour over disgrace, and propriety over indecency.

And it was the last one that made me leave.

The last one causing my current state of unhappiness.

It also made all those previous wonderings of *how*, completely irrelevant. Because who cared how it happened? Only that it did, and it was the best thing that could've ever happened to me.

But now I had nothing, and I couldn't stop scratching at the scars, wondering what caused me to deserve seventeen years of heaven with a girl I'd give everything for, only to endure the worst thing I'd ever imagined by giving the greatest sacrifice I could.

*Her.*

She was my greatest sacrifice.

And I did it to protect her from so many, many things.

But the question was back. Taunting me. Tormenting me.

*How.*

How did she get into that backpack in the first place?

It was night. She was a baby. I didn't know where she slept, but surely, she had a crib with bars or a room with a door. The backpack was discarded where it always was by the door. It wasn't a plaything for a child and it wasn't sanitary for a baby.

But somehow, she'd ended up in it.

How had Della been in that bag at the exact same time I decided to run?

Was it purely coincidence? Did fate know far more than we did, understanding that Della wasn't born for the Mclary's but for *me*? For me to learn how to love. For me to have someone to hold. For me to protect and treasure and focus on rather than spiral into a place I shouldn't go?

Or...had Mrs Mclary put her there?

Had she seen my test run the night before, watched me steal the meagre rations I'd managed, and somehow put her darling daughter in the stuffy, weathered ex-army bag?

And if she did, that changed my question from how to why.

*Why* did she give up her only blood?

*Why* did she tell her husband to shoot me and specifically mention what I could have in my stolen bag as I ducked and bolted through their cornfields?

The only two answers I could come up with were:

One, she wanted me and Della dead and figured she could kill two birds with one stone, blaming me when they walked to my gunshot body and noticed the bullet that killed me also killed their daughter.

Or two, Mrs Mclary wasn't as evil or as complacent as I thought. Maybe she knew I was about to run and figured I was a better chance for Della than her husband ever was. The same husband who raped young girls when he believed his wife was upstairs asleep. The same husband who went to church and sang before God and donated at least an acre of produce every season. The same husband who was pure filth decorated in small town trust and lies.

Regardless of my questions, it didn't change the fact Della ceased being theirs that night and became mine instead.

Every year from the first to the last, I loved that girl as if she were my very own blood, sweat, and tears. Girl made from my bones. Child made from my heart. Woman made from my soul.

The perfect mirroring piece that reflected everything I'd never had, loving me as unconditionally as I'd loved her, making me believe that questions didn't matter when it came to us.

We were too important. Too perfect for one another. Too connected.

There was no argument. No denying. No elaborating the absolute truth. It didn't matter if she was six or sixteen; our bond was unshakeable.

Which was why leaving her was worse than the worst thing I could do. Why walking away wasn't just painful, it was suicidal.

I'd come alive the day Della became my family, and I died the day she ceased to be.

And it was my fault.

For so many years, I'd told myself my love was innocent.

I'd clutched onto my lies.

I'd hoped I could keep her, regardless of how my heart silently changed from protector to traitor.

But then, I woke up.

I saw the truth.

I understood the facts.

I tore out my godforsaken heart.

And my questions didn't matter anymore.

Because all I knew, all I wanted, all I could bear was redemption from everything I'd done wrong.

And for the first time in my life, I wished she'd never been in my backpack, after all.

# *Chapter Two*

## DELLA

## 2018

LET ME ASK you a question.

Why exactly are you still here?

Didn't I vow never to write in you again? Didn't I close your document, bury the file, and shove aside all memory of Ren Wild and the secrets I was stupidly sharing with you?

Yet…here you are, still lurking on my desktop, a judging little icon begging me for an ending.

But I manage to ignore your taunting. I keep my mouse pointer well away from your pain and open a new file labelled Assignment Version 2.0.

Or that's what I did for the past little while, at least.

I earned an extension when I had nothing to hand in to Professor Baxter. I blamed the flu—which normally wouldn't be a homework-delayable excuse—but I have a bit of a reputation at college, you see.

The reputation of being a quiet, diligent student who enrolled the very afternoon she finished her high school exams. The moment I was free, I walked out of those halls and marched to the university a few blocks away. They weren't open for new admissions yet, and I didn't have my results from English, math, and science—not to mention any legal identification.

But that didn't stop me.

I practically got on my hands and knees for a chance to attend. To know I had a place to go, an institution to hide in because I no longer had anyone to call my own.

They were strict on no special treatment, but something in my desperation must've swayed them because my pleas were answered nine days later, and I was accepted into the creative writing course that I'd coveted for a while.

And, thanks to skills used to fibbing about our truth, I was able to extend the deadline for providing personal documentation, enrolling without proving who I was.

*All I cared about was a new adventure that would keep my thoughts far from Ren—for however long it lasted.*

*Not that anything had that power…but I had to try.*

*The second I entered campus, I gathered a reputation that stuck.*

*I was known as the earliest arrival and last to depart. I studied with sheer-minded focus. I never answered back. I was hardworking and didn't make trouble.*

*Along with an academic reputation, people made assumptions about me as a person. They knew me as slow to smile and last to laugh. A reputation for being a loner who would rather celebrate her upcoming eighteenth birthday on her own, rather than risk her heart by asking friends to fill up the hole inside her.*

*They say I'm lonely. They call me sad. They murmur sympathies when they find out I'm almost eighteen, live alone, and have no family—*

*Anyway…why did I even open your file?*

*I have no ending to give you.*

*He hasn't come back.*

*It's been two whole months since he left.*

*One graduation in the past.*

*One birthday in the future.*

*And no one to love or kiss or—*

*You know what? That's not important.*

*What is important is I didn't die when he walked out the door.*

*Bet you thought I slept through him leaving. Did you picture me waking up after a good night's rest thinking everything would go back to normal after I'd stripped naked and kissed him?*

*Are you insane?*

*Of course, I didn't sleep that night.*

*I know Ren. Or at least, I knew Ren.*

*I knew I'd pushed him to his limit and there were only two places he could go.*

*One, he would stew all night. He'd weigh the pros and cons. He'd blame himself, his parenting skills, his lack of discipline, and beat himself up for doing something wrong. And if, by the dawn, he hadn't figured out there was something between us that wasn't mere unconditional love, then he wouldn't have been able to look at me again—for fear of what he'd become—and he'd leave.*

*Or two, he'd watch my naked body stroll bravely away after kissing him, and think for a moment. Just a moment. A delicious awareness-crackling moment when he realised he loved me too. And not in just a brother-sister kind of way, but an earth-moving, I-have-to-have-her-right-now kind of way. He'd run after me, shove me against the wall, and his lips would taste so sweet because it would be the first kiss he bestowed instead of the other way around.*

*Two options.*

*But I knew in my heart which one he'd choose.*

*And I'd known the instant the door clicked, and I padded in my cupid pyjamas to stare at the money left on the coffee table, the unfinished note explaining nothing, and the woodsy, broody smell of Ren fading in the air, that I was right.*

*He'd chosen option one.*

*My heart didn't know how to beat anymore. My lungs didn't understand what air was.*

*But tears?*

*They'd vanished.*

*Not one droplet escaped as I stared at the door, wishing,* begging *for him to return, and gather me in his arms.*

*I waited all night until the sun slipped through the curtains, gently kissing everything awake. Its kiss wasn't kind to me though, because it gave me the first day of many without him.*

*If someone had touched me that first dawn, I wouldn't have been able to keep it together. I would've broken on the outside as spectacularly as I broke on the inside.*

*But there was no one to touch me.*

*No one to tell me it would be okay.*

*I couldn't be a child and scream until my heart stopped suffocating. I couldn't destroy everything so I could purge the destruction inside me.*

*All I could do was cling to routine and head to the bathroom for a shower. I dressed in my school uniform. I ate some peanut butter toast with the crusts cut off. I gathered my school bag and walked the three blocks to school. I paid attention in class. I smiled at fellow students. I escaped the moment the bell rang. I slung my backpack up my shoulders and strolled to the supermarket close to our—my—apartment. After I chose a two-day-old lasagne that was discounted in the deli, one packet of Oreos, and an iced coffee, I walked back home. I ate, I watched TV, I did some homework, and I went to bed.*

*I did all that.*

*I, I, I.*

*Me, me, me.*

*And not once did anyone suspect that my world had just fallen apart.*

*Not once did I cry.*

*Not once did I scream.*

*I bottled it all up—the heartache, the agony, the bone-deep cracking—and I swallowed it down like a pill I didn't want to take.*

*And there it sat—a breathing, seething thing dark in my belly, blocking my usual appetite for adventure, food, and love.*

*Blocking me from feeling.*

*Blocking me from screwing up again.*

*The next day, I repeated the day before.*

*And the tomorrow after that.*

*And the tomorrow after that.*

*Until a week had passed and I hadn't died.*

*My worst nightmare of Ren leaving me had come true, and I was still alive.*

*And I hadn't cried.*

*Not once.*

*Not even a little bit.*

# Chapter Three

## DELLA

## 2018

*I CAN'T SEEM to go on my computer without somehow clicking on your icon and exposing a nightmare.*

*I should've deleted every word I ever typed, but last week, when I wrote to you against my wishes, I slept a little better.*

*I didn't wake drenched in sweat, fearing someone had stolen into the apartment while I rested. I didn't lie in bed in the morning, frozen solid with the thought of yet more faking, more living, more existing without him.*

*It was as if I had a friend again.*

*Two months and one week is a long time to be on your own with no one to talk to. I'd started this assignment with a new lease of hope. I'd stupidly believed by writing about him, I could make him come back. Every day I gave you my secrets, I clung to a fantasy that he'd somehow feel me spilling our life story and come back to reprimand me.*

*But when the due date with Professor Baxter came and went, and I claimed the flu to write a hasty tale of a girl with two parents who weren't monsters, I shut up all that pain again.*

*And I suppose you caught my lie, right?*

*I said I never cried.*

*And I didn't.*

*Unless you count the times I cried while writing this stupid assignment.*

*Anyway, I don't have the energy to type anymore today.*

*These memories are too painful. My tale too familiar.*

*I'm no longer part of a pair.*

*I'm singular.*

*Just Della.*

*And I have a life that I'm wasting.*

*A life that Ren gave me.*

*As much as I hate him for leaving, I can't destroy what he gave me.*
*I'm going to move on.*
*For him.*
*Even if it's the hardest thing I've ever done.*

# Chapter Four

## DELLA

## 2018

*IT'S BEEN ANOTHER three weeks.*

*Three months since he left, and it hasn't gotten any easier.*

*But…I actually have something to write about other than Ren.*

*To be fair, my life has been pretty mundane since the night Ren walked out the door. I've crammed as much as I could into daylight and night-time hours, doing my best to delete Ren piece by piece.*

*I've stopped asking myself ridiculous questions as I fall to sleep in an empty apartment.*

*I've given up trying to find answers I'll never earn and accept that what I did was unforgivable.*

*I shouldn't have kissed him.*

*I shouldn't have tried to change us.*

*I shouldn't have demanded more.*

*I'm nothing but numb bones, dazed heart, and paralyzed soul.*

*Who knows…maybe I'll always torture myself with that night. Maybe I'll always feel wretched for hurting him.*

*I just had to push and push, and when he had nowhere else to go, he did the one thing he was best at. He'd run from the Mclary's because they were monsters who tortured him; now he'd run from their daughter because she'd hurt him too much to repair.*

*I have nothing.*

*Nothing but regret and minutes upon minutes of time to contemplate the* What Ifs. *The* What If *I'd let him go to bed and given him a few days to analyse how he felt? The* What If *I'd just been honest and said, 'Ren…you know I love you, but what you don't know is I'm* in *love with you. Now, before you freak out, it's nothing to be afraid of and I* understand if you don't feel the same way, but just in case you do…just in case some part of you that feels a tiny spark like I do, then let's figure it out. We always figure things out—together.'

*And he'd say…'Okay, Della. You're right. I do love you. Now, get naked.'*

*And we'd live happily ever after.*

*That's the worst kind of torture, isn't it? The horror where every outcome and scenario delivers a happier one than the life you're currently living.*

*But it all comes down to choices.*

*I chose to sleep with David, and I chose to slug back a few glassfuls of wine to dull the ache of entering womanhood. I chose to embrace my recklessness, strip, and yell at Ren.*

*I was tipsy and hurt.*

*And I wish I could take it all back.*

*But you already know all this, so I'll stop.*

*The real reason I wanted to write is…I needed someone.*

*Summer is well and truly here, and Ren is not, and that's left me empty to the point where I'll do anything to fill up the darkness inside me.*

*I'm ill-equipped for adulthood where I return to an empty apartment every night, the couch still smelling of him, the air still laced with his voice, and the night still warm with his hugs.*

*The memories nick my heart with their tiny, painful blades—giving me a thousand cuts until I bleed out slowly.*

*It's so slow, I don't even notice I'm dying.*

*I've run my immune system down. And the week after I handed in my assignment, I got sick.*

*Just a simple flu—karma for lying about being ill—but it knocked me on my butt. I could barely get out of bed from the body aches and fever. I had no food and no way of getting to a doctor without sneezing over some Uber driver.*

*I stayed in bed for two days, eating dried Ramen noodles because I couldn't stand up to put the kettle on from shivering so bad, and sipping tepid tap water for my raging sore throat.*

*In the middle of the second day, I honestly thought I would die, and no one was left to care.*

*Ren…ouch.*

*God, the pain never gets any easier to bear.*

*Thinking of him is a syringe full of poison to the heart. Dare murmur his name and it's a mallet to my bones. Risk imagining him sitting here, wiping away fever-sweaty hair and kissing my brow while feeding me chicken soup, and it's a cannonball to my entire chest.*

*By the third day of curling up with chattering teeth, I knew I couldn't keep doing this. I wasn't dead, but it wouldn't take much to finish me if I didn't stop grieving.*

*Ren would be furious if he knew I'd gone from chasing everything to uncaring about anything, especially after all the sacrifices he made for me.*

*That was the only reason I managed to grab my phone, log in to Facebook, and look up all the Davids close to me.*

*It took a few page refreshes and an hour of stalking social media, but I found him.*

*The man I lost my virginity to.*

*Technology connects all of us and, for some reason, I despise that.*

*I hate the fact there's no barrier anymore. No corner to hide from prying eyes.*

*David was easy to find, but not Ren.*

*He's no longer in reception.*

*He's returned to the wild that lives in his blood.*

*I have no way of contacting him and, believe me, I've tried. I've tried everything but smoke signals.*

*And thanks to that butcher's blade to the heart, I needed someone even more.*

*His Facebook page said his full name was David A. Strait. His birthday was New Year's Day, he was four years older than me, and according to his relationship status, he was single.*

*Funny that I'd willingly searched for the man who took my girlhood—a man I knew nothing about—yet almost cried in relief when I found him.*

*My message was lacking and needy:*

Hi David,

You probably don't remember me, but I'm the girl who pathetically asked you to relieve her of her virginity. You took me up on the offer, and then got beaten up by the guy I was trying to forget. Remember that messy evening? If by chance I've jogged your memory, I hope it's not too forward to be honest with you again.

That guy? He walked out on me twelve weeks ago. I thought I was ready to survive on my own, but then I got sick. I hate that I'm asking you this and fully expect a hell no, but if you don't mind being kind to me one last time, I need your help. My address is Apartment 1D, 78 RuBelle Ave. I'm just a few blocks from your place actually—walking distance really...

*I coughed wet and ugly as I pressed send.*
*It showed as delivered a few seconds later.*

*For a few hours, I dozed with congestion in my nose and a continent the size of Africa sitting on my head.*

*I almost forgot I was waiting until my phone chirped with new correspondence.*

*Even though I knew it wasn't Ren. Even though I knew, knew,* knew *I'd never get a text from him again; it didn't stop my ridiculous heart from jumping off a building and hurling itself onto painful concrete.*

*It wasn't Ren.*

*But it was the next best thing.*

I'm on my way.
Love, David.

# Chapter Five

## DELLA

## 2018

SORRY IT'S BEEN so long.

I meant to tell you what happened when David appeared at my apartment, but the guilt...

The guilt of welcoming him inside, letting him sit on the couch Ren used to sleep on, offering him water from glasses Ren used to drink from, sharing the space that Ren used to share with me...

The guilt hurt even worse than the bone aches from the flu.

Not that I have anything to be guilty for.

I'm single. I'm alone. I've committed no crime.

So why does it feel like I've cheated so many times on Ren in the past few weeks?

Let me explain.

David arrived with store-bought mushroom soup, fresh ciabatta, and a pharmacy bag full of painkillers, decongestants, and throat lozenges.

I welcomed him in, almost hyperventilated having him in Ren's space, paid by Ren's money, made possible by Ren's sacrifices, and stiffened in his arms as he hugged me and said, "You can't stay here on your own. Pack a bag. You're coming with me."

I gave him complete control as he bundled me into some sort of Chrysler, and drove us silently to the very same house I'd lost more than just my virginity in—I'd lost Ren.

He guided me inside, past the tastily decorated lounge with wall stickers of life quotes, up the stairs and past the bedroom where we'd ended up screwing on the floor, to another at the end of the hall.

He welcomed me into his bedroom with its charcoal and black colour scheme, pulled back the sheets on a king bed, and cocked an eyebrow until I crawled exhausted into the offered cocoon.

He set up a tray and let me eat the soup in private and swallow a few pills before he returned with a box of tissues, a hot water bottle, and passed me the remote control for the large flat-screen above his dresser on the wall.

I camped in his bed for two days.

And this is so hard to admit, but...I felt something for him. Something warm and grateful and, when I could breathe through my nose and showered away the stickiness of sickness, I wanted to repay him for his unbelievable kindness.

So, when he asked me to stay, when he said he'd thought about me a lot and wanted to see what else was between us other than just a one night thing, I said yes.

I knew what I was doing.

I wasn't stupid to think I liked David enough after two days of him playing nursemaid to move in with the guy, but I was lonely, I was lost, and just like the first time David made me feel wanted, he had a knack at making me feel it again.

So...here is my latest confession.

For the past three weeks, I've been living at David's house.

Actually, right now I'm typing this ridiculous never-to-be-read assignment at the breakfast bar in his kitchen.

It feels like yet another betrayal to admit that.

But why should I suffer in a place that stabs me over and over again with memories of Ren when he left me so damn easily?

Why can't I run, just like him?

After I felt better, David took me home to gather some clothes, toiletries, laptop, and school gear, and we returned to his place, slightly awkward and a little afraid of what we'd just committed to.

I had no intention of letting the lease on my apartment go.

It wasn't just an empty home.

It was the last place Ren had shared with me.

I wasn't ready to say goodbye.

I only left because I was more afraid of sleeping another night on my own than sharing a house with a kind-hearted stranger.

If you're shaking your head, thinking I leapt straight into sleeping with him—you're wrong.

Three weeks and we haven't even kissed.

I'm innocent.

But at the same time, I can't lie to you.

I can't type the words that pigeon-hole David into the friendship-only box.

Just like that first night, there's a chemistry between us that simmers *rather than burns. It heats up my blood just enough to melt the frost Ren left inside.*

*In the past three weeks, I've learned the A in David's full name stands for Alexander. That his dad is rich from aluminium manufacturing, and his parents bought him this house close to the university so he'd be warm and safe to study. The three-bedroom place is all his, but he opted to share with a girl whose room we'd shagged in that night.*

*She'd been away for the weekend, and David's room had already been stolen by other party-screwers.*

*The third bedroom was storage and a gym—the same gym that kept David's body trim and taut rather than fierce and strong like Ren's, thanks to a life of physical labour.*

*The first night I met Nathalie—who went by her favoured nickname of Natty—my hackles rose. After all, I'd gate crashed her cosy love nest with David.*

*But my worries were for nothing.*

*Natty adopted me as her sister and had a flair at finding the worst movies but making them the best with commentary and snacks.*

*Turns out, I'm not the only one nursing a chronic case of a broken heart. We all were.*

*A house of rejected losers all banded together, banishing—or doing our best to banish—the nightmares who had scarred us.*

*Natty had been cheated on by her fiancé.*

*Me, you all know my story.*

*And David…well, he'd been jilted by the girl he'd fallen in love with while working the confectionary stand at the local cinema a few years ago—he didn't know she was married and he was the other man.*

*It destroyed him.*

*And, it destroyed me too because their tales ended with someone cheating on another.*

*Was that the only path for romance?*

*It hurt to hear their sad stories, but it also helped because I was no longer alone. I had two misfits to help heal me, and for the first time in my life, I stopped analysing everything I said and learned the novelty of telling the truth.*

*I held nothing back.*

*What I've told you, dear assignment, is what I told Natty and David over the course of three weeks.*

*They know who I am.*

*They know who Ren is.*

*They know my pathetic tale and life moves on.*

# *Chapter Six*

## REN

## 2018

LEAVING HER WAS the hardest thing I'd ever done.

Harder than living in the city.

Harder than existing at Mclary's.

The *hardest* thing, and I'd done it voluntarily.

Walking away with my back aching beneath a rucksack full of tins and bottles, tents and sleeping bags, I physically fought myself every step.

What the fuck was I doing?

This was *Della*.

We'd never been apart except for three incidents in our past, and each of those only separated us for the shortest time possible.

I loved her.

I *needed* her.

So why the hell did I walk away from her?

The forest ought to have filled me with relief, being back in nature's sweet embrace. The warbles of birds and clear air, far from city smog, ought to slip the stress off my shoulders like an unwanted coat.

But I found no pleasure.

I found no sanctuary.

Because I was alone.

Della was my home. She was it for me. She was my *everything*.

And I'd always known she'd leave me eventually—as she should. As it was meant to happen when a kid outgrew their mentor. I used that excuse over and over.

Me leaving her was merely quickening the inevitably of *her* leaving *me*.

But it didn't stop the pain.

It didn't stop the regret.

It didn't change the fact I no longer had the most important thing in my life, and I was slowly dying without her.

* * * * *

That first day, I didn't get far.

Trees weren't just landmarks guiding me deeper into their midst, but supportive friends, holding me up as I stumbled beneath heartbreak.

I'd travel a mile with my thoughts full of disgust at my response to seeing her naked. I'd stride onward with fists clenched and teeth clamped against nausea for ever thinking about Della the way I had these past few years. I'd punch a sapling for the lust masquerading as love and beg for a way to be free—to somehow find simplicity again.

But then, my thoughts would change, and all I'd see was the little girl I raised. The sweet, trusting blue eyes gazing at me with uncomplicated love as I brushed her blonde hair or fed her a piece of crisp apple straight from the Wilson's tiny orchard.

My confusion would vanish, and I'd backtrack at a jog, staring at the city line below where Della existed without me.

She was my responsibility.

She was mine, and I'd left her all alone, undefended, uncared for.

Who *did* something like that?

Who put themselves first when their entire life had been wholeheartedly promised to another?

I'd hate myself the most in those moments.

The moments where my love was once again pure and full of self-sacrifice.

I was being an ass.

I was reading into things that weren't there.

How the hell did I think I could abandon her?

She was my kid.

My best-friend.

Fuck, she *needed* me, and I ran away like a thief. A thief who stole her protection, familiarity, and comfort all because he couldn't handle his own demons anymore.

I thought I'd protected myself from the vile whispers in my head. I thought I'd found a suitable outlet for the prohibited dreams about a blonde goddess who kissed me, loved me, and told me it was okay to fall and fall hard.

The one-night stands had helped curb my desires but each one left me emptier than before. Each one, I itched with guilt. Each one, I thought of Della.

Della.

Della.

*Della.*

Fuck...

I couldn't do this.

I couldn't leave her alone, unsafe, uncherished.

But as I'd race to the edge of the wilderness, riddled with remorse, and inhale the stench of cities and humans, I'd freeze.

Flashes of naked skin and come-hither eyes would turn my body traitorous.

And I'd remember all the mistakes and sexual tension that'd been building between us for years. I'd finally admit that the buzzing awareness was more than bonded connection but unpermitted chemistry.

It wasn't right. It wasn't allowed.

Della was no longer a little girl I'd die for.

She was a young woman destined to kill me.

Kill me with the absolute unacceptable ability to switch my pure love into dirty lust and destroy any chance at being close again.

On the fifth time of returning to the forest's edge and getting nowhere, even while covering more miles in one day than I'd normally do in two, I had to stop.

I had to admit that I'd left to save her.

I'd run because what I was feeling wasn't fair to her. I'd promised to pave her future with everything she could ever want, but by staying, I was confusing her.

She owned me heart and soul, but she needed more than me.

She'd *always* needed more than me, and the countless times we'd grown up together, the many incidents that proved just how much I lacked and she excelled, meant my determination to do the right thing was a vicious dictator.

I'd been with her every step—literal and figurative.

I'd stolen a lot of her independence.

I'd been the one smothering her, and *of course,* her feelings toward me would morph into something neither of us could have.

She hadn't had the freedom to learn who she was without me there to teach her. I'd screwed her up. I hadn't been fair. I'd been selfish and possessive, ensuring I was the most important person to her—just like she was to me.

That was wrong.

I saw that now.

John Wilson was right. I'd ruined any chance at keeping her as my sister, and now, I couldn't have her at all.

I'd promised to raise her to the highest heights she could achieve, and I'd sacrificed everything I could to achieve that.

That was all this was.

My final sacrifice to ensure she'd forget about this puppy crush, delete her teenage confusion, and find true happiness.

She'd no longer be brainwashed or subconsciously pick up on my corrupt thoughts. She'd be free to make up her own mind.

That resolution gave me enough willpower to turn and finally leave the city lights behind. Tree silhouettes welcomed me, looking like a ribcage where my empty heart hung lifeless and torn.

Della had a crush.

That was all.

But my feelings...they were deeper than a crush, harsher than a fling. My feelings were dark and complicated and yet another reason why I had to leave.

I strode quicker with heavy boots, turning my back on Della, vanishing into the forest I would always call home and the only place that could make me miss her even more.

# Chapter Seven

## DELLA

## 2018

*EYES.*
*Yep.*
*Eyes.*
*I feel them on me.*
*Everywhere.*
*At the supermarket, at college, at the park—even at David's house.*

*It's been four months since Ren left, and I'm going insane. I think I catch a glimpse of him, but nothing's there. I smell him in the air, but no one's around. My skin prickles like it did whenever he was close, but I'm all alone waiting for the bus to school. I'm in class, and my fingers trail across my paper as if touched by a phantom caress. I'm in bed, and my body heats as if worshipped by sinful lips.*

*I feel him everywhere.*
*I think about him* **all the time**.

*And yes, that had to be in bold because it's a nightmare I can't stop.*

*I thought I'd accepted his disappearance. I thought I was stronger than this.*

*But, I'm not.*
*If anything, I'm getting worse.*

*Instead of feeling alone like I once did—utterly abandoned and unwanted and lost, I feel…connected.*

*The scattered pieces of me are re-centring, thanks to the illusion of him watching me.*

*Every night for a month, I've called his cell-phone.*

*I'll wait until David is in the shower so he doesn't see me feeding my addiction and send Ren a message. A simple: 'Where are you?' Followed a few hours later with silent tears: 'I miss you.'*

*No call has been answered.*

*No message delivered.*

*Ren is still out of range, still deep in his beloved forest, as far away from me as possible.*

*So, these eyes I'm feeling?*

*They're not his.*

*They can't be.*

*But it doesn't mean I'm not constantly aware of* something. *Perhaps my heartbreak has infected me and made me sick? Maybe my mind has finally snapped, and instead of choosing to forget him, it's making up stories to keep him close.*

*Either way, I hate it.*

*I can't win.*

*I wanted to be so much braver than this. So much stronger.*

*David and Natty moved on when their hearts were broken, so why can't I?*

*Why can't my dreams of him returning home and falling to his knees in forgiveness stop haunting me? Why can't I exist one day—just a single day— where I don't want to tell Ren what happened at school, or laugh with him about something stupid, or ask his advice on something important?*

*He was a part of my life ever since I can remember.*

*And I have to give myself some slack.*

*I haven't just lost a lover, because we were never lovers. I haven't just lost a friend, because he was never just a friend. I've lost a parent, a home, the only person I ever loved and relied on and my grief is crying out for all of them.*

*But, at the same time...my grief is changing.*

*I know I pushed him away.*

*I'm the one who needs to ask for forgiveness, not him.*

*But I am* angry.

*God, I'm angry.*

*Burning, growling, fist-shakingly angry.*

*Summer is well and truly here, and it's the hardest season because it's Ren's favourite. It was the time of returning to the forest—either permanently or just for weekends away. It was swimming together, and picnics, and horse rides, and hay baling, and browned skin, and sweat, and long nights with just a sheet, side by side in bed.*

*These days, summer means nothing special, and my routine of school, homework, and chores remains the same.*

*However, David asked me a few weeks ago when my birthday was. He knows enough about me that I was honest and said I didn't know the exact date. That Ren would pick one during summer and we'd go out for burgers and fries to celebrate a long-standing tradition of sharing an unknown birthday.*

*My heart stabbed me with its well-honed blade, only to patch itself up with yet another hastily applied and totally ineffective Band-Aid when David took my hand, smiled in sympathy, and said he'd take me out to dinner himself to celebrate.*

*He's willing to be a substitute.*

*He knows how much I miss Ren.*

*I tell him.*

*And if I don't, he hears it in my voice and sees it in my eyes.*

*He'd be blind and stupid to think I wasn't trawling the streets with my heart on a platter, looking for its rightful owner to come claim it.*

*I have another confession to make.*

*I'm still living at David's, but I moved into the spare room where boxes have been pushed against the walls and the gym equipment relocated to the garage. I didn't bother bringing my own furniture over, and I bought a cheap bed and dresser on sale that David helped transport home for me.*

*The apartment I shared with Ren is my dirty little secret.*

*David thinks I terminated my lease and sold everything I didn't need.*

*I lied.*

*I go there on the days when the loneliness and anger hurt the most. I sit on the couch where Ren kissed, hugged, and wiped away my tears, and rock around the never ending ball of sick, sick sorrow.*

*The rent money Ren left behind has been diligently used to ensure the space remains untouched by others.*

*I don't know why I do it.*

*I know he's not coming back.*

*It's a waste of money to hold on to something I haven't lived in for months.*

*So why is there this inability to move on?*

*Why do I keep distance between David and me?*

*Why do I cringe whenever he takes my hand?*

*And why…why did I push him away when he kissed me last week? Why did I freeze on the stairs as he caught my wrist, pushed me against the wall, and apologised just before pressing his lips to mine?*

*We've kissed before.*

*We've slept together once, yet he apologised as if he knew what he was doing wasn't what I wanted.*

*Home life has been a little strained since then.*

*Natty knows what happened because I told her. She encouraged me to go for it. That David was a good guy: sweet, kind, loving.*

*I'd laughed and faked interest.*

*While she was encouraging me to jump into bed with David, I wasn't picturing the boy she spoke about, but the boy from my past. I lived in my little fantasy where the man I went home to at night—the one I kissed in the dark and let enter my body—wasn't a sweet, kind boy like David but a tortured, determined man like Ren.*

*So, you see?*

*That's why I'm writing to you for the first time in a month.*

*David is taking me out for my birthday tonight, and I already know what he's going to ask.*

*He's going to see if we can go from room-mates to lovers.*

*And...*

*And this is so hard to admit...but I know what answer I'll give him.*

*Are you judging me?*

*Do you know what you'd do in my shoes?*

*Would you forever pay rent on an unlived-in apartment just because it's the only thing you have left of a boy who would forever own your heart? Or would you terminate the lease, accept the inevitable, and try to find happiness in any place you could?*

*I'll tell you what my answer is going to be.*

*It's yes.*

*I'm going to move on.*

*Or at least, I'm going to try.*

*If only it wasn't for those eyes.*

*The eyes that follow me.*

*The eyes that know me.*

*The eyes that somehow, somewhere, belong to the boy I'll never be free from.*

# Chapter Eight

## REN

### Previous Month

I TRIED LEAVING for three interminably long months.

Every morning, I'd pack up my tent, snuff out my fire, and stride from camp toward the horizon. And every evening, I'd end up at the same ash-scattered, tent-crushed earth I'd left nine hours before.

A perfect boomerang—unable to break from the forgone conclusion that I couldn't take another step farther from Della.

I was bound to her in sickness, health, love, and distance, and I physically couldn't survive with more miles between us.

After the initial few weeks of mindless wandering, I didn't even bother packing up the tent anymore.

I'd leave my belongings and hike all day, exhausting my body so I might find some reprieve in sleep from the never ceasing desires and mistakes in my head. I'd deplete every ounce of energy, so I didn't turn my cell-phone on and climb the largest tree for reception. I'd barely hunt or eat, so I didn't have the energy to message her things I should never say out loud.

I ate my secrets, and my unpermitted desires sustained me…barely.

Away from Della and free from the authoritative position I held in her life, I allowed myself to remember her in so many different ways.

I smiled when I recalled her as a baby, and her stubborn attempts to copy me.

I grimaced when I remembered her as an eight-year-old, desperate to know about sex and the terribly uncomfortable talk we'd shared.

I sighed when I relived the perfection of the long nights when she'd help me learn in the hay loft, and we'd sit so close, laughing by starlight, studying until she fell asleep against my side.

Innocent memories.

Memories I was permitted. Memories I was proud of because back then...I'd been true in my love for her. I'd been allowed to touch and kiss her because there was nothing more than the everlasting need to make her happy and keep her safe.

It was the years after that had me tossing in my sleep and dreaming things I wished I could stop.

The dream goddess who always opened her arms to me.

The blonde woman I wanted more than anything who always kissed me as deeply as I kissed her, who tumbled to the forest floor, who ripped off my clothes with the same gut-shredding passion I felt and cried out as I filled her violently.

Those dreams woke me hard and hurting and more tormented than I'd been in my entire life.

I only wanted to remember her as my Della, yet my mind kept plying me with fantasies that she could be my future, too. A future I'd never contemplated until the day she'd kissed me. The day she'd tangled herself up with my dreams and my heart—my stupid, *stupid* heart—shed its capacity at only seeing her as a child and saw her as so much more instead.

"Fuck!"

The trees were the only ones who heard my distress, who witnessed my disgrace as I fisted myself and worked out the disgusting desire from my body. I felt sick to my stomach as I came, not because I masturbated, but because my mind fixated on Della and that was a line I should never fucking cross.

Even though I struggled with two memories of baby Della and sexual Della, I knew in my soul there was only one journey I could take.

It was as if Della had an invisible hold on me.

There hadn't been any rope or knot binding me to her as I packed my bag and left the apartment that awful night, but there was now.

An invisible lasso that tightened every time I tried stepping farther away, yanking me back, keeping me firmly stuck.

Was this limbo or purgatory?

Was it punishment for leaving her so callously when she needed me the most?

Those questions kept me company on my long treks through the forest until I'd memorised every trail and recognised every tree.

More questions came at night. Questions I had no right to ask.

Was she with someone?

Was she happy with someone?

Had she forgotten about me when I could never, *ever* forget about her?

But it was the questions that sprang on me, heavy with guilt, festering with shame that meant I would never be able to move forward.

Not like this.

Not without checking on her.

Not without convincing myself that she didn't need me anymore.

I would rather be crushed knowing she'd deleted me from her world, than forever wonder if she was okay.

I couldn't handle the unknown, the never ending need to see her, the almost manic desperation to clear the air between us and somehow find closure to this entire convoluted mess.

I'd lost weight.

I'd forgotten how to breathe.

My bones were glass and my chest a forge.

True love was a vicious monster, feeding on my reserves, breaking me beneath its resolve to either kill me if I didn't obey or destroy me if I did.

I was glad the forest didn't have mirrors because heartbreak had not been kind to me.

But just because I'd made a mistake by leaving, and it'd taken me three months of mentally punishing myself for all the misguided, impure thoughts I'd been having, I could finally admit what I couldn't before.

Away from the city, free from society's judgment, I had no choice but to be honest with myself.

I wished I could stop it.

I begged for it not to be true.

But...the reality was, I was in love with Della.

Not just platonic, parental, brotherly, friendship love but bone-crunching, heart-pounding, air-stealing, delicious fucking love that broke me down until I no longer knew who I was.

All I knew was I couldn't keep doing this.

I couldn't keep living without her.

I needed her in my life in any capacity that she'd let me.

Even if it meant I'd have to walk her down the aisle as she married some undeserving prick, I would do it.

I would take whatever she gave.

I didn't make a conscious decision to pack up my tent that morning or turn toward the city instead of away. I didn't mean to leave my campsite or haul my possessions onto my back.

I wanted Della, but I still didn't know how to deal with that even as I struck off on different paths, passed unfamiliar trees, and weaved my way from wilderness to city.

The closer I got, the more my worry escalated.

Was she even there?

Was she still at our apartment, or had she moved?

Had she sought out Cassie's help and returned to Cherry River?

My boots travelled faster as scarier questions chased me.

What if she'd been hurt? What if she'd been taken or sold or abused while I'd been having a personal crisis? What if I'd put myself first, and she'd suffered because of it?

I would die.

By my hand or heartbreak's if that was the case.

How could I say I loved her when I'd done the exact same thing to her as my mother had done to me?

My mother had sold me because I was worth more to her as dollars than I was as her son. And I'd walked away from Della because I chose propriety and martyrdom instead of burying my own pain and focusing on giving her everything I had left to give.

I'd been so fucking selfish.

And I stopped walking.

I ran.

I ran as fast as I could.

I ran all the way back to the apartment, to Della, to fix this.

* * * * *

She wasn't there.

For two weeks, I stalked the street where we used to live, returning to the dilapidated shed Della and I had slept in when we first arrived in town, watching for any sign of her.

No one entered our apartment.

No landlord or new tenant.

No Della.

Rain or shine, I'd leave my temporary shack and travel into the congested suburbs and find a place in the shadows to watch.

And every day, my heart would sink a little more.

I'd focused on the wrong questions.

I hadn't stopped to ask the most important one.

If Della had moved on and left…where had she gone, and how could I find her? Would it be as simple as turning on my cell-phone and calling her? Would she talk to me? Or had she changed her number?

I'd left every dollar I had on the coffee table when I'd gone, so I had no funds to purchase credit for my phone. And for now, I had no intention of finding a job. I could hunt what I needed to eat or I'd steal if long hours in the city meant game was scarce. Not that I had an appetite these days.

I ran purely on confusion and regret.

Money didn't matter to me, and besides, I couldn't stop watching the apartment, hoping against hope that someday, some hour, she'd turn up.

On the fourteenth day, when she still didn't show, and no one else entered the space, I crossed the street, checked I went unnoticed, and descended the stairs to the claustrophobic basement apartment.

It took fifteen minutes, but I managed to pick the lock with the two knives from my boot, and my steps sounded criminal as I crossed over the threshold for the first time since saying goodbye to the love of my life.

The first thing that hit me was the smell.

Must and un-use and un-want. Dust bunnies sat together in corners as if the unsealed windows had encouraged a breeze to enter and do some cleaning. The kitchen tap dripped like it always did into an empty sink. Dishes sat on the rack waiting to be put into the paint-chipped cupboards.

After living so free in the forest where nature decorated with sunsets and moonlight, the space was abysmal and poky.

How had we lived so long in this small place?

Then again, everywhere seemed better when Della was around. We were happy in a garden shed or under the stars as long as we were together.

Rubbing at the sudden blistering burn where my heart lived, I strode through the tiny home. My hands clenched as my eyes fell on the coffee table where the note I'd scribbled Della still sat unfinished.

She hadn't moved it.

The cash was missing but that was the only thing changed in

the entire room from its faded brown couch to its ugly striped curtains.

No noise came from the bathroom or Della's bedroom, but I couldn't stop myself from following the corridor—memories of Della naked haunting my every step.

I sucked in a painful breath as I pushed open the partially cracked door to her bedroom. Her bed was unmade, like usual. Her bedside table droplet-stained from glasses sipped sleepily in the night.

Prowling to her wardrobe, I wrenched it open. Sucking back another pained breath, I noticed the clothes she favoured and often wore were no longer there.

One of the only signs that she no longer lived here.

Her toiletries in the grout-stained bathroom were gone. Her subtle scent of petals and flowers from working at the florist no longer noticeable in the stale air.

She hadn't been here in a while.

Yet she still paid rent; otherwise, our furniture would've been evicted and a new tenant living in our home.

*Why?*

And if she still paid rent but didn't live here, where was she?

My boots echoed off the corridor walls as I headed back toward the living room, and my eyes fell on the front door.

A sequence of events unfolded in rapid fire.

Of Tom arriving that Halloween to take Della to the dance.

Of her kissing him in the dark amongst witches and vampires.

Of my jealousy finally starting to make me notice my feelings for Della were changing.

Of yet more jealousy and absolute excruciating heartbreak as she called me the night she lost her virginity.

Of me storming over there, snatching her as if she were mine to snatch, and beating up the guy she'd chosen over me.

I couldn't remember his name. I couldn't remember much about that night other than my roaring agony.

I didn't know what I'd do if I saw him again.

*Wait...*

Something inside me bellowed with possession. Something that whispered the answers to my questions.

*Where is she?*

I knew.

I didn't know how.

I didn't know why.

But I knew where to start looking.
I bolted out the door.

# *Chapter Nine*

## REN

## Current Month

I'D BEEN CALLED many things in my life.

A boy.

A belonging.

A bastard.

But this was a new low.

I was a pervert, a peeper, an obsessed watcher who didn't have the power to stop.

For two weeks, I stalked Della every second of every day.

I knew her schedule. I knew her friends. I knew she had English on Mondays and lit class on Wednesdays. I knew she studied until late and watched movies with the guy she'd slept with—who I remembered was called David—and some black-haired girl I didn't know.

I knew she slept alone in her own room in a new bed, new sheets, new pyjamas, and genuinely laughed when David whispered in her ear at breakfast and smiled softly when he clutched her hand goodbye.

I knew she was sad and lonely and angry.

I recognised the tightness in her shoulders, the blaze in her blue eyes, and the stiffness of her step.

We'd been apart longer than we'd ever been, but I knew her better than I knew myself.

I might not be fluent in many things, but when it came to reading Della, I was a master. Every nuance and twitch, I understood. Every flick of her hair and sniff of her petite nose, I read the hidden message.

And the language she shouted was of serious rage.

She was a part of me, and her anger became my anger because I understood it.

I felt it, too.

I was angry that I'd driven us to this point.

I was angry that, until a month ago, I had full intentions to track her down, approach her, and get on my knees in apology. I had an entire script planned, written in my mind not on paper, burned into my memory as if scribed in fire.

I was going to pledge myself to her all over again.

I was going to beg her forgiveness for breaking my promise never to leave her like I did when she was a baby playing on that comfy rug with glittery goldfish and opinionated cats.

I'd left her even when I promised I wouldn't.

*I'd* done that.

She hadn't asked me to go, and despite the mess between us, my leaving was inexcusable.

But my carefully planned speech had faded the longer I watched her.

I couldn't take my eyes off her, loving her the way I was meant to with pride for her excelling at life without me, joy that she was studying something she loved, affection for the messy blonde curls, and warm-hearted sentiment for the ribbon fluttering in her strands.

The first day of watching her went too fast and, before I knew it, my stalking reached creepy levels until I couldn't leave unless her bedroom light went out and sleep meant she'd be in bed for the rest of the night.

I'd slink off, hidden in my shadows and shame, crawling into a sleeping bag and dreaming inappropriate dreams full of need, love, and passion.

At dawn, I'd return to her, an itch in my blood commanding me to be close after so long apart.

The next morning, I found her hugging David goodbye on the stoop of the white picket fenced house I could never afford, and her bare legs flashed me where I hid in the trees across the street.

She wore flip-flops, and wrapped around her ankle was the same tattoo I'd paid for on her seventeenth birthday. The one with its matching blue ribbon trailing into its capital R.

A year old and the ink was just as bright, just as damning as the night I cupped her foot and demanded an explanation— begging her to put me out of my misery, all the while knowing she was about to condemn me even more.

The tattoo sucker-punched me with so many things, and I didn't have the courage to approach her that day. Instead, I drowned beneath everything I'd done wrong and everything I didn't know how to fix.

The day after that, David kissed her.

It'd been the slap to the face I needed.

It woke me out of the trance I'd fallen into, shaking me with truth that I'd left her for months, but she wasn't a wilting flower entirely reliant on me to thrive. She was tenacious and brave and fiercely independent. Always had been—always looking after me just as much as I looked after her.

Of course, she wouldn't wait for me.

*Of course*, her anger would drive her to find other things…other people.

My insides wanted to curl up and die, but I refused to be weak. I refused to think of myself as the injured party when I'd been the one to walk away.

*I'd* done this.

I'd pushed her to find comfort from some other man. A man she'd already given herself to. A man who had every power to destroy me, and he didn't even know it.

When he kissed her, every muscle seized.

She didn't exactly kiss him back—not the way she'd kissed Tom at the Halloween party—but she didn't push him away, either.

She nodded to something he said while they stood on the garden path, and he cupped her pretty cheeks like I wanted to, her eyes glowing with a mixture of affection and tears.

I wanted to kill him.

But I was also grateful because he'd kept my Della safe when I had not. I wanted him gone, but I wouldn't hurt her again.

She'd chosen him.

I had to respect that.

That was my punishment.

I returned to my borrowed shack on government land, unable to stop reliving her kissing him. Kissing the boy she'd lost her virginity to.

Just like when I'd run, I was only thinking of myself.

I should be happy she wasn't writhing in matching misery.

She was alive.

She was healthy.

She was living.

Who was I to ruin that all over again?

If she'd moved on, then I would do everything in my power to spare her any more pain.

So, I settled in to watch, to study, to make sure what she'd said to me that night—the way she'd stared, and stripped, and kissed me—had been what I'd feared all along: a puppy crush. A silly infatuation. Nothing more than innocent flirtation that I'd turned into something messy and untrue.

I needed to see that so I could let go of these tragic needs driving me into an early grave.

But...if she loved me the way I was learning I loved her...could our relationship evolve? Were our foundations strong enough, our morals good enough, to risk losing everything just for the hope of something more?

A few months ago, my answer had been no. I wasn't willing to risk it.

But now...now, I knew I'd fucked up everything and lived with the daily torture of what it was like to exist without her.

I wanted her back.

Emotions had been the glue that sewed us together, and I refused to let them be the crowbar to pry us apart.

I'd lost Della the moment I'd walked out the door. I'd decimated her trust, her faith, and her affection, all because I wasn't brave enough to admit I felt something, too.

And now, watching her kiss men from a distance was all I had left, and as much as I despised myself, I couldn't stop.

I just *could not stop*.

I couldn't be away from her.

I couldn't survive not seeing her.

I wasn't proud of it.

I knew she'd become a sick addiction.

And for the first time in my life, I wasn't fighting to better myself but letting myself slide into a deep, dark place I didn't know how to climb out of.

Even at Mclary's, I'd never let self-pity destroy my hope that one day I would be free—either in death or by running away.

I knew what I should do.

Leave.

Like I said I would.

Stop this madness and let Della find her place in the world without me messing it up even more.

But...I couldn't.

I gave in.

I kept watching.

The days became a blur.

I couldn't stop myself trailing her to school, to the coffee shop, to the pricey house she shared with David and the girl.

My heartache robbed me of yet more weight because I couldn't tear myself away to eat. I had no money for vitamins I sorely needed. My body didn't feel right...it felt sick.

I truly was the villain and slid into even worse territory for stalking her.

It all became much worse the night of a muggy summer's evening when David led her from the house dressed in baby blue shorts and white open-necked shirt, holding my Della's hand as her cream sundress with a lacy collar fluttered around her bare legs.

Once again, her ribbon plaited in her hair and inked around her ankle reached into my chest and tore out my pathetic heart.

She was so fucking beautiful.

He led her to a Chrysler parked in the driveway, opened her door, then hopped into the driver's seat and drove off.

I couldn't follow them, so I waited in the street-shadows, wishing for something to chase away the time, bowing beneath the weight of constant jealousy, plaguing myself with worry about what she was doing.

I wasn't a smoker or a drinker, nor did I have money for cigarettes or alcohol, but I would've gladly given away every worldly possession to have something to numb my self-inflicted pain.

They returned a couple of hours later, the warm breeze blowing scents of grease and bacon across the street as they climbed from the car, laughing at some joke they shared.

On the quaint garden path, David grabbed her hand and spun her into him. "Happy birthday, Della Ribbon. I hope you were okay with sharing a burger with me and not with him."

Goddammit, my chest cleaved in two.

Her nickname.

Her birthday.

She'd told him.

I stumbled with a mixture of despair and starvation.

She gasped as David clutched her close.

I winced as my fingers burned to touch her like he was.

She flinched as he bent his head to kiss her.

I barely controlled my growl as his body pressed against hers.

Their lips met, and this time…Della kissed him back. Hot and wet and needy—the same way she always kissed when trying to deny the truth and buy into a fantasy.

The same way the woman from my dreams kissed me. The same way I kissed her: with naked desire that sprang from desperation for love as much as a lust-filled connection.

With wet lips, he kissed his way along her jaw, then whispered something in her ear.

Her back straightened, eyes widened, and indecision flickered over her face.

But only for a moment.

Just a single moment where I knew she thought of me before pushing me out of her life like I'd pushed her out of mine.

And then, she nodded. "Yes."

Yes to what?

Yes to ripping out my heart?

Yes to tearing apart my love?

They vanished into the house, leaving me in pieces on the pavement.

That night, her bedroom light never turned on.

However, two shadows danced over David's curtains until late into the evening.

Two shadows having sex.

Two shadows of two people where one who meant the world to me had taken my hopeful heart, tore it out with reality, and left it to bleed out alone on the street.

I'd stalked her for long enough.

I'd seen enough to understand I no longer stood a chance.

As their birthday night of fucking finished, and their bedroom light went out, I turned and walked away.

I was twenty-eight.

She was eighteen.

And it was over.

I sent a prayer for her eternal happiness—the only thing I could give her for her birthday—and walked away.

I didn't go back.

# Chapter Ten

## DELLA

## 2018

*I SLEPT WITH him.*

*How could I?*

*How could I sleep with someone when my heart still belongs to another?*

*How can I be so cruel by leading David on when I might never be able to return his feelings?*

*I have no answers for you. I have no answers for me.*

*The blistering truth is, the night I slept with him, I sat in the shower once he was asleep and sobbed my damn eyes out.*

*The worst part?*

*I felt like I owed him when really, I wasn't ready.*

*He was so sweet, taking me out for a birthday burger and fries. So understanding when he let me list each and every diner Ren had taken me to, including the last one when he'd agreed to let me get a tattoo—the same tattoo I can't look at now without wincing with agonising regret.*

*He was so gentle as he took me home, kissed me, and asked if he could give me my present in his bedroom.*

*It wasn't an invitation for sex even though he'd touched me all night— grazing his hand with mine, kissing my cheek when I made him laugh about my five-year-old birthday and the incident at school about skinning Frosty the bunny.*

*Natty gave me a Cheshire cat grin when we returned, and David guided me up the stairs with our hands entwined. She winked and gave me a big thumbs-up as she slowly vanished from view as I reached the landing. Her encouragement made me feel semi-normal, as if entering David's room wasn't a direct slap in the face of Ren's memory.*

*But Ren wasn't here.*

*Ren had never kissed me the way David had.*

*Ren had never been interested in me the way David was, so I did my best to push him from my mind and planted a grateful kiss on David's lips as he gave me a jade green scarf and matching nail polish for my birthday.*

*That kiss turned to another.*

*Which evolved to another and another until the nail polish and scarf fell to the carpet and David whispered, "I want you. Do you want me?"*

*His voice wavered with uncertainty and need; a potent combination of authority and fear. Knowing he was as terrified as I was allowed me to be braver than I might've been. It allowed me to thank him in one of the only ways I could.*

*I nodded—not trusting my voice—and moved toward the bed.*

*As he stripped me, kissed me, touched me, rolled on a condom, and slid inside me, I did my best to keep my heart and mind with him.*

*But I wasn't successful.*

*For weeks, I'd hoped I would be able to move on, that the gentle affection I had for David would suddenly explode into the all-encompassing craving I've had for Ren for as long as I can remember.*

*But the simmer never became a burn.*

*If anything, it grew less and less as I acknowledged that I wasn't ready for anyone who wasn't Ren. I wasn't being fair because I was so far from the realm of being okay it was laughable.*

*The sex was fine.*

*But his hugs made me empty, and his kisses made me lost.*

*Afterward, David spooned me and my chest ached unbearably. My tears slowly trickled inside me until they clogged my throat with silence. And when his breathing finally slipped into slumber, and I was free to be honest with myself, I tore out of his embrace, bolted to the bathroom, and barely contained my grief as I wrenched on the shower and hurled myself under the hot spray.*

*My theory was the water would hide any escaped sobs and camouflage the sadness pouring down my cheeks.*

*To be honest, I didn't even know why I cried.*

*It wasn't like I'd cheated on Ren. It wasn't like I had any other sexual experience to judge other than sleeping with David on Natty's bedroom floor.*

*I was eighteen and so messed up by the boy who'd raised me that I was a wreck after having such a lovely evening with a man anyone would be lucky to date.*

*But you know what?*

*You know what I've kept tucked inside where all dark, disturbing secrets live?*

*The real reason I cried that night?*

*It was because I felt* him.

*I've felt him for weeks.*

*Every day, the sensation of him being close gets worse.*

*Eyes everywhere.*

*On the street, in my class, in my dreams.*

*A yearning that matches mine. A pleading that mirrors mine.*

*And I know it's just my mind playing tricks on me, but dammit, I have this feeling that if I turn quickly enough, I'll catch Ren behind me. This constant awareness that if I just breathe his name, he'll miraculously appear, just won't let me move on.*

*I'm stuck in limbo.*

*I'm becoming unhappier instead of happier.*

*I'm becoming lost instead of found.*

*And I need to do something…soon, because if I don't, I'm afraid of what I'll become.*

*I say I'm strong, but the reality is, dear assignment, I'm not.*

*I'm brittle and fragile and made of spun glass where my insides are nothing more than swirling smoke looking for a crack to escape, to hitch a ride on the wind, to fly into the forest, desperate to find the boy who stole my heart and beg him to make me whole again.*

* * * * *

*Six months.*

*Six eternally long months.*

*Nothing much has happened. I haven't slept with David again. Things are a little weird, but we continue to co-inhabit well enough.*

*I haven't had the energy to write.*

*But something changed, and I have news.*

*Funny, how honesty is always the worst weapon, isn't it?*

*I've turned to you as a sounding board because I have no one else to talk to. Natty is on David's side—as she should be. David is doing his best to date me—as he should with our history. And all along, I keep my secrets until I can tell you.*

*Normally, I write on a park bench while waiting for the bus after school, or in a coffee shop during lunch hour, but the other night, I stupidly left my computer on standby in the lounge, not password protected like normal, and David read everything.*

*He saw what I wrote about sleeping with him.*

*He saw how sad I was.*

*How empty and angry and confused.*

*I offered to leave, but David didn't kick me out. He didn't walk away from me, but he has withdrawn his offer of dating.*

*He said it was his fault to push for something he knew I wasn't ready for. That he understands I'm not over Ren, but will continue to support me as a friend.*

*He's correct, of course, but having him confront me so calmly with no blame or ridicule made me feel even worse.*

*He knows what it's like to love and not be loved in return, and to my utmost horror, I've done it to him again. Not that he's in love with me, but there* is *something there. Something that could become* something, *if you know what I mean.*

*Anyway, I'm running out of time, my Uber will be here soon, and I'm taking you to my old apartment. I'm going to print off every stupid word and burn you like I should've done the moment I knew I couldn't hand you in.*

*I've told David I'm having the afternoon away to get my head and heart on the same page. That I'll return in better shape and ready to stop moping around his house.*

*My printer is still gathering dust in my old room.*

*The clothes I don't wear still in my wardrobe.*

*The bed I don't sleep in still waiting for a dreamer.*

*It's time, don't you think?*

*Time to stop this—all of it. Time to cancel the lease on somewhere I'm not living, time to patch up the heart I'm not using, and finally put the past where it belongs.*

*Behind me.*

*Oh, my Uber is here.*

*I had other things to say, but I suppose they're unimportant now.*

*Farewell, assignment.*

*This is the last you'll hear from me, and I want to say thank you before I let you go.*

*Thank you for being a shoulder to cry on. Thank you for being the only one who truly understood how I felt about Cassie, Ren, David…everyone.*

*Just thanks, for everything.*

# Chapter Eleven

## REN

## 2018

THE EVENING DELLA slept with David I forced myself to stop being ridiculous.

I sucked up my pride, rubbed out my bruises, and trekked the few blocks to the abandoned apartment that my cash still paid for.

The lonely space breathed a sigh of relief as I jimmied the lock again and stepped into the musty, unloved lounge. It needed someone to comfort, just like I needed someone to comfort me.

I meant to do some dusting, return to the borrowed shack, and grab my backpack. To have my first shower in a while—if the water hadn't been turned off—and eat if the pantry still stored food.

But that was before my feet guided me to Della's bedroom, and my eyes fell on her unmade bed. Images of her sitting cross-legged while doing her homework slammed into me. The memory of her blue-dyed hair so glossy and bright. The sounds of her laughter as I pulled her ponytail. The feel of her arms around my waist and her cheek on my chest—

Fuck, it was too much, and every chore and task faded beneath the immense blanket of exhaustion.

I wasn't proud of it, but I fell face first onto Della's bed, wrapped myself up in her blankets, and inhaled her pillow.

I slept for two solid days, waking briefly to drink water straight from the tap and gnaw on a few stale crackers from the kitchen. All my body cared about was dreaming, and I woke angry and hard when my dream goddess refused to visit me—almost as if being in Della's domain meant my loyalties to her returned to loving her as a brother, rather than the complicated tangle I now accepted.

Unfortunately, once my body caught up on sleep, it became determined to reveal how badly I'd neglected it. Rundown immune system and no weight reserves meant a simple cold found me a very comfortable host. Within a few hours, the congestion and headache turned to fever and coughing—cursing me with the flu.

I got sick.

And I couldn't do a damn thing about it.

I spent a week combating lungs full of oppressive agony, and hugging a burning chest that charred me to ash.

At some point, I feared I wouldn't get better. That I'd fall down the sickly slope into pneumonia like I had when I was fifteen.

But, through some miracle, the hacking coughs slowly abated and the burning slowly cooled, morphing to a wheeze I could cope with.

When I felt semi-human again, I returned to gather my things in the forest. Afterward, I cased out a local convenience store for staples, and spent two full days spring cleaning the apartment.

To start with, I didn't want to spray the tropical scented disinfectant just in case I deleted any smells of Della, but she hadn't lived here for so long that no whiff or note of her was left.

Della had paid utilities as well as rent, which meant I had hot water to wash and gas to cook with. I wanted to thank her for wasting money on something she no longer used—almost as if she'd known I'd return and need a place to stay.

When I wasn't staying busy with chores, I tailed her.

I'd promised myself I wouldn't go back.

I broke that promise.

Countless times.

I couldn't help it.

After I was better, and more publicly acceptable, I walked to her shared house in much cleaner clothes than before, and watched her go to college. I waited outside like all those years ago when she first went to school, and followed her home again.

I slowly drove myself insane, keeping her constantly in my thoughts, all while she returned to David every night.

By the end of the second week, I couldn't do it anymore.

Any of it.

I couldn't keep stealing supplies so close to home unless I wanted to get caught. And I couldn't keep stalking unless I wanted to keep sliding into that dark, dismal place I couldn't climb out of.

I needed money.

I needed to learn how to exist without her so I could put myself back together again and be the parental figure Della needed, not the off-the-rails, rejected lover I had currently become.

The next day, I headed to a supermarket two blocks away that I hadn't stolen from and read their advertisement board for employment. I wasn't deluded to think I'd find a perfect farmhand role, but I was prepared to do what was necessary to get my life back on track.

The only two positions available were a window cleaning gig or a barman at a local nightclub. No way could I be cooped up in a darkened cesspit with writhing bodies and pounding music.

That left the window cleaning job.

I memorised the number then asked to use the supermarket manager's phone to arrange an interview. I knew nothing about washing windows, but I needed cash, so…

The owner was a spindly looking pothead whose dad had bought him a franchise once he'd dropped out of school with no prospects. He wanted someone to run the bookings and basically handle the entire business.

I bullshitted enough that I got the job, earning cash under the table with a bonus for each new contract I signed.

My first pay cheque was used to purchase a cheap pair of jeans and a couple of t-shirts, replacing the holey, discoloured things I'd lived in for far too long in the forest.

The next lot of cash went to topping up my long-suffering cell-phone, and it became a thing of torture as I stroked the buttons and read old messages from Della that I'd never seen.

At the start of our separation, she wrote to me often. Telling me stories of classes, exam results, how much she missed me, how much she cursed me, how much she was sorry.

Then they became less and less. Until now, she didn't message me at all.

Now, it was my turn to curb the all-consuming need to get in touch. Lying in her bed, I wrote text after text that I never sent.

*I'm in town.*

*I'm in our old apartment.*

*I miss you.*

*I want you.*

*I love you.*

*I'm* in *love with you.*

I deleted them all, needing more time so I didn't do something I regretted, something we couldn't survive.

Before I knew it, another two months had passed, pushing me over the six-month anniversary of leaving Della. Even though I still saw her every day—if only for snatches of time between window washing jobs or after work before dusk fell—I still missed her more than food, shelter, and freedom.

At least, she had a routine and friends. She had movie nights and dinners out. She had a life that I didn't want to ruin, and it gave me all the more incentive to stay out of it.

I hated that I watched with horror every night until her bedroom light turned on, not just his. I held my breath to see if she'd sleep with him again, and exhaled in utter relief when she didn't.

It was sick.

I knew that.

But it didn't change anything.

And, as much as our distance slowly robbed me of life and purpose, I didn't let her know how much I wanted her.

How much I missed her.

How deeply I cared.

How fucking screwed up I was...over everything.

# Chapter Twelve

## DELLA

## 2018

DAMMIT, THE APARTMENT *still smells of him.*

*I haven't been here in so long, but the moment I opened the door, it felt as if I'd never left.*

*It feels lived in.*

*I was expecting dust bunnies and cobwebs, but the floors are freshly polished and the corners neatly clean.*

*I know I said I wouldn't write to you again, assignment, but I had to tell someone.*

*I think I might have to go see a professional. Admit I have a problem. Talk to a doctor, maybe.*

*This level of delusion can't be real, can it?*

*I feel him watching me. I prickle for no reason. I stiffen at the slightest noise. I believe, no matter how insanely impossible, that he's close by.*

*And now this?*

*I truly am losing my mind.*

*My bed was made when I came home, and I swear I left it a mess.*

*The bathroom smells like tropical disinfectant, not the faint must of mould that lingers in the grout around the tiles.*

*How is that possible?*

*Why do I keep deluding myself this way?*

*He's gone!*

He's gone!

*I need someone to scream that in my face and then maybe the folded threadbare towels will make sense, or the fact that if I stand still and inhale, my nose fills with his woodsy, wild scent instead of stale passing of lonely time.*

*I smell him.*

*And I don't know what to do anymore.*

*I came here to put things behind me, yet everywhere I turn, the past keeps dragging me back.*

*I haven't said it out loud since he left—not that I ever said it out loud—but sitting here in my bedroom that Ren helped decorate, looking around the apartment Ren helped make a home, I can't pretend anymore.*

*I'm still in love with him.*

*Even more than before.*

*I'm still furious at him.*

*Growing hotter by the day.*

*And I'm afraid.*

*I'm so afraid I'll never be able to get past this, that my future is a merry-go-round of prickled skin for no reason, smells of Ren in the air, and the unnerving sense that he hasn't truly gone, after all.*

*Maybe he died out in the forest, and his ghost is haunting me.*

*Maybe this is what everyone goes through when they lose someone so damn special.*

*Either way, I can't do this anymore.*

*I came here to burn you, and that's what I'm going to do.*

*And then, I'm going to sell every piece of furniture and leave.*

*I can't be in this town another moment.*

*Screw my creative writing course. Screw being brave. Screw lying. Screw everything.*

*I can't do it.*

*I can't stay.*

*I'm running...just like he did.*

*It's finally time to say...goodbye.*

# Chapter Thirteen

## REN

## 2018

STEPPING INTO THE place I used to live with Della was excruciating.

Every day was the same; the pain never got easier, or the sensation that I was missing something fundamental any gentler.

She was the reason I went to work.

She was why I remained in a city I couldn't stand rather than return to the forest I loved.

And she didn't even know I was back because I was too much of a pussy to face her. I wasn't ready to accept her anger at my weaknesses, to bear the brunt of her disappointment, or to stare into her eyes as I lied about what I felt for her.

I wanted that lie to be truth when I next saw her.

I wanted to hold love in my heart and no lust. I wanted to hug her hard and feel connected and comforted and not consumed with the desperation of spilling everything.

Of confessing that I loved her in a totally different way.

That I couldn't exist without her.

That I was willing to do anything to have her back.

I hated how incredibly wrong it was to fall for the girl I'd raised, yet my body said it was unbelievably right. That it had been waiting for that moment to finally come alive and shout *yes* to finding everything I never thought I'd find.

My eyes glued to the carpet where she'd fearlessly stripped and offered every secret and vulnerability. And just like every day, I cringed in horror knowing that, despite the fact she'd moved on and my vow to pretend my love hadn't changed for her, if I could rewind time, I would gather her close and kiss her.

I wouldn't wait for her to kiss me.

I wouldn't make her put her entire heart on the line.

I would meet her halfway because our entire lives had been a partnership, and it was up to me to carry half her burdens.

My boots were heavy and droplet stained from washing windows as I trudged down the tiny corridor to her—*my*—bedroom.

*Wait.*

I froze as the sounds of splashing water came from the poky bathroom at the bottom of the hall. Light glowed beneath the door.

*What the hell?*

I'd grown so used to having sole use of this place, I hadn't considered what I'd do if she suddenly returned.

I backed up, my heart racing into overdrive.

*Shit.*

I'd caught her in the shower.

I didn't know her to shower at dusk—she was normally a morning person—but if she'd had a long day at college or a fight with David or whatever other reason had brought her here, I supposed it was only natural. Then again, I had no right to know her routine anymore.

I'd *left* her.

I wasn't privy to her heartaches. She wasn't a virgin, after all. She had the man she'd chosen warming her bed at night.

Once again, that knowledge harpooned me, and my steps faltered. She'd grown up beneath my nose and, by the time I'd noticed, it was too late.

Everything was too fucking late.

A painful cough ripped from my lungs.

Turning around, I meant to head back to the living room and out the door, but a stack of papers sat on her desk beside the cheap laptop I'd bought for her birthday a couple of years ago. A few of the keys were missing and the Wi-Fi capabilities were shit, but the thing was well used ever since Della decided to take her skills at telling stories, and my past of sharing tales, and enrol in creative writing.

The laptop hadn't been on her desk when I left this morning. She'd brought it with her.

Was it an assignment?

Was she hard at work on a project, and this was the printed

results ready to hand in tomorrow?

Looking back at the bathroom door, the sound of running pipes and groaning water pressure said I had enough time to spy.

I shouldn't.

I should run before it was too late.

Just the action of stepping into her room uninvited—the same room I'd slept in for the past few months—and glancing at the discarded bra on her dresser, the pink panties on the floor, and strewn jeans on her bed made my hands clench and belly knot with dangerous things, but the fat stack of pages and bright green Post-it note on top beckoned me forward.

My eyes widened and my heart beat with a different panic as I noticed my old lighter propped on top with a sketch of a fire and the words, *'It's been fun cutting out my heart, but it's time for you to burn. I'm ready to leave and be done with this.'*

The words were written in marker, deep and black and full of sharp pain.

Leave?

She couldn't *leave*.

Where would she go?

Who would be there to keep her safe?

I stopped breathing as my eyes fell to the title page beneath.

*The Boy & His Ribbon*
*by*
*Della Wild*

My heart froze as the title harpooned me in the chest.

She didn't.

She couldn't.

She *promised*.

Our secrets were our lives.

No one must know.

No one must guess.

I'd taken her against the law.

I'd kept her from everyone's knowledge.

I'd fallen in love with her even though she was practically my kid.

*And yet…she's written it all down.*

Every sordid, broken, pure, delicious thing.

I couldn't stop my shakes or urgency as I grabbed the paper, tossed off the lighter, and ripped over the first page.

# Chapter Fourteen

## REN

## 2018

I'D NEVER BEEN the best reader—no matter how much time Della spent teaching me—yet reading that manuscript, I absorbed the words through my fingers as well as my eyes.

The story leapt from the pages, latching sharp fangs into my heart. Every emotion and carefully fabricated lie ripped apart my life, dousing me in blistering honesty, pouring its black and white truth into the wounds it left behind.

It wasn't just words that sliced me, but Della's voice. Her vibrant honesty. Her fierce tenacity reading aloud the secrets she'd written.

*...that was what he did to me, you see? He made my entire life a jewellery box of special, sad, hard, happy, incredible moments that I want to wear each and every day.*

\*

*I can honestly say Ren is my favourite word.*
*I love every history attached to it.*
*I love every pain lashed to it.*
*I love the boy it belongs to.*

\*

*To me, Ren was magical.*
*He might not have been able to read and write, but he was the smartest person I knew.*

\*

*I wish I could paint a better picture of how much I looked up to him.*
*How much I worshipped him.*

*How much I loved him even then.*

*

*Amazing what love can make someone do, right?*

*In my toddler brain, I associated him calling me Ribbon with his admittance of loving me. He'd accepted me as his own. He no longer needed to remind himself that I wasn't born to be his.*

*

*Sometimes, and don't judge me for this, but sometimes, I would do something naughty just to have him yell at me. I know it was wrong, but when Ren yelled, he drenched it with passion.*

*

*How many times do you think a person can survive a broken heart? Any ideas?*

*I would like to know because Ren has successfully broken mine, repaired it, shattered mine, fixed it, crushed mine, and somehow glued it back together again and again.*

*

*I was jealous that he was close to another when I was supposed to be the only one. I was angry that he turned to another for comfort and didn't come to me. But most of all, I was in shattered pieces because I wasn't enough anymore.*

*

### I'm in love with Ren Wild.

*It looks even worse in bold, doesn't it?*

*It looks like a life sentence I can never be free of…which, in a way, is exactly what it is.*

*

*But what I do know is I will always love Ren.*

*I will always be in love with Ren.*

*And I also know I will never have him.*

*

*Why do I do this to myself?*

*Why do I insist on slicing through the sticky tape on my constantly breaking heart and stabbing it over and over again?*

*Can you answer me because I'm honestly at the end of my limit.*

*

*The next time Ren and I ran, I wanted it to be for good. I never wanted to tie him to a new place so I could go to school. I never wanted him to feel as trapped as I did. I wanted to be free because maybe, just maybe, away from people and rules and constant reminders, Ren might slip enough to realise he loved me, too.*

*

*That was my true performance because he never knew how much I sobbed*

---

*the moment he closed the door, promising to be home soon.*

*I sobbed so much I couldn't breathe, and my tears were no longer tears, but great heaving, ugly convulsions where hugging myself didn't work, where lying to myself didn't work, where promises that it would get better definitely didn't work.*

*I'm sure you can probably guess what I did next?*

*If you can't, then you've never been in love with someone who was off making a future with someone else.*

My breath roared in my ears. My limbs turned shaky and liquid.

I only had minutes to read, but I skimmed as fast as I could, absorbing letters of pain, heartache, and confusion.

I recognised the moments she wrote about.

I remembered the attitude she gave me around Cassie. The jealousy she tried to hide. The possessiveness she never stopped nursing. The obsession of keeping our family just us and no one else.

I had no fucking idea her withdrawal and moods were because she thought I'd replaced her with Cassie. I was so naïve to think she hadn't seen me sneaking off to make out time and time again.

*Fuck.*

Even with the kiss she'd given me when she was thirteen, I'd believed her when she said it was purely growing pains and learning what attraction was.

An experiment, she called it.

I'd *believed* her when she lied point-blank to my face.

I'd chosen to trust what she said rather than focus on what her body language told me. What her eyes screamed. What her sighs whispered.

How could I be so fucking *stupid?*

How could I be so blind?

How had I not seen how distraught she'd been the night I went out on that second date with some woman I couldn't remember? How had I not heard her tears or run back to her to stop her from losing her virginity instead of forcing myself to believe I was doing the right thing by finding comfort in arms I was allowed rather than dying for the ones I wasn't?

My hands curled around the pages, wanting to wring her neck for years of bullshit, while at the same time, wanting to clutch her close and say I finally understood. Understood the unrequited pining. Understood the burning jealousy at the thought of anyone else having her but me. Understood the epic heights of such sweet agony and the almost addictive properties of loving someone you just can't have.

The night she lost her virginity, I'd done that. I'd pushed her into doing something final by believing I was the only one hurting. That I was the only one struggling with right and wrong.

*Fuck!*

I spun around, one hand latched around the pages and another tangled in my hair.

I needed to get the hell out of here before I did something unforgivable.

But…everything locked into place.

My heart stopped beating. My body stopped shaking. I swallowed a groan as Della stood dripping wet in a towel, glowering at me in the doorway.

We stared.

And stared.

And *stared*.

I didn't move.

She didn't move.

I hadn't heard the shower turn off.

I didn't feel her arrive.

I'd been too focused on learning the years of pain I'd put her through to focus on the present.

She'd been in love with me. Was she still? When did she know? How long had she lied? How badly had I ruined this?

Slowly, my heart tripped into beating again, wary and worried, quiet and quick.

With blazing blue eyes and wet blonde hair plastered against creamy shoulders, she padded barefoot toward me.

I stumbled backward, my knees giving way at the delirious perfection of seeing her again, of her seeing me, of us being alone together—away from others and judging opinions.

My lips parted to speak, to say something that could delete the years of agony, soothe months of hardship, and have her love me the same way she did before I'd stupidly run.

But my voice no longer worked, my lungs no longer operated. She closed the distance, bringing familiar smells of vanilla and melon until she reached out and snatched the pages dripping with secrets from my hands.

I flinched as if she'd punched me in the gut.

Tears glittered in her gaze as sadness so deep and cloying seemed to blur her before me. "You read them…" Her whisper fissured with soul-breaking disbelief.

And for the first time…I saw her.

*Truly* saw her.

Not as a baby.

Not as a toddler.

Not as a child.

I saw her as Della.

*Herself.*

Her own creation.

A creation I'd had no hand in, no part in nurturing or raising. She was no longer mine; she belonged only to herself, and she'd utterly crushed me beneath her written honesty.

"Ribbon," I breathed. My voice shook. My hands curled into fists as I took in her wild, wet, blonde hair, the sharp wings of her collarbone, the swell of her breasts beneath the towel, and the long willowy strength of her sun-kissed arms and legs.

The first time I'd used her nickname in far too long.

But I had no choice.

The word was torn from my entire being as I stood staring at the most stunning creature I'd ever seen.

How had I prevented my eyes from seeing?

How had I believed she was merely pretty—just my little Della who needed me to survive?

How had I convinced myself that she loved me only as a friend when everything between us flared hot and forbidden with years of pent-up desire?

She was never innocent like I believed.

She was never pure like I hoped.

She was *none* of those things.

Not anymore.

She was sin and sex and such sizzling chemistry, my entire body burst into flames.

I couldn't take my eyes off her.

I couldn't breathe as explosion after explosion hit me, realisation after realisation, acceptance after acceptance that I'd loved this girl since I'd stolen her yet…here now, this very fucking moment, I fell head over heels, madly, desperately, horribly in love with her, and it fucking *ruined* me.

Her words…her confessions…I didn't stand a goddamn chance.

I shot forward, grabbing her tight and clutching her to me.

A hug.

Our first hug in so damn long.

Her body was unyielding—no longer open to my touch. She was braver, stronger, sexier, and having her in my arms, my body shook off the shackles I'd always locked tight and fell away.

I hardened, I groaned, I buried my face in her hair and allowed myself to shake with fear of losing her.

She didn't move in my embrace. Her back bowed as I pulled her closer. Her breath caught as I wedged us tighter, no longer keeping propriety between us, allowing her to feel how affected I was having her in my arms, wanting her to know I was done lying to her and myself.

That I felt something I shouldn't feel.

That I'd felt it for years, and this was my confession after reading all of hers.

My hips rocked against hers, seeking an answer, desperate to know it wasn't too late as I burrowed my nose into her hair, inhaling her, kissing her, wanting to kiss her lips but unable to let go long enough to pull her face to mine.

I was close to breaking.

Emotionally, physically, sexually.

My mind was full of heat and sin, a clawing hunger that had nothing to do with sex but everything to do with finally showing her how I felt about her—how tortured I was because of it.

Holding her again, hugging her after years of miscommunication, bullshit, and dancing a dance we didn't understand, I felt as if I'd returned home, and the one person who was home no longer knew me or invited me in.

I was cast out into the cold, and my fingers dug harder into her skin as I shook my head against her rigidness, the coldness, the unbreakable ice she bristled with.

Pressure tingled in my spine, goosebumps prickled my skin, and a heaviness that could only be described as regret filled my eyes.

Tears distorted my vision for all the waste, all the mess we'd put each other through by not talking to one another. Not being brave enough to admit there was something more.

There had *always* been something more.

There had always been fate puppeteering our lives as if we were its own personal entertainment where survival fell away in favour of sex and two people who loved each other more than life itself were forced to break apart to stay bound by society's rules.

"Della." I forced myself to unwrap my arms and step back. My body howled at the distance, but I couldn't touch her when she didn't want to be touched.

"Please, Della..." I didn't know what I asked for, but the brittle unhappiness on her face snapped into rage-filled indignation. "I'm sorry."

*"Sorry?"* She laughed once, shattering the shocked silence between us, deleting her tears, and choosing rage over disbelief. Instead of stepping into my arms like I needed her to, instead of kissing me as I was begging her to, she hefted the heavy pages of her manuscript and threw them at my face with all her might.

They hit me square in the jaw, shredding my chin with paper cuts, sending me reeling backward as A4 snow fluttered to the floor.

"What the—" I rubbed the impact zone, wincing in pain.

"How *dare* you!" she seethed. "How *dare* you walk back in here and think you have any right to read what is mine? How dare you touch me after years of avoiding my hugs? How dare you, Ren! How fucking *dare* you!"

Her fury roared in my ears, and I backed up as she hit my chest with fist after tiny fist. Tears streaked down her face, mixing with errant droplets from her shower. Her bare toes dug into the carpet, pushing her forward, giving her power to defeat me.

"Get out!" Her cheeks turned red with hatred. "Get out. *Get out!"*

"Della! Wait—" I tried to grab her wrists as she pummelled me, but I didn't succeed. "Let me explain." Every time I touched her, my fingers seared with need. Having her so close made my body crave and harden and do things I'd always forbidden it to do around her.

It was a traitor, but then again, so was my goddamn heart.

She continued hitting me, her hair flying in damp curls. "There's nothing to explain. You left! You left me alone. You *left* me, Ren! I've cried myself to sleep, desperate to earn just *one* more hug from you, and now you're somehow here and I want nothing to do with them! You have no right to hug me. No right to read something that was never yours to read. How *could* you? That wasn't for you! That wasn't for *anyone*. It's not yours. It was *never* yours."

"Stop." Finally, I managed to grab her furious fists, gulping against the heaven of touching her. "What was never mine?"

Her eyes flashed, turquoise fire and navy brimstone. "*All* of it. None of it. It doesn't matter. Just…*get out!* Go back to wherever you ran to. I don't need you anymore. I *can't* need you anymore. This is too hard as it is." Her lips twisted into a grimace. "You're making this impossible for m-me—" Her voice broke as a sob stole her breath.

"Della. Fuck." Tugging her closer, I lost the ability to talk.

Words evaded me. Apologies and explanations and questions. Only my heart functioned, and that was full of newness.

"You might not need me anymore, but I need you more than ever," I whispered, holding tight as she struggled. "I've been so blind. So fucking blind."

She stilled, her sudden frozenness unnerving. "*What* did you say?"

"I said I'm sorry. So unbelievably sorry."

"*Ha!*" She wriggled out of my grip, pushing me away. "I don't want your apology. I don't *accept* your apology. You leave after promising you never would, then come back at the worst possible time? No. Nuh uh. I won't let you make me feel as if I've lost my mind. I won't let you do this to me, do you hear me?!"

"Do what? Come back because I can't survive without you? Come back to tell you the truth that's been fucking tearing me apart every day since I left—"

"Stop it!" She clutched her hair. "This isn't real. I'm imagining this. I've finally lost it, and you're just a figment—"

"I'm not. I'm real." I grabbed her wrists, yanking her hands from her golden strands. "I'm here. You're here. And I want to tell you that what I read in those pages…fuck, Della. Why didn't you tell me?"

Her gaze fell to the scattered paper by our feet. Her face twisted with another complex recipe of hate and horror. "God, you *did* read it. How much did you read? That wasn't yours, Ren! None of it was. It was mine, and you've taken that just like you've taken everything else from me!"

My heart imploded into a black hole, sucking everything into it until my insides hollowed out with grief. I'd not only hurt the woman I loved, I'd ruined her.

*Just like I ruined myself.*

"I didn't mean to hurt you. I didn't mean—"

"But you did! You left."

"But I'm back now."

"Yes, and you read something that was private!"

"But it's *us*. You wrote about us. Me and you. If I'm not allowed to read it, then who is?"

"Anyone but you!" She threw her hands toward the ceiling. "Literally anyone—" Her rage abandoned her with another rib-quaking sob. "God, why does this hurt so much?!" She stifled her sobs as fast as they appeared, but not before slicing my heart with their razor-sharp agony. "Just...go away."

"I'm not leaving."

"Well, I don't want you here."

"Too bad." I crossed my arms even though I trembled with every urge to sweep her off her feet, gather her close, and rock her on the bed. She was angry, yes, but beneath her anger was heart-shattering pain.

Pain I'd caused.

Pain I needed to repair.

Wiping away wet tears, she narrowed her eyes. Her chest rose and fell with temper as she bit out, "What are you doing here anyway? Why now? Do you know how hard you're making this for me? I thought I was going crazy when I came back here. Everything smells of you. My bed was made. The shower clean. I thought I'd lost it. But now...now it makes sense." Her anger smoked into something new and condemning. "Wait. You were here before...weren't you? Oh, God." She froze, flinching with ice. "How long have you been back?"

I squeezed the back of my neck. I wanted to discuss anything else but that. She hated me enough without giving her another reason.

"*Ren?*" She stepped closer, bringing her fury until it gnawed into my flesh. "How long, Ren?"

I swallowed hard before admitting, "A few weeks."

"Weeks!"

"Maybe a couple of months."

"*What?!*" She spun around, her towel loosening around her fuming frame, teasing me with glimpses of skin as she snatched it tight and jerkily re-did the knot by her breasts.

I gulped back a wash of insane hunger.

This was dangerous.

Our fights always made me feel out of control, and this one was no different. Yet this time, my desire to rip off her towel and force her to understand what I was saying overshadowed my desire to stop arguing.

What I'd been trying to say all along.

If only she'd fucking listen!

"I couldn't leave you," I snapped, my own temper building to match hers. I hated that she'd turned this moment into something violent instead of the homecoming I desperately needed. I hated that I'd hurt her so much she couldn't forgive me like she usually would. And I hated that ravenous appetites did their best to unhinge me and make me forget that I might be ready to accept that I wanted her in so many indecent ways, but first and foremost, I was her friend, protector, and caregiver, and she had every right to hate me for doing exactly what I said I'd never do.

"I abandoned you. I know that." I stepped forward, chasing her as she paced the small bedroom. "And you have every right to hate me. But, Della, I need you to listen. I came back because I couldn't stay away. I tried. I really did. I did my best to leave—to let you live your life without me ruining it even more—but each time I packed up my gear and hit the trail, I ended up doubling back until I found the same camp. I-I couldn't go. I couldn't stop what I feel for you."

If I expected a thawing in her temper at my inability to walk away, I was sorely disappointed.

Her cheeks glowed with a brighter red, her chest pink and flushed. She faced me head-on, scorn painting her face like vicious makeup. "You couldn't what? Go through with it? Turn your back on me? Your only family? Or you couldn't leave the comforts of the city after having running water and a salary for so long? Because I sure as hell don't think you came back for me!"

"I did. I came—"

"Don't you *dare* lie to me, Ren. Not anymore. I'm *done* with lies."

"Good, because so am I!"

"Fine!" she screamed. "So tell me what you came here to say and get lost!"

My gaze tripped to the floor where I stood on a page with the bold words **I'm in love with Ren Wild**, and my body jerked with hypocrisy. My own rage unfurled to treacherous levels as I pointed at the damning letters. "You're done with lies, huh? How do you explain this then? How do you explain every line you wrote and every confession you shared? You stand there judging me for leaving; you yell at me for daring to come back to tell you what I've wanted to tell you for years, and you pretend you have nothing to say in return."

I bent and snatched the paper, shaking it in her face. "How

long, huh? How many years did you live with me, laugh with me, love me all while lying to my goddamn face? Was everything fake between us, Della? *Was it?*" I threw the paper at her, watching it flutter and float to its fallen friends on the floor. "I don't know what's real anymore. I don't know what to do. I don't know how to fix this. All I know is…you're as much to blame for this as I am."

"How do you figure—" She huffed in disgust. "Are you saying I *didn't* love you? That I pretended to care about you even though you've been the only person in my life since I was a baby?"

"No—"

"Are you saying that I lied to you when I was a kid and told you I loved you? That I made it up when I said I was happiest teaching you in the hayloft or that my heart didn't splinter when I watched you with Cassie? What, Ren? What part of our life together am I lying about?"

"I'm not saying—"

"You are." She planted hands on her hips, showing off the swell of her breasts and the tormenting shadow of her nipple so close to being revealed if the towel slipped just a little more. "Then again, maybe you're saying that for seventeen years, I didn't care about you? That you weren't the most important person to me?" Her tears started anew, fresh and glittering. "That you weren't my world, or that I didn't need you, or that I didn't miss you every damn night since you left? That I didn't curse myself for everything I'd done, every mistake I made. That I didn't wish I could turn back the clock and change so many things. That I didn't beg for a chance to make it all better, to find a way to stop my heart from switching in its affection, to somehow seek a way to stop all the pain and—"

Angry sobs interrupted her tirade, giving me time to grunt around my own agony, "I'm not saying any of that—"

"Then what *are* you saying?"

"I'm saying you lied about how you loved me! A-and I…I lied, too."

Silence plummeted us into frigid waters, causing the fire between us to smoke and billow.

Her chest rose and fell as breathing bordered hyperventilation. We glowered at each other, truth bright and fragile and hesitant—almost as if disbelieving this was the moment we came clean.

*The* moment.

The moment we'd been running from for so fucking long.

Our eyes locked, clutching hard with the knowledge that this time...this time, we weren't shoving it under the rug, or pretending we hadn't just confessed, or running from the truth that none of this meant anything other than teenage hormones and miscommunication.

We were through with bullshit.

And it hurt to understand we'd both been hiding for so long. Both forgotten how to be honest. Both missing in a sea of deception.

Her eyes downcast, argument raging and fading while honesty made her hiccup just once. She glanced at the bold line I'd pointed at, the printed permanent reminder that I wasn't making this up. That for years, I wasn't picking up on signals that weren't there. That I wasn't going slowly insane.

I'd been reading her truth. But I'd been too afraid to face mine.

"Oh," she finally whispered, shrugging sadly. "Yeah, that."

My heart fucking shattered.

This time, I swooped toward her with more than just the need to touch her but with the desire to fix everything. To tell her she wasn't alone. Not anymore.

Grabbing her cheeks, I ran my thumbs over her cheekbones as I pushed her the final distance to the wall where her back pressed and her breath caught, and I lowered my head to nudge her nose with mine. "Yeah, that," I murmured.

My heart.

Fuck, my heart.

It cried at finally touching her in a way I'd wanted to do for so incredibly long. My body cursed for so many incidents where we could've solved this with conversation and not ran away.

Her teeth chattered beneath my fingers as she shook as much as I did. We'd always shook when we fought. Always been so affected by the other's temper that our worlds were in disarray until we stopped.

The familiarity of such a thing. The realisation that this wasn't just a girl I was in love with but the one person who'd been there every step of my existence made it hard to breathe.

I sucked in air greedily, lungs useless, panting against so many things while doing my best to chase away my trembles even as my entire body went weak and wobbly for finally holding my Ribbon this way.

The fallen papers crunched beneath my boot as I shifted my weight, leaning into her, seeking an answer. "Why didn't you tell me?"

She flinched, her eyes closing beneath an avalanche of pain. This hurt.

*Everything* hurt.

"Della...please." My calloused thumbs caressed her silky-soft skin, catching on her young perfection with my older imperfection.

Ten years separated us.

Ten years was an eternity when she was a babe and I was a boy, but now...it no longer held such power. I refused to let it because I didn't know what I'd do if I couldn't touch her the way I was touching her now.

She laughed quietly, full of torture and tragedy. "I did tell you. In a roundabout way."

"You didn't."

"But I did." She dared meet my eyes. "I never understood how I could touch you, hug you, kiss you, and you never knew. I didn't know how I could hide my jealousy when you were with Cassie or later with your one-night stands. I lay awake at night analysing every sentence I said to you, amazed that you never heard what I'd been shouting for longer than I could remember."

She pressed her face into my right hand, daring to donate a kiss on the edge of my work-worn palm even as her eyes flashed with resentment. "Is that what you came back to hear? To hurt me a little more? To force me to admit that I've been stupidly in love with you for years, and there was nothing I could do about it?" Her blue gaze burned. "Is it, Ren? Because fine, you got your wish. Whatever you read...it's true. I started writing it for college, but then I realised you were right all along. I can never tell people our story because they won't understand. To start with, I was more afraid of them seeking you out and putting you in prison for kidnapping, but now I'm more afraid that I'd be judged for falling in love with someone who raised me. I'm horrified of what they'd say, the looks they'd give, the disgust on their faces because, even though I understand it's morally wrong, I can't help how I feel."

She kicked a foot-trodden paper, her body wriggling against mine. "I'm sick of feeling like I have to hide. From you and everyone else. I'm sick of lying to David that one day I'll get over you. I'm sick of watching you self-destruct by sleeping with a parade of women when I was there all along. Wanting you. Waiting for you. Begging you to just open your stupid eyes and *see* me—"

My boot thudded heavily as I took the final step into her. My leg between her legs. My hips to her hips. My body against her body. My heart pounded as I cupped her cheeks harder, willing her to understand. "They're open now. Believe me. I see you." My fingertips burned as I forced myself to be gentle.

She froze, inhaling quick. Her eyelids fell to that sultry stare I had no power against, and this time, I didn't fight it. This time, my gaze latched onto her parted mouth, and I couldn't do anything else. I collapsed against her, I breathed in her delicious, familiar scent, and I pressed my lips—

She tore away, ripping her face from my hold and ducking beneath the cage of my arms.

For a second, my brain couldn't figure out what had just happened. That the kiss didn't connect. But as I spun around to face her, my jeans tight with unrequited desire, and my mind a fucking mess, I gulped back pure agony as she shook her head, wrapping tight arms around herself as more tears cascaded down her cheeks. "I-I don't know if you do. If you truly saw me, Ren, you'd understand that this—"

"This what?"

"Whatever this is won't fix what you've been running from."

"Don't you think I don't know that? That's why I'm here, Della. Aren't you fucking listening? I'm in love with you, too. Goddammit, can't you tell? Can't you see how much I'm breaking?"

That dreaded stifling silence fell again, numbing everything as she gawked at me. My words didn't seem to register, bouncing off a force field designed to protect her heart, but then they stabbed into awareness, and she crumpled in place, wincing and crying, shaking her head with panic. "What sort of cruel joke is this? You missed me in the forest so figured you'd get me back by telling me what you think I need to hear?"

There was no hope in her gaze, no joy like I hoped; only resignation and age-old grief. "I know you, Ren. I know you'd never let yourself think of me any differently than the way you always have. I'm your Little Ribbon. Untouchable. Protectable. Something to be adored but never touched. Oh no, *never* touched."

I closed my eyes briefly, unprepared for the depth of pain her mistrust caused. "I don't know how to make you believe me. I'm *in love* with you. I'm head over fucking heels for you. I have been for years. How can I make you see that?"

I spilled my darkest secret with my eyes still closed, and when I opened them again, she was closer to the door and farther from me, her gaze tormented with new thoughts. The same dangerous light she'd had when she cornered me with the idea of going to school the first time, of the suggestion we share a last name, of the fight when she didn't want to go back to the city after months of bliss in the forest—glowed bright and savage, ready to destroy me.

I knew that look.

It was a look that petrified me because I never won against it.

My hand rose, imploring her not to run or do something we'd both regret. "Della…"

She shook her head again. "Don't."

"Whatever you're thinking…stop it."

She licked her lips, her forehead furrowing deep. "I just remembered what you said."

"That I'm in love with you?"

"No. Before that. The truth."

"That is the goddamn truth. I love—"

"Stop it, Ren! Okay, just *stop* it!" she shouted, her tone snippy and sharp. "I can't deal with this. You're spouting nonsense that makes me think you hit your head. And that's after you admitted that you've been back for months. *Months!*" Her voice thinned until it was soundless. "You've been watching me, haven't you? I wasn't imagining it."

I hung my head. "No, you weren't."

"Every day?"

"Yes."

"How could you? How could you do that to me?"

I didn't understand how I'd hurt her, but I put aside my questions and bowed to hers. "Because I couldn't stop myself. I couldn't stand to be away from you."

"But you *left!*" Her voice rose with a breakable octave. "You left me. You walked out that door."

"I know."

"Ugh!" She blinked back tears, her body wobbling with sadness and rage. "Want to know why I don't believe that you're in love with me? Because if you were, there is no way you could wait so long. Months, you've been back. Months where you watched me and made me think I was going insane. Remember all those times growing up when I knew you stared at me and I stared at you? Remember how in-tune and aware we were of each other?

"I knew that day when you needed help counting and

charging up those hay-buying customers. I felt you looking at me over acres of paddock. I've woken up at night to you watching me. Just like you did with me. I've spent a lifetime learning how my skin prickles when you think of me. Did you forget that, Ren? Did you forget that I might have been lying to you for years, but you've just tried to do the same with me in the *worst* possible way?"

I shook my head. "I-I don't understand. I needed time to figure out how to tell you—"

"No, you needed time to do your best to convince yourself it wasn't real."

"If you know it's real, why are you arguing?"

"Because you didn't come to me the *moment* you returned. The difference of loving someone and being in love, Ren, is loving someone can be full of obligation and self-denial. But being *in* love makes you selfish and greedy and *hungry*. It turns you into a self-serving monster because you can't breathe unless you have the one person you need."

She laughed coldly. "I know because I've lived in that emotion for so damn long. I've hated myself for how much I wanted you. What I did to myself thinking about you. How I used other boys to scratch the itch that was you. But you? You watch me from afar. You selfishly know I'm safe, watching me, studying me, all while I'm left wondering if you're even still alive! How could someone who says they're in love with another do that, huh? How could you stay away when it's taking all I have not to rip off my towel and pull you down onto my bed even while I hate you?"

I staggered under her condemnation and the mental image of her tumbling naked on her bed. "Fuck, Della."

I didn't know what I cursed at. The brutal honesty of her latest confession or the barbaric, almost primitive need to climb on top of her and force her to believe me. To crawl inside her body and soul and growl into her ear while I took her violently. *'See? I am telling the truth. I do love you. I love you so much you make me goddamn insane.'*

But I shook away the dark brutality, taking my turn to be the sinner with secrets. "Regardless of what you think, I *am* in love with you, Della. And I stayed away because I-I—"

"What? *Tell me!*" she screamed, her sudden outburst ratcheting up my temper to uncontrollable levels. She'd successfully threaded lust with rage, and it was a cocktail I no longer had any power over.

"I wasn't ready, okay?! *Fuck*, I don't think I'll ever be ready to accept that I've fallen in love with the child I stole. That even now, I struggle seeing you as Della, grown-up and filled out, an adult in your own right, and not buckle beneath the image of you when you were five years old with your beautiful blonde hair and fascination with your ribbon."

I dug my hands into my scalp. "It makes me sick, okay? It makes me want to burn out my eyes for ever seeing you naked as a kid or hugging you when you were a teen. It makes me want to cut off my own cock for ever getting hard around you, for all the inappropriate thoughts I had about you, for despising the boys you dated, for wanting to die knowing you let another fuck you when all I ever wanted was the freedom to love you in that way."

My temper cindered into exhaustion, leaving me breathless. I shrugged brokenly with palms spread in surrender. "How can I admit such things to you, Ribbon? How can I stand here and confess that I've jerked off to images of you? That when you were still innocent, still untouched, still so fucking young, I was using other women to somehow find a way to remain honourable and not crawl into your bed? Do you know how many times my willpower almost failed? Do you know how many dreams I've had? How many times I've had you in my arms and on my lips, only to wake up and find it was all a fantasy?

"It was everything I could do to hide such things from myself, but you...I could never tell you because I couldn't stand for you to think of me as a monster. For you to see me as others' would. A paedophile. A beast. A twisted-up son of a bitch who would rather put himself first than the child he'd sworn his life to."

My breathing came ragged as she took a hesitant step toward me.

However, this time, instead of disbelief, there was a sliver of something, a fledgling hint of hope, an aura of satisfaction of finally, *finally* hearing my truth. "How long?"

I shook my head. That was one secret I wanted to take to my grave.

But she came closer, her towel slipping farther, her eyes getting softer. "How long, Ren?"

"It seems like forever," I moaned, shaking my head again, begging her to let it go.

Her fingers fluttered on my overly hot forearm. Sweat covered me from fighting and declaring. My energy was gone. I was more exhausted than I'd ever been in my entire life, but still, she didn't let it go.

"Please...I need to know."

I looked up, flinching at just tasting the words. My tongue burned with wanting to lie, to add on a few years, to not make myself such a child-stealing savage. But she'd been honest with me, and now, it was my turn to be honest with her.

Hesitantly, I raised my hand, cupping her cheek for the second time, grazing my thumb once again over the delicate bones that swooped up toward stunning blue eyes. This time, she didn't jerk away, and I stared so damn long into her that I became lightheaded and terrified.

My voice was barely a whisper as I admitted, "Since you kissed me."

She tilted her head, biting her lip as if her emotions threatened to drag her under, but not before she got her final answer. "Which time? The kiss that drove you away or the kiss in the stable at Cherry River?"

I closed my eyes.

I'd been given an opportunity to hide the worst of my transgressions. I could say it was the kiss she'd given me when she was seventeen—so close to eighteen that it was no longer illegal to fall in love with a minor.

But...I couldn't do it.

Tonight had been a truth-tearing hurricane, and I had no choice but to murmur, "When you were thirteen." I sighed with every sickness and shame I'd carried for five interminably long years. "The night you woke me up kissing me."

*"Oh."*

One tiny sound as she jerked and fell.

I wasn't prepared for the way she crumpled. The way her legs gave up supporting her. The way her body shoved aside her anger and tumbled pliant and welcoming into my arms. And I definitely wasn't prepared for the way her eyes welled with a different kind of tear.

A tear full of heartache and years of hiding; a glistening, glittering joy that infected my heart until I felt forgiven. Understood. *Redeemed.*

Somehow, without saying a word, she gave me absolute absolution.

"I thought you hated me for that."

"I did." I pressed my forehead to hers, needing to be close, needing to sit down. "But not for reasons I made you think. Not for reasons I made myself believe."

"You saw me that night? Truly saw me."

"I saw that my feelings toward you were changing. That there was something unsaid between us. Something that wasn't allowed. Something that only grew bigger and more incessant as we grew older."

"Is this real?" she breathed. "Did you honestly just say you fell in love with me the night I fell in love with you?"

My knees quaked as I backed toward her bed, holding her tight and forcing her to trip with me. "I think I fell in love with you the day I returned for you in that house where I'd left you as a baby. The moment you saw me, you crawled so fast. You knew you were mine, and I was yours, even then. I'd never had anyone be so excited to see me. So innocent with their affection. So trusting that I'd keep her safe."

I sat down heavily. The instant the mattress held my depleted weight, Della spread her legs and climbed onto my lap, her towel opening indecently, revealing naked heat-flushed skin that I desperately wanted to drink.

But I forced myself to keep my eyes on hers, adoring the way her legs wrapped around my back and her arms looped around my neck and our foreheads remained glued together, our eyes so close, our lips so near.

This was all so new, and yet, so heartbreakingly familiar.

This was Della.

She was my home.

"I'm not saying I fell in love with you in this kind of way," I murmured as our lips inched closer. "I'm saying there are so many ways I fell in love with you. Most of them pure and utterly unconditional, but that night in the stable, the night you entered my dreams and made me plummet...that night was different."

Her chest rose and fell, her nipples pink and tight in my peripheral vision as her towel fell away, draping damply over my arms where I hugged her.

She breathed quicker, harder, as our mouths crept ever closer, quietly, tentatively, afraid that any moment this perfection would shatter, and we'd wake from yet another life-tormenting dream.

"I'm sorry I made it impossible for you to stay," she whispered, looking deep, deep into my eyes, all that trust and affection and connection back in place.

She was home, just like me.

She'd returned to being the girl I would kill for and the

woman who had every power to kill me. Only this time, there were no shields. No blockage of honesty. No slurry of lies. The way she looked at me was unlike anything she'd done before.

I'd caught glimpses, sure. The nights in the forest after she'd run away. The moments before I'd head out for a shallow night of pleasure with unknown women. The seconds before I'd climb into bed and she'd stare at me from the corridor as I turned out the lights.

Glimpses and glances—windows into the world of just how desperately she loved me, the same world I'd been hiding from her.

"You didn't make it impossible. You were trying to make things better by pushing me to admit what I was afraid of." I brushed back her hair, my body hardening, heating. My mouth watering, tingling.

Our lips drew closer still, magnets intent on connecting.

A new kind of energy crackled around us—just as dangerous and potent, but this time, it was passion, not rage.

Passion I never believed I was permitted to feel around her.

Passion I never thought I could earn.

I basked in it, loving the spark and sizzle of her body pressed against mine. Of the wondrous anticipation of where this was going, the build-up of seventeen years of living in each other's pockets, of being each other's everything, of finally coming full circle from friends to possibly more.

More than I could ever deserve.

The first graze of mouths was barely there. A whisper of touch. A kick of taste. But my heart ran away, galloping and pounding as wild as our shared surname and just as feral.

Della jerked in my arms, sucking a shaky breath. Her legs squeezed around my waist, her arms twitching around my neck. "Ren?"

My eyes were too heavy to keep open. They went half-mast. My body aching. My mind messed and incoherent. "Yeah?"

"I want to kiss you."

I licked my lips, groaning beneath my breath. "Yeah, me too."

"But...you need to know something."

The back of my neck strained with pressure, desperate to press my mouth to hers and devour any more words. I no longer wanted conversation. I wanted something so much less innocent that damn conversation. "What do I need to know, Della Ribbon?"

She shivered as I ran my fingers up her naked spine and ducked to press a kiss on the very same collarbone that had tormented me for most of my life.

Old memories crackled like ancient TV channels, overlapping the Della I had in my arms with the baby I'd carried in my backpack.

I jerked and shoved the disgusting comparison away, doing my best to silence the voice hissing that this was wrong. That I had no right. No permission.

"You kiss me," she murmured, her back bowing, pressing more of her skin into my mouth. "And that's it. There's no going back. No way I can stop loving—"

I didn't let her finish.

My arms banded tighter, and my chin arched up.

And I kissed her.

Hard.

Deep.

Wet.

Long.

I kissed her for all the nights I'd wanted to kiss her but couldn't.

I kissed her for all the years I'd needed her but daren't.

And she kissed me back.

Just as hard, deep, wet, long.

Her taste.

Her softness.

*Jesus Christ.*

She moaned into me, her tongue darting out and licking mine. Her body writhing on my lap, her weight and movement rubbing against the rigid hardness in my jeans.

I wanted so fucking much to shove aside my clothing and consummate this newfound acceptance. I wanted to propose to her and marry her and never let her go again.

But as our kiss turned from exploration and newness to uncivilised grinding and gasping, the same crackling, snowy memories came back.

Of Della laughing as I cannonballed naked as a fifteen-year-old into the lake.

Of Della crying when she was stung by a bee and my seventeen-year-old self sucking out the stinger and kissing her wound all better.

Of Della reading aloud the sex education book when I was

eighteen and just as lost as I'd ever been, finally realising that she was so far above me I could never get her back.

*Boom, boom, boom.*

*Reminder, reminder, reminder.*

I tore my lips from hers and shot up.

Twisting sharply, I placed her on the bed and yanked out of her embrace before her eyes had fully opened and her lips fully noticed they were no longer being kissed.

"What?" Her eyes instantly filled with blue terror. "Ren...no." She scrambled to her knees. Naked as the day she'd torn off her dress and forced me to see that she was no longer a virgin. No longer untouched. "Don't do this. You promised."

I backed away, pinching the bridge of my nose, unable to stop the torrent of recollections.

Of Della riding Cassie's horse for the first time and falling off.

Of Della giggling at something Patricia said only to stop laughing when I went in hearing distance.

Of Della watching me with a heart-stealing look as I chopped firewood shirtless.

Della.

Della.

*Della.*

Always there, always mine, and now, I didn't know how to separate past from future.

"I-I—" I balled my hands, forcing myself to look her in the eye. "I want you, Della. You know that now, and I have no intention of lying to you. I'm in love with you. I want to be with you. But right now...right now, I need to work through this, okay? Can you give me time? Can you understand how hard this is for me?"

She stood, fumbling for her towel and holding it as a barricade in front of her. "I understand because it's hard for me, too. Don't you think I have the same memories? Of you kissing Cassie? Of you younger and softer and nothing more than an uncomplicated farm boy who made me fall in love with a single smile?"

I held up my hand. "I know this is unfair, but our situations are nothing alike."

"They're *everything* alike."

"No." I shook my head firmly, scolding her like a child when, only seconds ago, I'd been kissing her like a man. What role did I play in her life anymore? Disciplinarian or partner? Father or husband? "They're not alike. At all."

Stalking to the door, I wrenched it open before saying softly, "I raised you, Little Ribbon. In my heart, I hold so many elements of love for you. I've fed you from my own fingers. I've washed your body. I've held you tight while you cried. I know we aren't siblings, but somewhere along the way, I did love you as a brother. I need to untangle that love before I can move on as…as—"

"As my lover?"

I winced. "Yes."

"Are you sure you want to be? This isn't just you running away again?" Her eyes sparkled with another wave of unshed tears.

I hated that I'd let her down all over again, but I wouldn't be honest with her if I didn't tell her how hard this would be. How difficult I found it separating all the Della's I knew, and *somehow* learn to allow myself to love all of them after she'd been off-limits for so long.

But I also knew if we were going to do this, we couldn't do it here.

We couldn't do this where people knew us as relatives.

We couldn't do this where we might be caught.

"Do you still have the same phone number?" I asked, my fingers clutching the doorknob, holding myself in place, stopping me from running back to her and shoving her down on the bed.

From this distance, all I wanted was her, but I knew the moment I touched her my world would shatter, and I'd drown beneath memories determined to make me vomit for taking a sweet, innocent girl and turning her into something sick with want.

"Yes." She hung her head. "But I won't be here when you get back. I have to go back to David's. I only came here to burn that." She arched her chin at the scattered forgotten papers, trodden and crumpled on the floor.

My chest ached at the thought of her going back to him, but I had no choice. "Don't burn it. And give me a few hours. I'll text you, okay?"

She looked up, forlorn and afraid but resilient just like I knew her to be. "A few hours? I thought you were going to say a few days."

I smiled sadly. "I've wasted more than enough days not having you. I have no intention of wasting anymore."

She smiled, wider than before. "Okay, I can accept a few hours."

"Thank you." My eyes drank her in, imprinting this Della, the *new* Della into my mind first and foremost as I backed out the door, promising, "I'll be in touch. And when I do…we're going to talk. You're going to help me understand that there was no other path for us. That it was always going to be this way. That we were always meant to be. And then…we're going to leave."

I didn't wait for her reply.

I had some soul searching to do.

I had some compartmentalizing to sort.

And I needed to do it now.

Because once I did.

I could have her.

And my complicated world would finally be complete.

# *Chapter Fifteen*

## REN

## 2018

DELLA: *ARE YOU ready to talk about this?*

The glow of my cell-phone screen lit up the night-shrouded park where I rested. The bench made my ass flat from hours of sitting, watching the sun go down. Pruned bushes and carefully controlled trees granted a sense of home, but nothing was wild about their regimented flowerbeds.

I'd meant to move. I'd meant to text Della hours ago, but once I'd opened the gates of so many stored memories, I couldn't rush it.

It was a curse to have a good memory.

I didn't have to strain to pull up image after image of Della as a two-year-old, five-year-old, ten, fourteen, sixteen. I knew her body and scars from falling off horses and clumsy incidents better than I knew my own. I knew more about her than any lover should. And I didn't like how that made me feel.

Was it right for me to want her body that I'd seen grow from so small to so stunning? Was it disgusting to admit, even though I'd carried her as a child and cared for as a baby, I saw her as more than just my responsibility and legacy now? I saw her as my other half. My future. Everything I'd ever been searching for.

I guess I'd *always* seen her as my other half; I just didn't have the lust component to go with it. It made sense now why I'd always felt lonely even when she was in my arms—because some part of me knew it wanted more but couldn't have it.

Sighing heavily, I pressed reply. The alphabet spread out on an on-screen keyboard, waiting to transform thoughts into messages.

Thanks to Della, I could read, write, spell, and wrangle technology enough to be proficient. Even when we'd moved away from the Wilsons and our regular study sessions were replaced with long hours at the milking shed and Della traded me for other boys, I hadn't stopped learning.

Instead of Della being the one to choose which textbook or subject I'd study, I merely went through her school rucksack on the nights I wasn't exhausted and read science books, math, English, then stole a few pieces of paper to work out the answers before checking mine against hers.

She'd caught me once or twice and had rushed over to kiss me. But then, she'd remembered that kissing wasn't exactly permitted anymore and would pat my shoulder with a strained smile instead.

I knew she was proud of me for continuing my studies, but I didn't do it for me. I did it for her. I did it so I could converse and calculate and not have to rely on her because I knew my job as her caregiver was almost over, and she would leave me for better things.

And when that day happened, I couldn't afford to be illiterate without her.

Then again, I'd left her before she'd left me.

And now...now there was a chance we would never be apart again.

My heart cramped with a hope so vicious it made me shake.

My fingers typed slowly, deleting my regular typos, hoping my spelling was on point. I wanted to be honest with her. I needed to be. She needed to know just what she was getting into because this was me putting everything on the line. This was me ripping up my world when I still didn't fully understand if I could.

Me: *I don't know if I'll ever be fully ready. If this was happening to someone else, and not you and me, how repulsed would you be if you knew the man was contemplating sleeping with his own kid?*

*Goddammit.*

I sat forward, digging my elbows into my knees and wiping my mouth with my hand.

*Fuck.*

Seeing it in black and white, reading how foul that sounded, I very almost dry-heaved. What the hell was I doing? I'd been driven by my desire for so long that I'd forgotten what this actually entailed. What sort of sins we were about to commit. What sort of mess we were about to create.

This wasn't me.

I wasn't this self-obsessed.

I ought to be her father figure.

I ought to be better—

Della: *First, I'm not your kid. I never felt like you were my father, and there was never any confusion about what we meant to each other. Second, forget about everyone else. They don't matter. I couldn't judge on another's life just like I don't want them to judge us.*

My head hung as I ran my fingers over the touchpad. She was right, I supposed. For some reason, we'd always clung to the boundaries that we weren't blood or related, almost as if we knew eventually we'd want more than just friendship.

Before I could reply, she sent another.

Della: *You told me this afternoon that we were going to talk. And we're talking. But if I'm honest, I don't think this can be rationalised by text message. You asked me to help you understand that there was no other path for us. That it was always going to end this way. That we were always meant to be. I'm not just saying what you want to hear, Ren. I truly believe that. And the only way to come to terms with it is to just...trust me, trust you, trust us.*

I sighed.

Her message was a lot kinder in black and white than mine had been. She'd successfully thrown my own words in my face, making me see there was no other choice for us. Even if she hadn't kissed me and firmly imprinted herself into my dreams, I would have eventually fallen for her because a man like me, I didn't love easy. I didn't trust easy. It'd taken me seventeen years to even admit I was ready to put my heart on the line in a romantic sense rather than family.

Cassie had known that about me. She'd sensed that I would never care more for her than gentle affection because I was too afraid to open myself up to pain.

Della was the only one worth risking such agony.

And as much as I'd vehemently deny it, I'd already been hurt by the Mclary's which sort of gave Della permission in a strange, unfathomable away.

She was the only one allowed to hurt me in the future.

I opened a new window and typed slowly:

Me: *Are you willing to let me work through this? Do you understand it won't be an overnight switch for me? It's going to take time.*

The moon hung heavy above, reminding me that it had been too long since I'd been in the forest. As much as I needed to live in the apartment to stay close to my addiction of stalking Della, I'd had my fill of cities.

I hadn't liked living here when Della was finishing school. There was no way I wanted to live here while we figured out whatever we were about to embark on. We'd had a near miss with her principal with rumours of her being in love with me. A mere rumour almost separated us. Now it was fact, we stood every chance of being ripped apart.

This had always felt like a temporary place. A chapter that didn't quite fit.

If it was over and we could go home...*thank God.*

Della took her time replying, and I reclined against the pigeon-crapped bench, exhaling hard.

Della: *I can't promise I won't get frustrated. I can't say I won't get mad if you kiss me, then pull away. But what I can promise is, I've wanted this since I was thirteen, and if you need another thirteen years to accept that I was born for you, then so be it. I'll be patient.*

I chuckled quietly, wincing as it turned to a cough.

I doubted she meant to be funny, but even now, her temper came through something as impersonal as a text. Somehow, it made me feel better—as if I wasn't such a monster to contemplate such a crazy idea as taking her for my own.

Me: *If we do this, we can't do it here.*

Della: *I know.*

Me: *Don't say you know as if nothing else matters. We need to think about this. You're in college. When does your course end? You're with David. How will he take you breaking up with him? What about your job at the florist? We have an apartment and furniture to get rid of. Are you prepared to say goodbye to another home?*

It took much longer for me to type such long sentences than Della, and my leg bounced as I pressed send, nervousness trickling through my blood. It wasn't a simple matter of running like previous times. We had things holding us here. We had bills and people. Or at least…Della did. She was more adult than I was in this scenario, and once again, my mind tripped down memory lane, feeding me images of her young and innocent and untouchable, doing its best to unhinge my resolve that this was what I wanted. No matter how hard.

Della: *I've already written regarding my course and withdrawn, stating a family emergency. I used part of the rent money to pay for the first semester—which I doubt I'll get back. But where we're going, we don't need the cash. I quit my job a while back. I'm not dating David; he turned me down when he realised I wasn't over you, and the apartment is easy. Terminate the lease, put our furniture back on the street corners where we got them from, pack a bag and…let's go home.*

My heart pounded as a breeze kissed my cheek, tugging me toward the black spaces where the city lights didn't reach. The darkness full of leaves and rivers.
Home.
I knew where my home was.
Did she?

Me: *Home means no running water, no supermarkets, no roof. Are you sure you want that?*

Della: *I don't know if reminding you of a younger me is a good idea, but on the night of my seventeenth and your twenty-seventh, I gave you that tent. Remember what I said?*

I groaned under my breath. That was one memory that wasn't just remembered but polished daily and treasured. She'd let me see behind her fakery that night. She'd painted a future that I'd desperately wanted, even while believing it could never happen.

Me: *You asked if I intended to stay here and said we had to start thinking about our future. That you wanted to return to the forest, and that's why you bought me that tent.*

Della: *And you asked if I was sure. You made a point to tell me there would be no boys, no jobs, no school. No future out there in the wilderness.*

Me: *And you set me straight by saying there was no future apart from with me.*

I looked at the moon again, tension slipping away. I was torturing myself about wanting Della as deeply as I did when, for so many years, I'd already been living with the same sin. I'd already accepted the mess, even then. And I wouldn't do anything to jeopardise it now. Not when we were so close.

My lips curled into a hesitant smile as my mind raced with everything we'd have to achieve. Every goodbye we had to finalise. Every beginning we were about to embrace.

Standing from the bench and striding toward the apartment, hopefully for the last time, my fingers flew, and I sent.

Me: *Pack a bag. We leave in two days.*

# Chapter Sixteen

## REN

## 2018

TWO DAYS

Forty-eight hours to delete our entire existence as the Wilds.

Della and I kept our distance while we systematically dismantled our world. She focused on selling, donating, and sorting through her stuff at David's house, while I lugged our fifth-hand couch up the steps of our place, and dragged it to the same street corner we'd salvaged it from.

My body proved just how badly I'd treated it the past few months and the residual cough from the flu made tasks last longer than I wanted.

I didn't like that Della had refused to sleep at our apartment, insisting that she owed David too much to abandon him without explaining and they needed a proper goodbye.

The urge to forbid her—the desire to beg her to be with me instead, proved I needed to keep my possessiveness in check. I'd never stopped her from hanging with her friends before.

I wouldn't start now.

Instead, I threw myself into my tasks, doing my best to tie up loose ends quickly so Della was mine and we could leave.

Scrawling a hasty poster, I announced a one-day garage sale and opened our apartment to anyone who wanted cutlery, crockery, bedding, an ancient TV, decrepit motorcycle, and anything else we couldn't carry.

I made sure to wash and pack clothes for both Della and me. Winter jackets, summer t-shirts, and every season in between. She still had her bag that we'd bought when we left the Wilsons, and I studiously ensured our rations and belongings were evenly distributed, even though I put all the heavy stuff into mine. The two pots for cooking, the many lighters I couldn't function without, the multiple knives I carried even though I constantly had at least three on my person at all times.

Della messaged me on the first day of our self-eviction from this city and said she'd called the landlord, cancelled our lease, and asked for our returned bond to be paid in cash. We didn't have a fixed contract anymore, so we weren't breaking any rules, and I left her in charge of cutting off the electricity and gas, leaving the apartment as dark as the forest on my last night in so-called civilisation.

With Della staying one last night at David's, I bunkered down in the empty space, lying on a thin yoga mat I'd stolen a few months ago in the very same sleeping bag I'd washed and prepared for our upcoming disappearance back home.

All that existed from the life we'd created in this apartment were empty walls and lonely carpet. Not one plate left in the cupboards, not a single blanket left in the laundry.

All gone.

My phone buzzed in the darkness.

Della: *I know we said I'd swing by our place and stuff the rest of my clothes into the backpack you have prepared for me, but…David has requested you come here.*

I shot upright, jack-knifing off the floor.
*What the fuck for?*
Ignoring my chugging heart, I wrote back:

Me: *What did you tell him? Is he planning on killing me? Does he have a gun?*

Della: *What? Don't be ridiculous. He won't kill you. And I told him the truth. He already knew it anyway.*

Me: *Goddammit, Della. I feel sick about this already without being judged by him. I'm the guy who raised you, who is now stealing you into a life of uncertainty, and who stole you from him. Of course, he wants to kill me.*

Della: *He wants to understand. That's all. Love hasn't been kind to him either, Ren. And you did beat him up, after all. You kind of owe him an apology.*

Me: *I beat him up because he stole you from me.*

She took a long time to reply, and I could hear her thoughts as if they were my own. *He didn't steal me. You pushed me into his arms. He didn't take my virginity. I gave it to him as I was over being hurt by you.*

My shoulders slouched, and I reclined back into my sleeping bag, cursing myself all over again. By the time her message buzzed in the dark, I was ready to agree to whatever she wanted if only to try to make amends to her, David, and frankly, even to myself.

Della: *Closure, Ren. I think we both need it. I think you need to understand what we're doing. You need to accept that we're leaving together— just like old times. But unlike old times, we know exactly what we're going to do out there...alone. You can't lie to yourself anymore. You can't imagine a life of happiness with us side by side and believe it will be like before. It will be better. Because this time, we aren't lying. We ARE going to sleep with each other. We ARE going to learn about each other on an entirely different level. And if you can't accept that in front of David, then...I'm actually terrified that you'll never be able to accept it. What's to stop you from changing your mind if this gets too hard? What if you can't stop the images of me as a kid when you see me naked? What if you break down the moment you slip inside me and can't go through with this? Where does that leave me? What will that mean for us? I want this, Ren. You have no idea how MUCH I want this. But I'm also so scared because if this doesn't work, if you can't accept it, then I'll lose so much more than just a lover. I'll lose you all over again, and not having you was the worst thing I've ever endured.*

My breathing was loud and heavy. My eyes flying over her message again and again. We were no longer talking about David. She'd somehow opened the vault of her terrors and shared them with me. I hadn't stopped to think how hard this would be from her point of view. I'd returned to her, told her I was in love with her, flipped her entire world upside down, and asked to take her away from the people who knew her, all with only a vague promise that we would try for more.

There was no guarantee this could work.

I couldn't promise I could get past my ethics.

Of course, she panicked and didn't believe me.

Of course, she doubted me when I'd kept so many boundaries between us for so long.

I didn't know if I'd ever be able to make her see that my mind was made up—even if there would be struggles along the way. I was willing to work through them because I'd do anything required to keep her.

Once again, before I could put my thoughts in order, she sent another message.

Della: *Sorry, Ren. I...I don't know where that came from. Just please, tomorrow when we leave, come collect me from David's. Say goodbye to him and Natty. Hug me in front of him. Tell him what I've been telling him for months. Let him be the first to see you do mean this. That I'm not imagining it. That this is real. Please...*

The glowing phone lit up the empty bedroom where Della had slept innocently for so many years, all while I'd banished myself to the pull-out couch, desperate for distance. Certain that if I could keep physical distance between us, it would manifest into emotional distance, too.

*It never did.*

It'd only made my need for her increase because all my life, I'd been used to sleeping with her beside me, of her breathing in the night, of her warmth in the dark.

And I'd forbidden myself to have that comfort the moment her kiss changed everything.

Was it weak to admit that I'd been living a half-life since the day we left Cherry River? Was it twisted to acknowledge that I'd gone from having affection and kisses from the one person I loved more than anyone, to months on end of no touch, all because I couldn't understand how a hug could hold so many different languages and complications?

I wasn't fluent enough to hug her while pretending it was platonic.

I wasn't brave enough to touch her while masking every unsaid craving between us.

And now, Della wanted me to hug her in front of David.

But that wasn't what she was asking.

She was asking me to stop pretending. Begging me to stop fighting, to finally permit myself to sink into those cravings, knowing full well I would never be able to swim back out.

She was afraid I could walk away from her after this.

Afraid I was about to steal her entire life and leave her broken when I realised I couldn't do it, after all.

But it was the wrong thing to be afraid of.

What she should fear was the part of me I'd kept hidden from her.

For seventeen years, she'd brought out the best in me. She'd nurtured my sense of honour, duty, and devotion to the point where she didn't know any different.

She never glimpsed the other part of me.

The part that had steadily grown worse the longer I denied myself what I wanted.

The savage part.

The violent part.

The first person to see it was Cassie.

After our first time having sex, she'd chuckled and told me I was far more dominating than her other lovers. That the boy who used to flinch when she kissed him was no more.

She said I had a tornado wrapped around my heart—tightly coiled and mostly contained until it came to sex.

At the time, I'd denied it.

It made me sound like a monster, even if she tried to assure me it was just a primitive part of me taking over. That it was normal. That some men were more aggressive than others. But as we sneaked into the stables again and again, I'd learned something new about myself.

She was right.

I couldn't stop it.

The Ren who would give his own life to save Della's vanished during sex when he no longer thought about others but himself. Only himself.

I hated it.

And as I shared hollow fucking with faceless women to rid that steadily building desire for Della, I couldn't ignore it any longer.

I wasn't as noble as I liked to believe.

In all aspects of my life, Della came before me. I sacrificed everything I could for her. I gave her the clothes off my back, the sweat off my brow, and the promises from my heart.

Nothing was too much.

No request too crazy.

But when it came to sex…I wasn't giving.

I wasn't selfless.

I wasn't soft.

And that was yet another thing that kept me awake at night, because even if I could come to terms with sleeping with Della, how the hell could I ever tell her that the Ren she knew would not be the Ren she loved when I was inside her?

I trembled in my sleeping bag as I shoved aside such thoughts and focused on putting her mind at rest even while mine rode a stormy sea.

Me: *Okay, Della. If you need a public display of affection, I'll do it. I'll come to his place tomorrow once everything is done, and I'll hug you in front of him. I'll lay claim to you. I'll kiss you if that's what you need. But then, we're leaving, and we're never coming back.*

I didn't mention my rapidly building concern that, once we were in the forest, surrounded by all-seeing trees and all-knowing birds, things would change once again.

That the fight to see her as my...*lover*...and not just my friend, was just the first of our many problems.

Hopefully, by the time we were alone and ready to do whatever it was we'd do, I'd have that part of myself under control. And she'd never have to see me as anything other than her sweet, protective Ren.

My phone vibrated just as I rolled onto my side, ready to rest so I wasn't wired from lack of sleep tomorrow.

It would already be hard enough; I didn't need to be fighting exhaustion.

Della: *I never want to come back. Kiss me. Hug me. Let him see that this is real, and you can take me wherever you want, for however long you want, any way you want. And yes, that's a thinly veiled sexual innuendo. The kind that I've been dying to say to you for years. To be free to finally do it...I have to keep pinching myself to believe it's real. Until tomorrow, Ren. Xxx*

My body hardened at the thought of kissing her again, followed immediately by the nauseous feeling of doing something wrong.

Here she was messaging me things we'd danced around for years, all while sleeping in the same house as the boy she'd lost her virginity to. Strange how actions had driven us to this place, and they were about to drive us to somewhere new entirely.

Sighing heavily, I adjusted myself before typing two words.

Two terrifying, exhilarating, life-changing, heart-winging words.

Me: *Until tomorrow.*

# Chapter Seventeen

## REN

## 2018

MY BACK ACHED from carrying two sets of camping gear.

One clinging to my shoulders, the other dangling from my hands.

Two over stuffed backpacks. Two sleeping bags. Two wardrobes for two people about to say goodbye to buildings and bills and people.

Unlike when I was a kid—fearing I didn't belong and would be noticed—I boldly wore my earth tone t-shirt and cargos. Wanting them to see that I didn't bow to fashion or conformity, that I only wore clothes for one purpose: practicality.

My pockets were full of matches, lighters, knives, and first-aid kits.

I had enough snares and traps to ensure we didn't need a supermarket for weeks and enough packets of rice, pasta, and other easy-to-cook things that meant we could vanish into the woods and never been seen again.

Not by this city or its inhabitants, at least.

*Good riddance.*

Coming to a stop outside the house I knew well, the same street where I'd stood and watched Della with despicable shame, I couldn't take another step.

My boots—complete with yet another knife tucked by my ankle and tramping socks protecting toes from blisters—froze to the pavement. I physically couldn't open the white picket fence or stride up the pretty garden path.

The same path where David had hugged and kissed my Della.

The same path where I'd carried Della from accidentally punching her the night I tore her from David's bed.

*Fuck.*

The front door swung wide as Della bounded from the house, her blonde hair secured in a ponytail, her lithe body encased in sturdy jeans, dusky pink t-shirt, and matching hiking boots.

No dresses or stupid sandals.

An outfit to run.

A dress code of living in the forest.

*We're really doing this.*

My stomach clenched for the fortieth time since I'd handed back the key to the apartment, done one final sweep of the place, tossed out the last of our accumulated junk, and made my way here.

Early afternoon and our lives were about to swerve into terrifying territory—not because we were homeless again, but because I was petrified of what would happen the moment our tent was erected and the stars announced our bedtime.

Would we sleep together tonight?

Was I ready?

Would I ever be?

She didn't stop until she flew to the gate and unlatched it, granting me invitation to step onto another man's property. "You came."

"Of course, I came." I scowled, unable to stop my stress from tainting my voice. "This is hard enough without you doubting me and acting surprised every second."

She smiled, dipping her head. "You've been gone for six months, Ren. You'll have to get used to me poking you at random times just to make sure you're real. I missed you." Stepping toward me, she ducked around the backpack I held in front of me, slotting her body into mine. "I missed you so much—you have no idea."

My fingers tightened on the rucksack straps, desperate to drop it, but propriety still commanded I keep it as a barrier between us, even as my heart yearned to gather her close.

My temper softened at the pain on her face. "I have some idea, Della." Ducking to kiss her swiftly on her cheek like I'd done for years—an innocent peck that was permitted—I murmured, "I missed you, too. Enough to make me face things I never wanted to face."

She stared into my eyes, studying me. "In that case, I'm glad you left."

"What?"

"I'm glad because if you didn't, maybe you'd never have…"

"Been brave enough to admit it?"

She nodded.

My fingers clenched on the straps, begging to release so I could cup her cheek.

But then, I looked up.

And there he was.

*David.*

And all my tenderness vanished beneath seething temper.

Arms crossed, lips thin, eyes narrowed as he glared at me from the front door. He judged me in ways I'd already judged myself.

Paedophile.

Sick fuck.

Blasphemer.

It didn't help that I agreed with him.

The urge to hit him all over again thrummed in my fists. Della noticed my quaking, turning to look over her shoulder. But as she twisted against me, I remembered what I'd promised her last night.

A hug.

A declaration.

A vow to this new direction.

She wanted me to accept this. *Us.* Well, I wanted to make him pay.

My fingers released the straps and, as the clunking sound of a survival-filled bag tumbled to the pavement, I reached for her in ways I'd never reached before.

My arms latched around her, holding her deep against me, forcing her to inhale me, feel me, accept me as my boots nudged against hers, and I hugged her so damn hard.

She made a noise of surprise as I deliberately slipped one hand to the back of her head and one to the bottom of her spine. Once I had such a dominating grip on her, I splayed my fingers through her hair, fisted the ponytail dancing down her back, and spread my touch along the top of her ass. In one seamless move, I pulled her hair down to tip her head up and pressed her hips shamelessly into mine.

She gasped as I held her prone and helpless, but I didn't kiss her.

I captured her in ways I ought to go to hell for.

And I looked up toward the man watching my every move. The man who'd had what I never could. And I let go of everything decent as I waited for him to understand he'd never have her again.

Not a single touch.

Not another *anything*.

This wasn't about me.

This was about some caveman insanity driving me to stake ownership in absolutely terrible ways.

My fingers tightened in her hair, fighting off the whispers that this was wrong, ignoring the man I truly was—the man who would *never* lay a hand on Della this way.

But then David's eyes flared with surprise and darkened with rage, and nasty triumph spread devil-hot blood through my veins.

I couldn't stop myself.

After all, I was only doing what Della had asked me to do. To lay claim on her. To prove, once and for all, that I was hers. What a shame that I lost sight of that and used a moment that ought to be pure as a weapon to destroy my competition.

And once David was fully aware how Della melted in my arms, submitted to my harsh hold, and feathered her breath with lust, I ignored him and looked down into the blue, blue gaze of my Little Ribbon.

She trembled hard, her chest panting, her gaze wild.

Images of her, young and innocent, tried to delete the pinpricked red cheeks and sinful invitation.

I shook my head, squeezing my eyes from the messy double imagery. I focused only on one Della. The one I held. The one who begged me to finish what I started.

And then, I kissed her.

Right there.

In public.

Where anyone could see.

And something brittle shattered between us.

Something that wasn't wholesome but filthy and twisted and held shades of black and grey and red, red desire all wrapped up in punishment.

I was punishing her for making me need her this way.

And she was punishing me for making her wait so damn long.

The kiss started with a crush of lips and bruise of mouths, but it quickly turned from explosive to desperate.

My fist yanked down on her hair, forcing her mouth open as I struggled to hide that violent side of me.

She groaned long and low as I kissed her deep and dark, full of disgust for what I'd done and drowning with desire for what I needed.

My body tightened, tingled, tangled, and my mind went from a single thought to crazed with memories of threading my fingers through Della's hair in simpler times. Of brushing back curls as she slept as a four-year-old. Of wiping away sweat as she battled chicken pox as a seven-year-old.

And fuck, I was *appalled* with myself.

I pushed her away.

I wiped my mouth.

I picked up her backpack, forgotten on the street, and shoved it into her arms.

She stumbled, blinking back passion, dazed with being taken, and licked her lips as worry and fascination and that strange light I didn't like assessed me as if she didn't know me but very much wanted to.

"What was that?" she breathed, stepping toward me, forcing me to trip back.

"What was what?"

"That kiss."

"The kiss you asked for." I cleared my throat, choking on yet more lies. "The promise I made to show you that I won't go back on my word."

David strode down the path toward us; Della rushed in a whisper. "That was more than that, and you know it." She cocked her head; her ponytail messed from where my fingers had ruined it. "That wasn't you. That was—"

David arrived in hearing distance with blond hair and distrusting blue eyes, and she cut herself off, smiling sweetly at him. "Hi."

I wanted her to finish. I wanted to tell her that it *was* me. Just a me she'd never seen before.

But David looked me up and down, his arms crossing harder over his preppy-boy chest. Ignoring Della, he grunted, "Hello."

My spine straightened, muscles tightened. "Hello."

We glowered as if we were about to go to war to win the hand of some maiden we both could never hope to deserve.

Della inched between us, closer to me than to him but still playing mediator. "David, I want to re-introduce you to someone. Now, before you say anything, you already know my story, and at the time, you said you understood. I'm asking you to remember your understanding and not—"

"It's okay, Della." David let his arms uncross and dangle by his sides. "I get it." His jaw clenched in a way that said he didn't get it, but to his credit, he held out his hand for me to shake.

I studied him, not quite ready to let bygones be bygones. Della inconspicuously kicked my boot, and I flicked her a glance.

This meant something to her.

And my entire life was based on the undying need to give her whatever she wanted.

No matter how hard.

I shook his hand firmly, friendly, and my anger swirled into shame. "I know what you must think of me." David opened his mouth to say something, but I snapped, "And believe me, you have every right."

We broke apart as he said, slightly surprised, "Look, I only need to know two things, and then I can let what happened between us go. I can overlook how sad Della was the night she came to me for…comfort, and I can accept that she'll be safe…out there." His eyes trailed to the city's horizon where the barest glimpse of trees beckoned.

"All right." I nodded. "But first, I want to say something." The words tasted sour, but I forced myself to continue. "Thank you for being the one Della ran to that night. I caused her pain and, out of anyone she could've chosen, I'm glad you were the one to help soothe it."

I glanced at Della, my heart kicking at her wide shock and besotted disbelief. "I never told Della, but I blamed myself. Every damn day. And I left because I was selfish. I only thought of *my* pain, not the girl I'd promised to keep safe." I tore my gaze from Della's, glaring at David once again. "You kept her safe when I didn't. And for that…I'll always be grateful."

I owed him that.

A thank you and an apology.

But I also owed him a warning.

My ability to accept that I was the reason Della ran into his arms only stretched so far. I could be magnanimous because we were leaving. We would never see him again, and that was the only reason I could lower myself to second best before him, to curb my anger and play meek.

But if we *ever* crossed paths again, if he ever tried to take what was mine…it wouldn't end so civilised.

David shared a look with Della before clearing his throat. "Eh, thanks."

I nodded sharply, the heaviness from my backpack reminding me that streets weren't my home, and it was time to leave.

Holding up his hand, not as judgmental as before, he said, "Okay, the two things I need to know are—"

"David, we talked about this last night." Della butted in. "And I told you, time and time again, nothing inappropriate happened. You know that. That's the whole reason I came to you in the first place. He refused to do anything inappropriate. *Please*...don't bring it up again."

"I know what you said, and I trust you. But I want to hear what he has to say." Pinning me with a glare, he added, "So, *Ren*. First thing I need to know is did you ever touch her improperly? Ever. In all the years you grew up together. Not an 'oops' as you were helping her from the pool or a 'whoops' when you were tucking her into bed?"

I stood taller, disgusted. "What sort of sick bastard do you think I am?"

"The one who's taking a child he raised and hiding her in the jungle to do whatever he damn well wants."

My chest puffed up, my hands clenching. "First, it isn't a jungle. Second, she's no longer a child. Third, I never *once* looked, touched, or thought of Della in any way other than brotherly affection until she—"

I cut myself off.

A kiss at thirteen was still a terrible thing to admit. It didn't matter that the moment it all changed, it wasn't my fault but hers. *She'd* been the one to ruin us, destroy me, and corrupt every day from there on.

And who knew?

If she'd never kissed me at the exact same second when I was having the most incredible dream of my life, I might never have had to fight changing thoughts and switching needs.

But she had, and I couldn't confess her age or mine when it'd happened.

Della put her hand on my arm, squeezing gently. "Ren, it's okay." Turning to David, she sniffed. "You know enough. You don't need to know anymore. And as for your second thing, I can guess what you're about to ask."

"You can?" He raised a fair-coloured eyebrow.

"Of course, she can guess," I interrupted. "Everyone can

guess what you really want to know. I want to know, too. But there isn't an answer. Not yet, anyway."

Della gave me a sad look, her fingers feathering on my arm again, this time in worry rather than consolation. "Does it scare you?" she murmured.

I completely forgot about David as I drank her in, saw her panic, tasted her concern. Unable to stop myself, I cupped her cheek softly. "I'm fucking terrified. But…we don't have a choice now. We've gone too far to go back."

She pressed her face into my hold, her gaze glassing liquid before she nodded. "I know."

David sighed. "I guess you have just answered my question."

We both turned to him, my hand dropping from her cheek. I'd forgotten how in-tune Della and I were. I didn't know what it was—a lifetime lashing us together, heartstrings knotted together, or just a sixth sense.

Our connection used to wow me as a boy and now undid me as a man.

"You want to know what happens in the end," I said quietly, staring him down. "You want to know if I'll keep Della happy for the rest of her life. That this isn't a mistake. That we aren't doing something sick just for the hell of it. Am I right?"

David swallowed, his face falling in a way I hadn't expected. "I care for Della, and for the past six months, I've hated you for hurting her. But you're right. It *is* sick, and I don't agree with it. And I hope to God I'm wrong, but I don't think it will work between you. However, I also know you care for her. I see that. I just hope you understand what you're getting into."

My stomach clenched. "I know."

"No, I don't think you do." Anger turned his voice sharp. "You share the same last name. How's that going to work now you're no longer able to be called brother and sister? You know Della better than anyone, but how is it going to feel when you can't separate the past from the present? What happens when it all goes wrong? What about when people find out?" He forced out a breath, reining himself in. "Look, you're right. There is no answer. And I can't protect Della from future heartache. It's not my place. I just hope you know what you're doing. Seeing as you're supposed to be the parental figure in this scenario."

*Fuck.*

His words rang in my head.

It wasn't anything I hadn't thought about before, but he'd

returned all my revulsion and fear. What *would* happen when we could no longer use the same name? Was that why I was forcing her to leave? So the next town we came across, I could introduce her as my *wife* and not my sister?

*Christ.*

I spoke the truth when I said it was too late to go back, but maybe it was suicide if we continued going forward.

Dread settled acidic in my belly as David shrugged at Della. "Sorry, Del. I know I said I'd just say goodbye, but I couldn't help it." Gathering her in a hug, he kissed her cheek. "Forgive me?"

She sighed. "Nothing to forgive. I'm sorry I put you in this situation."

"Don't be." His eyes glistened. "I'm really glad you found me that night."

My hands curled, reminded yet again that David had touched her.

"I'm always here if you need me. Just please...be careful. Okay?" He kissed her one last time, then stepped back. "I want you to be happy, regardless if I don't agree with how you find it."

Giving me a cool look, he pointed toward the road. "Now, get off my property."

Snatching Della's hand, I helped her slip her backpack onto her shoulders and yanked her through the white picket gate. "Be my pleasure."

Letting her go, I expected Della to take her hand back. Instead, she latched her fingers around mine—five of hers to my four—and tugged me forward. "Come on, Ren. Let's go home."

# Chapter Eighteen

## REN

## 2018

WE'D WALKED FOR miles.

At the start of our journey, we'd cheated and used our remaining coins to catch a bus to the city limits. Another few miles up the road, and we would've passed the dairy farm I used to work for. Even this far away, the air was tainted with the smell of silage and cow manure.

Instead of heading that way, we'd cut across some farmer's paddock, jumping over fences and ducking through wire until we approached the outskirts of the forest.

The trees were thin and sparse on the border, steadily growing thicker and taller as shadows swallowed them up. Fallen leaves scattered on the ground while the scent of must and mulch soothed a little of my heartache, welcoming me back.

Della paused as I stepped into the embrace of bracken and branches. We hadn't talked much since leaving David. Our conversation stuck to impersonal topics such as where I'd stored the rest of our cash, if I gave the apartment key back, and how many supplies we had before we had to return to a town.

My answers had been soft and monosyllable, my mind still hung up on David's questions. I needed to do this. We had no choice but to try. But what if...?

What if we realised we didn't work as lovers?

Where would that leave us? How would we ever go back to being family?

I waited for Della to look up at the towering trees, glance over her shoulder, then stride toward me with resolution.

Joining me in the shadowy world, she asked quietly, "Are you happy, Ren?"

I jolted, my heart forgetting its own woe and focusing on hers. "What?"

She dropped her eyes. "Are you happy?"

"What sort of question is that?"

She looked up, annoyed. "One that you're not answering."

"Of course, I'm happy. You're here. I'm happy whenever you're around."

"That wasn't my question, and you know it."

I sighed, dragging a hand through my hair. "I *am* happy, Della. But if you're asking if I'm happy about what we're doing, I can't give you that."

Her shoulders slouched. "Why not?"

"Because I don't know if I am yet."

"Oh." She flinched, breaking me all over again. I wanted to hug her, but after years of denying myself, I didn't remember how to just reach out and take her.

"I don't want to lie to you, Little Ribbon." I closed the distance between us, capturing her hand. "We both need to adjust. I'm sure if I asked you if *you* were happy, you wouldn't be able to give me a direct answer."

"I could." Her fingers twitched in mine. "I am. *So* happy. But I'm also petrified that any second now, you're going to say this was a terrible mistake and march me back to David's."

"Believe me." I chuckled darkly. "I won't ever take you back to David. You're mine. You always have been."

"Phew. I thought you forgot that part." She half-smiled and walked into me, wrapping her arms around my waist.

"Never." I allowed my embrace to envelop her, pressing my chin on the top of her head, smelling the subtle scent of melons. "You'll always be mine, and I'm beyond happy to have you with me in the forest again. Is that enough for now?"

She nodded against my chest. "It's enough."

We stood together for a long while, once again committing to this and gathering courage to continue. Once we'd settled our heartbeats, we broke apart, striding deeper into the forest.

Our boots snapping twigs and backpacks creaking were the only sounds as we ventured farther. We didn't talk—almost as if we were afraid of conversation and its power to make us wonder what would happen when we stopped for the night.

And now, we'd stopped.

For the past twenty minutes, Della had gathered firewood while I'd erected the tent that she'd given me on my twenty-seventh birthday. The same birthday she'd gotten her ribbon tattoo and I'd started a year's disaster of sleeping with women I didn't like, want, or need.

I'd despised myself for being so weak I'd sought companionship with women I couldn't even remember.

Della dumped her armful of branches beside a fallen trunk I'd dragged into a small clearing to be a bench. Strolling over to me as I fixed the final tent peg into the ground, she put a hand on her hip. "Did you use this one while you were gone or our old one?"

"This one." I stood, stretching out the kink in my back, cursing the aches in my chest. Just like old times, her gaze drifted to the bare flesh below my t-shirt and above my belt.

And just like old times, my heart smoked in desire and I shut down the aching in my blood.

But…I didn't have to shut it down.

Not anymore.

How long would that habit take to break?

Della licked her lips as I lowered my arms. "I want to kiss you again, but I don't know how."

She seemed to melt into the forest floor. "Yes, you do. At least, you did before." Her gaze darkened. "You still haven't answered me about that, by the way."

"And I'm not about to answer you now." Closing the distance between us, I gathered her close, used my forefinger to tip her chin up, and pressed my mouth gently to hers.

Technically, our third kiss, but it punched me in the chest just as violently as our first.

I kept my mind locked on her. This Della. Right now. No Little Ribbon. No childhood recollections. No memories of anything but *this*.

Her breath caught as I kept the pressure soft and coaxing, even though everything inside said to crush her to me and let go of my control. No one was around. No one would know. But *I* would know, and that was the main issue we'd have to overcome.

Her tongue crept along my bottom lip, making my body harden. She arched up on her tiptoes, kissing me deeper as she slipped her tongue into my mouth.

My thoughts tried to flicker, a hologram of a little blonde angel laughing in the hay.

I groaned, licking her in invitation, killing the image.

"God, Ren." Her arms looped around my neck as I dropped my finger from her chin and hugged her flush against me.

Our heads switched sides as our tongues danced and lips slid. Magic sparked from everywhere, electricity hissing, chemistry burning.

I couldn't catch my breath as we clung to each other, kissing and kissing, losing track of time, not caring our boots crunched leaves as we stumbled together and righted, tripped together and stabilised.

And even though we attacked each other with a kiss, even though my mind threw memory after memory at me, and Della's hands clutched my hair and tugged, and my fingernails dug into the soft curves of her hips and yanked her closer, we didn't try for more.

We were happy conquering this small but unbelievable task. Learning each other, recognising each other's flavour, remembering each other's body in an entirely different way than the way we'd known before.

I sucked her bottom lip, biting gently as her leg pressed against mine, wedging against my hardness.

Her control snapped, and she tried to crawl into me.

I responded.

I couldn't help myself.

Wrapping my arms tighter, I somehow marched her back and back, kissing and kissing, until her spine wedged against a tree, and I leaned into her.

Her fingers tugged viciously at my hair. My hips thrust in response, disobeying me. Her teeth nipped at my bottom lip, like I'd done to her, her tongue frantic for more.

Our kiss became frenzied and so fucking hot, I couldn't stand it.

Breaking away, I held her at arm's length as I struggled to get my breath back around the sudden vice of my lungs.

Her eyes were so dark they were navy, her pupils as wide as a cat's. "Wow." Tracing her mouth with a trembling finger, she shook her head. "I always knew kissing you would be extraordinary, but I had no idea how much."

I coughed, then murmured around a throaty groan, "Kissing you is better than I could've imagined."

"You're saying you imagined kissing me?" She looked up beneath thick eyelashes.

I dragged a shaky hand over my face. How could I answer

that?

"The truth, Ren. Did you?"

I laughed under my breath, tortured with honesty. "Yes. I imagined it."

"And?"

"And what?"

"Is it like you imagined?"

My voice thickened as I swallowed hard. "Better. So much better."

She gave a flicker of a smile, slightly nervous, kind of shy, but entirely sexy with the utmost power to drop me to my knees. "I'm glad."

"Glad you're destroying me?"

"Glad I'm not the only one feeling this."

"You're not." I took a hesitant step toward her again, brushing aside a wild curl like I had so many times in the past. "I feel it too. I have for years."

She rose up, kissing me innocently on my stubble-covered cheek. "I can't tell you the relief it is to hear that." Ducking away, she headed toward the four-person tent she'd bought me. The brown siding and green stitching camouflaged it perfectly in the rapidly falling dusk.

Dragging her backpack toward her, she sat on the fallen tree trunk and pulled out a packet of pasta and carbonara sauce to make an easy dinner. I wasn't fooled by her calmness. She acted as if our kiss hadn't just scrambled her up, but her body couldn't hide the jerky motions or shaky breaths.

Yet another reason evolving our relationship came with pitfalls. We couldn't hide. We knew each other too well.

"You still haven't told me, by the way." She looked up as she tossed me a lighter from the bag, pointing at the piled firewood to start a fire. "About what happened at David's."

Fisting the fire-starter, I strode toward the pile, dropped to my haunches, and set about making a stack with kindling. "Told you what?"

I knew fully well what.

The kiss.

The way I held her.

The mistake.

I cringed. I hadn't been myself. I ought to have stared David in the eye, told him to mind his own fucking business, and carted Della away. But she'd asked me to stake my claim. How could I deny her that when she obviously needed it?

"Ren…" Her tone raised my eyes.

I sparked a flame, holding it to the dried leaves and tiny twigs. I didn't know how to reply, so I shrugged instead. "There's things about me that—" I cleared my throat. "Look, I was jealous. You asked for a public display of affection, and I gave you one. Can we just leave it at that?"

She narrowed her eyes. "What things don't I know about you?"

I groaned under my breath, hating that she could finish my sentences. "The same sort of things I don't know about you."

This was turning out to be as awkward as talking to her about sex that first time. That damn book and its pornographic images. The stilted, strange conversation about penises and vaginas.

Once again, my heart suffocated with repugnance for what I was doing. How was any of this right when I'd taught her what sex was only to contemplate showing her a decade later?

"What don't you know about me?" Her nose wrinkled. "You know everything there is to know about me."

I pinned her with a stare. "Not everything, Della."

It took a moment for my pointed words to land, but when they did, she blushed. The pink flush wasn't something I often saw on her, and it made my body crave to touch her all over again.

"Oh."

"Yes, oh." I focused on nursing the baby flame into a cheery blaze before falling back onto my ass and resting my elbows on my knees. Twirling the lighter in my fingers, I said carefully, "I know you intimately, but not in…that way. I don't know what you like. I don't know what you need to find…" I coughed. "Pleasure."

Her cheeks reddened even more. "Do you want to know?"

It was my turn for my skin to heat. "Is that a trick question?"

She laughed quickly. "I can tell you…or show you."

I fisted the lighter, squeezing it hard, remembering exactly how the night had gone when she'd begged to be enlightened on sex. She'd taught *me*, not the other way around. She'd read words I couldn't read and explained things I didn't understand.

No fucking way would I repeat that embarrassment or be reminded how far out of my league she truly was.

"I'll learn for myself." I growled. "I don't need a lesson."

"I'm not saying you do."

"I know I've leaned on you a lot in the past for reading and maths and things, but in this topic, I don't need any guidance. Got it? I won't be able to handle this if you start teaching me—"

She held up her hand, worry painting her face. "I didn't mean—"

"Leave it, Della." I stood, swiping at leaves stuck to my jeans. "Let's just focus on dinner, okay?"

"No, not okay." She stood too, her chin arched. "I get that this is hard for you, but it's hard for me, too. You say there are things about you that I don't know? Well, guess what? There are *so* many things I don't know about you these days. You've been steadily pulling away from me and hiding so many parts of you that this feels wrong. I have all these memories of you where you're covered in sunshine, an open book, but now you seem in the shadows and covered in clouds. You say you leaned on me, but you never did. I taught you because of my own selfish desires, not because you needed help. So don't withdraw into yourself and paint this any worse than it already is."

Striding toward me, she balled her hands. "You've taught me so much, Ren. You've literally taught me everything I know. Don't you think it feels weird knowing you'll have to teach me what you like, too? How you like to be touched? How rough, soft, deep, and fast you like it?" She sucked in an angry breath. "This is new for both of us. Just because I've accepted the idea of being with you for far longer than you have of me doesn't mean I'm not having the same thoughts as you. Not struggling with memories of you teaching me how to drive the tractor or your innocent face before you earned hard edges."

She stopped, breathing hard.

Time ticked on as our argument faded, but we didn't make a move to patch up the wounds left behind.

Finally, she whispered, "I'm tired. Can we just go to bed?"

*Bed?*

I gulped, eyeing the tent.

Unlike the previous one we'd shared, there was more than enough room for two adults without touching. The double wings meant we could be entirely separate while our bags were in the middle.

She caught me studying the two pods and huffed painfully under her breath. "Don't worry. I have my own sleeping bag this time; you don't have to sleep so close to me."

Ripping a tawny-coloured bag with highlighter pink zippers from her backpack, she ducked under the tent awning and threw herself into the left wing.

I stood there wondering what the hell happened and how the fuck it all went so wrong.

I hated that we'd had yet another fight, but that wasn't new. Our tempers always seemed to ignite around each other. But the fact that she'd curled up tight, fully clothed and hurting made me wince because she was right.

I'd been wrapped up in myself once again. She was Della. She was the reason I was alive—the sole purpose for why I'd been placed on this earth: to protect, cherish, and care for.

And I'd just made her upset.

Again.

Moving our belongings away from the fire and placing the pasta back into its pouch, I bent and undid my laces before kicking off my boots. I didn't strip anything else. Not my belt, socks— nothing.

If I did this, I needed to be fully clothed.

Tonight was not the night we fell into sex. Neither of us were ready.

Unfurling my own sleeping bag, I crawled into the centre pod, unzipped it and spread it over the two yoga mats I'd brought with us. Once it was flat, I reached into the wing where Della lay curled up tight and grabbed her ankles.

"Hey!" She squirmed as I yanked her through the small alcove and into the main one. "Let go."

Ignoring her, I didn't stop until she lay beside me, then unzipped her sleeping bag, all while my eyes burned into hers, daring her to stop me.

I kind of wanted her to stop me. I wanted her to hit me because I deserved to be hit. I wanted her to curse me because I warranted being cursed. But most of all, I wanted her to fight because if she did, I could fight back and release some of the hissing lust in my veins.

Almost as if she sensed how close I was to snapping, she stopped wriggling as I rolled her out of the warmth, smoothed the now-open bag on top of us, pushed her onto her side facing away from me, then lashed my arm around her waist and yanked her firmly into my front.

The moment her solid, familiar weight kissed mine, I groaned under my breath.

Right.

Wrong.

*Home.*

Pulling her as close as I could, I didn't hide the fact that I was hard, shaking, and fighting the hardest I'd ever had to fight not to tear her clothes off and teach *her* a lesson for a change.

A lesson about me.

A lesson about how much I wanted her.

She moved in my embrace, and for a dreadful second, I thought she was trying to get away, but then she moaned softly and pressed her hips deeper into mine.

My fingers dug into her flat stomach as I buried my nose in her hair.

I couldn't stop myself from rocking into her, allowing that one element of sex to manifest where I thrust fully clothed, hinting that in that moment, the way I liked it was torturously slow and tormentingly erotic.

She shivered as I nuzzled her ear, breathing hotly. "Don't run away from me again, Della. Got it?"

She brought her arm up, her fingers threading in the hair at the bottom of my neck. "Only if you promise the same."

Nipping at her earlobe, I grumbled, "Never. Whether this works or not, I'm not going anywhere. You have my word."

# *Chapter Nineteen*

## DELLA

## 2018

*THEY SAY LOVE can be the worst test of all.*

*I tend to agree with them.*

*First, Ren left me.*

*Then he came back for me.*

*Second, Ren stalked me.*

*Then he told me he loved me.*

*Third, Ren told me to pack and leave.*

*Then he warned he needed more time.*

*My heart…wow, it had been given its every wish and fantasy in one painfully, truth-filled argument, only to be told to press the pause button.*

*I hope you don't mind me scribbling this in a notebook instead of on my laptop—I sold it, you see. I wiped it clean and got a couple of hundred dollars for it from a fellow student. No point bringing it with no socket to charge and a backpack already heavy with important things.*

*Not sure why I'm writing, really.*

*Then again, what's happening between Ren and me is all so new, I want to keep some structure in my life, and writing things down is it.*

*After a manic couple of days getting rid of the things I had at David's, cutting off utilities, and assuring Natty and David that I knew what I was doing, I'd believed the test would be over.*

*I thought stepping into the forest would be our fresh start.*

*A new beginning where we could forget the past and be two adults and not two children. Where love would finally nod with pride and say, 'Okay, I made you suffer enough, now crawl into that tent and get busy.'*

*It didn't quite work that way.*

*When Ren had said he had it harder than me accepting this new us, I hadn't agreed. We'd both grown up together. We both had memories and love and connection that no amount of time or distance could steal.*

*I'd been hurt that he could say that, to be honest.*

*But now, after tasting his kisses and knowing the exact moment when he stopped kissing me and started thinking of the past, I agreed he did have it worse than me.*

*He was right.*

*He'd raised me. He'd seen me in every stage of cute, embarrassing, plain disgusting, and everything in between.*

*And that was the difference.*

*I'd been raised by him; therefore, I worshipped him.*

*I'd seen him in every mood of possessive, angry, distrusting, hardworking, and forever untamed.*

*Two very different ways to see somebody.*

*One practical and parental. One fantastical and fanciful.*

*Funny, how my memories don't just see a skinny boy with nine fingers, dirty and wild—I only remembered power and strength and the undeniable safety I felt in his presence. I didn't remember Ren as a teenager with a zit on his forehead and the Mclary cattle brand on his hip—I saw him as lanky and incredible and not afraid to plough an entire field on his own.*

*I'd never seen the ugly messiness of life that he had by raising me.*

*So, yes. He was right.*

*I didn't have to overcome as much to be able to kiss him.*

*I had no fear we were doing something wrong.*

*My only fear came from his fear and, for once, I wouldn't make it worse on him.*

*I wouldn't push him.*

*Not this time.*

*Or not for as long as I could help it, anyway.*

# Chapter Twenty

## REN

## 2018

FOR TWO DAYS, we learned how to be friends again.

Mornings, we ate breakfast of squashed bread and jam, packed up our gear, and walked until exhaustion made our backs sway and bones creak. Nights, we'd stop, set up our home, then cook harmoniously, eating pasta and canned supplies by moonlight and sharing tales of the past few months as we caught up with what we'd missed.

It was exactly what I needed.

To find my friend again.

To accept that there was no place, no person, no scenario I would rather have than this, right here, with her.

By the time we found the meandering river that had been our faithful friend since leaving Mclary's all those years ago, we were both ready for a bath and itching for clean clothes.

Summer was still in the air even though autumn was only days away. Muggy temperatures and no breeze found us deep in the forest. The sun teased low in the sky, not quite ready to go to bed as we finished putting up the tent.

Della wiped her brow with the back of her hand.

Blonde curls stuck to her sweaty neck. Heat glistened on her upper lip. Leaves clung with foliage fingers to her ponytail, choosing her over their branch and willingly committing suicide.

The polish of house living and city conveniences had faded from her skin, leaving her as wild as I remembered, slipping back into the surname she'd given us.

"Ren?" She waved a hand in my face, snapping me back to

the present and out of my daydreams of licking away her heat, pushing her onto the ground, and stripping her free of every sweat-wet piece of clothing.

Clearing my throat, I ran a hand through my hair. "Yeah?"

"I asked if you want to go for a swim."

Glancing at the narrow river, the babble and bubble hinted it might be too shallow to do anything more than sit and sluice.

Pointing downstream a little, she said, "The current is calmer there. I reckon there's a place deep enough to submerge, at least."

"Okay." My heart picked up into a pounding tempo. Bathing had been a regular thing with us even when we were young. When age didn't matter, we'd skinny-dipped with no thought of doing anything wrong. But then, my body had changed and become a master over my mind, and I'd refused to be naked around Della.

And now...what was the correct protocol?

She saw my wariness, laughing gently. "Underwear stays on. Is that what you were about to say?"

I half-smiled. "Would you be shocked if I suggested naked?"

She blinked. "Were you?"

I swallowed. "I don't know."

Her shock faded under a thin glaze of disappointment. Ever since I'd hugged her two nights ago, keeping her trapped in my arms almost the entire night, we hadn't discussed when or how we'd leap over the divide from family to lovers.

I didn't know how to bring up the subject and didn't know what to say if I did. Della had relaxed around me but only on topics we both knew were safe. The moment we stared too long, or that sneaky, burning lust became too painful to ignore, we suddenly found other tasks that urgently needed doing.

I knew why we'd gone nervous.

We'd missed each other so fucking much, and here we were, living the life we'd clung to, all the while about to jeopardise it.

I had everything I could've dreamed of, and it made me hate myself because not once had I asked how she felt about quitting her writing course or if she missed any of her friends.

I couldn't bring myself to ask either because I wouldn't survive the answer if she admitted she wanted those things more than she wanted me.

"I'll make the decision for you." Grabbing the hem of her t-shirt, she ripped it over her head, dislodging her ponytail and its decoration of leaves.

My breath caught in a sharp cough as my eyes drank in her

slim figure and black sports bra. The fullness of her chest was a perfect handful, the shadows of her belly enticing me to touch, trace, and torment.

Never taking her eyes off me, she kicked away her boots, unbuttoned her jeans, slid them down long legs, and pulled them off with her socks.

Standing in black bikini briefs, looking athletic and strong and so fucking gorgeous, I very nearly stumbled with desire for her.

The scraps of material were the only things keeping me from seeing her—*all* of her—and I both thanked them for their discretion and cursed them for their barrier.

"Your turn," she whispered, swaying a little as her hands reached up and undid her ponytail, letting rivers of gold pour around her shoulders. The flash of blue ribbon beckoned me forward, and I stole it from her fingers, wrapping it around the back of her neck and pulling her toward me.

"You're beautiful," I murmured, pressing a kiss to her mouth. "I don't know how I ignored that fact for so long."

She gasped, surprised by my swift affection; a step behind my lust.

Before she could catch up, I broke the kiss and dangled the blue ribbon in her face. "This looks familiar." I smirked. "Not a day went by that you didn't wear this in some way." My gaze drifted to her bare foot where the inked one with its cursive R still caused my heart to clench. "Didn't you ever wonder why a piece of satin lasted eighteen long years?"

Her forehead furrowed. "Huh?"

"Think about it." I stroked the blue, dragging it through my forefinger and thumb. "It lived in the elements, got wet, dirty, knotted, and crushed. Yet it never fell to pieces. Never tore when I tied it in your hair, never unravelled when you wound it around your wrist."

Her head cocked. "What are you saying?"

"I'm saying, I couldn't exactly let your favourite thing fall apart now, could I?"

Confusion shadowed, then was chased away as comprehension lit up her face. "You replaced it?"

I chuckled. This was one secret I *could* share with her. Giving her back the ribbon she so desperately treasured—even now as an adult—I headed to my backpack that rested against a gnarly looking pine.

Throwing her another smirk, I reached into the side pocket

sewn tight for protection of wallets or other important things and pulled out a circle of cardboard that had well and truly seen better days. The printed label and name of the colour had long since worn off, the edges frayed and torn, but there, in the centre of the wheel, was a depleted length of blue satin.

Her eyes widened like an owl's as she dashed toward me— careful where to put her bare feet on the bracken-littered ground—and snatched it from my grip. "Where did you get this?"

Spinning it in her hands, she pulled out the pin holding the ribbon from unravelling and compared it to the one wrapped around her fingers. "Oh, my God. It's the same. Mine is faded and marked, but it's the same colour."

I chuckled, loving her disbelief. "My longest secret. I've had that since I was fourteen. I'm guessing there's only a few years left before it runs out."

"What? *How?*"

"We were living at Polcart Farm, remember? I'm not sure you will, seeing as you were so young—"

"I remember," she interrupted. "I remember Snowflake, our cow, and the TV channel with the puppets."

I ignored the squeeze of my ribcage and sharp stab of my heart as I recalled Della bouncing in front of the TV with her chubby toddler legs growing each year to an adorable little girl chasing after Snowflake in the field.

A crest of simple affection and absolute unconditional love made me feel wretched and wicked all over again for thinking of her in the ways I did now.

Squeezing the back of my neck, the enjoyment of sharing my secret faded somewhat. "You were four. That ribbon of yours was falling apart. It tore in half one night when you were learning how to tie a bow around my arm. My ears are still ringing with how loudly you cried."

Her shoulders rounded. "I don't remember that."

"It's because I never told you that particular story. I didn't want you to think your ribbon was an imposter." Pinching the wheel back, our fingers kissed and I stroked her softly. "I adored how much you loved that silly piece of blue. And when you finally went to sleep with your face all blotchy from screaming and your breath all short from bawling, I snuck out to find you a new one."

"Where did you go?"

"Into town. It took all night to find a house with two old folks, a man who liked to tinker with cars in his garage and a woman who liked to scrapbook and had a room full of ribbons, buttons, beads, and stickers." I smiled sadly, remembering the treasure trove of stuff that Della would've adored. "I wanted to steal everything for you, but I only took what was most important. It wasn't a perfect match. But it was close enough."

Holding up the ribbon, I let memories paint my voice. "That night, I took the two torn pieces of your ribbon, measured out a new length the same, then spent the rest of the darkness hours doing my best to make the bright blue of the new one look as weathered as yours. I stomped it into the gravel on the driveway. I dragged it through mud and washed it semi-clean. I crumpled it and abused it until it didn't look so perfect anymore."

I shrugged. "You woke up the next morning panicked, tears already welling, but I told you it was just a bad dream. That nothing had happened to your ribbon. See? There it was, intact and looped through your hair. The relief on your face, Little Ribbon." I sighed. "It was worth the sleepless night and dirt beneath my nails to be able to take that sadness away. I didn't know what it was like to love something that fiercely—not until you came along—and I didn't want you to know what loss felt like. Not then. Not when you were still so young."

Tears welled in her beautiful blue gaze, tumbling down her cheeks like the babbling river behind her. "I had no idea."

"Why would you? I never told you."

"But…how did I never notice?"

"Because I didn't wait four years to give you a new one next time. Every year, a few days after our birthday, I'd cut a fresh strand, rub and fade it, then swap it while you were sleeping. Sometimes, the blue was brighter, and you'd study it as if confused. But you never thought to ask why."

Her arms came up, her fingernails scratching my scalp as she grabbed my hair and yanked me down to her mouth.

Her kiss wasn't soft with desire. It was sharp with gratefulness.

Born from innocence, tainted with confusion, but wholeheartedly flavoured with love. Deep, blistering, *endless* fucking love.

"I didn't think it would be possible to care for you any more than I already do," she murmured against my mouth. "You've just broken my heart, Ren." She kissed me again, mixing salt from her tears.

I wrenched back, fear icing my insides. "What?" Grabbing her biceps, I demanded, "Why would you say something like that?"

She hung docile and crying in my hold. "Because you were always so damn selfless. You *always* put me first. You sacrificed everything you could for me. You would've done anything I asked, and it wasn't enough."

Swiping at her tears, she growled as if furious with herself. "It wasn't enough that I was your everything. I wanted more. I wanted no other woman to have you. No one ever to own your heart. I was so *selfish* compared to you, and I made you unhappy in your own home. I pushed and pushed you. I dropped hints I knew you would refuse to acknowledge. I never thought about how I made you feel. All the while, you were replacing my ribbon every year because you loved me so—" She couldn't finish, her tears coming fresh and fast.

Crushing her to me, I kissed her brow, her hairline, her ear. "Caring for you was the easiest thing I've ever done, Della. Raising you was the best thing I've ever achieved. I'm so fucking honoured to have had that privilege."

Pushing her away a little, I bowed my head to stare hard into her eyes. She needed to hear this, and she needed to hear it now.

Before I did what I could never undo.

Before I broke the final filament of my self-control.

"I might have been selfless when it came to you, but I promise you I am no saint. I'm hungry, Della. So fucking hungry, and I need you. But you need to know that the Ren you know— the boy who would kill himself if it meant keeping you safe—that Ren has a flaw. His selflessness comes at a price."

Her gaze danced in mine, desperately fishing for what I struggled to tell her. "What price?"

"I don't think I can be that selfless anymore."

"I'm not asking you to."

"You're not getting it." I dug my fingers harder into her arms. "When it comes to sex, I'm not…gentle. I only think of myself."

Heat drenched her eyes, making the blue turn to sapphires. "I'm glad. You deserve to put yourself first for a change."

I shook my head, sharp and quick. "You still don't understand."

"I don't need to understand." She ripped herself out of my hold, swooping up to kiss me again. "I need you to show me." Her lips bruised mine, her tongue tasted me, and her breathless beg undid me. "I wasn't going to do this. I promised myself I wouldn't push you again. But please, Ren. Show me. Don't be so nice to me.

I need you to do that." She kissed me harder, wetter, faster. *"Please."*

*Fuck.*

I very nearly snapped.

I attacked her back, kissing her brutally, swept up in her pleas, drowning beneath vicious desire, but...just like a couple of nights ago when she'd slept stiff in my arms as if unused to being touched by me, we weren't ready.

I was hungry; that wasn't a lie. But beneath my hunger lurked childhood memories just waiting to pounce and condemn me. Under no circumstances did I want to feel sick while making love to Della the first time.

I hadn't told her my flaws to give myself permission to treat her without care or attention. I was selfish, yes, but then again, I'd never had sex with Della, and I wanted it to be different.

I wanted it to be special.

I needed it to be the best goddamn thing we'd ever experienced, and until I was mentally more stable and Della more trusting that I wasn't going to run again, it would be a mistake.

Her tongue stole into my mouth, licking away the remaining shreds of my willpower.

She made sleeping together seem like the easiest thing in the world, while it felt like the hardest thing I'd ever have to do.

I kissed her back—I couldn't help myself—but my thoughts tangled once again, taking the sting out of the whip of urgency.

We'd spent our entire lives together.

And, if I had my way, we'd spend the rest of eternity.

There was no rush if I never planned on letting her go.

I *couldn't* rush.

Because I hadn't fully come to terms with this.

I hadn't found a truce between the old me and the future me. The brother and the husband. And I needed to because it wouldn't be fair to either of us if I didn't.

"Della..." I groaned as she hooked her leg over my hip, doing her best to climb me.

"Kiss me back, Ren." She licked my bottom lip before sealing her mouth on mine again. "I want you. Now. Please."

"Christ..." I melted and hardened and wanted so damn much to give in to her. I might have spent a lifetime looking out for her, but she'd mastered the art of commanding me. Whatever she asked for, I found it extremely hard to deny.

But this...it had to be right.

"Stop, Della." Grabbing her shoulders with harsh fingers, I put distance between us, making her stagger back before finding her balance. Her face was wild and wistful and tugged on every heartstring I possessed. "Not tonight."

"Why not?"

"Because I need more time."

"To do what?" She blew a curl from her eyelash in a frustrated puff. "To torture yourself a little more?"

I scowled. "No, to find peace. To accept the fact that I have so many memories of you at every stage of your life, and to find a way so they don't drive me insane when I finally do let go."

"I know those are legitimate concerns, and I understand because I understand you...but you need to get over that, Ren." Swatting away my hands, she crossed her arms. "The past isn't going anywhere. It's always going to be a part of us."

"I know. But do you honestly want me to take you when I'm not emotionally ready?"

"I don't think we *will* be ready until we've had sex."

I coughed, hating the need in her voice. She'd always been braver than me—always willing to leap before looking. But I wasn't wired that way. I hadn't had that privilege when raising a kid at barely ten years old. "Well, I think it would be rushing if we did it now."

"And I think we're just tormenting ourselves by waiting."

"Unfortunately for you, it's not your choice." I stood to my full height, glaring her down. "Don't push me until I'm ready, Della."

"Push you? I'm trying to *help* you!" Her arms uncrossed only for hands to plant on her deliciously curvy hips. "You're turning sex into this huge thing, when really, it's just an act."

"Just an *act*? Is that what this is? A quick fuck to you? How stupid of me to treat it as the biggest thing in my life. I didn't know I was just some guy you wanted to screw to get out of your system."

"You know that's not what I meant."

"Do I? You're the one getting mad at me for being honest." Once again, our romantic moment spiraled into a fight.

Were we always destined to clash?

I didn't remember fighting this much before. I didn't like it then, and I despised it now. But I wouldn't bow to her temper. No matter how much my body agreed with her to get it over with.

Sex between us shouldn't be a 'get it over with' kind of thing.

It should be the best fucking thing in the world.

My anger swirled hotter, annoyed she couldn't see that sleeping with her was something I never believed I could have. It was the one thing I didn't feel worthy of. The one gift I didn't know how to take. And to have her give me permission so flippantly, well, it hurt.

It killed, actually.

She cheapened it when I wanted it to mean so much.

"You said you'd be patient," I said coldly.

"I did. But I also said I'd be frustrated." She sighed again, looking up at the purple slashed sky as if beseeching perseverance. "God, I'm sorry, Ren. I promised myself I wouldn't do this, yet here I am making a mess of everything again." Her voice softened, regret tightening her eyes. "You call yourself selfish...but look at me." She chuckled a little. "Okay, you need more time. How much time?"

"I don't know."

"But it won't happen tonight?"

"No." I shook my head firmly. "It won't."

"Can't blame a girl for trying." Her shoulders slouched. "Ugh, I'm being a bitch." Rubbing her face, she moaned, "Forgive me, Ren. I don't know what came over me. I just...I thought we'd come out here, and I dunno...act like a pair of bunnies." She shrugged with a roll of her eyes. "I should've known it wouldn't be that easy. I even understand *why* it's not that easy, so just put this moment of weakness down to the fact that I'm madly in love with you, and it's taking everything I have to keep my hands to myself."

I laughed quietly. "Madly, huh?"

"Completely." She smiled shyly. "Utterly. Totally."

"I'm madly in love with you, too."

"Now you're just teasing me."

A small smile tilted my lips, glad our fight had vanished, leaving us drained but connected. "There's plenty of time for that. Teasing. Kissing. Fucking. I'm not going anywhere, and neither are you."

"Well, a girl only has so much patience before she goes a little crazy."

"You're already crazy. Crazy for me." Moving closer, I pulled her into another hug, loving the familiar simplicity, grateful she swooned into me. "Believe me, Little Ribbon, this is the hardest thing I've ever done. Saying no to you when you're so damn beautiful and willing? God, it's pure agony." I nudged her chin up with my knuckles, staring deep into her eyes. "But when I take you, Della. I want my mind to be clear. I want to be with *you*, not the past. I want to fully accept us, not feel torn between right and wrong."

Kissing her softly, I murmured against her lips, "When I'm inside you, Della Wild, I want to only have one thought, and that's how much I fucking love you."

She sighed into our kiss, snuggling closer. "When you say things like that, I can be patient. For just a little longer."

And she was.

For a few more days, at least.

# Chapter Twenty-One

## REN

## 2018

SEVEN DAYS SHE gave me.

One week to accept the unacceptable and change our entire relationship.

We didn't end up swimming that night; the river was too shallow, but we did manage to bathe and wash a few pieces of clothing. Although I wasn't ready to sleep with her, it didn't stop my eyes from roaming over every inch as she soaked herself in the swift current.

I'd stupidly blocked myself from finding the best pleasure in the world, but I clung to the hope that when I finally did let go, it would be entirely worth it.

That night, we slept in just our underwear, sandwiched together in the tent, nuzzling and kissing as if we'd always been so close. I loved that each time we kissed, it was a little easier, my mind a little quieter, my heart a little less confused.

In the morning, as we packed up our camp and headed back on the trail, I grabbed her and pressed her against a tree. My hands roamed to her breasts as I kissed her hard, driving myself against her, drowning with a sudden crippling need to take.

Her moan snapped me out of what I'd done purely by instinct.

Backing up, I waited to be persecuted beneath memories of Della as a baby and Della as a child. But...nothing came.

No sick sensation. No regret. Only awareness that, for the first time, it'd felt perfectly normal to grab and manhandle her because I wanted to, and she was mine.

There was nothing wrong with that.

In fact, there was everything right, and I froze because I'd held her, kissed her, and touched her—in ways I never thought I could—and not once had my thoughts tried to ruin me.

My capacity for change had finally started, and the sick sensation was taking a back seat to the rapidly growing lust I struggled to control.

"You can do that again...if you want." Della smiled behind a golden curl, her lips still pink from my kiss.

"If I do, I won't be able to stop."

She groaned, "Say that again and *I* won't be able to stop."

Taking her hand, I chuckled. "Patience is a virtue."

"Not when it's making my heart work overtime and my body behave like a horny cat."

Tugging her into a walk, I chuckled. "A horny cat? I have no idea what that feels like."

She gave me a dirty look. "Oh, really? You want me to believe you've never felt like you want to jump out of your skin at the barest touch. Never wanted to scratch someone or pick a fight just so you can be attacked and have it lead into the roughest, sexiest moment of your life?"

I stared at her dumbfounded.

I'd known Della was passionate—I'd seen her kiss other men, for God's sake—but maybe my waiting wasn't just about putting the past in the past and accepting our new dynamic, but also about figuring out who she'd be in bed before I got her there.

Was she like me?

Was she aggressive or tame?

Did she expect our first time to be beneath a blanket of stars with gentle snuggles and sweet missionary, or did she secretly crave what I did?

A messy, filthy, violent affair that left us bloody and oh-so-fucking satisfied?

Letting her go, I stepped in front of her, following the narrow animal track. "I've been many things, Della, but I can't say I've been a cat."

*More like a wolf.*

*A starving one.*

Clearing my throat from thoughts full of thrusting and wetness, I said, "Let's get going. Think you can keep up?"

She snickered behind me. "Think you can keep avoiding this subject for much longer?"

I scowled into the trees. "I'm fully aware I can't."

"Good." She sniffed with a mixture of smugness and joy. "Because I'm going to be a good girl and not push you, but it doesn't mean I'm not going to make you fully aware just how much I want you. How watching your butt right now turns me on so much. How your boots cracking twigs makes me hot. How your smell makes me we—"

"Della," I snapped, spinning on her and pointing a finger in her face. "Thin ground, Little Ribbon. Behave yourself."

With a flash of mischievous blue, she stood on tiptoes and bit my finger, running a warm, silky tongue around the tip.

I groaned.

Loudly.

My cock instantly sprang into the hardest, most agonising erection I'd ever had.

I dropped my hand as if her saliva was gasoline and her teeth the match. My entire finger burned and, *fuck*, it wanted more.

She licked her lips, her eyes hooded and hazed. "Okay, Ren. I'll do what you say."

The temptation and invitation behind that innocent, obedient phrase almost had me yanking off my backpack and shoving her onto her knees right there in the middle of the forest.

Brushing past me, incinerating my body with hers, she whispered, "I'll behave. Guess we better get hiking, huh? The sun won't last forever."

Words vanished.

Humanity disappeared.

I was an animal, pure and simple, so damn hungry for the girl I'd always loved.

I couldn't take my eyes off the way the sun dappled her hair, glinting on her ribbon, or the way her body glided through greenery as if she was part forest herself.

A quick flash of her bounding through the trees when she was nine or ten came and went, but instead of defiling the new love I had for her, it layered my heart with a heat that unravelled me and stitched me back together in an entirely different way.

Someone who was okay with this.

Someone who could finally admit Della Mclary never *was* a Mclary because she'd always been a Wild.

I wanted to tell her just how much I loved her. Just how much I would *always* love her. How I'd had an epiphany, and I knew within my very bones I'd never leave her, hurt her, or do anything other than defend, cherish, and adore. I pitied anyone who ever came between us. I feared what I'd do if anyone ever tried to—

"Coming, Ren?" She looked over her shoulder, nonchalant and willowy.

Her gaze met mine, playful and happy before they darkened in response to the shadows swirling inside me. The shadows of possession and dominion that clenched my fists, already angry with phantom ideals that might try to ruin this.

"Ren?" Her voice lowered, the expression on her face one of seriousness and trust. "Everything okay?"

I might've grunted something in response, but she'd well and truly won. She'd shown just how right she was. Sex *was* just an act. Because we'd already surpassed mere pleasure and flesh. We were joined on so many levels, and nothing else mattered but that.

"Fine." Marching toward her, I coughed and pointed ahead. "Let's keep going."

I was fucking captivated by her.

Utterly bewitched.

But I wasn't prepared to spill the contents of my heart when I didn't fully understand it myself.

"Okay…" Her forehead furrowed, but she obeyed, and I spent the rest of the day in agony, eyes fixated on her gorgeous ass as she strode ahead, my body in a perpetual state of thick, black desire.

Served me right.

I wanted her.

I could have her.

So *why* was I waiting again?

\* \* \* \* \*

Every day, we travelled deeper into the forest, following the river and leaving behind the city we'd called home for so long. At night, we were pleasantly exhausted and returned to the ease of before when Della would ask for a story, and I'd willingly conjure past events we'd shared.

Even though I'd fully accepted the inevitable and just how screwed I was by falling in love with this woman, I hadn't initiated anything past a kiss.

And Della remained true to her word and didn't push me.

It'd become a silent joke, kissing, grinding, driving each other to the pinnacle of tearing off clothes and consummating but then pulling back at the last second.

Making out with Della was the best and hardest thing I'd ever done. Best because I never knew kissing could be pure fire, that a tongue could make me lose myself, that a fingernail dragged down my spine could almost make me come. And the hardest because I couldn't let go...not yet.

We'd had almost two decades together, yet this element of touching and kissing was entirely new, and I wanted to learn everything I could before I jumped a grade. I wanted to be fluent in her moans. I wanted to know her levels of need.

Already, I knew her legs spread whenever I grazed my fingers along her lower belly. Her gasps became heavy whenever I'd tuck aside a curl and murmur in her ear how much I wanted her.

But it wasn't enough.

I wanted to know what made her snap.

And on the fourth night, I found the spot as she spread out her sleeping bag while I kneeled at the bottom of the bed and pulled off my t-shirt. Her bare leg flashed me, her ribbon tattoo with its R, bright blue and taunting.

Without thinking, I flipped her onto her back, grabbed her ankle and dragged her freshly river-washed foot to my mouth.

She froze as I pressed a kiss on the ink, brushing my nose against her soft skin.

"Ren..." Her head fell back as I kissed her again, slipping my tongue out and licking the length of the ribbon all the way to the cursive capital of my first name.

I nipped her.

"Holy..." Her entire body crackled and sizzled with desire.

My fingers tightened on her ankle, holding her still as I licked the length again. "You got this to torment me."

Her foot arched in my hold, her legs widened, her hands fisted in the sleeping bag. "No—"

"You got this because you were in love with me."

"Y-yes." Her breath caught as I nipped at the R again, scraping my teeth over the fine bones of her foot, fighting the feral part of me that wanted to clamp down and bite hard.

"You fantasied about me touching you."

"Every night." Her eyes met mine, blazing. "All the time."

I almost gave up there and then.

My body had never felt so wired or hot or greedy.

The little boy shorts and t-shirt she slept in could so easily be removed, and her body feasted on.

But as much as I cursed waiting, I fucking adored the

anticipation, and I licked her tattoo once more before placing her foot down gently. "You very nearly ruined me, Little Ribbon."

Unzipping my jeans, I slipped out of them and didn't bother hiding the raging erection I sported.

She licked her lips, eyes locked on my tented boxers. "And now you're doing the same by teasing me so badly."

I didn't say anything.

I just wanted to bask in the heady drunkenness of lust and the unbelievable knowledge that I'd earned everything I'd never dared hope to earn.

Crawling beside her, I wedged her back into my front and breathed as hard as her.

And we just lay there.

Trembling with need.

Cooking with desire.

Fully aware we were playing a very dangerous game.

And we were utterly addicted to it.

# Chapter Twenty-Two

## REN

## 2018

BY THE SEVENTH day, that intense desire meshed with carefree laughing. We'd found a balance of friendship and chemistry that made me trip even deeper into love.

Every day, we tramped until our bones ached, and we'd make our home in the wonderful heart-warming high of being just us again. Whenever I looked at her, I wanted to explode with affection. Whenever she looked at me, my body begged to override my hesitation.

Her eyes had the power to send electricity fizzing down my spine and between my legs. Her laughter had the magic to make my chest ache and body throb. And when she stopped in a small clearing at twilight and shrugged off her backpack, she turned to me, not with relief at finding somewhere to rest, but with a demand I could no longer ignore.

I knew.

Even before she opened her mouth.

I *knew*.

With suddenly shaky hands, I pushed at the straps and let my bag slam to the forest floor.

The air changed. The trees froze. The creatures silenced.

"Della…" I didn't know if I spoke in warning or acceptance or denial. Whatever I was feeling was drowned out by the overpowering appetite in my blood.

I wanted her.

I wanted her more than I could stand.

Taking a step toward me, Della reached up and undid the

blue ribbon in her ponytail. The gold mass plunged around her face, making my mouth dry and my cock pay utmost attention.

"We haven't put up the tent," I groaned, breaking beneath the heavy pressure in my chest. The pressure that was done waiting. The pressure I'd been living with for so fucking long.

"I don't care." She bent and undid her laces, kicking her boots away, not fussed where they landed.

My knees trembled to move—either to her or away from her, I couldn't quite decide. Thanks to the week of teasing, I didn't trust myself around her. I didn't know my limit of self-control anymore. I didn't know how spectacularly I'd snap and what would happen if I did.

She'd always been my Della, but right here, right now, I was hers. Well and truly hers.

A slave to his queen, enraptured and caught and begging for her mercy. I was ready to kneel before her, but that final part of me that didn't fully trust he could have this perfect life, the tiny sliver that still believed he ought to love her the way he always had, gave one last attempt at propriety.

"We're dirty. We need a bath." I spread my hands, revealing the mud-smudges and grime from hiking all day.

"I don't care about that, either." Her voice lost its sweet melodic tone, slipping straight into sin.

*Goddammit.*

I couldn't compete with that.

I couldn't deny her or myself any longer. She'd put a curse on me, deleting any other arguments or delays, keeping me pinned in her stare.

She stepped again, and my cock swelled to an agonising hardness. I coughed around a groan. "Della...you're making this impossible for me."

"Good."

"What if we're rushing—" Even to my ears that excuse was empty.

I was ready. So fucking ready.

"We're not." She wrapped the ribbon around her wrist, tying it quickly.

"At least let me put up the tent."

"No."

"We only get one first time, Della."

"And I can't wait any longer."

"I'm not sleeping with you without a bed." If there wasn't

something soft to support her, I didn't know what sort of state she'd be in once I'd finished.

"Too bad we don't have one."

"If you gave me a few minutes, I could set it up." I pointed helplessly at my bag. "At least let me—"

"I can't wait another minute, Ren." Her hair glittered in the fading light as she shook her head. "All day, I've been counting. Just another minute, just another minute. And now, we're here. And I have no more minutes."

My heart lurched. "Our minutes seem to be up."

"They do."

"What does that mean for us?" My voice was smoky and hot.

"It means you made me do this. You made me this way. I promised I wouldn't push you, but Ren...you've been torturing me. When you licked my tattoo...? *God*, I can't stop thinking about it. I'm in a state of permanent wetness."

I choked on the sudden avalanche of lust. "Della—"

"Too much for you? Too honest?" Her cheeks burned with the same sexual fever I suffered. "Too bad. You're to blame."

I chuckled darkly. "Me? It's you I can't keep my hands off. It's your fault I constantly need to touch you, kiss you."

"So do it."

"I don't know if I can be gentle." I shook my head. "No, I *know* I can't be gentle. Not after—"

"I'm not asking for gentle." She smiled thinly, almost angry with me in her desire. "I'm asking for you to put me out of my misery. No more teasing. We face this. Together. Right now."

I gulped as I stepped toward her, already lost. "Face what we've been running from for years?"

She nodded sharply. "No more running."

I sucked in a lust-heavy breath, coughing once. "No more running." I stepped again. Entirely entranced by the violent hunger lashing us together. It was so damn powerful it muted everything else.

No thoughts. No accusations. No fear.

Just us.

As it had always been.

My mind raced, already drunk on images of how good we'd be together. Of how she'd feel as I slipped inside her. Of how hot and wet and—

I was too far gone for more memories to find me. Too twisted to let echoes pull me back. But in some shred of rationality, a voice entered my ears with warning.

Not Della's or mine, but Cassie's.

*Protection.*

The night I'd lost my virginity. The night I'd learned about condoms and STIs and unwanted pregnancies. Thanks to that lesson, I'd never slept with a woman without a condom. It was paramount. It was law.

*Christ.*

It took every strength, and then some I borrowed from the devil himself, to step back. "Shit, we can't do this."

"What? Why?"

Pinching the bridge of my nose, I did my best to swallow back hot, hungry rage. The rage that very much wanted to forget about the rules and take her anyway. "We don't have protection. I didn't bring any."

What was I *thinking*?

Why did I forget something so important—almost as if I'd banished the very idea of sleeping with her, believing it would never happen no matter how much I wanted it to.

I'd done this deliberately, even if I denied my moronic logic.

Della blinked calculatingly, holding up her hand. A single condom rested in her palm. "I did."

"Where did you get that?"

"Does it matter?"

I ought to feel absolute horror that my last attempt at ensuring this was right had just been eradicated. But all I felt was relief. Sheer, indescribable relief.

It was the final straw.

The last hint to show I was ready.

So, *so* ready.

I dropped my hand, giving her a grateful smirk. "Thank fuck for that."

She laughed unexpectedly, her lips spread over perfect teeth. "Even if we didn't, I wouldn't have been able to stop. Not now."

"Me neither."

"Good."

"God, you've made me hard."

She sucked in a breath. "And now you've just made me even wetter."

If I thought the forest was quiet before, watching us shed away every shackle we'd imposed, I was wrong.

Now the trees vanished, the river disappeared, and all I saw was Della. We'd just been graphically honest, yet a joke mixed present with past, making me chuckle under my breath. "Thank everything holy, I taught you to always be prepared."

Her laugh turned to a breathy moan. "Ren...if you don't touch me soon, I'm going to combust."

I lowered my head, watching her with half-hooded eyes. "I like seeing you like this."

"Like what?"

"Desperate."

She took another step. "So, so desperate."

"You have no idea how filthy my thoughts have become."

"If they're anything like mine, I have some idea."

"Fuck, Della." I balled my hands, matching her step with one of my own. "Is this real? Are we really going to do this? It isn't another dream? Because I've dreamed of this. So many times."

"Touch me and find out."

My hand raised, crossing the final distance, tingling with intensity to touch the one girl I'd loved forever.

I'd always known Della was special. But what I hadn't known was every year I fought to keep her safe, I was ultimately protecting every dream I'd ever had. I'd had the privilege of raising her, but really, I'd been creating a future I'd never be able to deserve. Every winter snowstorm and summer rain shower, forest adventure and paddock picnic had all been leading to this.

I'd been searching for something all my life, and it had been under my nose the entire time.

*Her.*

My past, present, and future.

The only path I could have taken.

It wasn't a choice anymore.

It had *never* been a choice.

I stumbled toward her as she stumbled toward me, both starving for touch. Even before my fingers landed on her arm, they stung with electricity so sharp it crackled between us.

Our eyes locked as I whispered, "If we do this, it's no longer just a fantasy."

"I know."

"We do this, and everything changes. Forever."

"I know."

"If I touch you, I'll never be able to stop."

"God, touch me then." Her eyes fell shut as we met in the middle of the small clearing.

Having her that close undid me to the point of forgetting everything else.

I didn't care about the repercussions anymore.

I'd literally exhausted myself to the point of not being able to fight.

There was nothing to fight against...only something to fight *for.*

"Open your eyes, Della." I growled as the savage part of me licked its lips for what it was about to taste.

I was seconds away from giving her every disgusting sin I'd lived with. I needed her to understand that by tempting me this way, I would no longer have any control.

Her eyelids fluttered upward, her gaze heavy and heated.

We stared into each other, stripping ourselves bare.

"Tell me to stop," I begged. Even on the cusp of no return, I pleaded for salvation.

"I can't." She bit her lip, looking me up and down with such pain-filled greed, my belly clenched. "I'll never be able to do that."

Everything about me burned. On fire. Seconds away from erupting into fury. "You've always pushed me. Forever tested me."

"And you've always indulged me. Forever protected me," she breathed shallowly, her gaze locking onto my lips. "I'm sick of you protecting me."

Our chests brushed as I sucked in a breath, knowing it would be my last one for a while. I was about to drown in her. And I didn't care if I damn well suffocated. "If I kiss you now...it's all over."

"Stop trying to scare me off and do it."

"So bossy." I smirked.

"I don't know how else to tell you I want you, Ren." Her eyes flashed with temper. "I don't want to talk. I don't want to stop. I don't want you to treat me kindly or gently or softly. I want you to show me. I want you to take me, just like you said you—"

I snatched her into my arms and kissed her so damn hard our teeth clacked.

I showed her.

And then I showed her again.

And again.

I kissed her harder than I'd ever kissed her.

I let our week-long foreplay drag us down and down, deeper and deeper where heartbeats and blood reigned and the only thing we needed to do was connect.

Connect in the most primitive way possible.

She cried out as I plunged my tongue past the seam of her lips, forcing her to accept me, commanding she dance to the same feral song.

We fought to get closer—her wedging into me and me bowing over her. My hands turned to claws, holding her cruelly.

Nothing was enough.

No scratch intense enough. No bite painful enough.

There was nothing civil about us.

We were animals.

Dirty, filthy animals that had reached a dirty, filthy level and had nowhere else to go.

Teeth and nail and sullied, snarling lust.

Lowering her to the ground, I didn't care we had no tent or shelter. I didn't care sticks and leaves would be part of what we were about to do.

*I didn't care.*

I had no *capacity* to care.

The only thing that mattered was getting inside the one person I needed more than air.

Della went without a fight, letting me brush aside as many twigs as I could before pressing her onto her back and smothering her instantly with my weight.

She squirmed beneath me as I grabbed her jaw and kept her still so I could deepen the kiss to exquisitely harsh.

With my free hand, I shoved up her t-shirt and cupped her bra-free breast with eager fingers. Her back arched, revealing the perfection of bare skin. Her legs kicked out wide, welcoming; her hips raised off the ground, seeking.

My brain short-circuited.

A flicker of persecution needled me as my hand drifted down the delectable length of her belly, ripped at her belt, and tore at her zipper. Image after image of Della in similar undress. Of her changing after late night baling and getting covered in prickly dried grass. Of her sitting on a rock by the pond in her swimsuit, pretending to be as worldly as Cassie but failing for being so young.

Bang. Bang. Bang.

Caution. Caution. Caution.

Even though I loved that little girl with all my heart, I no longer bowed to her.

I bowed to this new mistress instead.

I wasn't clutching that child or kissing someone I shouldn't be kissing. I wasn't committing some heinous act, or stepping over lines that should never be crossed.

This was Della.

Girl and woman.

A girl with a ribbon in her hair, and now a woman with a tattoo on her foot.

I was kissing my goddamn soulmate, and who fucking cared how we'd met or how long we'd known each other? Fate had decided to throw us an unconventional beginning by giving her to me the moment she was born.

Her lips parted as I kissed her with renewed violence, ignoring sudden breathlessness and overwhelming heat.

Moaning, she slung her arms over my shoulders as I managed to unzip her jeans and yank at them without finesse. Frustration bubbled as the tight material refused to move. "Are you trying to kill me?"

She smiled beneath our kiss, her lips stretching tight with the same kind of delirium I suffered. "You mean…you need help stripping me?"

"Don't taunt me, Della. Now is not a good time."

"Why? Because you're a little worked up?"

"Because I'll die if I don't get inside you."

"Oh." She blushed, pleased and sexy. "In that case…"

I glowered as she pushed me away and hooked her fingers in her jeans. With a coy, almost shy look, she shoved them down her legs, leaving baby blue bikini briefs.

I groaned.

"Do you have to be so fucking gorgeous?" I fell on her again, kissing, attacking, worshipping. Her heat promised me all kinds of sinful things as I ran my hand between her legs, just once, unable to stop myself from claiming.

She jolted as my fingers trailed over her inner thighs, wrenching her knees apart to give me more room to settle between them.

Keeping my weight on my elbows, I fisted her hair, morphing the kiss from deep to downright devouring. My body ached with a fever born from needing her so badly. With our mouths locked, I pressed my hips into hers, surging upward, searching for every part she'd give me.

My hand lassoed around her neck, squeezing for that perfect taste of submission.

The flash of surrender that I so desperately needed.

Her mouth popped wide as I held her tight.

Our eyes locked.

For a second, she stared as if she didn't know me then, in a wash of pure acceptance and obedience, she corrupted me with bliss.

She licked her lips, arching herself deeper into my control.

"Fuck." I fell on her again, holding nothing back, driving her into the dirt, squeezing her gorgeous throat, stealing everything I could.

I wanted to treat her as kindly as I'd always done, but she knew me now.

She knew enough to understand I wouldn't be sweet.

Not in this.

I reached between us for my own belt. "Don't move. I won't last much longer if you move."

But she disobeyed me, wriggling a little higher to slip her hands over mine and grab the buckled leather instead. "Me."

That simple possessive word made me harder than I'd ever been. "*Christ*, Della."

A thunderstorm percolated in my blood. Rumbling thunder and crackling lightning gathered like eager sinners in my lower belly, howling at her to do whatever she damn well wanted.

I couldn't breathe as her shoulders bobbed, her hands busy below. The tug of her yanking the leather through the buckle, the slight give as it fell to the sides, the incineration of her fingers on my sensitive skin as she unhooked the button and eased my zipper down.

And when she touched me…when her fingers feathered over my hardness for the first time. When she bit her lip as if shocked and awed that I'd finally, *finally* permitted such things. When her touch turned from feather to forceful and she wrapped her fingers around me, I motherfucking broke.

My mind fractured, and I sucked in lungsful of tainted air.

And by breaking, memories I'd been ignoring drowned me.

Of Della teaching me to read.

Of Della smacking a kiss on my lips under the mistletoe that first Christmas at the Wilsons.

Of Della…

Della…

Della.

*Fuck.*

I panted as if I'd run to Mclary's and back. My eyes saw double. My heart beat triple. But even though I bordered obsession filled with disgust for what I was doing, I couldn't stop.

For a week, I hadn't remembered.

Now, those memories were determined to play a part—to ensure we were prepared for the aftermath of pleasure. To prove we were ready to accept that we could never go back, only forward.

I accepted.

I wholeheartedly flung myself into the future and fisted both hands into her hair, smashing her lips to mine.

I stole her breath as my tongue dove deep, tasting her, condemning her.

She writhed, her legs scissoring tight around my waist, caught up in the whirlpool of erotic thirst and carnal hunger.

Our bodies strained with violence, already grinding, punishing, needy.

For years, I'd suspected Della was just as volatile as me when it came to sex, and now, I knew. She was just as unleashed. Both of us dangerous. Both highly unstable.

A fatal recipe.

Beasts driven to mate on the forest floor.

She nipped my lip, digging her nails into my scalp.

With a rumbling groan, I attacked her again, twisting in a vortex of young Ribbon and the present. My touch turned nasty, bruising her as I tried to take and take.

We kissed hungrily, savagely.

I wanted to hurt her for the power she had over me.

I wanted to punish her for making me this crazed.

Della slid a hand between our tight, overheated bodies and grabbed my cock, jerking me with vicious command.

I snapped and kissed her again, teeth and tongue and torment.

Deeper and deeper, over and over.

She cried out as twigs and debris scratched her while I devoured her. Thorns and sticks were nothing compared to the delicious pain her nails granted as she fought me back, bruise for bruise.

There was nothing gentle about any of this.

Both of us drunk on wildness and frenzy.

And when our battling wasn't enough, I bit her bottom lip. Hard.

Too hard.

She cried out, pulling back with a look of fiery desperation and a thread of wariness.

I'd told her I couldn't control myself. But as fresh air filled my nose and common-sense returned, my heart became master over my traitorous body, dousing my lust with ice. "Ribbon...I-I'm sorry."

She breathed as hard as me, quicksilver desire in her eyes. "I'm not." Rearing up, she captured my mouth again, enslaving me to her for life.

Our mania reached a new level of velocity.

All the years between us, each precious in their own way, were now barriers we had to smash apart *immediately*.

I needed her instantly.

She needed me urgently.

I loved that we both raced to the same chaotic beat.

Her body wriggled beneath mine as she shoved her underwear down her legs.

I froze, knowing she was naked, and I only had to lean back to look.

I wanted to look.

I *desperately* wanted to look.

But if I did, this would be all over.

Everything about this was too much.

*Too much.*

Della didn't pause, moving to undress me fast and ruthless, almost as if she wasn't sure I'd go through with this. Grabbing my jeans and boxer-briefs, she inched them down my ass.

I shivered as her fingers kissed my bare flesh and couldn't stop my hips from arching, giving her room to shove aside the unwanted clothing. Once they were mid-thigh, she fell back, then wrapped slim arms around me, pulling me tight.

I hissed as my eyes snapped closed against the most *incredible* thing I'd ever felt.

Her naked against my naked.

Her heat against my hardness.

I groaned low and loud as she burrowed closer, my hands balling where they wedged into the ground.

Her arms looped around my neck, her lips on my ear as she breathed, "You didn't look."

I knew exactly what she meant. "I couldn't."

"Why not?"

"Because I'm barely holding on as it is." Inhaling her gorgeous scent of wilderness and melons, I grunted, "Seeing you naked...fuck, Little Ribbon."

Her right hand slid from my shoulders, following the contours of my chest, leaving a trail of fire in her wake. "You didn't let me look, either. Can I?"

All my life I'd given her what she wanted. How could I deny her now?

I gulped as I pressed off her a little, her eyes searing my cock as she melted into the ground. "Look at us, Ren."

My jaw clenched as I looked down to the trimmed dark blonde curls and glisten of Della and the steely hard cock of me.

It didn't matter I'd seen her body grow through every stage. It didn't matter she'd seen me go from boy to man. All that fucking mattered was how perfect we looked together now.

"You're making me lose my mind." My hips dared to press closer, making me hiss again against the blistering heat of her.

"I lost mine years ago." She sucked in a breath, her hand shaking as it continued its path down my chest.

My heart suddenly crucified me, hating me for all the wasted moments we could've shared. "Why was I so blind?"

"Because your morals were killing you." She smiled softly. "But also because you knew it wasn't right. I was too young. I wasn't ready."

"And you're ready now?"

"This is the best moment of my life. Does that answer your question?"

I bent to kiss her, my back tight with tension, keeping me aloft. "I love you, Della."

"I know."

"I've loved you since that first moment I found you."

"Liar. You hated me."

I chuckled. "I wish someone could cuff me around the head as a ten-year-old and tell him his entire world was in that backpack."

"Well, your entire world wants you to stop talking and touch her."

She successfully stole every word, slamming me back into the swirling speed we'd shared before.

Her fingers locked around me, making me jolt. She shivered as if touching me affected her more than any summer breeze or dusk-shrouded forest ever could.

I'd had a lifetime of being held by her, loved by her...but this? It was fucking *everything*.

My hands moved as she touched me harder. Digging my left hand into the dirt, I ran my right down her side, my thumb kissing the side of her breast.

I wanted to mark her, brand her.

She moaned, her hand twitching around my cock.

I wanted to take my time and fondle her, lick her, bite those perfect nipples, but there was a demon in my blood howling for other things.

Dropping my touch down her waist, I marvelled at the shape of her, then lost my goddamn mind as I found the pulsating heat between her legs.

No barriers.

Just satin and silk and everything Della.

I disintegrated.

*Everything* ached.

My thumb found her clit, and my finger, shit, that drove into her with no sweet sonnets or requests. I couldn't help myself from spearing deep, twisting my existence with how perfectly hot and wet she was.

Her back arched as I withdrew, smearing her slipperiness against my other finger, rubbing her clit just once before I drove both into her.

I drove so hard, her body inched higher up the bracken littered ground.

Her mouth opened wide. "Holy fu—"

"Enough talking, remember?"

Leaves crackled as she squirmed. Breaths panted. My mind was awash with greed.

The wondrous sensation of being inside her ought to be enough. I ought to linger in this magic and take my time learning what she liked.

But it was too late for that.

"Condom. Where is it?" I bit out, thrusting my fingers deeper.

She searched blindly in the dirt beside us, finally holding up the foil packet.

"Put it on me," I snarled, thrusting fingers into her body while my cock wept with punishment. If I didn't get inside her now, I'd come. I was so close. *Too* close.

Her hands trembled as she ripped the foil, grabbed the

rubber, and cupped my length.

I growled under my breath as her tiny touch rolled the condom over me, squeezing my base as if determined to make me explode.

Knocking her hand away, I ripped my fingers from her and angled my hips.

"Tell me to stop, Della." My voice wasn't my own. It was black and dripping and demonic.

"Never." Spreading her legs, her hands landed on my ass, pulling me into her.

A small ribbon of blood decorated her arm from a sharp twig.

A shadow of a bruise marked the creamy flesh of her throat.

I wanted to feel bad.

I didn't.

The first welcome of her body blew my existence into tiny smithereens, and I no longer cared about the pieces. I didn't care if I'd be the same person after this. I didn't care about right and wrong.

This was right.

So, *so* right.

I fell on her, crushing her into the earth as I pushed inside her. I wasn't slow. I wasn't gentle. I was everything she'd made me become.

She tensed beneath me, her body tight, unyielding.

Parts of me cried for what I was doing, for the desecration of the purest thing I'd ever loved, while most of me rejoiced at finally finding the one person I'd been searching for.

"I'm sorry." My mouth slammed on hers, and my hips shot forward, driving through that tightness until her body gave way in a rush of welcome, her legs wrapped around my hips, and her moan filled my lungs.

She wanted me.

And I took her.

Hard.

Fast.

Ruthless.

My eyes snapped closed as everything inside wanted to erupt. Her heat. Her scent. The fact that this wasn't some faceless, nameless woman I couldn't stand but the girl I'd loved my entire life. The girl I'd die to deserve.

My heart swelled to four times its size, suffocating in its ribcage, desperate to sacrifice itself to her.

I was the luckiest bastard alive.

Connected.

Finally.

Together.

*Finally.*

Shock crashed over us that we were no longer separate, but one.

Tearing my mouth away, I locked eyes on hers and begged to see what I needed to see. The same violent fire. The same undeniable desire. Plucking a leaf stuck to her cheek, I groaned, "Look at what you're making me do."

"I don't care."

"I'm inside you."

"I know."

"I'm fucking mad for you, and you're wedged on the forest floor. You're bleeding for fuck's sake."

She smiled as if I'd given her the best gift in the world. "I know."

I laughed, groaning under my breath as my cock throbbed in her body. "What else do you know, Della Ribbon?"

"I know that you're inside me. And you're just delaying what you truly want to do."

My eyes hooded. "And what's that?"

"You want to fuck me."

My entire body rippled in impending release. "Quiet. You'll make me come."

"Well, you shut up and fuck me."

I thrust once, both of us hissing with searing pleasure.

"I can't believe—" My voice hitched as I thrust again. "—we're talking at a time like this."

"I can't believe you're *still* talking." Her hips rocked up, rubbing herself on me. With a sexy moan, she dug nails deeper into my ass. "Shut up, Ren."

I kissed her, speaking into her lips. "You're such a menace."

"And you're a tease."

I laughed again, awed that even in this new act we could joke like old times. "Tease? Oh, I'm many things, Della, but I'm not a tease."

My knees dug traction into the leaf-littered earth, driving into her again, deep, so deep.

Her head fell back, and her fingernails dug into my ass, yanking me harder into her.

I stared at her in total fucking awe.

How had I never seen?

How had I never known?

She was my other half, not just in friendship and family, but in everything else, too.

"You want me, Della Ribbon?" I murmured, my cock throbbing inside her.

"Yes. God, yes."

I moved.

I thrust hard, driving her into the ground. "Have me." *Thrust.* "Have all of me." *Thrust.* "You already have my heart. Now you have my soul."

I thrust in anger for how true that was.

I bent to kiss her again, and something snapped inside her. The same thing that'd snapped inside me. She bit me, pushing my shoulders and fighting against me to roll me onto my back.

For a second, shock rendered me pliant, and I rolled over, staying inside her, pressing her hips down onto mine. I coughed, unable to comprehend why I was on the floor instead of her.

She sat on top of me, her eyes heavy and lips swollen, and although she looked absolutely stunning with leaves crowning her tangled hair and dirt smudging her cheek, she didn't belong up there.

She belonged beneath me.

Rolling again, I pinned her to the ground, grabbed her wrists, and slammed them above her head. My hips rolled, locking her in place. "I call the shots, Della. Not you."

Something flared in her eyes as she struggled to free herself.

I only fucked her harder, my fingers tightening around her wrists as I thrust fast and deep. "Argue and I'll argue back." My face contorted with black agony as I let go a little more, biting her neck, arching my hips until every inch of me pounded into her. "Then again, fight. Let's see what happens if you do."

A look of rebellion etched her face, then melted into pure, glittering lust. "You think you're punishing me?" Whatever fight had been there siphoned into utmost surrender. "Ren, you're giving me exactly what I need."

Something hot twisted in my belly, bathing in her submission.

The need to own every part of her made me slip straight into the animalistic aggression I tried to hide.

I couldn't stop it.

I'd *never* been able to stop it.

But with her so beautiful and aroused beneath me—fighting back, matching my thrusts, biting me, scratching me—I'd found my equal.

I'd found home.

"What are you doing to me, Della?" Rearing up, I ploughed into her. Not caring she inched upward, dislodging twigs and leaves with each thrust. My knees burned from digging into earth. My back cramped for bowing into her, forcing everything I could inside her. "I promised I'd never hurt you. And now you've driven me to the worst."

I was a rough lover, but this...seeing her come undone in the most basic way possible, covered in earth with the scent of nature all around us, I lost it.

Dropping on top of her, I didn't care she bore my full weight or that I'd trapped her, smothered her, captured her.

She was mine, and she'd take what I gave her.

"Hurt me because nothing has felt this good in my *life*."

Grabbing her around the neck, I kissed her furious and vicious. My fingers twitched to squeeze. My nails ached to mark.

"Make me come, Ren. *Please* make me come." She moaned as I drove into her with all the finesse of a raging bull.

Burrowing my face into the crook of her neck, I drove again and again. "You've ruined me. Fuck, you've ruined me." Harder and harder I rode her until the forest was full of skin slapping and animals rutting.

She cried out as I thrust faster, crueller, driven by her fight and surrender.

"Della." My forehead crashed against hers as I panted and raged, wanting to climb deeper, cursing her and myself. *"Fuck."*

Pinching her wrists with my left hand, my right soared down her body, squeezing her breast with nasty fingers before finding the place where we were joined.

We were wet and messy and scorching hot.

It turned me on.

*Christ*, it turned me on.

I couldn't catch my breath as I found her clit and rubbed.

Her back snapped up. "Oh, God!"

"Shut up. Just shut up." I rubbed harder, all while plunging my tongue into her mouth in time to the plunging between her legs.

Her nails punctured my ass, riding with me as I rode her.

Every roll and twist and thrust of my hips, she matched me

until I didn't know who fucked who.

Leaves flew. Birds scattered. And it was no longer about love but war.

"Ren!" Her body tightened, her legs spasmed around my hips, and the delicious heat of her pulsed with release.

I lost everything that made me human.

I only lived to make love to this woman.

I only existed to be hers.

My orgasm brewed full of pain and exquisite intensity, pushing me over the edge.

We clawed and cried and thrust and fucked, and my entire world changed being inside her. My soul switched owners as the thunderstorm that had teased me from the beginning finally found its matching cloud and erupted into existence.

My release ripped howls from my chest, vows from my heart, and promises from my soul. And I knew, without a shadow of a fucking doubt, I would never be whole again unless I had Della.

She was it for me.

I belonged to myself no more.

I'd officially handed over my life, and I was done fighting.

Forever.

# Chapter Twenty-Three

## DELLA

## 2031

*A NEW MANUSCRIPT, a new page, a new story.*

*It's been a long time since I wrote down our tale. Too long since I've felt the keys of a laptop beneath my fingers and sat alone with my memories.*

*So many, many memories.*

*To be honest, I don't even know where to begin.*

*I did scribble now and again into that tatty notebook I took with me, but once Ren and I slept together, I forgot about everything else.*

*I didn't* need *anything else.*

*It was like the past story of our lives was over, and we had a new story to look forward to.*

*Does that make sense? It was the end of an era. Forbidden, unrequited love no more.*

*I will admit that I worried a little once we finally 'did the deed.' I worried that Ren would struggle with our new connection. I worried we'd still have roadblocks to overcome.*

*I needn't have worried.*

*Once Ren took me on that forest floor, filling me so full and hard that I had external and internal bruises for days, he committed himself to everything he'd been fighting.*

*His protectiveness became fiercer. His love deeper. His commitment truer than it had ever been.*

*That first time—that magical time—we both walked away (or rather limped) with cuts and scrapes and a togetherness that meant we could barely stop touching long enough to put up the tent.*

*From that moment on, we were insatiable.*

*Desperate and hungry and crazily in love.*

*Being in love with Ren Wild…words can't do it justice.*

*When he finally took me—when he finally woke up and saw he wasn't the only one with a wildness inside him—we reached a level that sometimes scared me.*

*The depth of love I felt for him.*

*The depth of love he felt for me.*

*It demanded our hearts beat to the same rhythm, our bodies be near, our minds be in-tune, our breaths be in-sync. I'd never felt anything like it. And I still feel it today.*

*His fears that he was selfish and unkind when it came to sex were totally unfounded. He couldn't accept that, after a life of doing his utmost to protect me, it was okay to be rough.*

*Wanting me as savagely as I wanted him didn't make him any less of a saint.*

*In fact, his darker desires made perfect sense. He bent over backward to put my needs before his own, but when it came to sex, he took his own pleasure too.*

*And there was absolutely nothing wrong with that.*

*Sleeping with Ren that day in the forest was my third sexual experience, but it might as well have been my first. Where Ren treated me like a queen in every waking moment of my life, when he got me beneath him—I was his to use as he saw fit.*

*He snapped and growled and dominated. He swore, which he painstakingly never did. He bruised me after making a vow to protect me from everything. He took control over what he wanted rather than sacrificing everything. When he thrust, he forgot about me and became obsessed with me at the same time. And when he made me come, that was the true gift because I'd never come before.*

*I craved—even before I knew what I needed—to be punished.*

*I needed to be punished because I'd fallen in love with a man I shouldn't, and a part of me always needed that discipline.*

*Only Ren understood because he had that same sin. Ren was the only one with the power to make me feel wholeheartedly female, and I worshipped that man with every inch.*

*I look back, and I'm actually jealous of myself. Jealous of that perfect time. Jealous of everything we were about to enjoy, endure, and explore.*

*There is so much I need to tell you. So many, many things.*

*And I will.*

*I'll get around to it because I'm not leaving anything out.*

*I can't, you see.*

*I have to write it down because I never want to forget. I never want to forget every minute of every day—not just passing flashes that make an impression.*

*Flashes like sleeping with Ren that first time.*

*Flashes like every day thereafter and every day in between.*

*Life is so fast and stuffed full of surprises that I'm afraid if I don't write them down, they'll disappear just as child amnesia deletes your earliest memories.*

*And it's more than just a drive to immortalize Ren with ink on paper. It's a necessity because these pages are our photo album.*

*Back when we were younger, we didn't have the luxury of cameras and video recorders. There are no pictures of us as we grew side by side. But there are words. And they are just as special because they're painted with all the love and connection I was feeling at the time. They not only show an image but let me borrow those emotions and relive it.*

*As for the other assignment—the one I was going to burn just before Ren walked back into my life? Well, that's here beside me. Almost two decades later, and I still have it. Ink smudged and paper torn but still intact and treasured.*

*Ren never let me burn it.*

*He tucked it safe and kept all three-hundred-and-ninety-seven pages wedged in his backpack the entire time we travelled.*

*This story is no longer about a baby and a boy who were never meant to be family, but a woman and a man who were always destined to be soulmates.*

*But before I get started, I want to say a few things.*

*First, I'm well aware I'm breaking another writing rule. Not only am I shattering the fourth wall, but I'm also talking to you from the future. I have the benefit of knowing how this tale turns out.*

*I know the ending.*

*I know the journey we take.*

*And you'll have to excuse me if I slip now and again. You'll have to forgive me for any spoilers because it isn't intentional. It's hard keeping things tucked up inside, desperate for their time to shine, my fingers cramping with desire to fly over the keyboard and release sentences and descriptions of the best man I've ever known.*

*But as much as I want to just blurt out everything, to let you know what happened when we travelled back to Cherry River, to whisper the name of someone so unbelievably special, to reveal if Ren and I got married...I can't.*

*It wouldn't be fair, because like any story, there is a beginning, a middle, and an end.*

*You know our beginning.*

*You're about to know our middle.*

*And our end...well, that's not finished yet, so you'll have to be patient.*

*What I can give you are incidents.*

*Five incidents that are crucial to this tale.*

*Just like I teased you with the four times Ren and I were apart, this time…there are moments.*

*Wonderful moments.*

*Horrible moments.*

*Moments that make up a life.*

*Five of them.*

*One, two, three, four, five.*

*Some I loved.*

*Some I hated.*

*One that hasn't happened yet.*

*My advice?*

*Watch out for them.*

# Chapter Twenty-Four

## DELLA

## 2018

"STOP," I COMMANDED, slipping from the tent and stretching out the kinks in my spine. My entire body felt used and abused and oh-so-delicious.

Sex was my new favourite activity.

And I wanted a second round immediately.

But first...there was something that'd been bugging me since I saw Ren bathe in the river that first night.

"Why?" Ren turned to face me, his t-shirt dangling in his hands, low-slung cargo shorts already hiding the parts of him I wanted to explore. "What's happened?"

Padding barefoot toward him, I ran my fingers along the visible ribs interrupting the perfect shadows of strong stomach muscles. "I've wanted to ask you for the past week. When did you lose all this weight?" My heart clenched, suddenly terrified. "You're not sick, are you?"

He cupped my chin softly, his gaze molten caramel mixed with coffee. "No, I'm not sick." His hair was longer, teasing his forehead with sable bronze thanks to summer turning the strands light.

I could stare at his perfect face with its strong nose, powerful jaw, and thick eyelashes for an eternity and still find things to love about it. "Then why can I see your ribs?"

"Because I didn't exactly have an appetite when I left you."

I accepted his fleeting kiss before he let me go to sling his black t-shirt over his head, hiding the skinniness that wasn't there before. To be fair, he hadn't eaten as much as he normally did these days. I'd put it down to the sexual tension between us and the fact that my own belly was tied up with string.

But I didn't like seeing Ren skinny. I didn't like feeling as if I hadn't taken adequate care of him.

Following him as he wandered around camp, I asked, "You're saying you didn't eat the entire time we were apart?"

"I'm saying love was cruel, and my mind fixated on other things." He stopped and faced me. "I didn't want food, Della. I wanted you."

My skin burned with pleasure.

I knew it shouldn't, but in a way, that made me feel better. I hadn't forgiven him yet for leaving me, or for stalking me for months and not letting me know he was back in our apartment.

Three months we wasted.

Three long, horrible months where I lived unhappily with David, unable to stop the sensation that Ren was close by, all while he crashed in our apartment alone.

"Is it bad if I say you deserved it?"

He chuckled, running his hands through his hair. "Is it wrong that I love hearing you say that?"

"Say that I'm glad you suffered?"

"I deserved to suffer." He gave me a rueful smile. "I made you suffer by breaking my promise and leaving."

"We both know why you did."

"Yes, and I was selfish. I was only thinking of myself. I didn't know how to deal with what I felt for you, and I was weak enough to run." He coughed a little then gathered me in a hug filled with electricity and desire.

His soft lips pressed a kiss to my hairline. "Never again, Little Ribbon. You're stuck with me."

"And you're stuck with me." My smile faltered a little—just a flicker—but enough for Ren to frown.

"You okay?"

"Yes, just...*you're* okay, right? You're happy and healthy and you'll put on weight again and stop that little cough you do sometimes?"

He grinned. "I love it when you care."

I swatted him. "I care all the time."

He nodded, falling serious. "Look, I had the flu while we were apart and I haven't fully shaken the cough, that's all. And as for putting on weight, I've already filled out. You make my appetite come back because I need all the energy I can to keep you satisfied."

My cheeks pinked. "You kept me satisfied well enough last night."

His chocolate gaze turned dark and rich. "You too." He licked his lips. "Last night was..." He sighed with a little huff of indescribable bliss. It made my stomach flutter and heart leap for joy. "It was amazing, Della."

He kissed me again, distracting me from another niggling question.

He noticed, nipping my bottom lip before pulling away with a resigned look. "Something else?"

"Umm..." I shrugged. "I need to ask you something."

His frown spread. "Ask me."

"I know we're both surviving on no sleep with no small amount of shock for what we've done but..."

"But..."

"Well, after fighting your feelings for me for so long. Now we've, eh, crossed those boundaries, are you still happy?" I ducked my gaze. "Are you happy you—"

"Ah, Della." Scooping me into strong arms, he rested his chin on my head. "I was honest with how I struggled to come to terms with loving you this way, and now, I'll be honest again." His voice dropped to a smoky murmur. "For the first time, I don't care about any of it. I can stand here with my head proud and tell the sun to go guilt-trip someone else for a change. Last night was the best night of my life with the only person I have ever loved. As far as I'm concerned, it was the first time for both of us. No one else compares because no one else ever came close to how I feel about you. And now that I know who you are beneath that bossy, brilliant girl I raised, you're in trouble because having you once won't be enough. Having you twice or three times or even a lifetime will never be enough, do you hear me?"

Pulling back, he stared as deep as he could into my heart. "I'm not just in love with you, Della. You're the only reason I'm alive. Loving you gave me purpose. And now you've completed me by giving me something I never dared dream of, so to answer your question, yes, I'm happy. So fucking happy I'm going to explode."

I shivered in his arms. "Okay then. Good."

"Fine." He grinned.

I raised my chin, my eyes fixating on his beautiful lips. "You know...after a declaration like that, you can't expect me not to want to get you back into bed." Standing on my tiptoes, I brushed a soft kiss on his mouth. "Take me into the tent, Ren."

He groaned, "Don't tempt me. It was hard enough untangling myself from you this morning."

Last night—after we'd orgasmed and slowly realised the enormity of what we'd done half-undressed, smeared in mud, and scratched with leaves in the middle of an empty forest—we'd petted and stroked and laughed at the sudden glorious freedom of being together.

That dazzling freedom drenched us in a high that made us shake and laugh and giggle like silly children as Ren pulled free, disposed of the condom, then plucked me from the gound.

The river was too shallow to swim, but we were able to wash off the stickiness and wilderness before eating a simple dinner of roasted fish, then snuggling up like we always did in the tent that took forever to put up, thanks to him grabbing me or me kissing him with our constant need to be close.

It was the best day of my life, but for some reason, we couldn't fall asleep. Too in awe of what had happened, too afraid that if we closed our eyes, we'd wake and it would all be a dream.

All night, Ren cupped my breast, rocked his front into my back, and wrapped his leg around mine. Our touches were allowed to be sexual. We were allowed to include our bodies as well as our hearts.

By the time dawn stole the midnights of darkness and used a different palate of shell-pinks and mandarin-golds, Ren and I were well and truly smitten.

Thank God, no one else was around because we were completely wrapped up in each other to the point of eye rolling.

"We have nowhere to be. No deadlines. No appointments. Why can't we just have sex for the rest of our lives?"

Ren chuckled, warming my heart with its husky melodic sound. "Because you didn't let me prepare. You pounced on me yesterday, remember?"

"I did nothing of the sort." I smirked, knowing full well that when I'd found that small clearing, I couldn't hold off the urgency anymore. The tingling, sparkling urgency that had steadily grown from painful to excruciating.

If Ren hadn't given in last night, I very well might've attacked him against his will.

"You won last night, Little Ribbon. Now you have to do what I say." Throwing me a heated look, he commanded, "Help me pack up camp. We're heading down river where the current isn't so fast and it's deeper to swim."

I followed him as he pulled the sleeping bags from the tent and started to roll them up. "And then what?"

He threw me a cheeky, deliciously dirty look. "And then, it's my turn."

# Chapter Twenty-Five

## REN

## 2018

DELLA HAD CHANGED my world.

And now, I wanted to change hers.

As we strode through the fading light to yet another campsite, I spotted a natural clearing where no sun was welcome, and no trees grew.

The river babbled in the distance, glistening in the twilight with invitation to wash away our exhaustion and relax. It wasn't as loud or as swift as our last stop. The surface calm and serene instead of choppy and chaotic.

The small cuts and grazes from sex last night marked Della's creamy skin as she strode ahead of me, her backpack heavy, boots crunching purposely, unaware I'd made my choice.

I wanted to feel bad about hurting her, but all I felt was absolute satisfaction and weird male pride.

"Stop," I said quietly hiding a cough as I slipped my bag to the ground and once again became bombarded by the tingling, incinerating chemistry that'd set up a constant vigil between us.

Della brushed away a sweat-sticky curl, breathing shallowly as she slowed to a halt and turned. She didn't say anything as our eyes locked, and we became caught up in a vortex of need.

"Don't." I kept my distance. "I'm doing my best to have camp set up before we give in this time."

"And how's that going for you?" She laughed as I tore at my bag's zipper and wrenched out almost every belonging in a rush.

"Good." I fisted the tent and shook it out.

"If you say so."

"Hold that tongue of yours, Della. I'm having you. Just give me a few minutes."

She smiled sweetly as I began the process of erecting somewhere to sleep—somewhere to take her where it was soft and safe so I could take my time and make her fall apart as spectacularly as she'd made me.

Disposing of her own bag, Della rubbed her lower back as she came to grab two sides of the tent as I unrolled it. She held it taut while I hammered in the pegs. Together, we inserted the poles, bending them until the nylon sprang upward, creating a roof.

The entire time we worked, my skin never stopped prickling at her proximity. And once we'd finished, she moved away and stripped off her t-shirt, leaving her in just a black sports bra and jeans as she twisted up her hair to encourage a breeze to cool her down.

My gut squeezed, my heart pounded, my mouth went dry.

All my life, she'd cared for me. She'd done chores I didn't ask her to, cooked food I didn't request, been there every step of the way. I no longer looked at her as two people—girl and woman—just her.

Della.

*Mine.*

Dappled in twilight with tiredness clinging to her skin, she looked so damn young. Too young to withstand the hurricane of lust in my blood.

But she *had* survived.

She'd fought me back.

She'd woken me up to the temptress she truly was, and I couldn't wait anymore.

We had a bed.

That was all we needed.

As she kicked off her boots and removed her socks, her ribbon tattoo with its capital R filled my vision, no longer condemning me but welcoming me.

I wanted to lick it again.

Bite it for good measure.

Stopping beside her as she turned to face me, I hovered like a love-struck fool, drinking her in, licking my lips at how I wanted to suck the sweat on her chest and run my thumb over the perspiration on her upper lip.

I was so fucking in love with her, I could barely stand it.

She looked up, shielding her gaze from the final light streaming through the trees. "Why are you looking at me like that?" She narrowed her eyes. "You don't look well. In fact, you look hungry." She stepped toward the bags. "I'll make you something to eat. You need to put on weight—"

Grabbing her around the waist, I shook my head. "I'm not hungry for food, Della."

She blinked, whatever tiredness she suffered vanished. "Oh."

"Yes, oh. You've turned me into an addict."

"I don't mind."

Nuzzling her nose with mine, I breathed softly, "It's my turn to ask you something."

"Okay…" She didn't help my concentration or self-control by fixating on my mouth. "What?"

"Last night…was it okay for you? Not emotionally, but physically?"

She laughed under her breath. "Seriously?" She melted in my hold, her eyes soft and glowing. "Good? That's a very underwhelming word for how great it was."

"I was rough with you."

"And I loved every second of it." She tilted her head. "What's this really about?"

Honestly, I didn't truly know. I'd shown her quick and explosive, but I didn't want her to think that was my only trick. And I didn't want her to think I was some idiot who needed affirmation that he'd performed well.

This wasn't about me.

This was about her.

This was about pleasing her, so she never looked elsewhere again.

This was about me ensuring my heart would never be broken when she realised I wasn't everything she hoped I would be.

"Last night was the best night of my life, Della. Is it wrong that I hoped it was the same for you?"

Her body tensed. "It was."

"Can I try to make it better?"

"There's no need. I loved every—"

"I had you pinned in the dirt while rutting into you like a savage. Tonight, I need to show you I'm more than that."

"I know you are." She pressed a kiss to my cheek. "I love you as a savage. That savage made me come for the first time, so believe me, I loved it just as much as you did."

"Wait." I reared back, holding her at arm's length. "What do you mean, the first time you came?"

She blushed. "I'm saying...I'd never come before."

"But..." My mind whirled on all the times she'd thrown hints and secrets in my face, daring me to rise to the bait, tormenting me on a daily basis. "You implied. You said—"

"That I'd made myself orgasm to thoughts of you?" She sighed. "Yes, I know. I wanted you to have that mental picture. Sorry." She winced a little as I glared at her. "The truth is, I *did* try. I've touched myself while thinking about you, but even though I wanted you enough to overlook certain rules, I could never get past the fact that you didn't want me. Every time I got close, I...I couldn't do it. The shame would be too much to bear, and I'd stop."

I rubbed my face with a hand. "So you're saying you've spent your entire life frustrating yourself and never finding a release?"

She laughed under her breath. "I guess you could say that."

"No wonder living with you made me on edge." I chuckled painfully, coughing once. "Every time I looked at you, Della, the way you stared at me almost brought me to my knees. The amount of times I lectured myself that I was imagining it, picking up on things that weren't there." I shook my head, reliving the agony of sharing a house with the one person I couldn't have. "You made my life a lot harder than it should've been."

She smiled sinfully. "Yes, but it meant I got you in the end, so I have no regrets."

I fell quiet, letting the past crash over me but no longer suffering the same guilt as before. Maybe Della was right, and everything had happened for a reason. Maybe I'd never let myself care for anyone else because I knew I'd never be able to share my heart with anyone other than her. And maybe she'd never made herself orgasm because all along she'd been waiting for me to—

I groaned, wedging my fingers against my temples as yet another tormenting thought appeared.

"What? What is it?" Della scooted closer. "You have that look again."

"What look?"

"The look that says you want to whip yourself for ever thinking about touching me."

"First, I'll never feel that way again. Ever. As far as I'm concerned, your body is mine just like mine is yours. And second, just because you know me doesn't mean you can predict everything about me."

"Well, you should accept that last night needed to happen the way it did. It was never going to be slow and sweet, Ren. We'd been edging to exploding for years."

I nodded, picking up on her wavelength just as I used to do when she was young. "It smashed through our perceptions. Changed the relationship between us."

"Exactly." She shifted to kiss my stubble-covered cheek. I hadn't shaved in a few days and didn't have the urge out here. "And now, stop changing the subject and tell me what you're truly thinking."

She was right. Last night was never going to be anything more than a feral battle because we had far too much history between us. History that held different dynamics and ages and pent-up secrets we hadn't shared.

Now, things were out in the open.

And we had so much to look forward to.

Cupping her cheeks, my touch sent goosebumps ricocheting down her arms. "I've taught you almost everything you know. Just like you've taught me."

Her breath came feathery and light. "Yes."

"Would it be sick of me to teach you something else?"

Her gaze hooded as she leaned into me. "Teach me what?"

I licked my lips, drawn to her, unable to stop the way her heart hooked mine. "How to come. Not just when being ruthlessly taken but with my fingers inside you, my tongue licking you, my cock fucking you. So many different ways. I want to be the one to teach you all of them."

She gasped, then shook her head slowly. "I-I wouldn't mind."

The shy happiness in her tone undid me.

Bringing her close, I kissed her hard. "Good answer, Little Ribbon. Let's start now."

# Chapter Twenty-Six

## DELLA

## 2018

REN'S KISSES WERE something made of fantasy.

Hard and rough. Swift and sexy. Deep and lingering. Whenever he kissed me, it didn't matter if it was a peck or a meal, he completely hijacked my thoughts and body.

And that was how I went from standing in my jeans and bra to him undoing my belt and zipper, pushing the denim down my legs, then reverently removing my black bikini briefs before pulling the sports bra over my head.

Once I was naked, he kissed me harder, plucked me from the ground as if I weighed nothing and carried me in arms that bunched and trembled with an intoxicating mix of love and lust.

My legs automatically wrapped around his waist, our lips never unlocking as he toed off his boots, kicked them aside, and marched fully clothed toward the gurgle and chuckle of the river.

He licked me deep and clutched me strong, trading dry land for a water-world as if he outran echoes from our past and bravely stormed into our future.

"What are you doing?" I gasped when he continued walking. Water sucked at his socks, saturating his jeans. His steps became wades as we traded the shallows to a darkened pool where the current didn't disrupt the crystal clarity of the surface.

Once there, he ducked to his knees and pulled me down into the cool, crisp embrace of the river.

His breath caught from the chill, a tiny rattle roughening his voice. "Making love to you."

Somehow, it felt as if he bowed to me. Worshipping me all

while his tongue said he planned to corrupt me with an evening of ecstasy.

The coolness of the running water stole the remainders of our breaths as it flowed between us, making our bodies tense. His eyes caught mine, hooded and heated as he grabbed my chin and pulled me back into a kiss.

I gasped into his mouth, shuddering from the sudden temperature change and the refreshing lick of liquid.

"You're sopping wet," I murmured, tilting my head as he kissed me deeper, and his fingers found their way into my hair.

"And you better be too," he whispered, hot and dark. "Because I'm sure as shit hard."

A lash of lust travelled from my heart to my core, tugging on strands and sensuality, preparing my body for whatever he wanted. "All you have to do is smile at me, Ren, and I'm wet."

He attacked me with unbridled need. His kisses were pure velvet violence. "Don't say things like that. I want this to last, not be over in seconds."

"Then stop seducing me so well."

We laughed together even as his hands stroked skin sore with cuts from last night's war. His palms explored my back and spine, fisting handfuls of my ass as he yanked me forward and onto the straining erection in his jeans.

"Do you know how often I've stared at this?" His fingers kneaded me. "How I'd dream of seeing you naked and in my bed?" His lips parted wider over mine, directing the kiss from shallow hello to deep dance.

I moaned as he kissed me like all women wanted to be kissed—hungrily, fondly, passionately.

We kissed all night.

We kissed for a second.

And as we kissed, he rocked up into my bare core, his zipper as cold as the river, his hands holding me firm.

We were in perfect alignment for sex.

Pity he was still so encumbered.

Our thoughts vibrated to the same frequency—just like always—because he pushed me down his lap, giving him room for his hands to fumble at his belt.

"Let me." I panted, partly from cold and mostly from need.

He clenched his jaw as I found his buckle and unthreaded the leather. I didn't tease; I was just as starving as him. Popping his button and drawing down his zipper, my hand vanished into his boxers before he could push me away.

Steel-covered satin and sheer power. Holding Ren so intimately was like being given the keys to immortality.

His head fell back on a groan, nostrils flaring, hips rocking, granting me all the magic in the world.

"I'm always so damn close with you."

"Is that a bad thing?" I gasped as his fingers trailed over my goose-pimpled thighs and dug into my flesh.

"Bad that I find you unbelievably gorgeous and can't help how much I want you?" He kissed me with a twist of silk and softness. "Never."

Rearing back a little, his arms criss-crossed as he grabbed his hem, and with eyes dripping with chocolate promise, yanked his sodden t-shirt over his head. With a grunt of strength, he tossed the wet material toward the shore.

"Thought you'd wash your clothes as well as yourself, huh?" I snickered as he gathered me to his hot, naked chest. His cock wedged against me, making both of us hiss in that deliciously depraved way.

"Everything about me is filthy, so yeah." He smirked. "Just trying to cleanse myself from needing you so badly."

"I don't think the river will help with that." I melted as he kissed me again, adding bruise upon bruise, rasp after rasp from all the other kisses we'd shared.

"I think you're right." Pushing me away, he ordered. "Go get the soap. Let's see if that works."

I swiped hair from my eyes, the ends floating in the water like kelp. "Now who's being bossy?"

"Only because I want to stare at you while you get it." His eyes glowed. "Go. Before I change my mind."

Burning up from the desire between us that even the chilly river couldn't douse, I turned and waded back to the shallows. Self-consciousness descended as water sluiced off me, preferring to stay with its friends than on my skin.

With my spine straight and belying the nervous butterflies in my stomach, I swayed my hips, revealing my back and bottom to Ren.

It wasn't like he hadn't seen me before, but this...it was different.

Without a backward glance, I headed toward the bags standing sentry at the tent's entrance. It only took a second to unzip the side pocket where painkillers, toothbrushes, and soaps lived, then spin to face the only man I'd ever love.

His arm was above his head, cocked back to toss his soaking jeans to the bank.

They landed with a loud splat beside me, his boxer-briefs on top, letting me know he was as naked as I was.

My heart fluttered as I stepped into the water.

Ren bit his lip, his right shoulder rocking up and down. I knew exactly what he was doing, and it made yet more lust bubble in my belly.

Reaching him, I kneeled and ducked my fingers beneath the surface. Sure enough, his right hand was latched around his cock, stroking himself. "Couldn't wait?"

He didn't even look ashamed, more like tortured. "You are far too stunning for mere mortals. Are you truly mine?" He took my hand, wedging it beneath his on his stiff cock. Squeezing both of us, he grumbled, "Feel what you do to me, Della? See what I've been hiding from you for years?"

I couldn't catch my breath at the raw honesty in his tone. The knowledge he'd hurt just as much as I had. The shared pain we were well acquainted with.

I'd seen Ren naked so many times.

His body was as familiar to me as my own.

But this was entirely new.

He'd shed the brotherly side of himself, allowing me to see him as a man and not just my protector.

He couldn't be any more handsome or tempting, and I wrapped my fingers tight beneath his, making him half-groan, half-snarl.

Desire snapped and crackled, making its way to form a fireball in my core.

Ren surrendered to my touch, wrapping his arms around me, dragging me close. "Come here." Our skin slipped and slid over each other as I floated onto his lap, and my legs wrapped around his waist.

Releasing his erection, I moaned as he rubbed against me, and we both almost buckled with pleasure. The soap in my left hand wasn't wanted as Ren purred into my mouth, rocking against me, fucking me even though we were still apart.

His fingers threaded through my hair, tugging my head back as he broke the kiss and nipped his way down my throat. He didn't let me go as my back bowed and water lapped over my head, drenching every inch of blonde.

His mouth was hot as he trailed kisses down my chest, then latched onto my nipple with furious need.

I cried out as he wrapped one arm around my waist, driving against me as his tongue swirled and teeth teased, slipping from one nipple to the other.

"God, please..." I writhed against him, needing him inside me.

*Now.*

But he didn't bow to my command. Instead, he sucked my breasts one more time before kissing his way up my throat and ending at my mouth with the longest, sexist kiss I'd ever been given.

I gave up trying to figure out what he would do next.

"Turn around," he murmured. "Turn around so I can wash you."

With a quick inhale, he unwrapped my legs, then spun me on his lap, pushing me outward until I floated on the surface. Gathering the thick weight of my hair, he lathered the soap and ran his strong fingers over my scalp, massaging gently, breathing a little easier thanks to familiar pastimes and recognisable comforts in the sex-storm we lived in.

My body didn't know if it should orgasm or melt. I was tangled with lust and trust, remembering all the other times Ren had washed me, tended to me, cared for me.

It made my heart burst and tears prickle as I whispered, "That feels so nice."

"And you feel too perfect to be real." Lathering more bubbles, his large hands worked over my shoulders, under my arms, over my breasts, and down my belly.

"Kneel," he ordered, pushing my body deeper into the water so I switched from floating to kneeling. "Turn to face me."

There was something so erotic about following his curt commands.

Once I faced him, he rubbed the soap once again, then trailed his hand through the water to the curls between my legs.

I jolted as he washed me gently, the slipperiness of soap washed away by the river, leaving me so much wetter than before.

Never looking away from me, he spread me apart, then inserted two fingers inside me.

I froze and tightened and quaked and liquefied.

He might've only given me two fingers, but it felt like two pieces of his soul. Two pieces that Cassie had bemoaned she would never have. Two pieces that no one else would ever own.

Just me.

*Only* me.

My mouth fell wide as he sank deeper. He hooked his touch inside me, pressing, rubbing, igniting the fuse that would eventually explode into a toe-curling orgasm. He didn't give me a moment to breathe, analyse, or decide if I wanted to fight back, submit, or melt into a puddle in his hand. All that mattered was I was his, and he was touching me in ways I'd always begged him to.

"Ren," I breathed as he gathered me closer.

"Shush." Never looking away from me, he studied my every twitch and sigh as if learning exactly what made me simmer.

And he found it with his thumb on my clit.

My back bowed, and a low moan spilled from me as he drove two fingers deeper.

He smiled, satisfaction glowing in his dark eyes. "You like that?"

"Uh huh." I nodded with desire-lethargy, my head heavy and eyes struggling to focus.

"Good to know." Pulling his touch from my body, he lathered yet more bubbles and dragged them over the sparse hair on his well-defined chest, swiftly washing himself before the soap disappeared to clean other areas.

I wobbled before him, shocked that he'd touched me so spectacularly, then acted as if nothing had happened.

"Oh, that's just mean." I pouted as ripples of pleasure still worked through my core, begging him to come back.

"It would be mean if I didn't plan on doing more." His hands finished washing, tossing the soap toward the shore. "But I do. An entire night of more."

"I would've done that," I said.

"What? Wash me?" He shook his head, jaw tight and eyes black. "Della, I'm seconds away from forcing you onto my lap. I couldn't stand you washing me. I barely have any control left as it is."

"I don't care. It's about time you let go of that lifetime of control. You just teased me. It's only fair I tease you." Wanting to make him as wound up as me, I pushed off the pebble-littered riverbed and floated onto his lap. "I need you, Ren." Wrapping my arms around his shoulders, he was too slow to push me away.

My core connected to his cock, and we stiffened.

"You're making me insane." He growled around a cough.

"All you have to do is give in." I ran my tongue around the shell of his ear, adoring the way he trembled. "You want me? Then take me. Right here."

My heart thrummed as his possessive hands splayed over my back like panther paws—velvet and heavy with a touch of claw. "You're a minx."

"And you're a martyr." Pulling back a little, I kissed his cheek and chin and finally sought his lips. "Please, Ren. Just a tiny thrust and you'd be inside—"

His hands shot to my hips, angling me perfectly so the tip of him hovered over my entrance. "Such a demanding little thing." He breathed as if he'd run for days, his eyes hotter than I'd ever seen. "Ruining all my plans."

I didn't know who made the first move—me with a quest of my hips or him with a probe of his, but somehow, we went from two people to the precipice of becoming one.

Nothing else mattered.

No other thoughts entered.

The world had vanished, and it was just us in our forest like always, on our own like forever, fighting the undying need to merge into one.

"You want this?" Ren strangled, slipping another inch inside me.

My forehead slammed to his wet, cool shoulder, unable to stop my teeth from latching into his skin. "Yes!"

"Goddammit, Della." He surged deep. "*Fuck*, you feel incredible."

Hard.

Fast.

Consuming.

My legs spread wider as my feet rubbed on pebbles and flotsam, not caring about anything but his hard length slamming inside me.

My hips rocked back, driving him deeper to that wondrous place.

"Don't move," he snapped.

Prickles of rejection kissed over my skin. "Why not?"

"Because I'm so fucking close to coming, and I forgot to put a condom on. You feel *far* too amazing bare."

His fist wrapped in my hair, pulling my head back until he could meet my eyes. I expected him to kiss me hard, to drive into me harder, but his face blackened with self-control. "I can't believe

I broke that rule."

"What rule?"

"Never have sex without protection."

My shoulders fell. I knew enough from sexual education at school and what Ren had taught me that STIs were a big reason rubbers were important.

But we'd been safe with others. Surely, we could be free with each other. "You're inside me. It's already too late."

He swore under his breath as I rocked on him.

"Stop, Della." His hand landed heavily on my hip. "It's never too late." The hardness of him throbbed inside me, his heartbeat matching the thick craving of my own.

Pushing me, his length slipped out torturously slow. Once we were two people again, he burrowed his face into his hands and yelled into his palms. *"Fuck!"*

I gave him a moment, hating the separation but familiar enough with Ren to know he followed rules—especially ones that protected me—religiously.

He stood upright, and the river went from lapping around his shoulders to barely covering his proud erection. "Let's get inside the tent. I'm assuming you have more condoms with you?"

I stood on lust-wobbly legs as Ren swept me into his arms. His eyes softened with regret. "I'm sorry. I didn't mean to ruin the moment."

"You didn't."

Kissing me softly, he whispered, "I'm just so terrified of hurting you. It would kill me, Little Ribbon. If I ever did anything to—"

"You won't." I wrapped my arms around him, sucking in a breath as he swung me into a horizontal position like a groom would his bride and carried me from the river. "You never will."

Pressing his nose to mine, he chuckled. "You always manage to bring out the best and worst in me. One moment, I don't care about anything but fucking you; the next, I want to lay you on a throne and pledge everything I can." He carried me toward our bags with hardened feet used to walking on twigs and prickly things. "Being in love really is a disease."

Placing me reverently by my backpack, I got my balance by clutching his biceps. "Love's a disease?"

He nodded, brushing aside my wet hair and palming off excess droplets from the river. Even brusque, having his hands on me was pure cashmere and desire. "When I'm with you, I have the cure. I feel stronger, happier, invincible. But when I'm not, I feel as if life itself could delete me, and I wouldn't care."

The intensity of such a strong moment infected both of us, and our eyes locked with oaths and vows. "I'm never leaving you, Ren."

"And I'm never walking away again. No matter what happens. We stick together."

Our lips sought each other, sealing our promises with silky sweeps of our tongues.

The heat of our skin helped dry us a little, but we didn't care about the rest as we pulled apart and I bent to unzip my bag. The sound of the zipper in the gloom made Ren wince, his senses on high alert.

Dropping my hand into the dark rucksack, I rummaged for a second before pulling out a box.

A familiar box with a familiar note stuck to the top.

"What the—" Ren snatched it from my hands. Squinting to read in the final threads of light, his basic handwriting decorated the top: *If you're going to do things outside my control, please be safe. Use these. At all times.* "Is-is this the box I bought you?"

My cheeks glowed pink. "Yes."

"But...how?"

I could guess what ran through his head. How many condoms had I used? Had I replenished the box? Had I used David's instead? I didn't want him having those thoughts. He'd end up on the moral seesaw again, wondering if he was wrong in taking me. We were in such a good place and I refused to let anything from our past ruin that.

My heart hiccupped as Ren battled beneath his mental struggle, and I stole the box back, cracking it open to reveal a neat regimented row of foil wrapped condoms glinting in the gloom. There were too many to count quickly or guess how many were missing. But Ren wouldn't need to guess. I would tell him.

"I only used two. Well, three, counting last night." I kept my fingers locked tight on the box.

"What?" He coughed. "How is that possible? I saw you kissing Tom at the Halloween party. I'd seen how passionate you were. I lived with you, for God's sake. As you slowly awakened to the idea of sex, it drove me mad every time you went out with your friends, not knowing what you were doing."

My insides smarted for how much I'd hurt him over the years, but I stayed brave because I owed him this. I owed him an apology. "You're forgetting that most of the time, I was in agony over you, Ren. I only used two; you have my word. One the night I lost my virginity, and one the night of my eighteenth birthday." I didn't want images of me sleeping with others in his head, but he needed to know the truth—that I wasn't some harlot, even if I made him think I was.

I never looked away from him. He deserved to be able to read the honesty on my face, not just hear it. "Yes, I lost my virginity because I was messed up over you. But I chose not to have sex again because I wasn't emotionally ready. I didn't sleep with anyone until that second time on my birthday. And I didn't do it because I wanted him. I did it because I wanted *you*."

He sucked in a noisy breath.

"For months, I'd felt as if you were near. My missing you was at an all-time high. I never wanted to be with anyone else but you. I'm a terrible person for using David when I never stopped loving you."

He made a sound as if I'd kicked him in the gut. "Della—"

"I don't say any of this to be cruel, Ren." I shook my head, wet strands clinging to my shoulders. "I'm telling you out of pure honesty because you never truly accepted that I could love you as much as you love me. You are my entire world. You ran because of me. And in some part of my mind, I'm worried you'll run again if this is too much to accept."

Sick, sick shame filled his face. "God, Della. You let me take you so roughly—you have cuts and bruises all over you—and it was only your third time?" He dug fingers into his hair. "Why didn't you...I don't know...?" He looked at me with pain and self-disgust. "I should've taken you gently. I should've remembered you are so youn—"

"If you call me young, we'll have a problem."

His lips thinned. "But it's the truth. I raised you, for God's sake. I should've been more careful." Backing away, he wiped his mouth with a trembling hand. "I pushed you into losing your virginity by being an asshole, and I'm the reason you did it a second time by watching you instead of having the balls to admit I was back in town. I-I don't know what to say."

"I don't want you to say anything. Words only get you into trouble."

"But I should have—"

"What? Waited until we were in some motel and gone slow? Ren, I love you. But when you start second-guessing yourself, you're really a pain in the ass, you know that?" Holding up the back of my arm where a pretty decent scratch had scabbed over, I said firmly, "I wear these with pride. Every second of last night was better than any fantasy I've ever had of you, and believe me, I've had a lot."

A twisted half-smile decorated his face.

"I was only able to come because you gave me exactly what I wanted, when I wanted it. Your strength. Your aggression. I need that because all my life you've been strong and aggressive in keeping me safe, and somehow, I've come to associate that with you loving me. If you dare touch me with kitten gloves and feather kisses, I'll just rile you up until you snap again." I chuckled under my breath. "And we both know how easy I can spark your temper. Don't make me prove it."

He rolled his eyes, tension slipping down his spine. "I always knew you were trouble, Della Ribbon."

"And I always knew you were it for me, Ren Wild."

He closed the distance, tugging the ends of my dripping hair, his knuckles brushing my nipples. "How is it that you turned out like me when I did everything I could to prevent it?"

"How is it that you see that as a bad thing when it's the best thing in the world?"

"It's not a bad thing." He gathered me close, one hand going between my shoulder blades and the other on the top of my bare ass. "It's a miraculous thing. We're so similar that I swear if I didn't have memories of being sold that day, or vague images of my mother, I'd be terrified we were actually brother and sister, and Mclary was my father, too."

I fake shuddered. "God, can you imagine it? A lifetime of lying about being siblings only to find out we actually are?"

His face darkened as troubling thoughts filled his gaze. Bringing me flush against his nakedness, he whispered against my ear, "Even if that were true, now I've had you, I wouldn't be able to stop."

Molten heat swelled between my legs.

"Now I've been inside you and found the girl of my dreams, I don't care if our blood runs the same. We share the same heart anyway. I'd live in sin and go to hell because I literally could never give you up." Ren tugged my hair, arching my neck so he could latch his lips and teeth onto my throat. "I thought I was sick before—wanting you after so many years between us—but I truly must be the devil if I can admit I would fight every law, rule, and enemy if they ever tried to take you away from me."

His lips made their way to mine, planting firm. A swift, dominant tongue slipped into my mouth.

My knees gave out as I surrendered absolutely. In that second, I felt entirely like a girl and not a woman. I felt young and being kissed by a much older, braver, purer person than I could ever be.

"Ren…" I moaned against his lips as his hand trailed down my body, dipping between my legs and finding how wet I was.

He growled beneath his breath, driving two fingers inside me as he wrapped his arm around my hips, holding me steady.

"Tent, Ren." I stumbled backward, wanting so much to continue what he was doing but quickly losing my eye sight to galaxies and shooting stars the longer he stroked me.

Ripping his fingers from me, he spun me around and pushed my back. "Get in."

As I tripped forward, he stole the condom box from my hand, fisted a single one, and tossed the rest to the side.

Slick sweat sprouted over my skin, full of needle pricks of anticipation as I ducked under the awning, and Ren followed me inside, almost as if he were as dazed as me.

Our sleeping bags were unzipped and ready to cocoon us.

"Lie down, Della."

Ren's command was full of wood smoke and kindling. "Now."

I had a physical reaction to him commanding me—a rippling squeeze of pure lust from my heart to my core.

Flopping onto my back, I looked up as he kneeled above me, his cock jutting out, his eyes wild as the feral cats we'd seen stalking us for our scraps.

"Open your legs." Ren sucked in a breath, biting his bottom lip when I did as he asked. He was as naked as a heaven-sent prince ready to corrupt me.

I didn't care I was exposed to him. I didn't care we hadn't fully cleared the air. All I cared about was Ren and the clawing hunger rapidly filling the tent with hailing fury.

"What am I going to do with you, my dear Little Ribbon?" Opening the foil packet, he plucked out the slippery condom and, without tearing his gaze from mine, rolled it down his impressive length before squeezing the base and hissing between his teeth. "You've seen me at my worst, my sickest, my angriest, and my saddest. But you haven't seen me when I'm so fucking hard I have no control." Letting himself go, he crawled toward me, settled between my legs, and bowed until his mouth hovered just above my core.

Every muscle in my body locked.

He smiled; his lips swollen from prior kisses, and his jaw covered with dark stubble. "No one has because no one has pushed me as much as you do. I'm weak against you, Della."

I licked my lips, loving his honesty. I was jealous of his past lovers, but I pitied them too because Ren never gave them what he was giving me. He wasn't just giving me his body; he was giving me his life, heart, mind, breath, and soul. He was giving me everything, and I took, took, took. I took all of him because he'd already taken all of me.

"You made me," I breathed. "I only exist because of you."

"No, you exist because the universe knew a ten-year-old kid with nine fingers and hate in his heart was lonely."

I cried out as his tongue licked me for the first time, stealing language, maths, history, and every other knowledge I possessed, leaving me empty apart from one thought. "Ren."

"Enough talking." His whipping whisper came just before his mouth sealed over me.

He didn't ease me into this new sensation. He didn't test and probe. He dined on me. He devoured me. He drove two fingers inside me all while his teeth nipped my clit, and the burning heat of his mouth never stopped.

I didn't stand a chance.

I had no control over the typhoon swirling and building, sucking up debris, cleansing my heart from all its maybes and uncertainties and blowing them around, focusing the eye of the storm into my belly.

Up and up, I flew.

Tighter and tighter, I gathered.

And when his voice shared his tongue, spearing into me and murmuring against my searing flesh, he smashed the old Della apart and gave this new one wings. "Remember that wish—" *Plunge, lick, bite* "—you made when you were five years old?" *Twist, tease, nibble*. "At the diner with the cupcakes?" *Thrust, consume, worship*. "Answer me, Della."

I shivered, unable to talk but desperate to reply. I nodded. I remembered, or at least I remembered the stories he'd told me. "I wished for us to never be apart. For you to take me everywhere."

"I'm ready to ensure that wish comes true." He licked me

again. And again. "You're mine, Della Wild. I'm going to take you places you've never been. Starting with making you come on my face."

The crude snap, the dirty vow, the darkness of his voice—they all added matches to the swirling wind inside me.

His mouth settled over my core again as his tongue laved and fingers hooked and those tiny flying matches inside turned into a spark, a flame, a roaring fireball that took me with no warning.

"*Oh*—" It was the only word I knew as Ren dug fingers into my thighs, holding me down and wide as he gave me no safety, no sanctuary, no reprieve from the torture he brought between my legs.

"God, you taste—" He bit me again. "You taste like Della. Like everything I've ever dreamed of."

And that was it.

I did what he said I would.

I exploded.

I unravelled.

I came and came and came.

And before the final breeze blew the fire out, Ren crawled up my body, slotted his hips into mine, and thrust inside me in one long, delicious impale.

We both cried out. Him low and guttural. Me high and needy.

This was truth.

This was us.

This was everything.

His hips pistoned into mine, driving me deep, shoving me into the sleeping bags, and the tent shook and creaked, and we clawed and snapped and bit, our hands never empty, our legs never untangled, our bodies as joined as they could ever be.

On and on, he fucked me.

On and on, I rode him.

And when a matching fire-breathing typhoon found him. When his body couldn't withstand the pleasure. When our hearts exceeded too much love and thankfulness and joy, he reared up on his hands…

…and roared.

# Chapter Twenty-Seven

## REN

## 2018

IT TOOK A MONTH.

A month for me to trust that this was real.

That I hadn't died and found my version of heaven. That I wasn't asleep and living in my dream. That I wasn't fantasising that Della was mine only to find I'd gone insane.

For four wondrous weeks, we stayed in the forest, swimming in chilly rivers, making love in glades, and eating the rest of our supplies before brushing off our hunting skills and living off the land.

Autumn well and truly arrived, turning the final mugginess of summer into the warning chill of impending winter.

T-shirts became sweaters and we snuggled for warmth as much as for sanity.

We walked far, sometimes leaving the river to climb up a hill for a better vantage point, and sometimes doubling back to a campsite where we'd shared a night beneath the stars, naked and writhing on a sleeping bag beside a cheery fire.

We didn't care what time of day it was or where we were—when the urge to be close overtook us, we didn't fight it. We'd spent far too long fighting it and were now making up for lost time.

Most mornings, I woke with Della plastered to my side—just like she did when she was little—her face tucked into my chest, her legs wrapped in mine. Those moments stabbed my heart with memories of a blonde cherub who always made me melt.

I found it hard to let such thoughts in—of Della playing with

Liam when she was six or seven. Of Della launching on my back while I raked freshly cut lucerne when she was eight or nine.

The guilt was still there, but not because I'd slept with her. The guilt was because she was so damn pure and had an entire life ahead of her. By accepting what had always been between us, I'd stolen that future from her. I'd shackled her with me, and I still struggled to believe I would be enough.

She'd always been so bright and brave and capable.

I'd always been distrusting, untalkative, and stubborn.

I'd given her everything to ensure she had an education, enjoyed fellow humans, and was prepared for a career she could be proud of. But by giving in to my feelings for her, I'd made all those sacrifices obsolete. I should've noticed just how similar we were. I should've stopped to *look* at her, not just manhandle her into a life people were told they should want.

As far as I was concerned, I would never live in a city again. I doubted I could. I'd reached my people quota the day I ran from Mclary's, and that hadn't changed just because I'd fallen in love.

But I also couldn't deny, I would live in a high-rise poky apartment if that made Della happy. If she wanted to work in an office and have overpriced drinks with her colleagues and become the bread winner, then I would agree, because I meant what I said: I was hers.

We'd stepped over every line we could, and there was no going back now. She was stuck with me, and no matter what sort of life she wanted—city or farm—I was limited to what I could offer her.

Wherever we ended up, I would forever be an unskilled labourer with no accolades to my name. I knew hard work, and I lived to cultivate and tend, but I would never be a man to wear a suit, own a laptop, or host dinner parties in his home.

At the moment, Della was as wrapped up in me as I was in her...but things always had a way of changing. When she grew sick of my overprotectiveness, or when she turned away my need to have her in my arms...what would happen then?

She was still so damn young—still forming into herself; unaware of her true wants and dreams. Compared to her, I'd always been the surly old man who would rather growl at visitors than welcome them. Would Della love me when she was my age and I was pushing forty not thirty? Would she still find me handsome with sun-weathered skin and a body that had seen better days?

At least those thoughts were few and far between—I could forget about any future worries because when I was with Della, she made me exist purely in the now. When her fingers touched my arm or her lips landed on mine, nothing else mattered.

*Nothing.*

And that was the best gift she could give me because for the first time, I was free from worry. Free from the weight of responsibility and concern for her future and mine.

"Ren?" Della cocked her head, her hands glittering in scales as she rasped the silver fish I'd caught.

I put down the snare I was making to catch dinner, giving her my undivided attention. Her hair was lighter from living outdoors, bordering white gold instead of sunshine. The blue of her ribbon peeked between the glossy strands, dangling a little over her shoulder.

"Yeah?"

"I know we agreed not to discuss it again, but…it's all I can think about."

I groaned, leaning heavily against the sapling I'd chosen to sit by. "Della, you know why I can't—"

"It's not enough. It doesn't feel complete."

I wouldn't admit that I felt the same way. That whenever I was inside her, I hated, *hated* having to pull out before I came. We'd gone through her box of condoms—the box I'd bought her and probably close to their expiry date—within the first few days of sleeping together.

Once they'd run out, we had no other alternative. To start with, I'd adamantly swore I wouldn't touch her again until we had more. That had blown into a massive argument where she threw logic in my face and made me agree that since I'd never had unprotected sex before her and she hadn't either—we were safe in that respect. However, I wasn't just worried about that.

I didn't want to hurt her, and I knew what would happen if we continued sleeping together with no protection.

She'd get pregnant.

And as much as I loved her, she was far too young to be shackled with a kid—I should know after dedicating my life to a child I hadn't planned—and far too naïve to think it wouldn't happen.

And out here? If she got pregnant, so many things could go wrong. Even if we headed back into town, we had no insurance or money to pay for hospital stays and baby check-ups, and I refused to put her in danger when it was avoidable.

"You got your wish. We're still having regular sex. It doesn't matter if I come on your stomach or inside you, it still feels incredible." I lowered my voice, giving her a dark smile. "Believe me, Della, that first time I felt you without anything between us, it took everything I could not to come that very second."

She huffed, not buying my attempt to redirect the conversation. "It doesn't feel complete, and I struggle to come, knowing you can't finish with me." She brushed away a tumbled curl with the back of her hand, decorating her forehead with a fish scale.

Seeing her in a stretched sweater hanging over her shoulder, jeans with holes and frays, and dirt beneath her nails with mess upon her face made me hard.

So damn hard.

I loved how wild she was. How the last name she'd baptised us with matched us perfectly. And because she was wild, she wanted our sex to be wild.

Three weeks ago, she'd crawled onto my lap while I was turning a spit-roast of rabbit and undone my shorts before I could stop her.

She'd been naked under one of my t-shirts, and it only took a second for her to squeeze me, jerk me, and make me hard enough to slip inside her. I'd become her prisoner the second I felt her wet heat, allowing her to take from me until…she stood as suddenly as she'd sat on me, her eyes harsh and dangerous.

It had been the night after our fight about the condoms, and she still hadn't forgiven me for not giving in.

Well, she won. And she won again when she looked me in the eye, then dashed away, barefoot and hair free, disappearing into the woods.

I wasn't responsible for what I did next. I wasn't myself as I tossed good meat into the cinders, clutched my open shorts to keep them on, and took off after her.

So many times we'd played chase when she was little. So many times I'd run after her when she was angry or cheeky or pissed, and because of those games, I knew how to play this one.

I knew how to track her. Knew the weaves and ducks she favoured. Never staying in a straight line, she used the undergrowth to hide her.

The small hitches of her breath and snaps of bracken as she navigated the gloom led me directly to her.

She didn't see me until it was too late.

And when I did…my behaviour was abominable.

Pushing her to the ground, I let out a savage groan as she landed on all fours, then, because she insisted on fighting me like an animal, I fucked her like an animal.

I speared into her from behind—just like all the farmyard creatures did—and the scream she made? Holy shit, I lasted mere seconds.

I thrust savagely until her entire body rippled with her release, and then I pulled out, fisting myself hard as I came all over her back.

The shame that crashed over me was entirely new. It wasn't about taking more than I deserved but going too far—for letting her push me until I snapped and only thought of myself. For getting so caught up in whatever war we'd been fighting that I'd hurt her.

But of course, Della hadn't let me stew, and once we returned to our camp in stony silence, she'd climbed my body and kissed me deep, murmuring that having me behind her, driving into her like a monster had been the best experience thus far.

I hated to admit that I'd fucking loved it too, and unfortunately for both of us, we became hooked on pushing our limits. Of using trees to stand against and rocks to bend over and riverbanks to writhe on. Nothing was safe from our insatiable love, and even now, the minor scratches from this morning's lovemaking still glowed on her palms from where I'd shoved her to her knees after she'd returned from washing in the river.

She made me a terrible person, but she also freed me in ways no one else could.

Sighing, I shrugged. "What do you want me to do? Get you pregnant?"

She froze. "Is that what you're afraid of?"

Why did this conversation sound eerily like the one I'd had with Cassie the night I lost my virginity?

Putting the snare down, I hoisted my ass up and went to her. Brushing away the fish scale on her forehead, I sat down and murmured, "I'm not afraid of it. I'm afraid of losing you to something that's full of complications and pain."

Her eyes searched mine, deep and almost wary. "I know it's early days, but we've never actually discussed our future."

"Our future now that we're together?"

She nodded shyly, looking back at the fish in her hands. "I

know it's technically only been a month, but it's been so much longer than that. As far as I'm concerned, I've been yours for eighteen years. But I never thought about having children until the exact moment you said you were afraid of it."

I clasped my hands between my knees, very aware how dangerous this subject could be. Before my dreams came true and I earned Della, I was adamant I didn't want any more kids. It'd taken a lot out of me to raise her right and fix all the things I did wrong. I wasn't exactly the best father figure for her. Look at us. We'd fallen in love despite everything telling us not to.

But in that moment, sitting beside her on a dead tree with the smell of smoke swirling around us and the sounds of happy birds serenading us, I had a flash of what life could be like if Della gave birth to my child.

Of another girl.

A girl who would once again own me completely, make me stress, make me proud, give me purpose—a legacy I could utterly adore. A legacy of both me and Della—a little girl who had her blue eyes and my dark hair and our cynicism of society.

And I wanted that.

Very much.

Just...not right now.

Tipping her chin up with my forefinger, I kissed her gently. A simple press of lips and love, not asking anything more than a quick connection. "I'm not afraid of it, Della. But I am selfish."

"Oh, please." She rolled her eyes. "Is this like when you said you were selfish in sex? Because you got that wrong. You never leave me wanting. You always—"

"I'm selfish because I've only just found you. I want to keep you for myself for a little longer. I want to share a world with you. I want to marry you. I want to give you everything you've ever wanted, and only then, once I've had you all to myself, will I be ready to share."

Her shoulders slouched as love glowed on her face. Love I still couldn't get used to. Love I would do anything to deserve. "Ren, we could have a hundred children and not one of them would steal me from you. I know women aren't meant to admit this, but you would always come first for me. I wouldn't be able to help it."

I chuckled against her lips as I kissed her again. "You've just proven you're not ready, either. You're the one being selfish, Little Ribbon. When the day comes that you love me so much that your heart has expanded for more, that's the day we'll start a family. But not before."

Standing, I held out my hand to pull her to her feet. "Because one thing is for sure. Our child will steal our hearts entirely, and I wouldn't have it any other way. I would want you to love our daughter more than you love me. I'll happily come second."

She weaved her fingers with mine until there was no space between us. "You have my word, Ren Wild, that I will forever love you. But if and when we have a family of our own, I promise they will be loved just as much as I love you." Walking into my embrace, she hugged me hard. "But I don't want a daughter. I want a son. I want a son exactly like you."

# Chapter Twenty-Eight

## REN

## 2018

"DO YOU KNOW this is probably only the third or fourth time we've been shopping together?" Della grabbed a can of nectarines from the supermarket shelf and placed it into the basket I carried.

"Supermarkets aren't exactly a rare occurrence." I smirked. "I happen to be well-versed in how to get into most of them undetected."

"Yes, and you didn't let me go on those adventures, did you?" She smiled, her blue jacket, jeans, and boots faded from forest-living, and her hair with its requisite leaf hidden amongst the gold.

"I didn't want you to be in danger," I said.

"No, you didn't want me cramping your thieving skills."

"That too." I reached for a packet of pasta, placing it on top of the canned nectarines. "Then again, when we lived in the city and we had cash to pay for things, you did most of the shopping."

"Only 'cause you worked such stupid hours. I mean, really? Who gets up before dawn?"

I rolled my eyes. "Are you forgetting I'm a farm boy? At Cherry River, I was up with the cockerels, and at Mclary's—well, it was be up before him or your ass would be beat and you'd have to spend the day in agony as well as exhaustion."

Her face fell a little, her gaze trailing to my missing finger. "You know, I don't think I ever apologised for what my father did to you."

I froze to the spot. "Why would you? You weren't responsible."

"I know, but now that I'm not so self-obsessed, I can see how hard it would've been for you to love me. Not only love me but keep me when you were running for your life."

I went to her as she turned to stare blankly at brightly boxed taco shells. Wrapping my arm around her, I kissed her temple. "What's really going on, Della? Why are we talking about the past when we're both so incredibly happy in our present?"

Wedging herself into my chest, she breathed me in, shaking a little. "I don't know. Being back in a town? Having other people watch us? Wondering if they know? Afraid that we'll be caught and the past few wonderful weeks will be over?"

Putting the basket down with our carefully chosen supplies, I hugged her close, breathing into her ear. "No one sees us. We're invisible."

Other shoppers strolled past, some looking at us and others not caring at all. I wouldn't deny I'd felt the same fear Della did as we left the forest, backpacks, and tent and followed the animal tracks out from the trees toward the country doorstop where the only things on Main Street were a bar, pharmacy, doctors, pet store, diner, and supermarket. Oh, and a knickknack store that claimed to have more junk than K-Mart at half the price.

However, we wouldn't be here if it wasn't for Della's insistence. We didn't need food, but fresh fruit and baked goods would be nice. And we didn't need medicine, but we had come to see a doctor.

The prickle of being around people again was worse after being on our own for so long, but Della had insisted, and I couldn't refuse.

Besides, I wasn't against getting some more painkillers for the ache that hadn't left my chest. It'd been months since I'd had the flu yet an occasional cough still lingered, annoyingly persistent.

"Della, look at me." I pulled back a little, waiting until her chin popped up, and her eyes met mine. "No one knows who we are. We're just two strangers to them. Two strangers kissing in a supermarket."

Her lips parted in a gasp as I bent my head and captured her mouth with mine. Her back rippled with tension under my palms, her eyes wide and worried. But then I deepened the kiss and her tension melted away, trusting me to keep her safe, slipping into the lust we always suffered.

Her eyes closed, and my body hardened, and this was a bad, *bad* idea because I couldn't just keep the kiss at publicly acceptable;

I had to lick her, taste her, clutch her as close as I could so she felt what she did to me.

Only when her breath caught and someone cleared their throat in disapproval did I let her go. The kiss upset my balance. I expected trees around us not shelves with overly sugary cereals. I was all the more aware we were in a place I hated. But at least I'd helped Della with her anxiety, and she gave me the biggest smile with pink-pleased cheeks.

"Kiss me like that again, and we'll be arrested for indecent exposure." She looked me up and down as if she'd rather eat me than the food on display.

"Look at me that way for much longer, and this town expedition will end as quickly as it began."

She laughed softly. "Thank you. I needed that."

"I know you did." I wiped my bottom lip where her taste still lingered. Honey and chocolate from the Toblerone bar she'd opened and snuck a piece before we'd paid.

"Okay, so we're done here, right?" I coughed once and picked up the basket from the floor. Another tube of toothpaste, sunblock, painkillers, and a range of perishable and non-perishable foods. We used a basket to select what to buy so we didn't fill up a cart and forget we had to carry it for miles.

"Oh, almost forgot!" She dashed back to the toiletry aisle while I made my way to the checkouts. At least today I wouldn't be stealing. The cash I'd saved before leaving and the deposit on the apartment we'd had refunded were more than enough to keep us going for a couple of years before the dreaded concept of employment knocked on our strange holiday-honeymoon.

As I placed the basket on the conveyor belt behind an elderly woman counting out coupons, Della tossed three boxes of condoms on top of our innocent fruit and veggies.

"Three?" I raised my eyebrow, flicking a quick glance at anyone who might've seen. I didn't care that we were buying condoms. I cared that they'd figure out Della was the one person I should never be sleeping with.

"Tina told me a couple of years ago that the pill takes up to a week to become effective, and if I have a tummy upset, secondary precautions are needed, too." She gave me another coy I-want-you-right-now kind of look. "I won't last a week, Ren. And don't pretend you will, either."

I gritted my teeth as the checkout girl stole our basket and started scanning things before tossing them into plastic bags.

"You're forgetting I exercised self-restraint for years. I can manage a week."

She pinched my ass as I pulled out a bundle of cash from my back pocket. "That was before."

*Before.*

Such a simple word, but it held so much history.

"You're right." I smiled, loving the way she stood close, her eyes twinkling with joy—joy for just sharing something as mundane as shopping with me.

Clearing my throat, I tore my gaze from hers and looked back at the cash in my hands. Handling the money shot me back to the time Della had helped me tally up and charge for the hay bales at John Wilson's place.

Not for the first time, I thought about him. How he was? Did he get another farmhand? Was his family okay?

And not for the last time, I wondered what he'd say now that I'd broken that self-restraint and claimed Della.

Would he understand?

Would he condemn me?

Would he say *I told you so?*

His warning of finding a way to keep Della as my sister ran through my head as the teller reeled off a figure, and I handed her a bunch of notes. I'd failed in that respect, but really, looking back...I think he knew. He knew there was something more between us, and that was why he'd sent us away.

Because eventually, even if we'd stayed there, we would've fallen into bed, and things would've gotten messy. Especially with Cassie in the mix.

"Have a pleasant day," the checkout girl said blandly, already scanning items of the customer behind me.

I grabbed two bags and Della took one as we left the supermarket with its annoying beeps and bright lights and stood on the pavement where the sun reminded us we were wasting one of the last days of camping weather by being cooped up inside concrete and steel.

"I don't want to be much longer, Little Ribbon."

"Me neither." She placed her well-used and scratched aviators on to avoid the glare and strode purposely toward the doctor's. "How is this going to work, do you think?"

I shrugged. "Same way we've always done it. Our name is Wild. We'll pay cash. We lost our driver's licenses, so have no identification, yada yada."

Slowing to a stop, she looked at me, biting her lip. "Hey, Ren?"

My heart pumped faster—as it always did when she looked at me like that. "Yeah?"

"On the form, if they ask what our relationship status is...um, what do I put?"

Goosebumps scattered over my arms as the answer I'd always given her delayed upon my tongue. *'I'm your brother.'* That wasn't just incorrect anymore, it was undermining everything good and perfect that'd happened between us.

Putting the groceries down, I tugged her bag free to join the rest, then ran my fingers through her hair until I fisted two handfuls right there on the street. "I never got to give the speech I'd prepared when I came back to find you. I had a whole promise laid out. How I'd come back because I couldn't live without you. That even if it meant I couldn't have you, even though it would rip my heart out and leave me bleeding until the day I died, I'd gladly walk you down the aisle on your wedding day. I would've given you away to another man, Della, because that was my job in your life. To ensure you had everything you ever needed in which to *live*. To be happy."

I trembled as I kissed her softly. "But then I read your manuscript, and I realised *I* could be the one to make you happy, so I said other things. So much more important things." Digging my fingers harder into her hair, I murmured against her mouth, "So, if they ask who I am to you...there's only one thing you can say."

"What's that?" she breathed, shivering with matching goosebumps.

"That you share my last name. That you own my heart." I kissed her hard and fast, long and lingering. "Tell them...you're my wife."

# Chapter Twenty-Nine

## DELLA

## 2031

*WHEN REN KISSED me that day on the street, he didn't know it, but he gave me every hope I'd been nursing since we'd fought with the truth and gave in.*

*Our last name was as much his as it was mine, and I didn't want to change. But how could we not when Wild had been a sibling address, and these days, we were so much more than that?*

*I'd teased with the idea that it could be our married one, sure, but until Ren said the words I'd been fighting, I didn't think it was possible.*

*He successfully made me float on air, wrapped me up in daydreams, and sent me gooey with desire.*

*After that, I didn't really care what we did as long as he was always near.*

*We went to the doctor, filled in forms, ignored side glances when we said we had no I.D, and proudly ticked the 'married' box without an ounce of shame.*

*To start with, the doctor refused to see us without some form of identification.*

*But Ren quietly took him aside and had a few words. I didn't know what transpired, but after an hour or so wait, I was ushered in to see a doctor who asked my sexual history, if I was aware of the health risks, and prescribed me the pill to prevent pregnancy.*

*I asked for more than just three months' supply, but he was adamant my blood pressure should be checked before a refill was given.*

*At the time, it frustrated me, but then I remembered it would be winter, and we'd most likely be holed up somewhere close enough to a town not to be a nuisance.*

*After we'd filled the script at the pharmacy next door, taken another handful of condoms from the fishbowl on the counter saying* 'Free: help your frisky selves,' *my stomach growled, and the diner with its sun-bleached specials in the window and paint-chipped green door reminded me of all the times Ren had found ways to make simple excursions into life-affirming treats.*

*Looking back, it was yet another moment I had no choice but to write down.*

*Mainly because of what happened next.*

*I'd dragged him into the grease-infused restaurant all while he grumbled and kept his eyes glued on the horizon where the tips of the trees waved at us in the chilly breeze. I'd forgotten how unsociable Ren was. After living in the city for so many years, he'd relaxed enough not to hanker for freedom or give the impression he was a trapped animal amongst a cage of glass and brick. But he'd been in his element for too long, and it was a visible chore for him to stay away for long.*

*I felt the same tug to leave, but I also had the tug of hunger. Taking pity upon him, compromising like a good couple, we agreed to order takeaway cheeseburgers and curly fries, eating the naughty but oh-so-good meal in the tiny park across the street.*

*Once our bellies were full and fingers salt-dusted from french fries, I stood and expected him to march directly back into the wilderness with me trotting to keep up.*

*However, his eyes landed on the junk store with its vow to beat K-Mart with its merchandise and prices and, with a determined look, he dragged me into the overly cluttered store with its scents of candle wax and plastic toys, smiling as if he had a secret.*

*This is why I had to write this.*

*This is why I was so madly in love with him.*

*"I want to buy you something."*

*"Okay…" I narrowed my eyes. "What do you want to buy me?"*

*"Something you're not allowed to see until I've found it."*

*I looked around at the overflowing baskets of tea-towels and dog collars. This place had everything from shampoo and cookies to Easter and Halloween decorations. "And you'll find it in here?" I raised an eyebrow. "What exactly are you up to?"*

*"Call it…a gesture of a future eventuality."*

*I laughed, drawing the attention of the mid-twenties cashier sucking on a lollypop. "I think we need to get you back into the forest. The city is infecting you with retail therapy and commercial advertisement."*

*"You did say shopping with me was a novelty." He smirked. "While I find what I want for you, you find me something."*

*"Like what?" My heart sprang into action, acting nonchalant but*

*already rushing with images of finding the perfect gift. We'd shared many birthdays, but apart from my ribbon tattoo that Ren paid for, and the willow horse he carved back at Cherry River, we had no keepsakes or mementos. Not that we had space.*

*"Go on." Ren pointed down an aisle full of ugly porcelain vases and weird bachelorette party gimmicks—let me tell you there were a lot of penises: penis straws, penis shot glasses, penis aprons, and unicorn horns shaped like dildos. "You trying to tell me I'm missing an appendage you want, Ren?" I couldn't stifle my snicker. "'Cause you know, I rather like playing with yours so I can see the allure—"*

*"Honestly, Della." He grabbed my bicep, yanking me into the aisle and away from the nosy sales keeper. "You always know how to get a rise out of me, don't you?" His voice was brash with temper, but his eyes glowed like chocolate syrup.*

*Things with wings erupted in my heart as I stood on tiptoes just as Ren's mouth crashed down on mine.*

*He kissed me so fierce and swift, I stumbled backward, directly into a shelf of penises with wind up legs that all bounced and whirred from the unwanted collision.*

*We broke apart, laughing as penis after miniature penis committed suicide off the shelf.*

*"You break it, you pay for it!" a voice yelled from the front of the store.*

*Ren and I only laughed harder.*

*Funny how memories like that—the ones that are so simple and stupid—are the ones that stick in your head with such clarity you can transport back to every smell, heartbeat, and yearning.*

*I want to share every detail, but I also want to rush and tell you what Ren bought for me and I bought for him. Because, honestly, they were two gifts that became our most treasured belongings. No mud, snow, dust, or grime could make us remove them. Even now, I still wear it. Even now, after so long.*

*"Ten minutes, Little Ribbon." Ren kissed the tip of my nose. "And no peeking at where I go."*

*"I have no idea what to get you, so I'll be using those ten minutes wisely, not stalking you."*

*"Good."*

*"Fine." I grinned. "See you at the cash register."*

*"No, see you outside. Here." Forcing a twenty-dollar bill into my hand, he kissed my cheek as if he couldn't not kiss me whenever we were close. "Pay for what you find and meet me on the street."*

\* \* \* \* \*

*Sorry, I let memories take over and forgot to type.*

*Who knew writing about something so silly would be so utterly heart-breaking—not because it was sad but because it was so* good?

*So perfect.*

*So sweet.*

*I was so incredibly lucky, and I'm just glad I recognised just* how *lucky, rather than take Ren for granted.*

*The older I get, and the more I grow, I'm always struck by two things:*

*One, no matter my age, I always feel the same. No more adult than child or wise than stupid. I keep expecting myself to snap into a grown-up, but it's never happened.*

*And two, nothing beat just hanging out with Ren.*

*Nothing.*

*No trip or gift or fancy new experience.*

*Nothing could beat just existing with the love of my life.*

*Remembering is almost bittersweet, but I suppose I better finish this particular chapter before I close my laptop and go in search of the very man I'm writing about.*

*I'll skip over the mad rush through the carnival ride of junk and pointless figurines and*

*not bother to mention the adrenaline rush of finding such a random, childish, and exquisitely perfect gift that Ren would no doubt roll his eyes at and laugh in that affectionate, perfect way of his. The way that opened his entire face from suspicion and ruthlessness into a window of trust and devotion.*

*I couldn't stand still as I waited for him on the curb and spun to face him when the junk store bell jingled.*

*In his hand rested a small, brown paper bag.*

*He gave me a half-smile. "This feels like a ridiculous idea now."*

*"I think it's the best idea you've had in a while."*

*"You're saying I lack good ideas, Della?" He narrowed his eyes, but behind his fake annoyance, laugher bubbled.*

*"Well, you have to admit the best idea we've ever had was sleeping together—and that was mine, so you're welcome. You can thank me later, but right now, you're handing over my present."*

*"You're saying all of this, our relationship, the fact that I told you to call me my wife, was* your *idea?" He put the shopping bags on the ground, delaying giving me the gift just like he had when he'd presented me with that tea-towel wrapped horse.*

*Delay tactics were Ren's way of pretending he wasn't nervous by covering it up with bluster and brawn.*

*"Yes, all mine. Been my idea for years." Shooting my hand out, I held up my own paper bag. "Stop changing the subject and swap."*

*He huffed dramatically, playing along with the familiar way we joked and ribbed. "I don't know why I put up with you most of the time."*

*"Too late now. You married me."*

*His face lost its joviality, slipping straight into steely sternness. "Not yet I haven't. But I'm working on it."*

*My tummy let loose a torrent of floating balloons, filling my insides with helium.*

*"Here." He passed me the gift, taking his in return. "It's not much. But it's a promise of more."*

*I don't mind telling you—mainly because you'll have figured it out for yourself—but I wasn't good at delayed gratification. I should've clutched that paper bag and paused in that moment. That delicious, perfect moment where the happiest future I could've ever imagined teased.*

*But I didn't.*

*I was too impatient.*

*I ripped at the bag and tears instantly appeared as I tipped out a ring with a blue gemstone dancing in the sun.*

*It wasn't real.*

*It wasn't silver or gold or sapphire.*

*But it was the best thing I'd ever received.*

*Ren's shadow fell over me as I swiped at the tears trickling down my cheeks. "I didn't mean to make you cry, Della Ribbon."*

*"I know. Sorry." I looked up with a watery smile. "I just…Ren, I—"
I shook my head, grasping for words on just how perfect he truly was. How grateful I was that I had his heart. How I'd never take him or his thoughtfulness for granted. Ever. "I just…I love you so much."*

*He smiled, tilting his head like an eagle would while pitying a poor mouse for falling in love with him. An eagle who could soar away at any moment and kill that little mouse with just one talon. "I know."*

*Taking my hand and the ring, he slipped it onto the finger where engagement rings belong. "This is exactly what it implies. We've messed up the usual steps of a relationship. We met young. We loved each other in so many different ways before the one that truly mattered. But now that I have you, this is the only way forward. If it's too soon, tell me. If you're having second thoughts, better put me out of my misery now. But if you want me as much as I want you, then you don't even have to give me an answer because I've already made it for you."*

*Tugging me into his arms, he kissed me sweet. "Will you marry me, Della Wild?"*

*I shuddered in his embrace, more tears falling. "I gave you my answer the day I was born, Ren Wild." Standing on tiptoes, I met his second kiss, deepening it until the street vanished, leaving only silky tongues, hitched breaths, and hands straining to touch secret places. "Yes. A thousand times yes."*

*I could finish this chapter on that line. It holds quite a punch, and you all know how much Ren's random proposal meant to me. But I want to tell you what I got Ren.*

*Pulling back from his arms, I was the one to open his bag and pull out the baby blue leather band with nine diamante letters threaded onto it—letters I'd chosen from tiny boxes full to the brim with alphabets and shapes, painstakingly deciding the best, simplest message for him to wear. For everyone to see.*

*He burst out laughing as I opened the clasp and hoped it would fit his large wrist.*

*It did.*

*Barely.*

*Stroking the glittery word-charms, he gave me a look so completely humble and awed I felt as if I'd given him the keys to my forever rather than a simple gimmicky bracelet.*

*And in a way, I had.*

*Because forever would never be enough. Not with Ren. Not with my soulmate.*

*Cupping his wrist, I kissed the springy hairs of his skin right above the bracelet. The charms blinded me with their crystal glitter as I breathed, "Della Wild Loves Ren Wild Forever."*

**DW  RW4EVA**

---

# Chapter Thirty

## REN

## 2018

WE STAYED IN the forest until the second snowfall reminded us that as much as we'd adopted the wilderness as our home, we had yet to find ways to grow fur coats and hibernate in warm burrows.

The cold ruined everything, making bones ache and lungs burn and bodies bow to nasty viruses.

The sooner we were warm and out of the elements, the better.

We had cash for a rental, but without furniture and other belongings to furnish it, we didn't bother putting ourselves through the stress of real estate agents and reference checks.

Not to mention, we didn't want to lock ourselves into a long lease when we had no intention of staying past the last frost.

I suggested finding another government owned hut on a tramping trail, or searching for an uninhabited building like we did with Polcart Farm, but Della took my ideas and one-upped them, suggesting we could have a toasty, furnished place away from main cities and only pay for the months we wanted.

I didn't believe her, but the day we headed to yet another tiny town to buy thicker jackets, she topped up her phone credit, and showed me an online site that rented holiday homes that usually fetched a premium in summer but were offered at great rates during winter.

Together, we sat in a cosy coffee shop beside a gas fire and ate delicious apple and cinnamon muffins while scrolling through housing options.

We were there for hours, searching, discounting, debating pros and cons of each. Some were too close to the city, others were semi-detached or had the owner living on site. Most were totally impractical for loners like us, but finally, after a second muffin, we narrowed it down to three.

One was a few miles from a local town and decorated in country chic with yellow everything; two was a rambling big place with weathered furniture and bare wooden floors; three was a two-bedroom cottage with whitewashed floors, handmade daisy curtains, and the comfiest looking couches with a fireplace.

For four months' hire, it would take a big chunk of our cash, but if the two-bedroom cottage lived up to the pictures, it was totally worth it.

Della—ever the resourceful and happier to deal with strangers—called the number and arranged to view the property the next day. We spent the rest of the afternoon heading back into the forest, packing up our belongings, and having a final dinner of fish and rabbit.

The next morning, we left the trees and met with the agent.

The moment we stepped inside, we knew.

This was our winter nest, and we paid cash upfront in lieu of not having credit cards. The round, blue-rinsed hair woman asked for a bigger bond seeing as we didn't have the necessary paperwork, but after chatting to us and showing us around the quaint, cosy cottage, she handed over the keys and happily gave us instructions on how to work the oven and washing machine.

That night, Della and I made love for the very first time in a bed.

The foreignness of clean cotton and soft springiness of a mattress added a sensual element to our otherwise rough encounters. Our thoughts were on the same wavelength once again, and our touches were softer, our kissers longer, and when I slipped inside her, our connection was deeper than it had ever been.

I adored her to the point of stupidity.

I'd wake in the night with horrors of losing her. I'd stare, completely bewitched at odd times during the day, even if she was doing something as mundane as washing the dishes.

I had no power over myself anymore—she had it all.

And I was glad.

I was glad whenever the fake blue gemstone gleamed on her finger. I was glad whenever the diamante letters on the leather bracelet she gave me caught my eye.

I was glad for all of it.

I was grateful for everything.

I was so damn lucky.

Normally, I despised winter.

But that one...I didn't mind it so much.

Not with warm beds, roaring fireplaces, and Della.

In fact, I didn't mind it at all.

# Chapter Thirty-One

## REN

## 2019

SPRING ARRIVED WITH a vengeance, thawing the frosts and banishing the snow as quickly as they'd arrived. The weather reports said it would be one of the hottest summers on record, and both Della and I couldn't wait until the last day of our agreed cottage rental where we could leave for the forests we loved so much.

Living in the cottage had been an experience I wouldn't forget, and we'd become a little too used to having a comfy house with a pantry full of food and a freezer crammed with everything we could ever need.

The first week after moving in, we'd spent a few days setting up with supplies, so when the snow fell, we wouldn't have to leave unless we wanted to.

And sometimes, we wanted to, despite the cold.

On the mornings when the sun twinkled on virgin snow and birds sang in white-capped trees, we'd slip into warm clothing and go for a walk. Sometimes, we'd kiss by the frozen river, and others, we'd tease and torment until we practically ran back to the cottage and couldn't tear our clothes off fast enough.

Those were my favourite days.

The ones where we forgot about ages and education and futures and society.

A simple existence where we ate when we were hungry, slept when we were tired, and fucked at any time or place we wanted.

Nothing in the cottage had been free from our escapades. Not the smooth bamboo kitchen bench—where I'd hoisted Della onto it, bare assed and panting. Not the claw foot bathtub that was big enough for two—where Della had gotten on her knees and blown me.

Not even the woodshed was free from us screwing like the bunnies Della wanted us to become. I'd ended up with a splinter in my ass, but I didn't care, seeing as Della was a master at tending to my injuries.

A couple of days before we were due to hand the keys back, we washed all our clothes, sorted through our supplies, ate the rest of the food that we couldn't take with us, and prepared to hike for the rest of the season.

I felt like a creature crawling from its den after a winter of bunkering down.

I was itching for exercise. I was ready for adventure.

I wanted to be a wanderer again even though I also wanted other things.

Things like being able to officially call Della my wife. Things like officially making our last name Wild and not just a word we'd chosen.

My belly clenched whenever my attention landed on her hand and the gaudy blue ring I'd bought. The promise I'd made and the need to make her mine was a constant desire.

I hadn't told her, but one night, while she slept beside me, I'd used the final internet credit on her phone to research how to get married. The information bombarding the screen made my brain bleed, and the prices some people were willing to spend made me sick.

The thought of a party with hundreds of people watching a very private moment turned me right off, but even the civil service ceremony with just a single witness wasn't open to us.

Basically, we couldn't get married.

Not unless I found a way to get us birth certificates, and we became real people and not just lost kids in the system.

It was a complication that had always been on the back of my mind, but I had no clue how to rectify it. It also didn't help that the diamante letters of my bracelet had already lost some of its glitter, the tiny gems falling from their metal surroundings.

In the dead of night, deep in my nightmares of losing her, I feared it was a sign that if I didn't find a way to make her my wife soon, my entire future would be in jeopardy.

I didn't care the jewellery couldn't stand up against time, I would wear it until it disintegrated and then somehow resurrect it because it'd become almost a good luck charm, promising me a future where Della would always love me, just like she promised.

Despite my desires to make her mine on paper as well as in my heart, we left behind the cottage where we'd found so much happiness and, for the first time, I was open to the idea of putting down roots.

A place to call our own.

A bed to keep Della warm.

A house we could raise a family in.

# Chapter Thirty-Two

## REN

## 2019

2019 WAS ONE of my favourite and equally unfavourite years.

Summer was spent skinny-dipping, travelling, fucking, learning, laughing, and living in every precious moment.

It didn't matter we had no life luxuries. We didn't care our bathroom was open air, our shower was sometimes shared with fish, or our bedroom was a flimsy thing that was useless against storms—nothing could scare us away from the joy of being alone, entirely self-sufficient, and free to love how we wanted to love.

Our need for each other seemed much more accepted out here, rutting against trees and rocks, driving each other to pinnacles I doubted a house with pretty painted walls could contain.

We had solar lanterns that lit up our tent when we wanted light and solar chargers for phones we didn't care about. We made do with what the sun wanted to give us and only ate what we foraged and hunted for months on end.

I never asked if Della missed her friends or school. I never regretted spending a lifetime ensuring she had an education, only to yank her away from one the moment I fell in love with her.

We belonged together.

End of story.

And I'd take on the entire universe if it ever tried to take Della away from me.

Then autumn arrived.

Bringing with it more than just its pretty colours of copper and bronze—it heralded my worst nightmare and the reason we left the forest much earlier than we planned.

It all started with a storm.

A particularly terrible storm that ripped our guy-ropes from the ground and scattered our tent pegs in the undergrowth.

Trees cracked as they were uprooted from the earth. Animals screeched as their homes were destroyed. And at some point in the howling, slashing rain, Della crawled into my arms and I hugged her close, keeping her safe from whatever crime we'd committed against Mother Nature for her to hate us so.

It took thirty-six hours for the worst to pass, and everything we owned—including us—was soaked.

The nylon of the tent and its rain sheet couldn't withstand the torrent and I worried keeping Della from a sturdy house was the right choice.

Eventually, she'd want more than this.

And she'd be fully within her right.

What if she'd gotten hurt?

What if *I'd* gotten hurt?

What if I wasn't around to protect her?

As we sorted through our littered and destroyed campsite, nibbling on things we salvaged and drinking fresh rainwater, we did our best to find the tent pegs and tangled guy-ropes, and at some point with our bodies muddy and spirits dull, I made the decision that we needed to be closer to civilisation and not a week's walk from anywhere.

And thank God I did.

Because a day after we arrived at a campsite, only a few hours' walk from a town, Della got sick.

Really sick.

Fucking terrify me and make me bargain with the devil sick.

We didn't often get viruses, and if we did, it was mainly from our quick excursions into towns and touching coins and menus contaminated by other sick people.

But this was different.

For days, she vomited every morning, stayed grey for most of the day, and complained of aching stomach pains that even copious amounts of painkillers couldn't stop.

I didn't understand how Della got the stomach flu and I remained untouched. We ate the same things. We were careful about what we cooked. But whatever illness struck, it chose her and chose her hard.

By the end of the fourth day of watching her vomit, and suffering fear and utmost helplessness, I couldn't handle it anymore. Her assurances that she was getting better were bullshit, and I'd had enough.

I couldn't listen to her being so ill or watch her gorgeous body become gaunt with malnutrition from not being able to keep anything down.

She had to see a doctor.

*Now.*

Della was so weak her protests had dwindled to nothing apart from the occasional groan when her tummy hurt and a half-hearted swat when I helped her into a jacket and jeans and tugged her from the camp.

I left behind our belongings, not caring about a single thing.

Nothing mattered.

Only her.

All I took was a smaller rucksack we had for emergencies and stuffed it with our cash, Della's manuscript, toothbrushes, and a spare set of clothes in case we were delayed for a night or two.

Della followed me slowly, her steps laboured and her skin ghostly. I tried to help her. Tried to offer support and even carry her as we headed down the steep animal tracks to the rye paddocks of some farmer and cut through his land.

But each time I reached out, she pushed me away with a shake of her wobbly head. "I'm fine, Ren. Don't worry about me."

But I did worry.

I worried a whole fucking lot and had never been so grateful to see a road when we finally travelled four hours and found a painted path and not a muddy track.

My temper was short from fear, and my patience at her unwillingness to let me help depleted. I was furious at her for getting so ill—as if this were her fault—but mainly I was livid at myself for letting her assure me it would pass, when obviously, it was only getting worse.

If anything happened, I'd never forgive either of us.

"Come on, Della." My voice was clipped as I held out my hand, hoping now she was on the road she'd quicken.

But if anything, the opposite happened. The moment her boots found level concrete, her shoulders slouched, and she seemed to fade before my eyes.

"Fuck." Marching to her, I scooped her off the road and cradled her close. "I'm never going to forgive you for this."

She smiled weakly. "For getting ill?"

"For not letting me help."

Her head thudded against my chest and stayed there as she closed her eyes, no longer even pretending she was strong enough to fight me. "You're helping now."

"Yes, and you're about to pass out on me."

"Nuh uh." She yawned as she clutched her lower belly. "I'm still here."

"You better stay here too, Della Ribbon. Otherwise, I'll—" I cut myself off, drowning beneath vicious promises and violent vows.

"What? Otherwise what?" Her eyes opened to a dull blue laced with pain.

I coughed hard, averting my mouth until I stopped. "I'll murder and cheat and steal and commit any crime imaginable if it means I find a cure for you."

She smiled, her hand cupping my cheek briefly before it tumbled back into her lap. "I love you, Ren."

"And I love you, even though I despise you right now."

Laughing softly, she stayed content in my arms as I lengthened my stride and marched toward the larger of the towns we'd been in recently. I didn't care sweat rolled down my spine beneath my jacket, or my heart beat in terror at the colourless sheen on her face and the sticky temperature of someone unwell.

I was used to walking. I was fit and normally had good endurance, but each step my chest seemed to switch from its familiar ache to a discomforting twinge.

I coughed and strode faster, ignoring my pains and focusing entirely on Della's.

It took too long.

It didn't take long at all.

She was too light and motionless in my embrace.

The town welcomed us up ahead as we passed road signs stating speed and population. "We're almost there, Little Ribbon. You'll be fine soon; you'll see."

I coughed again, cursing the breathlessness of panic.

*Please let her be fine.*

I kept my thoughts on pleas rather than the curses I wanted to shout.

As I stalked down the main highway, the tiny buildings slowly became recognisable landmarks of a church and hall and convenience store.

With every step, I bargained with fate not to take her from me.

I wouldn't hesitate to kill for her if it came down to it.

If a sacrifice was needed, I would deliver with no hesitation.

I would sell my own soul.

Maybe I'd put this curse upon her by loving her too goddamn much. Maybe I should feel regret for stealing her away and keeping her all to myself. Perhaps I should repent in some way.

If I should, then I would go to church and apologise to God while we were in this town. I wasn't a religious man, but if it meant Della was cured, I would do fucking anything.

Glancing at Della, I hugged her closer.

*Doctor.*

*Fast.*

My legs lengthened again, ignoring my fatigue. I would walk until I was dead if it meant I could save her. Keeping my chaotic thoughts to myself, I didn't speak as bare farmland gave way to congested streets, hazy in the hard-to-see dusk light. Streetlights suddenly turned on, ready to combat the darkness as I climbed the curb and scanned the shop fronts for a doctor.

Nothing.

Only a row of clothing stores, hairdressers, a florist—which reminded me of the one Della used to work at—and a few other stores with knick-knacks and magazines.

I had no intention of wasting time walking up and down, searching.

More sweat ran down the inside of my jacket as I coughed and spotted help.

"Excuse me." I stepped into the path of a blonde woman pushing a red stroller. "Where is the nearest doctor?"

She peered up, the fading light behind me blinding her a little. Her lips pursed as she looked at Della in my arms. "She okay?"

"I'm fine." Della clipped weakly. "He's just—"

"She's not fine. That's why I need a doctor." This woman had precisely two seconds to tell me what I needed. Otherwise, I was asking someone else who wouldn't waste my time. My heart palpitated strangely, starving for air and salvation. "Where can I find one?"

"Ren. Manners," Della hissed.

My back stiffened as I glared at her, then spat out. "Where can I find one, *please?*"

Della snickered, somehow deleting a little of my horror at her being ill and absolutely helpless to help her.

"I'll deal with you later," I said under my breath. "Behave."

Della blew me a kiss, then winced and clutched her side. "Ow."

Instantly, any patience she'd granted me flew down the goddamn road. My lungs became blades, puncturing my chest. "Do you know, lady, or are you just wasting my time?"

The woman sniffed as the baby inside her stroller grizzled. She rocked it softly. "I'm thinking. Look, you won't be able to see a general practitioner. It's past six p.m., and that's when they all close around here. But there is an urgent doctor's and afterhours surgery."

"Where?"

"Two streets over on Jordan Road."

"Which way?" Moving out of her path, I waited until she pointed to her right down a road where shopkeepers carried in signs and pushed racks of merchandise back into their stores.

"Down there. Take your second right. It will be on the left side of the street halfway down."

I remembered to be polite before Della told me off again. "Thank you." I broke into a jog, following the woman's directions.

My heart skipped a beat.

I looked down at Della and my entire body churned with sickness. Her skin was a ghostly pallor, her lips thin as she winced again.

*Christ.*

*Please, please let her be okay.*

I coughed and ran faster.

# Chapter Thirty-Three

## REN

## 2019

"MR. WILD?"

"Yes?" I looked up from where I had my face buried in my hands in the waiting room of the afterhours. It had cost a small fortune, countless explanations why we had no I.D, and finally, nasty threats for someone to treat her regardless that we didn't have the necessary paperwork.

If my threats hadn't worked, I was prepared to hand over every dollar just to have someone examine her and tell me how to fix this.

"Can you come with me? Mrs Wild asked if you could join us."

Terror shot down my limbs as I stood and stumbled after him. The long hours spent waiting in the yellow plastic chair had numbed my ass and made me stiff. "Is she okay?" I coughed into my hand. "She's been away for ages."

"I know. I'm sorry for the wait." The doctor had thick black hair and tanned skin, hinting he had Indian blood somewhere in his lineage. "We had to do a small procedure."

"Wait, what?" I slammed to a halt, dragging the attention of other worried husbands, wives, and parents from their own woe to focus on mine. My blood drained to my toes. "What procedure?"

The doctor narrowed his eyes, looking me over. "Are you quite well yourself, Mr. Wild? You look a bit under the weather."

"Forget about me. I'm fine." Stepping into his bubble, I growled. "What about Della? Where is she? Tell me what you did."

"I think it's best if we discuss this in private, don't you?" The doctor smiled encouragingly, waving away my temper as if he was used to husbands losing their shit.

He wasn't that much older than me, which didn't help with my trust issues. What the hell would he know? What was his experience?

"Where's my wife?"

Such a strange but perfect word. A word I had no right to use in the eyes of church and law, but every right in the eyes of our togetherness.

"Just this way, please." Buzzing his badge against a locked door, he guided me down a white corridor smelling strongly of disinfectant until we reached a room four or five doors down. Pressing the handle, he pushed another door wide, letting me enter first.

I eyed him carefully as I stepped inside, only to break into a jog the moment I saw Della.

She smiled the instant I arrived, holding up her hand for me to grab. "I'm sorry you were stuck out there, Ren. And I'm sorry for making you worry the past few days."

"Nothing to apologise for." Brushing aside her hair, my fingers came away hot and clammy from her skin. "What's wrong? What's going on?"

My heart couldn't figure out what pace it wanted to settle on. Fast and furious, braced for bad news, or slow and sedate, buried beneath hope that all of this was a mistake.

"Please, Mr. Wild. Take a seat." The doctor motioned at a grey vinyl chair in front of his desk. The ugly wood was wedged against the wall with apparatus and a computer blinking with important scans and who knew what else.

There was no earthly way I could leave Della's side where she lay on a starched bed hoisted high. "Tell me. Immediately." I squeezed Della's fingers, my heart choosing fast and furious as the doctor nodded.

"Mrs Wild has mentioned all her symptoms, and we've done a few tests."

"Tests? What sort of tests?" I glanced back at Della, my vision going wonky with worry. "Ribbon?"

"It's okay, Ren. Just calm down. I'm fine. Let him explain. Okay?" She brought my hand to her lips and kissed my knuckles, somehow injecting me with a much-needed dose of serenity. "You're all sweaty."

"Yeah well, you got me worked up."

"Well, I'm fine so relax, okay?"

My heart leapt on a trampoline instead, double bouncing and triple beating. "I'll relax when I know what's going on."

All I could think about was the nightmare of her being in the hospital with complications from chicken pox when she was younger. I couldn't do a thing to take away her pain or make her heal faster.

I hated it then, and I *despised* it now.

Della murmured gently as if I was the one in peril. "I wanted Doctor Strand to tell you because he'll do a much better job than I could."

Forcing myself to stay rational, I turned to face the doctor. "You have my word, I won't interrupt. Tell me. What's wrong with my wife?"

Doctor Strand cleared his throat, giving Della a gentle smile. "Technically, nothing should be wrong in a couple of days, but we will need to monitor her until that time. Mrs Wild has chosen outpatient therapy, so I expect to see her daily for the next seventy-two hours to ensure things are okay."

"Fine." I wouldn't focus on the complication of such a request or the deeper concern of why we had to stay in town. Obviously, whatever was wrong with Della was worse than I feared. "It's not stomach flu, is it?" I cringed, not wanting an answer even as I craved one.

"No. I'm afraid it's not," Doctor Strand said. "It's an ectopic pregnancy."

"*What?*" My world tilted, sending me stumbling against the bed holding the most beloved thing in my life. "What does that even mean?"

"It means a fertilized egg is growing outside the uterus. The baby can't survive and it will lead to life-threatening internal bleeding if we don't stop it."

I couldn't focus on the words life-threatening without wanting to be sick.

"How? How did this happen? She's on the pill." Frowning at Della, I asked, "You've been taking it, right? We had an agreement—"

"I know. And I am." She squeezed my hand. "But about a fortnight ago—just before the storm—I had an upset tummy. Just once. I didn't think anything of it, and we didn't have sex that night. By the time you woke me up in the morning—"

She blushed, flicking a glance at the doctor and saving him the details of just how I'd woken her up by slipping inside her warm, soft body as she moaned, still half asleep.

"Anyway, I didn't remember that we should probably use alternate protection." She hung her head. "I'm sorry, Ren. I know this is my fault."

"Don't, Della." I shook my head. "It takes two to cause this. I'm just as much at fault as you."

She smiled gently. "Regardless, it was enough for me to get pregnant." She winced. "I'm truly sorry."

"Stop saying that." Looking back at the doctor, I commanded, "Why has she been so ill? Women get pregnant all the time. Why is my wife struggling so much?"

"It's a possibility she has another condition called hyperemesis gravidarum, but those symptoms don't usually show up until week four or five. And she's not that far along. We'll cross that bridge when she next wants to have children, but for now, we need to deal with this. Unfortunately, the pregnancy can't be permitted to continue."

My mind didn't know which word was more important to latch onto, so I let them all go in a stream of incomprehensible gibberish.

Della was pregnant.

But she couldn't continue to be?

"I-I don't understand." I sounded like a fucking idiot.

Doctor Strand clasped his hands. "I don't want you to concern yourself with her vomiting. Sometimes these things just happen."

"How can we make it un-happen?"

"By removing what the body is obviously trying to reject." He gave Della a supportive smile. "The small procedure we've done is an injection. I've given her methotrexate, also known as trexall. It will stop the cells from growing and allow the body to reabsorb the pregnancy."

He rushed as I opened my mouth to ask more questions. "I think she's only nine or so days along, so the medication should be effective. There's always the risk of it not working, in which case laparoscopic surgery is our next option. However, we prefer to use mexthotrexate to prevent damaging the fallopian tubes, which may cause complications for future conceptions.

"I require Mrs Wild to come in daily to monitor her hCG levels until they're back to normal. The good news is she isn't far along, and I have confidence she'll make a full recovery once the pregnancy is terminated."

Clearing his throat again, he threw a kind look at Della before focusing on me. "I have already advised Mrs Wild of the side effects, but you should be aware, too. The injection can sometimes cause cramping, some bleeding, nausea, and dizziness. I recommend she take it easy and spend a few days in bed. Think you can keep her there?"

I didn't know if he was trying to make a joke to cut through the tension or if he was serious. Either way, Della wouldn't be leaving a bed the moment I found her one.

"Is she free to go?" My mind already leapt ahead, problem solving and planning. Where the hell would we sleep tonight?

"She is. I've made an appointment to see her in the morning."

Della swung her legs over the bed, her feet dangling high off the floor. "I'm fine, Ren. Honestly. We'll just treat it as a mini-vacation, and then we can go home."

I smiled and let her believe I accepted that, when in reality, I was already committed to staying close to town for the next few months. Autumn had already arrived. We only had another six to eight weeks of chilly weather before we would've been driven into civilisation by the snow anyway.

We were here now.

We would stay until spring.

Pushing me away a little, Della sprang to the floor, wincing and grabbing her stomach.

"Goddammit, let me carry you." Wrapping my arms around her, I tried to pick her up, but she shoved me back. "I can walk, Ren. Don't even think about it."

My jaw locked, but I wouldn't argue in front of a stranger.

"Thank you, Doctor Strand. I'll see you in the morning." Della took my hand, and together, we headed from the strong-smelling room and back to the waiting area.

I settled up, paid yet another small fortune, and accepted a card with a new appointment time for eleven a.m. tomorrow.

By the time we were on the street, thick darkness had fallen and even the restaurants were closed. I doubted we could find a similar cottage like our last one at this time of night. I doubted we could even find something to eat.

Della pointed at a quaint sign up ahead. "Look, it's a Bed and Breakfast. Let's crash there and sort out better accommodation tomorrow."

I froze.

The thought of sleeping in a house with strangers. Of seeing those same people in the morning. Of hearing them through the walls and sharing their showers.

*God, no.*

I honestly didn't think I could do it.

My feet actually backed away as everything inside me repelled against the idea.

I would rather sleep on the street. Naked.

But then Della flinched and hissed between her teeth, her face going white and hinting she wasn't as okay as she pretended.

She was ill.

She was tired.

And it was no longer about me.

It was *never* about me.

"Okay, Della. Bed and Breakfast it is."

# *Chapter Thirty-Four*

## REN

## 2019

I DIDN'T SLEEP.

Of *course*, I didn't sleep.

After we'd checked into the last available room in the five-bedroom Bed and Breakfast, I'd paced the small flower-decorated space like a caged rat. Thanks to my idiosyncrasies, I didn't have a hope in hell of relaxing in this place.

Just as I feared, the sounds of pipes groaning as another guest had a shower and the flush of a toilet a wall away drove me nuts.

I wasn't claustrophobic, but living so close to other people was past my very limited tolerance when it came to my fellow human race.

I didn't know how Della stood it, considering we both preferred trees and silence to buildings and chaos. Then again, she'd spent her childhood in noisy school classrooms and busy malls. Her natural habitat included both, while mine was firmly set in wide open fields with only a tractor and wind for company.

Doing my best to stay calm, I pictured emptiness all around me with no threats to listen to and no people to suspect.

But it didn't work.

I despised being so close.

I hated that we weren't free to go where we wanted.

I cursed how, even now, even though almost two decades separated me from Mclary, I still had the occasional panic attack that demanded I run.

The day I'd had my first attack—when John Wilson closed the door at Christmas to give me my first pay packet—I'd wondered if I'd outgrow them.

And I had, to a degree.

But my childhood had made me distrustful, and the loner who had run when he was ten was just as happy on his own with Della now that he was twenty-nine as he had been as a boy.

I was simple.

I needed Della.

That was it.

Nothing else required.

And the thought that she could be taken from me by something as idiotic as this?

It made me fucking *rage*.

It was exactly what I'd feared happening. It was why I never wanted her pregnant in the first place.

I paced again, checking the bathroom for intruders—as if they could climb through the tiny window—doing anything I could to stop my temper from building and latching onto the one person I shouldn't be angry at but was suddenly insanely furious with.

By the time I entered the bedroom again, my fists were clenched, my heart beating chaotically, and I itched for a fight—anything to expend the sick-fury and never ending need to keep Della safe.

I couldn't fight her body from hurting her.

But I could fight—

"Ren." Della noticed my unravelling self-control. How could she not with my pacing and jumpiness and longing looks out the window?

"Ren, come to bed."

Bed? Lie down? Sleep? Let my guard down when other people slept so close? In the same *building* as us?

"Can't." I flung myself into the high-backed chair with an orchid decorated ottoman, swallowing a cough.

The meagre supplies I'd brought with us meant we'd at least been able to clean our teeth after the landlady kindly brought up some ham sandwiches and a few chocolate cookies as an evening snack.

She seemed nice enough, but so did anyone who wanted to lull you into a false sense of security.

"Ren, the door is locked. We're safe."

I narrowed my eyes at the flimsy lock and the flimsy door and its flimsy hinges. If someone wanted to come in, they could. No problem.

Conversation was good, at least. It gave me something else to think about instead of the undying need to scream at Della.

She huffed as if she didn't quite understand me even though she should. Of all people, she should understand *exactly* what I was struggling with.

She cocked her head. "You didn't have a problem sleeping at the Wilsons, and they were just across the driveway."

I clutched the armrests hard, forcing myself to stay on this subject and not yell a totally different one. "To start with, I was sick and didn't have a choice. And by the time I was better, I'd learned to trust them."

"Well, trust that nothing will happen here. We're just guests like everyone else. We'll checkout in the morning, and everyone will go their separate ways. No one cares who we are."

I did my best to relax, but the tingling anxiety continued to zoom in my veins. Needing to change the subject—to prove to myself I wasn't a monster who screamed at Della when she wasn't well—I asked gently, "How are you feeling?"

Her face fell as she plucked at the pansy bedspread with its copious amounts of pillows.

"I'm okay. I just keep hearing the words 'you're pregnant.' You know?" She shrugged, a gleam of tears springing from nowhere. "I thought I'd feel happy if I ever heard those words. But all I felt was terror. The pain...if this is what it feels like to be pregnant, I don't know if I can—"

"Stop it." I leaned forward, digging my hands into my temples and wedging fingers into my hair as if could prevent her from speaking. "Just...go to sleep."

Her gasp spoke volumes of how I'd shocked and upset her. "What do you mean? Wait. Are you *angry* with me?" Shifting higher in the pillows, dressed in just her t-shirt and underwear, she demanded, "Why are you acting like this?"

"Like what? Pissed off that you're in pain and there's nothing I can do about it?"

*Stop it, Wild.*

*Just stop it. Before you go too far.*

"Forget about it." I raked my fingers through my hair and let them fall to my knees. I'd been the one to work myself up. I'd made myself feel sick and out of control. Not her. "I'm sorry. Go to sleep, Della. Get some rest."

A long pause before she muttered, "I won't be able to sleep

unless you get into bed with me."

"I can't."

"You can. It's just a bed, Ren. They've washed the sheets. They've—"

"It's not that."

"Then what is it because your temper is driving me—"

Swooping to my feet, I growled. "I can't touch you. I can't lie beside you. I'm the reason you're in agony. Why did I put so much responsibility on you, huh? To not even bother supporting you with taking the pill at the right time every day, making sure you were okay, ensuring that things like this didn't happen. You're so fucking young. Far too young to get pregnant, let alone a complicated one. What does that even mean? Is it because I carted you out to the wilderness and thought I could keep you healthy and happy? Is it because I didn't give you what you needed as a kid and your body is all messed up now? *What?*"

My roar found every corner of the room and bounced back amplified. "I mean it, Della. You're only nineteen. How did I think it was right to touch you? Let alone *sleep* with you?! I'm sick. I'm perverted. I'm the reason you're in agony and…and, I don't know how to make it right."

I stalked to the door, then back to the window, needing open spaces and trees. My lungs begged for fresh air. "I'm *furious* at you for putting yourself in danger this way, but it's me I should be angry at."

Punching myself in the chest, I seethed, "All me. I knew getting involved with you would be a bad idea. I'm ten years older. I should know better. Maybe it was me, huh? Maybe it was my screwed-up sperm that made you pregnant where it can kill you. Goddammit!"

Breathing hard and struggling, I stood in the centre of the room, desperate to pick up the confessions I'd just littered all over the floor, but unable to move.

Most of my issues didn't even make sense. All I knew was I was horrified, terrified, and pissed off at everything.

Della sat stonily in bed, her chin high and eyes bright. "How can you say that? How can you say *any* of that? Loving me was a bad idea? Screw you, Ren. It's not your job to make me swallow a damn pill every day! It's not your fault that the pregnancy is ectopic. None of this is your fault!"

"I didn't say loving you was a bad idea. I said *sleeping* with you was."

"And I said *screw you!*"

"Della—" My heart punctured for how my worry twisted my words. "Look, all I'm saying is, I should've kept myself in check. I shouldn't need you the way I do. I shouldn't expect to have you every day. Sex is a health risk. Especially when you're still so young."

"If you say I'm young again, we're going to have a serious issue, Ren Wild." Della sat on her knees, the blankets discarded. "Girls have babies when they're fifteen, for God's sake. Sometimes even younger. I'm not young. I'm fully grown, and you're forgetting it's not just you who wants sex every day. I initiate as much as you do. It's not your job to treat me with silk gloves and hold me at arm's length when you need me as much as I need you!"

My temper roared back into cyclonic heat. "No, *Della*, it's my job never to send you to the goddamn hospital!"

"And you didn't! What happened is a freak thing. Even the doctor said these things happen randomly with no rhyme or reason. It's not your fault."

"Not my fault?" My temper coiled and snapped. "*Not my fault?* Okay, let's just see what *isn't* my fault." Holding up my fingers, I counted on them as I spat, "You grew up with no parents. You lived a lot of your childhood totally homeless with a kid who knew nothing about nutrition or health. You trusted everything I did when most of it was wrong—"

"Why the hell are you re-counting the past now? This has nothing to do with any of that!"

"Shut up and let me goddamn finish, Della!" My snarl was the harshest I'd ever been with her, but I couldn't control it anymore. We'd been together for a year and a half, and in that time, I'd remembered the past often. Most of the time, I loved thinking of her as younger and older. Proud rather than disgusted to have the privilege of loving her in so many different ways.

But now?

Now that reality had slapped me in the face, I crippled beneath blame.

Heavy, *terrible* blame.

I'd always believed my choices had been made with her best interests at heart. I'd always put her first. Always fed her over me if there wasn't enough food. Always wrapped her in my jacket if hers wasn't warm enough.

I'd screwed up many times raising her, but I'd like to think I'd been honourable and true.

But...I hadn't.

My choices had always been about me.

And that had never been more obvious.

"You were happy at your creative writing course. You were working on your future. You had everything I wanted you to have, and what did I do? I took you away from all of it!"

Pacing again, I struggled for air. "I didn't ask if you wanted to live in a goddamn tent. I didn't discuss with you what you thought about abandoning everything. I ran the moment it got hard between us, and I snatched you for mine the moment I knew I couldn't survive without you."

Della shifted again, her forehead furrowed, and hands balled.

I didn't know if it was from pain or anger, but I had no hope of stopping everything I'd bottled up. These dirty, awful conclusions that had whispered cruelly in my ear as I'd sat in the doctor's waiting room. Waiting and not knowing if I'd be told good news or bad. Waiting and not knowing what was wrong with my Della and what I'd done to cause it.

Because it had to have been me.

Because I should've known better and not been so fucking selfish.

"I love you, Della. And I'm so fucking sorry I did this to you. I'm sorry I have no money to keep you healthy. I'm sorry I have no career to build you the house you deserve. I'm sorry I somehow got you pregnant and now you're sick and in pain and there's absolutely *nothing* I can do about it. I'm sorry for all of it, but you should know that when it comes to you, I'm useless. I wanted you, so I stole you. I loved you, so I kept you. I didn't stop to think that by making you mine, I owed you more than I ever did before. I owe you a life that everyone else has. I owe you a stable environment. I owe you a man who can fucking provide and who isn't afraid of humanity, for God's sake!"

"Ren, stop—"

"No!" My eyes narrowed to sniper scopes, a cough exploding from my lips. "Let me finish." My chest rose and fell, spikes stabbing my lungs as I inhaled with even worse admittances. "With you, I'm the rawest form of myself. I obey no laws, I follow no rules. If someone hurts you, I *will* hurt them back, ten times worse. No, a thousand times worse, because you mean more to me than anything. I would *kill* for you, Della. My entire purpose on this earth is to love and take care of you. I've been doing it for almost twenty years, and I plan on doing it for another twenty and beyond. But how the fuck can I mean that when *I'm* the problem? All this time, I believed I was protecting you from them when I should've been protecting you from myself!"

Dragging a hand over my mouth, I shook my head as a future I'd always wanted incinerated into dust with reality. "What if we do end up having a family, huh? What happens when you're in labour and about to give birth? Do I expect you to suffer on your own and deliver in a forest that hides your screams? Do I think I can just drop you off at the hospital when it's time with no I.D or money, and a few hours later, we'll walk back to our tent with a goddamn new-born? A new-born who needs shelter and safety and a mother who is healthy and happy and has a bed and a shower and a fridge and a roof—"

"Ren!" Della climbed off the bed, flinching as another wash of agony worked through her. "Enough. None of that matters. We're not having children yet. It's fine—"

"But don't you see? It's *not* fine. It's shown me just how precarious all of this is. How I've been so fucking blind and wrapped up in this fantasy that we can stay wild and not suffer any consequences. How did I not see this? How did I not understand that this life can never be permanent? It's too risky. I need a job. I need to provide for you. I need to stop being a creature who thinks a tent is a suitable home and be a man instead and build you the life you deserve—build you a future we both want and a future we can't have unless I grow the fuck up."

My pacing ended by the chair, and I collapsed into it, all my rage depleted. All my terror shared. All my worries tainting the air just like they'd tainted my mind.

Pinching the bridge of my nose, I murmured, "I just can't stop thinking that I did this to you, and you're the one paying for my mistakes. That this would never have happened if we'd just stayed in our old apartment and figured this out in a place where humans are meant to live, not drag you halfway across the country with nothing."

"Ren." Della cut in. "Ren, look at me."

It took a monumental effort, but I did.

She sat on the side of the bed, whitewashed and tear-streaked.

Our eyes locked, and the love I felt for her poured free in painful waves, obliterating my anger, commanding I go to her.

I couldn't fight it.

I'd never been able to fight it.

I needed her as much as she needed me, and I'd fucking shouted at her while she was ill.

*Christ, I'm a bastard.*

Storming toward her, I climbed onto the mattress—boots, knives, and all—and pulled her into my arms. Tucking her back under the covers, I kissed the top of her head and breathed in her delicate scent of pine and earth and air. "I'm sorry, Little Ribbon. I didn't mean to say all that. I'm just…I'm so scared of losing you."

Snuggling into me, she wiped her tears on my chest. "I know this is hard for you. I guess it would be hard for anyone when they first hear they're pregnant and what it all means. But you can't believe that you took me into the forest against my will, Ren. I love our life. I love our tent and simplicity and freedom. If I didn't, I would tell you."

My breath still came fast and haggard, but the crazed terror faded a little as I hugged her harder. My heart stopped its fanatical beating, slipping back into a rhythm I knew.

She kissed my t-shirt, whispering, "You didn't do this to me, and you *do* provide for me. You've provided for me all my life, and no one could've done it better. So please don't worry about the future, Ren. And please don't think you'll ever lose me because you won't. I promise."

"How can you promise something like that?"

"Because I know love transcends blood and bone. Yes, eventually we will die, but we're bound to one another. For eternity." Kissing my t-shirt again, she worked her way to my collarbone and whispered into my feverish skin. "You have my word if, heaven forbid, anything happens to me, I'll wait for you to join me. Death isn't our ending, Ren. Promise me you won't stop sleeping with me or prevent us from having a family one day because you're afraid of life itself. And all the rest of it—the house and money and things—it will work out. You'll see."

I held her for a long time, her heart thudding against mine, imprinting her shape and curves against me, allowing our connection to eradicate my fury and accept that I wasn't truly angry, just petrified.

Finally, I kissed her hair. "Thank you."

"You don't have to thank me."

"I do. I don't know what I'd do without you."

She smiled up from my arms. "Well, lucky for you, you'll never have to find out."

Echoes of her promising that we'd always be together, even

past death, made me clutch her as hard as I could.

She squeaked a little in protest, but I tipped her chin up with my knuckles and kissed her lips. I'd wanted to keep the kiss tame and sweet, but the moment I tasted her, my tongue crept into her mouth and hers met mine in invitation.

A quick kiss turned into a sensual make-out, our lips gliding, tongues dancing, hearts kicking.

And when I finally pulled back, my chest burned with the same promise she'd given me. "You have my word in return. If anything happens to me, I'll wait for you to join me. You're mine, Della. Always will be."

She relaxed, breathing easier. "Good."

"Fine," I murmured, like we usually did at the end of an argument, releasing the final tension.

Reclining into the pillows still fully dressed, I waited until Della found a comfortable position with her head on my chest and body spooning my side before I stroked her hair with shaking fingers. "Now, go to sleep, woman. I'm not going anywhere."

It was a promise I kept all night.

I didn't undress, and I didn't sleep, but as I held the girl who was my everything, and she slipped into slumber and her body went lax against mine, I whispered into her moonbeam painted hair, "I hope to be the man you deserve, Della Ribbon. I hope I can give you everything your heart desires. And then, when we've lived a life rich in so many things, I hope I die before you. Because if I don't, I know I won't survive a day without you. I can't."

My voice hovered like smoke as I sucked in a gasp with how true that was. It wasn't an empty sentence. It was every truth imaginable, and, in some inexplicable way, I hoped whatever rules of fate governed our lives heard me and understood how deadly serious I was.

It was my prayer.

My penance for taking Della all those years ago.

She gave me a life and taught me how to be happy. And if she left me, I would no longer want that life without her.

It was selfish and cruel to wish such a thing, but I knew who was stronger out of the two of us, and it wasn't me.

Cradling her in the moonlight, I looked out the window at the stars.

I was her watcher and protector.

And I never let her go...all night.

# Chapter Thirty-Five

## DELLA

# 2031

THAT WAS THE *turning point for us.*

*The moment where life got in the way of our fantasy, bringing us both back to earth with a crash.*

*Still, to this day, I get mad at myself for ruining such an idyllic existence.*

*I wish I could rewind time and remember to use alternate protection. I should've told Ren that we might not be safe.*

*An honest mistake was the biggest catalyst of our lives.*

*But really...it turned out for the best.*

*Things were about to happen that meant our past and future blended in a way we never expected.*

*Surprises that we never wanted inched closer to being known.*

*Wishes would come true and promises would be kept.*

*And one of those life-changing five incidents crept ever nearer.*

# Chapter Thirty-Six

## REN

## 2019

THE NEXT DAY, I was better equipped after my meltdown the night before.

I kissed Della good morning, showered away my sleeplessness and worry, and focused on being the strong one and not some nutcase who wished upon a star, asking for something as morbid as death before another.

That was my secret, and she would never know just how fundamental she was to me.

That sort of pressure wasn't fair to anyone, and it was my fault I felt that way. My fault that she'd turned from my charge to my friend to my lover.

She didn't have the luxury of entering my life when I was fully developed with other significant relationships to lean on. *She* was my significant relationship in every way, and that sort of connection wasn't exactly easy.

Once I was dressed and Della comfortable with the TV on and painkillers in her system, I popped out like any normal city dweller, and bought her a chocolate croissant and coffee from the bakery two stores over, rather than eat with other guests.

At least, my body was back to being mine again with no breathlessness or palpitations. Stress had almost killed me last night and I refused to let it happen again. I would remain calm and reasonable, so I could provide the best possible care for Della.

When I returned, we ate breakfast in bed, laughed at some kid's cartoon, and reminisced about the bad reception and street-salvaged TV at Polcart Farm.

It was simple and lovely and filled me with false belief that she was on the mend.

I'd hoped she'd be able to keep her breakfast down, but ten minutes after finishing, she rushed to the bathroom and retched it all back up.

My temper built, cursing myself all over again, begging for a way to fix this.

Once she'd purged her system and her skin was once again the colour of a corpse, she protested weakly as I stripped her and myself, and for the second time that morning, turned on the shower and dragged her into it with me.

Running hot water was a novelty, and I didn't care how much we used if it granted Della some comfort.

I took my time washing her gently, massaging her scalp until she moaned, feathering my hands over her curves until her lethargy showed a spark of sexual interest.

When she plastered her naked, water-drenched body to mine and kissed me, I turned off the shower, bundled her in a towel, and helped her dress.

Sex was not something either of us should be indulging in right now.

By the time we sat back in the doctor's office and he checked her temperature, took a blood sample, and asked how she was feeling, his face went from kind to guarded, and my worry went from simmering to roaring.

My lungs imitated tiny sickles again. My breath catching with pain.

*So much for staying calm.*

With professional silence, he scanned the readings of her blood test, smiled a little too brightly, then said he'd like to give her another injection as her hCG levels hadn't changed and he'd expected at least a small drop.

It took everything I had to stay sitting and permit him to jab her with that needle. In a way, I wanted him to jab her with a thousand needles if it would make her better, but I also wanted to murder him for the bead of blood as he pulled the injection free and patted a Band-Aid over the puncture while Della kept her eyes tightly closed.

After another hour of monitoring, Della was cleared to return to bed.

Walking slowly, hand in hand, to the Bed and Breakfast, total strangers smiled at us seeing a couple in love, not a man distraught by his lover's pain.

At least we had a room and a bed, and after I'd ensured she was safe and warm, lying down with a glass of water close by, a bucket just in case she vomited again, a hot water bottle courtesy of the landlady, and the TV remote, I left her for the afternoon, taking my phone and hooking into the free Wi-Fi of a coffee shop, searching the same site where Della had found our previous winter accommodation.

I'd reached my limit staying with other guests.

But I couldn't go back to the forest.

Not now...maybe not ever.

Not after my epiphany last night.

I owed Della so much more, and I didn't want to return to her until I had a solution to our unknown future.

It took longer than I wanted. I wasn't nearly as adept with using a small screen with big thumbs and reading the descriptions as quickly, but just before dusk, I managed to narrow my search down to two suitable places that I wouldn't be tempted to bulldoze or bolt from.

An old manor house that offered cheap rent in return for physical labour to do repairs and a one bedroom container house planted on a hilltop where a local farmer grazed his sheep.

The idea of being close to livestock appealed to me. But the fact that the owner would pop around often to check on them turned me off. Besides, if snow was heavy this year, getting up and down a hill might be tricky.

Leaving the coffee shop as the sun painted the sky in a swirl of reds and coppers, I called the manor house number and spoke to a gruff older woman who said her husband had died five years ago, and the house was falling apart.

I told her I was happy to renovate, that I had experience with tools and was a diligent worker, but only if she agreed not to pop by and check on us.

She'd grudgingly agreed, mentioned something about writing a long list so we wouldn't have to be in constant contact, and gave me a time to meet the following day.

I spent yet another sleepless night in the Bed and Breakfast holding Della close, wincing when she winced and holding back her hair when she vomited. The sooner whatever drug the doctor had given her worked, the better, because I didn't know how much longer I could stand seeing her like this.

* * * * *

"Isn't it too big, Ren?" Della asked quietly as we drifted away from the grey-haired bat who'd met us at the manor house to give us the 'grand tour.' Not that there was anything grand about the place anymore.

The roof had partially caved in in the dining room, the eight bedrooms upstairs had a roost of pigeons sharing one and a nest of mice in another, and the kitchen was straight out of a time warp with a coal range to cook on and a sink that could fit an entire pig.

It was cold and drafty and frankly, I'd already made up my mind to say no. It wouldn't be fair of me to expect Della to camp inside a house all winter because we'd literally have to pitch a tent inside to ward off the breeze and bird shit.

But that was until the owner caught us coming down the impressive winding stairs and said, "There is, of course, an annex next door where I've been living for the past couple of years. It's got two bedrooms, warm and dry, which is where you can stay. I'm moving in with my daughter and just want to get this place sold but can't afford a builder to do what's needed."

"So you thought you'd rent it out, get money, all while your tenant fixes it up for you?" Della asked sharply. Her patience hadn't been the best, and I couldn't blame her with feeling the way she did.

The old woman narrowed her eyes, her spectacles perched on the end of a hooked nose. "It's a nice house. I was told people do this type of arrangement all the time."

I jumped in before Della could piss her off. "Look, thank you for your time, Mrs Collins, but I think—"

The woman held up her hand. "You seem strong, and I don't know about you, but winter can get awfully boring without a hobby or two." She crossed her arms. "Tell you what. You can live here all winter for free, and we'll work out what you owe me in rent once I know what sort of renovations you're willing to tackle. Fair?"

I hadn't let Della know how tight funds had become. What with her doctor's bills and the Bed and Breakfast, we barely had enough to cover one month's rent, let alone four or five.

At least, I could earn the roof over our heads. I could do enough work that ensured my labour ought to cover our stay. The place was far enough from the city limits not to be disturbed, and there was somewhere warm to go to at night.

"Can you give us a moment?" I smiled politely at Mrs Collins.

"Of course." She turned toward the large engraved front

door. "Take your time."

"Della?" Cupping her elbow, I pulled her into the large lounge, coughing at the dust swirling from the floor. The moment we were out of earshot, I told her the truth. "Money is running out. This might be our best hope at avoiding another winter with some coin left over to buy food."

"But, Ren. Have you seen the amount of work required?"

"I know. It's a lot but—"

"Do you really want to be working all winter?"

I laughed, running my thumb over her cheekbone, so damn happy there was some colour there for a change. We'd had another doctor's appointment, and he said her levels were dropping, which was a good sign. He still insisted she should be in bed, and the fact that she'd argued until I'd brought her with me to see this house had added a bit of friction, but it wouldn't be just me living here. She had every right to weigh in on the decision.

"Not sure if you remember, but I was happy working on Polcart Farm. Tinkering kept my mind off the short days and cold nights. I think this would be good for me."

"Would you let me help?" She smiled, kissing my hand as it cascaded from her cheek.

"Of course. I'd adore your help."

"Even up ladders and things?"

I frowned. "Within reason."

"Fine. You do the hard yards, and I'll paint and plaster and wallpaper and do whatever else you'll deem safe enough for me."

"So…you're okay living here?"

"As long as there is somewhere with a working toilet and a warm bed, then yes." She nodded. "Be kind of cool, actually."

"Should we go tell Mrs Collins?"

Della clutched my hand and stood on her tiptoes, pressing her mouth to mine. A faint line of sweat appeared on her upper lip, revealing she needed to be back in bed and resting. "Make sure we can move in tomorrow. I'm sick of you not sleeping in that Bed and Breakfast."

I chuckled, kissing her back. "Deal."

* * * * *

We moved in the next day after Della's doctor's appointment. Her hCG levels had once again dropped, and Doctor Strand finally looked more relaxed than tense around her. The cramps in her stomach weren't as bad, and the minor bleeding had stopped along with her vomiting.

The relief at seeing the cheeky spirit in her eyes and the sheer gratefulness at her quick kisses and sarcastic comments made my heart glow with happiness.

I didn't even care we wouldn't be returning to the forest.

Della was okay, and I wouldn't ask for more than that.

While we wouldn't be heading back into the trees we'd called home for so long, I did travel back to our campsite and collected our backpacks and belongings.

Della wanted to come, but I'd put my foot down before an argument could start.

Her hipbones stuck out and her flat stomach was concave from vomiting so much.

She was on the mend, and no way would I let her risk her health after the nightmare we'd just survived.

The return trip took me over eight hours, not to mention the pack up time. And I'd never admit—even under pain of death—but I had to stop a few times due to a frustrating case of breathlessness.

I feared by not having antibiotics to ward off the flu so long ago, I'd scared my lungs a little. I kind of wanted to take Doctor Strand up on his offer to take a look at me, but our funds were strapped, and I wanted to keep what we had just in case Della needed more treatment.

Besides, I was used to long journeys, and had far too much to do than worry about an occasional cough.

\* \* \* \* \*

One week turned to two, and we settled in.

In the cosy annex, we washed the curtains to remove any scent of its previous inhabitant, dusted the cute figurines of pumpkins and snow peas above the TV, and cleaned the tiny kitchen with its white countertop and wooden cupboards.

Della had a few more doctor visits, which ate into the final reserves of our cash, but she was finally given the all-clear along with a fresh prescription for the pill.

It'd been the longest we'd ever gone without having sex, and the night we celebrated her recovery—trying not to think about the fact that she'd actually been pregnant—we fell into bed together and finally gave in to how much we'd missed each other.

We made it last as long as we could, long and slow and deep.

And when it grew too much, we came together, hard and fast and wild.

Only to do it all over again a couple of hours later.

Two weeks melted into three, and I started working on the house.

By day, Della and I roamed the large corridors and bedrooms, making notes of what to tackle first, and reading through the list Mrs Collins had provided.

By night, we crossed the overgrown lawn, went past the weed-dotted tennis court, and hid in the small annex where the open fireplace crackled and popped, and I raided the terribly untended veggie garden by the old kitchen, pulling up long overdue broccoli and kale, leaving Della to use her internet trawling to turn them into a feast.

We'd become more adaptable—not just to outdoor living but to city living, too. When it was on our terms, neither of us felt trapped or ridiculed or afraid.

The town was nice enough with a couple of supermarkets, cheaper restaurants, and plenty of houses that looked like they kept their doors unlocked—if it came down to needing to 'borrow' a few things if our money ran out.

Mrs Collins was true to her word, and a week after moving in, she had three trucks deliver timber, paint, and fixings. The materials were stored in the old garage at the back, and that was one of the last interactions we had all winter.

She trusted us in her home and we trusted her to leave us alone.

Our bargain meant I had no intention of letting her down.

Her late husband's tools, stored in the workshop behind the four-car garage, were a candy box of ancient cranks and rusty hammers—a history lesson in gadget evolution, but they did the job.

Six weeks flew by, and I tackled the roof first.

Before the weather turned entirely disgusting, I ripped off the broken tiles, removed the rotten joists and bearers, and began rebuilding the ancient girl to survive another century.

Those were some of my favourite days—working in the attic with Della perched on old trunks, reading me stories from ancient diaries and dusting off porcelain-faced dolls and patching up bug-chewed teddy bears.

It did something to me watching her cradle the toys so lovingly, almost as if imagining the kids who had once played with them before time turned them to adult, then to dust.

I didn't have the guts to ask her how she felt about pregnancy after the pain she'd endured. Then again, I knew Della was a fighter and determined, and despite what had happened, she'd still want a kid…eventually.

And although I was still well acquainted with the terror of losing her, I couldn't deny I already loved her for the mother she would become. The way she'd hold our son or daughter. The way she'd kiss them and read to them and introduce them to the world that we viewed as harsh but would be so fantastical to them as we'd ensure they'd forever be protected and cherished.

That winter was just as good as the previous one in our cottage.

As we grew familiar with the manor house, we'd run the halls, have paint fights that turned into tickle wars, chase up the rambling stairs and indulge in still-dressed sex, rutting against a wall or over the arm of a hundred-year-old chaise.

Della was my other half, and the magic that existed between us meant the sad old house slowly shed off her cobwebs and stood from her ruins, prouder, prettier, braver than she ever had before.

# Chapter Thirty-Seven

## DELLA

## 2020

CHRISTMAS.

New Years.

Another year.

I wasn't exactly sad to say goodbye to 2019, thanks to the still sharp memories of an ectopic pregnancy, but there was so much good about the year, too.

Ren skirted the topic of what happened in a way that made me suspect he took it a lot harder than I had. Respecting his fears of losing me, I never truly described the pain to him. Never told him that as he carried me from the forest, I felt as if my ovary was trying to claw its way free, determined to drag my entire uterus with it.

Thanks to him, I was still alive.

Thanks to him, we had a chance at a family in the future.

And that was another reason I never told him what I went through when Doctor Strand said the words 'You're pregnant.'

How could something so good be so excruciating?

How could something I wanted be so utterly terrifying?

And how could I admit to Ren, that even though I knew the termination had to happen, I felt as if I'd killed our child in cold blood? What sort of life did we end? Was it a girl like me or a boy like Ren?

Sometimes, in those first few weeks, I'd stroke my phone with the urge to message Cassie. She was the one who'd helped me during my first period, and the only girl who'd confided in. I wanted to share my feelings. I wanted someone to understand that, even though I knew it had to be terminated, it still didn't stop the occasional nightmares of some ghost-child condemning me for choosing my life over theirs.

But I couldn't message Cassie because I hadn't told her about me and Ren.

Sure, I'd spoken to her since we'd gotten together but I always directed the conversation away from her questions of my love life and if David was still in the picture.

What I really wanted to talk about was the shadow slowly building inside me about Ren.

A shadow full of worry.

He'd put on weight since we'd been back together. He laughed and joked and ran and played and worked.

But he still coughed.

Not often.

Not all the time.

Just occasionally.

But my ears hated the sound and my heart twitched like a frightened rabbit every time he did.

Just like I never told him what I went through with the ectopic pain, I didn't confide my growing concerns over his own health.

To look at him, he glowed with vitality and hardiness…but when that cough appeared?

The shadow inside me grew bigger.

I was used to not having a sounding board to share my concerns, so our separation from society was nothing new, but sometimes I did wish I had someone to assure me that from here on out, life would be kind to us and grant long healthy days and never ending happy nights.

Despite the fact I kept a few things from Ren, and my worries chewed like tiny mice inside me, winter was great fun in that rambling, ramshackle mansion.

Ren had always been a hard worker, and that part of him came out loud and proud as he took it upon himself to renovate the entire property and not just the long list Mrs Collins had provided.

One month turned to two, then three; snow fell, ice formed, and we stayed warm thanks to physical labour. Some days, we'd focus on the bedrooms, lugging timber up the stairs to rebuild rotten walls, both of us learning how to plaster so it didn't look like Play-Doh slopped on the wall, and figuring out that paint didn't dry in the cold and caused ugly streaks that meant we had to sand and try again.

Other days, we cleared the overly cluttered living rooms of old magazine boxes and discarded dresses from a century ago, ready to rip up threadbare carpets and buff ancient floorboards beneath.

I loved every second because it meant Ren and I were together, like always.

Life couldn't get any more perfect.

Until spring arrived, of course.

And then it just got better.

We stayed far longer than usual, but whenever I brought up the subject of returning to the forest, Ren refused.

What he'd said at the Bed and Breakfast still governed him, and he was determined to provide more than just a tent even though that was all I really wanted.

Just him and long, hot days of freedom.

Summer came knocking with a vengeance, giving us an easier job of tackling areas of the house we'd left until last. And as ramshackle slowly became regal once again, the urge to move on returned, despite not knowing where we would move on to.

That traveller's itch and wanderlust was vicious once it arrived, and it hung a countdown clock over our heads, tick-tocking for a departure.

Almost as if she heard our growing restlessness, Mrs Collins left us a neatly penned note in the repaired letter box asking for a tour in one weeks' time.

We'd stayed longer than any place in two years, but even though Ren didn't want to make me homeless again, another reason we hadn't traded walls for trees was that he felt as if he hadn't done enough.

The house was immaculate compared to the state it was in when we first arrived. The roof was solid and watertight. The bedrooms rodent and pigeon free with fresh paint, beautifully sanded floors, and furniture that I'd painstakingly washed, waxed, and restored.

The downstairs was just as impressive with its polished chandeliers, spotless—if not still ancient—kitchen, and the lounge had a full makeover with new walls, re-tiled fireplace, replaced chimney flu, and an emerald rug the size of a small country we'd found in the attic and spent weeks airing out.

We were officially down to almost nothing in our wallets, but I didn't think I'd ever been so happy. Ren had even stopped coughing as often, thanks to having a proper house to protect us and regular vegetables in our diets.

Things were good.

Better than good.

But by the time Mrs Collins arrived for her tour, Ren and I grew nervous about showing her around.

It was her home, after all.

The photo album of her youth and scrapbook of her twilight years. Had we trespassed on those memories?

To start with, she'd listened as Ren explained what we'd done and nodded as we showed her room after room. Toward the end, though, her nods turned to trembles and the curt replies from a gruff woman became silent tears from a grateful widow.

We feared she hated what we'd done. That somehow, we'd overstepped.

But of course, we worried for nothing.

It took two hours and forty-three minutes to show her around, bypassing the gardens and tennis courts that we hadn't had time to tackle, and as we all stood on the repaired front veranda with peach roses perfuming the muggy breeze, she pulled out her cheque book and wrote us a figure that, even if we could've cashed the cheque, we wouldn't have felt comfortable taking.

Ten thousand dollars.

Probably her entire retirement kitty, judging by the patched-up blazer she wore.

Obviously, we insisted we couldn't take it.

Not just because it was too much, but because we had no way to cash it. No bank would touch us, no loan office would trust us—not without identification.

But even though it was a gift we couldn't accept, there was something special about being offered that cash.

Ren and I stared at the cheque all evening after Mrs Collins had gone, and somehow, in that moment of feeling worthy and valued, we turned to each other and said, "It's time to go."

The next day, we called to let her know the annex was free, and it wouldn't take a gardener much to tidy up the outside in order to sell the old girl for a tidy sum.

We left with freshly packed backpacks and aired out sleeping bags, leaving the cheque on her kitchen bench with a simple note saying thank you.

We were penniless and homeless, but our happiness made us richer than we'd ever been.

# *Chapter Thirty-Eight*

## DELLA

## 2020

"ARE YOU SURE, Della?"

I leapt into Ren's arms right there in the tiny office of Lo and Ro's Fruit Picking. "I'm sure. But only if *you're* sure."

He chuckled into my hair, holding me close, making my legs dangle off the ground. "Well, we just spent our last dollar, so unless you want to be in love with a thief, I suppose we don't have a choice." Letting me go, he smiled at Lo—a middle-aged woman with a baby boy tugging at her skirt and a sun-burned button nose. "We'll take the job. How long was it for again?"

Lo—short for Loraine—pushed a clipboard toward us with a pen. She, along with her husband, Ro—short for Ronald—owned a farm that grew apples, pears, and berries.

"Five to six weeks, depending on how quickly we strip the orchards before working on the greenhouse berries. We like to pick later in the season because we can charge more as fruit gets scarce with colder weather."

"Makes sense," Ren said as I grabbed the clipboard and began hastily filling in the boxes. Names? They were easy. Phone number? We had one of those. Date of births? Fine, we could fudge that. Most details were easy apart from three things.

"Eh, Lo?" I looked up, tapping the pen against the form. "We don't have a bank account or an address, and recently we were robbed, and they took our driver's licenses, so we don't have any I.D. Is that going to be a problem?"

I hated lying. I also hated how not having a piece of paper with our name on it had become a hazard in day-to-day living. But

I wanted this job, and Ren needed some cash in his pocket in order to feel as if he was taking adequate care of me, so I fibbed and hoped for the best.

Lo looked us up and down, judging our tale.

I'd never been the best liar and hated to do it to a woman who'd caught us counting our last coins on the dusty highway where she had a small wooden stall selling freshly picked apples and pears. She'd taken pity on us when we'd settled on buying three instead of four, mentioning if things were tight, she had a few fruit-picking jobs open.

We'd only been on the road a couple of days since leaving the manor house, and we'd yet to embrace the thicker forest as we didn't have the cash to fill up our backpacks with supermarket food. As comforting as it was to know Ren could hunt enough to keep us alive, I wanted more to my diet than just meat and the occasional wild vegetable.

When I'd seen the fruit stand, my mouth had watered, and I couldn't stop myself tugging Ren across the road and drooling over a gorgeous pear.

"Ah, gotcha. You're one of those." Lo finally nodded.

"One of what?" Ren asked, his hackles rising, a slight cough falling from his lips.

My heart instantly froze, and I studied him.

Searching.

Seeking.

Desperate to know why he coughed, so I could stop it once and for all.

Perhaps it was just allergies.

Maybe it was from living in storms and traipsing through snow for so many years.

"Backpackers." Lo pointed at our well-used bags. "I've had a fair few from overseas come through and want to be paid in cash as it violates their visa."

Sighing, she picked up her baby son from the floor and plonked him on the small desk amongst the boxes of pears, blueberries, and apples. "Okay, I can do cash. And your hourly rate will be a dollar more, seeing as I don't have to pay tax. I'll pay you every Sunday, cash in hand. Got it?"

Ren cleared his throat, hiding any remnants of his tension. "Wow, thanks. We appreciate it."

"Meh, don't mention it. Government takes too much these days and doesn't do anything worthwhile with it. Rather help out people who need it." Taking my unfinished clipboard, she scanned it. "Married, huh? So you want a co-cabin with no one else?"

Ren stiffened. "You mean, you offer accommodation, too?"

Lo smiled. "'Course. We're expecting dawn wake-ups and out in the orchard plucking by seven a.m., lot of transient folk don't want to pay for motels seeing as fruit-picking isn't exactly a long-term thing or pays the big bucks." Bending down, she rustled below the desk before pulling up a key with a carved apple keychain. "Cabin six. It's the only double free. Some people don't like it as it's the farthest from the communal showers and kind of on the forest edge. Heard it gives some tender-hearted folk the heebie-jeebies, but me? I love wildlife, and there's nothing to be scared of." Dangling the key, she raised a dark eyebrow. "So, you want it?"

Ren looked at me, and I looked at him.

This was entirely his choice.

I would happily live in the tent farther in the treeline if that was his preference, so he surprised me when he held out his hand and waited until Lo dropped the key. "We'll take it. Happen to like wildlife too, so think it's the perfect fit."

And it was.

For the final weeks of summer, we tackled yet another kind of job, and Ren—who seemed to glow with the dawn—relaxed back into the wild, serious, incredible man I knew and loved.

Together, we'd pluck ripe, plump produce and sneak one or two on our way to the weighing and packing station. By day, we'd work with other staff—some young, some old—and by night, we'd walk the rows between the orchard trees, inhaling the scent of life, lying on our backs in the grass and watching the stars with the songs of cicadas serenading us.

Occasionally, if we stayed out late and crept back through a sleeping, silent farm, Ren would snag my hand and pull me into the massive greenhouse. There, surrounded by strawberries and raspberries and every other berry imaginable, he would push me into the shadows, press me against a wall, and hoist up my skirt to slip inside me.

For a man who loved waking with the sun, his nocturnal activities never failed to steal my heart and make me melt. His kisses were as hot as the greenhouse, his fingers coarse from picking fruit, his harsh breath as sweet as the sugary berries around us.

Together, we'd rock in the dark in perfect harmony, faster

and harder as bodies demanded more, and fingers bruised, and teeth nipped, and hands clamped on mouths to silence our moans.

We were completely untamed and unashamed.

Utterly in tune and bonded.

Even with long hours and early wake-ups, Ren and I smiled often, laughed regularly, and fell into a pattern that only comes from being with someone for so long. We'd always been able to finish each other's sentences, but now, we barely needed to talk.

I knew with just one look if he needed a drink or quick massage to loosen the knot in his back. He knew with just a glance if I needed a kiss in the shade or more sun cream on my skin.

The long days equalled blissful dead-to-the-world sleep. I even grew accustomed to the delightful ache of hard work in my lower back and moaned in gratitude when Ren massaged the cramp in my hands from twisting apples off branches all day.

Our tiny cabin was perfect in its basicness with its whirring mini fridge, lumpy queen bed, and small discoloured sink.

Lo didn't just give us a job; she gave us something incredibly raw and pure, teaching us the ease of working the land and cultivating. Eating straight off the trees, sharing our skills to help each other, working our muscles until sleep was no longer a luxury but a necessity.

Not that Ren wasn't a master of that already with his past, or me, thanks to my chores of helping on a farm in my childhood, but this was something else.

This was Ren and me in Utopia.

It was how humans were supposed to exist.

I could've lived in fruit-picking paradise forever, but unfortunately, our life had a few bumps up ahead.

If I had known what was about to happen, I would've prepared myself.

But that was the thing about life.

You didn't know what to expect until it happened.

# Chapter Thirty-Nine

## REN

## 2020

THE PHONE CALL came on a Sunday.

I knew it was a Sunday—unlike most of my life when I had
idea what day or even month it was—because we'd just been
for our fifth week of fruit picking, and I'd agreed to take
out to a diner down the road to celebrate having some cash
up again. Plus, we hadn't enjoyed our shared birthday yet,
tradition was one we did our best not to break—especially
s no longer a teenager, and I was officially thirty.
old.

me days, I felt it.

'y when I recalled a TV show we'd watched a few
men who claimed their first million before they
show interviewed entrepreneurs and successful
naking me doubt I had what it took to be
what I was.

umber savvy or have any desire to be rich.

'd everything *I* ever needed, didn't mean
ssure on me to find a way to be more.
ash again—not much, but enough to
and travel in the final patches of
ll over again.

d, and we still didn't have a clue
ly thought of finding another
position—something I knew I

was good at and paid fairly well—but I didn't know how to go about finding those.

Of course, those worries became obsolete the moment the phone rang, diverting our journey onto a totally different path.

I had a razor in my right hand and a face cloth in my left, staring into the grainy mirror in our fruit-picking cabin, combating terrible lighting to shave the couple-of-month-old beard that I hadn't trimmed in far too long.

Poor Della earned red lips instantly from kissing me these days, and I was sick of itchy cheeks when I got too hot from working.

Della looked up from where she sprawled on the bed, already to go in a black flower print dress with her gorgeous hair loose and curly.

The phone rang again and again in her hand, all while she continued to stare at it rather than answer.

"You going to get that?" I asked, swishing my blade in the sink, ridding the hair it had already shaved from my throat.

"It's Cassie."

I spun to face her. "Why would she be calling?"

She shrugged. "We messaged last week. She said everything was fine. Just shot the breeze about unimportant stuff." She bit her lip, nerves dancing over her face as if she didn't trust Cassie even now.

The phone seemed to ring louder. "Maybe you better get it."

Swallowing, she shot me a look and pressed accept. "Hello?"

Instantly, her skin eradicated all colour, leaving her white. A hand plastered over her mouth. "Oh, God, Cas. I'm so, so sorry."

Abandoning my razor, I rubbed off the soap from my cheeks and crossed the room to her side. The tinny voice of Cassie drifted from the phone. She was crying, but I couldn't understand what she said.

Della's eyes welled with tears, spilling over and hurting my heart. Clutching her hand, I sat heavily on the mattress as she sniffed and nodded. "Yes, of course. We'll be there." Shaking her head at whatever Cassie had mentioned, she said firmly with a little wobble of tears, "No, not at all. We're family. We want to be there."

Another few seconds ticked past before Della sniffed again and straightened her back. "Okay, let me talk to Ren. I don't know where we are exactly or how long it will take to get back to you. Just…let me talk to him, and I'll let you know, okay?" Her eyes shot to mine, then more tears fell onto our joined fingers. "Okay, sure. Here he is."

With a shaking hand, Della passed me the phone. "She wants to talk to you."

I wanted to ask what had happened, but I had no time as I took the heavy cell and held it to my ear. "Cassie?"

Instantly, her cries became sobs, and the part of me that cared deeply for her sprang into an all-out blaze. "What is it? You okay? What can I do to help?"

I winced, glancing at Della, afraid she'd be jealous or hurt that I'd leap to Cassie's aid if she needed me. It wasn't romantic entanglement; it was purely friendship, and the knowledge that I owed her family not just my life, but Della's, too.

Only, Della just looked at me with adoration and trust, nodding for me to continue.

Cassie swallowed back her sobs, long enough to splutter, "Please come home, Ren. Please."

Before I could assure her that we would do whatever she needed—regardless if I knew why, she told me.

And broke my damn heart.

"It's Mom. She died this morning."

And nothing else mattered.

Not how we'd get there or how long it would take. Standing, I looked for the backpacks, but Della was already ahead of me, flinging open the single wardrobe and shoving our clothes into each bag.

"We're coming, Cassie. We're coming home."

# Chapter Forty

## REN

## 2020

IT TOOK US six days to cross the miles we'd travelled since leaving the Wilsons.

Between paying for bus tickets and hitchhiking, we managed to trade the still sunny skies of whatever small town we'd been picking fruit in for the cooler clouds of the Wilson's territory.

Della and I barely slept, and when we did, it was in a hastily erected tent with a muesli bar for dinner or something just as quick and easy.

Cassie had called twice since we hit the road. First, checking in to see where we were, and second to let us know the funeral had been arranged and we better hurry if we wanted to attend.

We travelled as fast as we could, even though I still felt bad about ditching Lo and her fruit-picking job after she'd helped us out. I'd broken my honour, and I hated that I'd do it all over again because Patricia Wilson had died.

*Gone.*

She was the only mother I knew.

The woman who'd shown me that not all mothers wanted to sell their children.

I couldn't think of her as…dead. It just didn't compute. It hurt too much.

"She's been keeping things from me," Della murmured, her head on my shoulder as the overnight bus trundled us the final distance.

"Hmm?" I opened my eyes. I hadn't been sleeping, but my brain was fuzzy enough not to follow. "Say again?"

"Cassie. I didn't want to pry as I've been keeping things from her, too. But…now I wonder if she was hiding the fact that Patricia was sick along with all the other stuff."

"What stuff?"

She shrugged, jostling me a little in the small, squished together bus seats. "I think she and Chip have had a rocky time. Some messages they're back together, others they're apart again." She sighed, deflating beside me. "I haven't been a good friend to her."

Moving my arm, I looped it over her, forcing her to rearrange before resting her head on me for a pillow. "The fact that you stayed in touch shows you're a better friend than me."

"You wouldn't say that if you knew what I've thought about her over the years."

I chuckled under my breath, halting a cough. "I think I have some idea."

"Believe me. You don't."

"Believe me. I do." My hands curled, reliving the suffocating rage and stomach-clenching helplessness when Della ran to David. "You're forgetting I've been in love with you for a long time, Della. I just kept it hidden. Just because I didn't let on, doesn't mean I wasn't in pain when I saw you with another boy."

"I put you through that just a couple of times." Her voice turned sharp. "Whereas I lived a constant nightmare with you and Cassie."

I flinched.

I'd wondered when this subject would come up.

For years, I'd felt the strain between Della and me back at Cherry River. At the time, I'd been too blind and stupid to understand that the discord between me and my tiny best friend was Della's heart breaking. When she was a little girl, it was broken because she thought she'd lost me by having to share me. And as a young woman, it was broken because she fell for me long before she should feel such things.

Kissing her hair, I cuddled her close. "I'm sorry for hurting you, Little Ribbon."

Her body stiffened in my hold. "You didn't—"

"I did. Countless times. I was just too clueless to see it."

She laughed softly. "I was five and you were fifteen when we first met the Wilsons. We couldn't have been expected to vocalise how we felt when we had no clue ourselves."

"You have a point, but I'm still sor—"

"Don't apologise." She snuggled nearer. "There was no other

path we could've taken. Our ages don't make any difference now, but back then, ten years was an ocean apart."

"It still doesn't change the fact that I hurt you. Then again, I don't fully understand why you were jealous."

"What?" She twisted to look up at me, her eyes a condemning blue. "How could you *not* understand? I was *obscenely* jealous."

"But you should've known there was nothing to be jealous about." I kissed the tip of her nose, braving her temper. "I remember telling you once that you were it for me. No one else ever came close. You've had my heart since you could barely say my name."

"Ugh, and that just makes me feel even more wretched." Her face fell as she tucked herself back against me. "Did you know Cassie once admitted she was in love with you? On a ride together. It was one of the things that pushed me into kissing you that night." She winced, a deeper blush working over her skin. "That was the day of my first period. I didn't have the courage to tell you, but Cassie...she looked after me."

"She loves you, too, Della."

"Not the way she loves you."

It wasn't news that Cassie was in love with me. I'd seen it—admittedly too late, but by the time I did, I hadn't slept with her in a long time. And I hadn't given it any thought because I had Della, and no one else mattered.

But I also understood why this conversation had happened. Della was feeling nervous.

And to be fair, so was I.

Not just because we were about to say goodbye to one of the best women we knew, but because we hadn't addressed the past.

Bracing myself, I asked, "Did you tell her? About us?"

My heart pounded for her answer, which didn't make sense as it wasn't like I wanted to keep our love a secret, but...Cassie wouldn't understand.

"Are you crazy?" Della shuddered. "That sort of information isn't something you announce via text."

"I agree it's something she needs to hear in person."

"I know." She rested her fingertips on my chest. "But it's even harder because her Mom just died. What sort of people would we be if we hurt her even more when she's been hurt enough?"

"Honest people." Staring ahead, I worried just what sort of shit storm we were about to walk into. "You're my only family,

Della, but the Wilsons...they come a close second. We owe them a lot, but don't think for a minute I won't tell her. I won't spare anyone's feelings from the truth."

Even as I gave her that assurance, I couldn't stop the thread of fear.

John Wilson had sent us away for a reason.

That reason being the town had seen Della and me grow up as brother and sister. Did we still run the risk of being separated by Social Services now Della was twenty? Could I still be arrested for keeping her, even though the crime had no doubt been filed with unresolved cases and not on a local cop's radar anymore?

Della's tension slowly crept back, chasing the same thoughts I did. "You said you couldn't go back. Do you think that still stands?"

I wanted to smile and shake my head and tell her not to be so silly. But I couldn't because I honestly didn't know. And not knowing was tantamount to danger.

I coughed and closed my eyes. "We made our choice. We're almost there. Guess we'll face any consequences together."

\* \* \* \* \*

My phone was almost out of battery by the time we crossed the town boundary, and memories bombarded me of the last time we were here. The night of panic as I ran down streets and investigated houses, thanks to Della running away.

The night she'd kissed me for the first time.

The night everything changed.

Della weaved her fingers through mine as our boots crunched on the road and our bags creaked on our backs. "The night I kissed you..." She gave me a sad half-smile in the pink light of a new day. "I felt something, Ren. I didn't quite understand it at the time, but I felt *everything* when I kissed you."

Bringing her hand to my lips, I kissed her quick. "You destroyed me that night."

"Would you have noticed me differently if I hadn't?"

It was a question I'd asked myself before, and even though I would never know for sure—never fully know if I would've continued loving Della the way I was supposed to or if she was always meant to be more—now our lives were entwined, it was hard not to believe all of this wouldn't have come true anyway. Kiss or no kiss.

"I wouldn't have been able to keep my hands off you."

She laughed quietly. "You know, two years ago, you wouldn't

have been able to say that. You would still be hung up on how wrong it was to want me."

"That's true." Looking down the road with only a few more steps separating us from the Wilson's driveway, I murmured, "But life is too short. Patricia just showed us exactly how short."

Della's shoulders rolled in grief. "I can't believe she's gone."

"Me neither."

"Cassie said the funeral is today."

I sighed, rubbing the grit from my eyes and exhaustion from my mind. "It's dawn. We have time to have a quick shower and dress appropriately."

Not that we had anything appropriate to wear. I didn't own anything black that wasn't riddled with holes, and the closest thing Della had to a somber dress was her charcoal-flowered one.

I coughed a little as we traded public road for private driveway. It ought to feel different, stepping back into a place where we'd grown up, but nothing happened.

No bells.

No fanfare.

Just a farm that I knew so well with tractors tucked up in bed and paddocks I'd explored a thousand times before.

The familiar blue and black letterbox proudly stated the Wilsons lived here. A manila envelope wedged in the slot, delivered by a postman who didn't know the tragedy that'd happened inside.

Della let out a heavy sigh as we crunched on gravel and moved toward the barn where we'd lived for so many years. The barn where I'd had my first blowjob, lost my virginity, talked about sex with Della, and every other nonsensical moment in between.

"Ren?" Della tugged on my hand, removing her fingers from mine. "I didn't finish saying what I wanted on the bus, but...I don't think we should tell anyone about us. Not yet."

I scowled. "It doesn't matter if we tell anyone or not. They'll know."

"How will they know?" The farmhouse came into view with its beautiful gardens and flowers that would no longer be tended to by Patricia. "People are used to us being affectionate. Nothing has changed in that regard."

"Oh, they'll know, Della." I rolled my eyes at her naïvety. "The way you look at me, and the way I look at you? That isn't something that can be ignored. It's obvious we're not just brother and sister. And besides, I'm not going to hide that I'm in love with—"

"Oh, my God!" a familiar, husky voice cried as the front door slammed open.

Cassie gawked at us for a second, her hair still the same colour of her bay horse, messy and long. Her figure was trim and toned, encased in cream silk pyjamas.

She was older than before.

Time worn, just like me.

"I can't believe it." Shadows etched her pretty face and grief gnawed her body. "Ren? Della? You're truly here."

Charging from the doorway, she winced and hobbled as her bare feet danced over gravel, then she threw herself at us. "You're both so much bigger than I remember!"

She clutched us in a three-way hug, both Della and I soothing the girl from our past. The girl who'd made our worlds difficult and taught us so much.

"Cas!" Della hugged her back.

My arms wrapped tight, breathing in a foreign smell of a woman I no longer had any feelings for apart from sadness for her mother and gratefulness for her friendship. "I'm so sorry, Cassie."

She squeezed us tight, her body quaking as she fought tears. A few seconds passed before she composed herself enough to pull away and smile fake-bright. "I couldn't sleep. There I was, staring out the window and thought I was dreaming when you guys appeared. At first, I didn't recognise you." She nudged Della. "You've grown so much." Her eyes landed on me with a flash of history and heat. "And, wow, Ren. Age has been kind to you."

I stiffened, but her quick assessment vanished as another tear welled and rolled down her cheek. "I'm so sorry for dragging you back here. I just...I really needed to see you both."

"Don't be sorry." Della shook her head. "We want to be here. We loved Pat so much."

Cassie's bottom lip wobbled. "I know. She was the glue of this family. I don't know how Dad is going to cope." Waving that concern away as if we were strangers to entertain and not family who understood, she looped her arm through Della's. "We have so much to catch up on. Any guys on the scene? What happened to that last one? David, was it?"

Her voice was too jovial and forced, hiding just how much she was hurting. "Wait, where have you come from? You're filthy. You been on vacation during school holidays or something?" She looked us up and down, growing suspicious.

Right there.

This was the moment to tell her.

To admit the truth that Della and I were in love, that I'd gotten her pregnant and almost killed her, that I was seeking a future that was everything she deserved.

Cassie ought to be told point-blank rather than wonder, because it was obvious *something* was going on.

I cleared my throat, cursing as yet another damn cough rattled my lungs. I daren't glance at Della. "We, eh—"

Della cut in. "David and I broke up, and I decided that I'd done enough study for a bit. Taking some time off." She kept her eyes averted as if ashamed to tell Cassie that we were together. Then again, ashamed wasn't the right word. Worried, perhaps? Afraid? "Ren kindly agreed to take me travelling for a while."

*What the hell?*

I could kind of understand omitting the truth, but outright lying?

That would spiral out of control and fast.

"But you love school." Cassie pouted. "And sorry about David."

"I'm not." Della smiled. "He was never the one." Sneaking me a quick look, she focused again on Cassie, but Cassie's attention had fallen on me. The way she studied me said she figured out something was different but couldn't understand what.

Giving me a soft smile, she said, "You look even better than you did the night you left, Ren."

I flicked Della another glance, assessing her level of acceptance and how I should respond. I nodded. "You, too."

Even in her grief, she blushed. "That's kind of you to say. I can't believe it's been so long." Jostling Della's arm, she whistled under her breath, brushing aside whatever tension had sprung up between us. "And you, little lady. You were thirteen when you kissed, um, well, when you guys left. I know you sent me pics, but you're stunning, Della. All grown up." Pecking her on the cheek, Cassie sighed. "Can't believe we're not all kids anymore."

I wasn't opposed to reminiscing, but there was a time and place, and dawn on the driveway, a few hours before Patricia's funeral, was not it.

"Liam home?" I looked at the farmhouse, not seeing any lights on in the bedrooms. "John?" I missed that old farmer. I wanted to offer him my condolences and thank him again for all he'd done for us.

"Dad isn't doing so well. I think he finally had a sleeping tablet last night after the doctor said he'd fall sick if he didn't rest. And Liam, he's okay. He lives in town now with his girlfriend, not here. You'll see him at the funeral."

A fresh wash of tears filled Cassie's eyes, and she smiled brighter. "Anyway, sorry. I'm sure you guys have travelled a long way. I mean, look at you, almost as dirty as the day you first arrived." Laughing at her joke, she let Della go. "Go on. Your room is still made up. Feel free to shower, and I'll bring one of Dad's suits over for you, Ren, and you can borrow one of my dresses, Della. Once we're all dressed, we'll have breakfast, and then…we'll go say goodbye to Mom."

* * * * *

Stepping back into our old one bedroom off the stables filled me with nostalgia and claustrophobia.

Nostalgia for all the precious memories I had of hugging a tiny Della, of telling her stories, of holding her when she was sad.

And claustrophobia for all the feelings I now had on top of those innocent ones. The memories of thrusting inside Della, of her cries as I made her come.

So many ways I knew her, and sometimes, it felt as if I knew too much. That I didn't deserve to know what she looked like as a ten-year-old as well as twenty. That I wasn't meant to hear her childish laughter blend with her adult chuckle.

Crossing the room and shrugging off her backpack onto her old single bed, Della was quiet as she stared at the dresser where we'd kept our things. The ribbon box from her first Christmas present Patricia had given her, and the willow horse I'd carved, still rested together.

A time warp to another era.

This room might've had guests stay in the years since we'd left, but it still smelled of hay dust and summer sunshine of our youth.

"Oh, wow." Della kicked off her boots and padded in her socks to a little shelf by the bathroom door. Picking up a silver photo frame with ducks waddling on the bottom, her voice wavered with tears. "It's us."

My temper wasn't exactly calm, thanks to Della refusing to tell Cassie the truth about us, but curiosity got the better of me, and I headed to where she stroked a time-bleached picture.

Looking over her shoulder, something reached into my chest and squeezed. Something pure and innocent and young.

I didn't remember John or Patricia taking a lot of photos around the farm, and this one had been taken without our knowledge, capturing a moment of utter simplicity that only made it all the more perfect.

"You're so pretty," I breathed, drinking in the sight of young Della with white blonde hair, blue ribbon tangled in whatever breeze had danced in her strands, and the yellow daisy top and skirt she favoured. Knobby knees and white sneakers and the most gorgeous heart-warming smile as she hung on the moss-covered gate, staring at me as if I held her every wish and promise.

And then there was me: lanky and awkward, still a teen with an aura of aloneness beneath the vicious veil of protectiveness for the little girl beside him. I had my hand on Della's shoulder, laughing at something she said, my entire body turned to face her as if I had to be wherever she was to survive.

Hay covered us, pink cheeks, and sweaty heat. Everything about the photo said summer fun without a care in the world but also throbbed with love.

So much fucking love between two kids who not only adored but needed each other past common-sense.

My anger vanished as I wrapped my arms around Della, hugging her back to my front and resting my chin on her head. She smelled of earth and travel and sleepless nights but she was still the girl I'd known for two decades. "I love you as much as I did then. Even more."

Twisting in my arms, she reached up and kissed me.

I expected my usual reaction.

The undeniable desire to give in to her, to grant permission, to take the kiss she gave me and deepen it into something more.

But familiarity gave way to a different kind of reaction.

I couldn't help it.

I reared back just as our lips connected.

And my heart that loved her as a woman threaded with a heart that had once loved her as a child. A heart that knew its boundaries. Knew its boundaries so well, it scrambled behind them and trembled in disgust.

It happened in a split second, but Della froze. She gasped, stumbling back as if I'd slapped her. "Ren…"

"I didn't mean—"

"Don't." Her hands balled. "Nothing has changed. Just because we're back here—"

"I know." Raking fingers through my hair, I coughed around

the sudden tightness in my chest. "It-it just happened. I didn't mean to pull away. I—" I dropped my hand. "I'm sorry, Little Ribbon."

Even her nickname in this place sounded blasphemous for all the knowledge I now had of her. The knowing of every dip and curve of her body—the same body I'd washed and healed.

*Fuck.*

My heart raced as more nausea filled me.

I'd raised her, for God's sake.

I'd lied to every person in this town and told them she was my sister.

Stepping onto the Wilson's estate, I'd been waiting for some sort of homecoming, some sort of nudge of welcome. But I hadn't expected to be bombarded by every emotion I hadn't dealt with before Della kissed me and ran away. Every emotion from a teenage boy struggling to keep his thoughts in check and honour intact.

My boots thudded as I took another step away from her.

And it broke something between us.

I hadn't meant to do it.

Even now, I wanted nothing more than to move toward her, kiss her deep, and assure her that nothing had happened.

But something *had* happened, and I didn't know how to fix it.

Della shook her head as if denying what I'd just done.

I raised my hands, wishing I could ignore the memories, the strict unbreakable laws I'd erected in this place.

But then Cassie's voice sliced through our agony. "Ren? Della?"

I spun to face the door where Cassie stood on the threshold holding an armful of clothes. Her hostess routine and sweet welcome was immediately blackened as she tasted tension on the air, assessing the complications throbbing between me and Della.

"Um…I brought you some clothes." Stepping gingerly into the room, she placed them on the bottom of the bed that had once been mine. The same bed where I'd woken up with my fist in Della's hair and her mouth on mine. The same bed where I'd dreamed of a girl I wanted more than anything, gotten hard thinking about, and never dared admit it was the thirteen-year-old asleep in the dark beside me.

*Shit.*

"Everything okay?" Cassie asked as she made her way back to the door.

If she didn't know something was going on before, she sure as fuck did now.

Sucking in a heavy breath, I growled. "Fine, sorry. Long trip." Marching toward her, I grabbed the door and began to close it. "We'll have a quick shower and be with you soon, okay?"

I shut it before she could reply.

I'd been an asshole to a woman whose mother had just died all because I couldn't control my thoughts from past and present.

By the time I turned to face Della—to try to fix what I'd broken—the bathroom door slammed and the lock clicked into place.

I barely made it to my old bed before my legs gave out, and I collapsed onto it.

# Chapter Forty-One

## REN

## 2020

THE FUNERAL WAS crowded with almost everyone from the small town paying their respects to a well-liked, wonderful woman.

As we stood beside the Wilsons on the church steps while they welcomed people to the service, Della and I stayed stiff and hurting, unsure how to breach the sudden gap that had appeared between us.

I was achingly aware of her.

She was flinchingly aware of me.

Our connection had switched from steadfast to fragile.

I wanted to grab and hold her. I needed to talk to her away from prying ears.

We had no time to clear the air and standing at the entrance to a religious service to say goodbye wasn't the time or place—not because Patricia was the one we ought to be honouring, but because the town insisted on giving us its own welcome.

Person after person smiled and said hello as they trailed into the church.

Exclamations of how big we'd grown, how pretty Della was, how tall I'd become. Along with questions of where we'd been, what we'd been doing, and if we were back for good.

Della's old teacher hugged her, then looked at me with strange curiosity, acting as if she knew why Della kept flicking me nervous glances.

Other so-called friends narrowed their eyes as if they knew a secret, and some girls from Della's grade seemed to find answers to their questions in Della's obvious tension.

I didn't like any of it.

I didn't like being noticed, and I didn't like being judged. And I definitely didn't like being estranged from Della at the worst possible time when we both needed each other.

Once the larger part of the crowd had entered, I inched closer to her, brushing her hand with mine.

Our skin sparked; the electricity between us crackling.

But she stepped out of my reach as one of Cassie's friends who'd offered to hop into my bed with no strings attached smiled at me and pressed a fake kiss to my cheek before heading inside.

Out here, away from our old room where so many memories clung to the curtains and the photo that immortalised two children who didn't know any better no longer condemned, I was clear-headed and disgusted with the way I'd acted.

I needed Della to understand I hadn't meant to pull away, and things were still exactly the same as before. Not letting me touch her made me almost suicidal with the need to drag her away from nosy townsfolk and demand she talk to me, to accept my apology.

But then the service started, and it no longer felt right to be hurting over a relationship I still had when the relationship I'd shared with Patricia was gone forever.

The Wilsons, Della, and I headed somberly into the church.

Halfway down the aisle, Della tripped on the carpet runner, stumbling in Cassie's borrowed heels.

I caught her.

The touch was purely instinctual to protect her from falling— cupping her elbow, lashing my arm around her, pulling her close.

I steadied her, fighting the urge to kiss her, all while standing in the aisle surrounded by busybodies.

Had I just revealed I was more than just an overly attentive brother? Would people know we were more?

My worries were answered as knowing eyes brushed over us, making my heart fist and lungs burn.

Of course, people noticed.

We weren't strangers here.

And our arrival back into their midst wasn't unseen.

John was right that people wouldn't understand, and Della was right to keep our relationship hidden.

Giving me a grimace, Della pulled away, and I coughed as if nothing had happened.

More eyes followed us as we continued to the front and the

pew reserved for close family. My back prickled as people stared at us. It was nobody's business, and I wanted to growl for them to stop, but I swallowed my temper, pushed the wariness from my mind, and focused on Patricia.

She deserved to be focused on.

Nothing else.

Sitting down, I kept my hands to myself and didn't reach for Della's as we listened to the priest give his spiel then, one by one, the Wilsons got up to speak.

Liam—no longer a silly boy who'd gotten naked with Della under the willow tree—delivered a speech of love and thanks that brought tears to everyone's eyes. Adam—the oldest son we hadn't met but was the reason for John's charity toward us—painted a picture of a mother he adored. Cassie—dressed in black and shaking with sadness—did her best not to cry through her delivery, and John...

The big, gruff farmer who took us in and gave us shelter. The larger than life, generous man who'd become my only father figure, managed two sentences before breaking into a sob.

It fucking hurt to see a grown man who seemed utterly invincible shatter into pieces before the coffin of his dead wife.

I never wanted to live through that torture.

I never wanted to bury Della and live alone, just waiting for the day I could join her.

Tears danced over my own vision, not for Patricia's loss but for John's pain at being left behind. I was selfish to be almost grateful that, thanks to the ten-year-age difference between Della and me, I would logically be the one to go first.

I'd spent my entire life protecting Della from sadness and agony, only to admit in this matter, I couldn't protect her.

I'd be a wreck, just like John.

Dressed in a too-big black shirt of his and too-short borrowed black slacks, my fists clenched as John held up his hands in surrender, shrugged an apology at the gathered crowd, then stumbled off the podium and crashed from the church.

Della flinched as the doors slammed closed, leaving everyone a little shell-shocked and slightly afraid.

The priest stood, saying the final words while Della chipped at the ice between us and touched my hand. Just a flutter, but it made me inhale as if she'd just given me air after a day of suffocating.

She wore a borrowed dress from Cassie—a black one piece

that hugged her every curve, making her seem older, wiser, sadder. "You should go to him."

I bent my head so I could whisper in her ear, "I don't want to step on Liam's and Adam's toes." They were his true sons, after all. However, looking where they sat next to Cassie, neither of them could console their father; the Wilson children were wrapped up in their own sad world of losing their mother.

John was on his own.

My heart hurt even more.

"You're right." Inhaling her scent of vanilla and caramel—recognising a shampoo she used to use as a child that was most likely still in the bathroom, restocked by Cassie or Patricia, I slipped from the pew as a hymn started. "You'll be okay?"

She smiled softly, her standoffish behaviour gone. "I'll be fine. You'll find me after?"

"Of course. We need to talk."

"I know."

Holding her blue eyes for as long as I could, I stepped from the church and winced as the heavy doors cut me off from her.

The day was overcast and grey, matching the melancholy mood.

Striding forward in my weathered boots that didn't match the black dress code, the top of my sock glinted with my well-used knife. Searching the graveyard with stone and cherub headstones, it didn't take long to find John on a bench beneath a tree with white flowers, his head in his hands and large frame quaking.

Was it right to intrude when he was obviously suffering? Would I make it better or worse?

Before I could make up my mind, John looked up, his red-rimmed eyes heavily lined and wrinkles more pronounced than before. His hair was whiter, his body not as fit, but the quick flash of power and authority he'd always had made him sit up straighter and clear his throat. "Ren."

We'd seen each other this morning after Della and I had finished getting dressed in borrowed clothes and joined the Wilsons in their kitchen. We'd all shared an awkward reunion over toast and jam with strong coffee. Conversation hadn't exactly been flowing, and apart from a clasped arm and bear hug, John hadn't talked to us.

I'd understood his silence.

His grief was a physical thing, throttling his voice and heart.

But now, his face lit up, focusing on me and not on his dead wife—grateful for a reprieve. "Sit with me, my boy." He snapped his fingers. "Sorry, not boy." Wiping away the moisture on his cheeks, he chuckled softly. "Della would kill me for calling you that. She was rather adamant your name was Ren."

I matched his chuckle, hiding a cough. "You're right. It was a pet peeve of hers. Probably because I told her over and over again that my name was Ren and never to use anything else."

I didn't think I'd told him much of my sale to the Mclary's, but sitting beside him, I offered up a piece of myself. "Her parents didn't care what my name was. As a baby, she would've heard them call me boy. I guess something deep-seated like that can have strange consequences."

John nodded, his eyes clearer, happy to focus on other things. "Sounds like that might be the case."

We sat in silence for a bit. Apologises and kind words danced on my tongue, but nothing felt right. I didn't want to hurt him deeper by saying the wrong thing. So I said nothing at all, hoping he knew how sorry I was in our shared silence.

Finally, he sighed heavily. "You lost, didn't you?"

"Excuse me?" Glancing at him, I raised an eyebrow. "Lost what?"

"The battle on keeping her as your sister."

Heat flushed my skin as I dropped my gaze to the ground. "Ah."

"Yes, ah." Reclining, he rubbed his mouth with his hairy hand and shook his head gently. "How long have you two, eh…"

"Two years."

"Are you happy?"

I looked at the sky with an almost wistful exhale. "I was until this morning." Looking at him, I shared my idiotic fears. "I screwed up a little. I guess being back here has tangled my thoughts somewhat."

"Understandable."

"I hate it. I hate this feeling of distance. I-I'm so afraid of losing her. I love her so much, but no matter how much I want to, I can't protect her from everything. One day I'll lo—" I cut myself off, horror drowning me. "Fuck, John. I'm sorry. I didn't mean. *Shit*—"

"It's okay." He patted my shoulder. "I get it. I feel the same way about Patty." He buckled as if someone had shot him. "*Felt*. I *felt* the same way about Patty." He swallowed a few times, getting his grief under control. "I loved that woman, and I know the fear you're living with because I've felt it myself. I think everyone feels it when they love something so much."

I slouched, cupping my hands between my legs. "How are you coping now the worst has happened?" It was a terrible thing to ask, but I had to know. I had to understand how broken I would be if Della ever left me. Either by choice or death.

John took his time, staring at the headstones in front of us. "I'm still alive, against my better wishes, but I have a family relying on me. I can't give up because I owe Patty to keep going. You can't fear the end, Ren. Not when you have so much to look forward to."

His words hovered between us.

I should've continued to let them hover. Instead, I blurted, "Della got pregnant. Ectopic. She got sick. It showed me just how much I've been avoiding the future, and that I can't anymore."

"I'm sorry." His gruff voice calmed me somehow. "You know, I never liked seeing Patricia pregnant. I know some men say it's the best thing they'll ever experience—seeing their wives fat with their unborn child, but not me." Shaking his head, his tone thickened. "I never relaxed until she'd given birth and was back at home happy, and bossy, and just as full of life as normal. Only then did I let myself focus on my new child."

I'd forgotten how easy it was to talk to John.

Forgotten how nice it was to have someone to confide in when I wrapped myself up in knots. Even on a day like today.

"Thank you." I nodded, coughing again. "That helps. Especially when I keep thinking I'm the worst man alive for hating the thought of Della getting pregnant, only to crave a family with her one day."

John smiled sadly. "You're not the worst. If you're anything like you were before, you're the opposite of worst." Slipping back into a reclined position, he asked, "So, I'm guessing your last name...you've kept it? Do you introduce her as your wife instead of your sister?"

My heart skipped. "Look, we can talk about this another time. I-I don't feel right. Today should be about—"

"Pat would want to know how you two are doing. Same as me. My grief isn't going anywhere, Ren. Believe me. It's nice to have a reprieve." He cocked his chin. "Go on. Fill me in."

I sighed again, amazed that in a few minutes of conversation, John had successfully brought up all my greatest fears and somehow given me freedom to discuss them. "Well, I put her through high-school. I watched her date assholes who didn't deserve her. I hurt her by sleeping with women, all while doing my best to fight what I felt for her—"

"And when did you know what that was?" His bushy eyebrow rose.

I cleared my throat, unable to look him in the eye. "The night she ran away."

"Yeah, I thought as much."

"That was why you said not to come back, isn't it?" I rubbed the back of my neck, unable to delete my tension. "You knew people wouldn't be able to accept that we'd lied after we went so far to make it the truth."

"I sent you away because you both needed to figure out who you were away from people who thought they knew for you." He looked at the rain-threatening sky. "I fell for Pat when I was young. Fifteen, to be exact. I knew I wanted to marry her the second she smiled at me, but it took almost a decade to convince her father I wasn't just trying to get her into bed."

I laughed under my breath, smothering yet another cough. "Seems you won."

"I did." He smiled smugly. "I was married to my soulmate for forty-eight years. And I didn't take a single year for granted."

I kicked at a pebble, wanting so fucking much to have what he had. "I want to marry Della. And I'm going to somehow. But no one knows who we are. We don't exist. We have no birth certificates or passports. How can we get married without that stuff?"

John flicked me a glance. "That will make it tricky."

"But...not impossible?" I hated that my heart beat quicker, tasting hope.

"Nothing is impossible." Giving me a watery smile, John patted my knee with his heavy paw. "I'm happy for you, Ren. I always knew you kids loved each other, and I'm not above admitting I was worried once or twice when I believed you were true relations. I'm glad you chose to fight for her and not go your separate ways." Tears glistened again. "True love is a blessing and so damn hard to find."

Placing my hand on his, I shared his grief. "Patricia loved you, too. You guys were a perfect example of a happy marriage when I didn't have any role models. She helped me and Della so much."

"That's nice of you to say." Letting me go, he stood with a weary sigh. "I suppose we better get to the wake, and then...you should probably tell my daughter that you and Della are no longer just siblings before she figures it out like I did."

Standing, I coughed harder than I had in a while. My eyes watered as I cupped my mouth, waiting for it to pass.

"You okay?" John asked, worried.

I smiled, shoving the episode away. "Yeah, sorry. Damn cough just keeps lingering."

"You were sick?"

"A while ago. Need some good ole' home cooked meals to get my immune system back in working order."

John's face fell. "Well the cook of the family has gone, so you'll be stuck with chargrilled things on the barbeque from me, I'm afraid."

I winced. "God, I'm sorry—"

"Don't. I know. Let's just keep talking about other things." He waved his hand as we slipped back into a walk. "So, when are you going to tell Cassie?"

"Della thinks we should wait."

"Wait?" He shook his head. "No, waiting doesn't work in this world, Ren. She'll be shocked, I'll admit, and maybe a little hurt, but she's in a good place now. Her and Chip are giving their relationship another chance, and little Nina will be coming in a few days. You can meet her. She's adorable. Patty loved that little tyke."

Following him through the graveyard, I asked, "Nina?"

"Cassie's daughter." He raised another eyebrow. "Her and Chip share custody right now while they figure things out. She's six, almost seven."

I froze, my inability to do fast math once again my downfall.

How long had Della and I been gone?

When was the last time I'd been with Cassie?

John must've understood the sudden whiteness on my face as he held up his hands. "She's not yours, Ren."

To go from shock to relief so quickly made my knees liquid. "Oh."

"I will confess, I did ask her. She got pregnant not long after you guys left. But she said you two hadn't been together in a while. That you'd pulled away from that part of the friendship, and had always used, eh, protection."

"Protection doesn't always seem to stop such things," I muttered, thinking of Della's complications.

"That's true but rest assured, Nina isn't yours. Even if Cassie didn't do a paternity test, you can see for yourself she's Chip's, purely thanks to the flaming red hair of her father."

Clasping an arm around my shoulders, he guided me into the church as if he were the one consoling me and not the other way around.

I let him be the patriarch—the role he played so well, for a little longer, but once we got to the wake, I stayed close by, monitoring his drinking, doing my best to change the subjects when his face grew blotchy and tears streamed silently down his face as he hung in the shadows.

He might have his own children, but if he let me, I would be there for him as much as they were.

We hadn't discussed if we should stay or go or what the Wilsons expected, but by the time nightfall smothered the farm and the wake was over with a fridge full of casseroles and leftovers, Della and I cut across the driveway, pushed our single beds together, undressed without speaking, and reached for each other.

We were too emotionally exhausted to talk.

Too physically drained to do anything more than hug.

We returned to an age of innocence, where skin on skin contact was purely for comfort and nothing else.

We fell asleep in our old room, entangled and entwined.

Just as before.

# *Chapter Forty-Two*

## DELLA

## 2032

DEATH IS NEVER *easy.*

*And it wasn't any easier just because we hadn't seen Patricia in a while or that we weren't truly her children. Patricia had been a large part of our lives, and Cherry River didn't feel the same without her.*

*Being back in that place…I wish I could warn myself.*

*Wish I could whisper what was about to happen.*

*It's so obvious from where I sit in the future, but of course, with the complications between me and Ren, the residual childhood jealousy toward Cassie, and the overwhelming aura of grief on the farm, all of us were preoccupied with other things.*

*Things like accepting John's invitation to stay and for Ren to resume his role running the fields.*

*We had no place else to be and no rush to leave and really, Ren had been searching for an answer to our future, and found a temporary one by brushing off his skills to work the land.*

*That first afternoon when he cleaned the rusty tractor from its cobweb jacket, greased ancient gears and cranks, and kicked her into a growling, diesel-coughing start, my heart fluttered with so many memories of him. So many memories of so many different Rens. Child Rens, teenage Rens, early twenties Rens, right to the thirty-year-old man I adored.*

*For a week, we spent our days alone, toiling in paddocks and debating what to do with grass long past its prime. Ren's frustration grew thanks to the lack of care since we'd been gone, and his determination to take on the workload now that John could no longer handle it burned with need.*

*He announced war on nature, pulling up weeds that hadn't been there before, liming entire meadows and harrowing others.*

For seven days, we didn't discuss what had happened when we'd first arrived at Cherry River, nor touched more than a sweet hug to go to sleep. There was always either someone too close or something more pressing to deal with.

Somehow, my request to keep our relationship hidden had backfired, and without thinking, walls were built and timelines crossed, so there was nothing to hide, after all.

No kisses to secret. No sex to avoid.

Cassie's suspicions faded as more days passed, and Ren and I acted no different than we had when we were thirteen and twenty-three.

Plus...I was worried.

God, I was so worried.

Ren's coughing hadn't stopped.

And I didn't know what to do.

I did my best not to hover or freeze when a small cough sounded and was almost glad of something else to think about when Cassie shared her own pain, revealing how Patricia had died of a sudden stroke.

No warning.

No signs.

Just woke up one morning, made breakfast as usual, and by the afternoon, she was gone.

She also confided in me about Chip and her daughter, Nina.

To say it was a shock hearing she had a daughter was an understatement.

I was angry she hadn't told me.

Hurt that after years of messaging, she'd kept her a secret.

But then again, I had no right to be jilted. I'd done the same to her.

I hadn't told her about me and Ren. I'd kept us a secret, too.

I'd spent my childhood knowing she was in love with him, just like I was.

I'd spent countless nights in tears while she touched him, just like I wanted. And, although we were all adults now and I knew Ren was mine, that sort of fear was deep-seated and nonsensical even as age made me wiser.

So, you can see why I asked Ren to keep our relationship hidden. Yes, I didn't want to hurt Cassie at her mother's funeral, but I also needed time to figure out how to apologise for thinking the worst of her all those years apart.

To admit that I was weak enough to be threatened by her.

She was the only one who truly understood what it was like to love Ren and not have him, and we would always share that in common.

But keeping the truth quiet was never going to work.

And on the seventh night, we were caught.

In more ways than one.

# Chapter Forty-Three

## DELLA

## 2020

I'D BEEN DRINKING.

Not a lot, but a couple of glasses of wine with Cassie had made my fears over Ren amplify until I sat on the pushed together single beds in our bedroom to wait for him.

Seething.

Stewing.

Spiralling into terror that the reason he hadn't touched me in a week was that he remembered what he had with Cassie. He remembered me as a little girl. He remembered too much to be with me.

Time had strange properties here. It had taken the seven years when Ren and I had lived alone and folded it so the two ends touched, forming a bridge from past to now and blurring everything in between.

I'd grown up a lot in the two years since Ren had claimed me. I'd grown to like myself more and stand up for the things I believed in. I'd blossomed into someone worthy of him, and I hated, positively *hated* that confident Della now bowed to a less confident one.

That my fears over his coughing made me mad at him.

That my concerns over his blasé attitude made me rage.

I knew what was happening.

My anger was founded entirely in terror, but it didn't make ignoring it any easier.

I'd started the week off blaming Cassie for my doubt, but sitting in the dark waiting for Ren, my heart showed the truth.

I loved Ren with every fibre of my being. There was no part

of me that would survive if anything ever happened to him. My entire life he'd been everlasting and indestructible.

And to have that faith punctured every time he coughed…to have panic fill me, drop by drop, until I was close to overflowing…it made my hands ball and heart quake and an almost manic desperation to have him touch me, hold me, convince me that my mind was running away with me and everything was fine.

I'd tried voicing my fears before, but Ren didn't tolerate my mother hen routine and he'd just kiss me, smile, and brush me off as if it were me with the problem.

However, this morning I'd woken with a new resilience and spent the day working beside him, holding oil cans and rags as he maintained the tractor's decrepit engine, helping thread the twine through the baler when it snapped on the overly thick grass, and generally proving to him that I wasn't a child he needed to be afraid of or a kid who couldn't handle life.

As always, we'd fallen into a comfortable pattern working together, and by evening we were so tired it didn't take much convincing for Cassie to get us to dinner.

The dining room looked the same as all the other times with one key thing missing.

Patricia's place setting and presence.

It was a wound that still bled, and conversation stuck safely on subjects of the farm.

Adam had returned to his wife and two children, and Liam had stayed in town with his girlfriend. So it was just the four of us, and John kept looking at where Patricia would sit, and Cassie kept looking at her father.

Once our meal was finished, I stood with renewed purpose, ready to tackle my concerns with Ren, but John asked for Ren's opinion on a new grass seed, and Cassie dragged me to her room where I learned yet more about her on and off again relationship with Chip the accountant.

From proposals to pregnancies to births and break-ups, I saw how much she cared for him and how glad she was they were giving it another chance.

The entire time she spoke, all I could think about was Ren. How he'd never once let me down, even when things weren't perfect between us. How he'd always put me first, even when we'd had nothing to our names.

And how, here in a place that meant so much to both of us,

everything that we'd created had been threatened, all because the past dared mingle with our present, making me wonder and worry.

And so, I'd had a third glass of wine before bolting from the farmhouse and cutting across the driveway—the same driveway I'd run across so many times before—and paced our bedroom, needing to end whatever distance was between us.

I *missed* him.

I missed him more than I could stand.

For twenty minutes, I'd paced before resorting to sitting on the beds.

I'd been waiting for an hour.

Waiting for a way to stop feeling so lost and alone and cast aside.

The door opened fifteen minutes later, swinging wide as Ren prowled in with a hand buried in his hair as if already stressed about sleeping in a room with me.

"You're back."

My voice wrenched his eyes up, squinting in the dark. I hadn't bothered to turn on a light as dusk steadily became night. I knew I seemed creepy, sitting cross-legged, hands tightly linked in my lap, my heart terrified and temper fuming, but I couldn't help it.

I'd reached my limit and we needed to talk.

"Della, what the hell are you doing?" Ren flicked on the overhead light, shutting the door behind him. "Why are you sitting in the dark?"

"I've been waiting for you."

"Okay." He frowned. "I'm here."

"You are." Unravelling my legs, I hopped off the bed and moved toward him. "A week ago, you refused to kiss me. Since then, you've barely touched me. I feel like you're avoiding discussing—"

"I haven't been avoiding anything." He straightened. "And I *have* touched you. We fall asleep touching every night. Plus, you know why we haven't talked—there just hasn't been the right time."

"Now is the right time."

He sighed. "Look, you're tired, I'm tired. Let's wait until morning so we don't say things we might regre—" A cough interrupted him.

My heart grew hot with dismay. "See? There you go again. Avoiding this. What are you so afraid of?"

"I'm not afraid of anything." His nostrils flared. "I think

you've wound yourself up and should calm down before—"

"Don't tell me what to do. I'm not a child anymore, Ren. You can't command me and expect me to obey." Storming toward him, I stood on my tiptoes and slammed my lips to his.

I wanted to fight.

The frightened part of me needed it.

His mouth yielded to mine for just a second before he pulled back…just like before.

My heart cracked.

"Della. Stop." He had the audacity to raise his hand and wipe his mouth as if what I'd done wasn't permitted. As if the past two years of countless sex, endless kisses, and numerous I love you's had never happened.

For a second, I wanted to run.

Another second, I wanted to hit him.

And then, in a final second, I nodded, accepted my hurt, and prepared to fight for what was mine.

"I won't let you do this." Stepping into him, I grasped his belt, tugging quickly at the leather. "I miss you, Ren. I want you. I'm worried about you and feel like you're not—"

"Della…" He tripped backward as I worked on unbuckling him, crossing the small room until his back smashed against the door, and I trapped him. "*Della*—"

I didn't stop until I unthreaded the leather and yanked the buckle free, discarding both ends the instant they were undone. "Don't 'Della' me. You know what you're doing, and it isn't fair." My fingers attacked his button then reached for his zipper in record time.

"What *I'm* doing?" His large, warm hand landed on mine, stopping my progress, gripping me hard. "How about what *you're* doing?"

"I thought that was obvious."

"You're upset." His fingers twitched around my wrist, his eyes shouting their love but his body rigid with refusal. "I get it. I know it's my fault, but whatever you're doing isn't the way to fix—"

"Please." I bit my lip, stemming sudden tears. "Please prove to me that nothing has changed when it's all I can worry about. Please let me make love to the only man I've ever wanted. Please convince me that this fear inside—this fear that is slowly growing—is completely crazy and irrational. I need to know you're okay. I need to know *we're* okay. I need—" I stopped as a cry spilled from my lips, revealing just how knotted I was over this.

Over our distance.

Over childhood fear that he didn't want me anymore.

Over adult terror that life wasn't infinite like fairy-tales but a war for every moment.

"Fuck." He let me go only to wrap me in his strong embrace. "Nothing has changed, Little Ribbon. I promise."

"Prove it." I stayed stiff in his arms. "Sleep with me."

A tormented chuckle bubbled in his chest. "I'm not taking advantage of you when you're like this. We should talk. Why didn't you tell me you were so worried?" The softness of his worn, blue sweater was warm, the thud of his heart familiar. My body responded to what it had always considered safe, and my spine relaxed even as I fought to stay angry.

"You know I love you. How many times have I told you that? Nothing can drive us apart, Della. I know I hurt you with my knee-jerk reaction when we first arrived, but nothing has changed."

He ducked and kissed me sweetly, tasting my tears. "See? I love you. I'm *in* love with you. Everything is fine."

I blinked, lips tingling and heart smarting. "Kiss me again."

"Not tonight."

"Why?"

"Because you're worked up over something I don't understand. I'm sorry about before, I truly am. But anything else you're worried about is completely ridiculous, and I won't be pushed into sleeping with you. Not when you're like—"

"My fears aren't ridiculous, Ren."

"I didn't mean they were."

"Is it ridiculous that I love you so much I can barely breathe at the thought of losing you?"

"What?" Temper lashed through his voice. "Why the hell would you lose me?"

"I don't know. You tell me."

"Is this about Cassie?" His eyes blackened. "Don't you trust me?" His question was soft but lethal, daring me to give light to my terrors when, up until a few days ago, I trusted him with my life.

I sighed, defeated and fully aware I was at fault. "Of course, I trust you."

"So, you're not driving yourself insane thinking I'm going to leave you for Cassie?"

I flinched. "I won't deny it was hard at first, but I know what we have supersedes all that."

"Then…" His head tilted, hair caressing his forehead. "What is this really about?"

"It's about us." I shrugged helplessly. "It's about me needing you and…and I don't like this distance between us." I looked down. "I was wrong to keep our relationship a secret. The longer we don't tell people, the more I worry it's even real."

His finger tipped my chin up. "It's real, Della. More real than anything in the world."

"I needed to hear that." I half-smiled.

He tucked a curl behind my ear. "You're forgetting *you're* the one who wanted to hide. I wanted to tell everyone the truth."

"I was wrong." Reaching for him, I brushed my mouth on his. "Please…take me to bed. Let's just forget I made a mess of this."

I chickened out.

I'd picked this fight to address that annoying little cough.

I'd stewed in stress so I would have the guts to order him to see a doctor.

But, somehow, none of that mattered anymore.

I just wanted him.

Inside me.

Around me.

With me.

Our lips touched before he shook his head with a soft groan. "I can't sleep with you in this room, Little Ribbon."

My eyes snapped wide. "Why?"

"There are too many memories here."

My heart fluttered, tasting progress. "So? Memories are just memories."

"Memories have a way of driving me insane." His tongue wet his lips, his gaze drawn to my mouth. His voice denied me, but his body reacted. "So many memories of so many things between us."

"But don't you see?" My hand landed on his chest, sliding down until I pressed my palm against his erection. "That's why we need to make new ones."

He hissed between his teeth. "Stop."

My bravery at addressing so many things had flown out the window, but I wouldn't let him deny me. Not in this. Not when we desperately needed to connect.

"I want you, Ren." Sinking to my knees, I tugged his jeans

and boxers down in one smooth glide. They bunched around his knees as his cock bounced free.

I didn't hesitate.

I licked him, inserting him into my mouth.

"Fucking hell." His hand fisted in my hair, holding me tight as he crippled under my control. "Della." His belly clenched as he rolled over me, hugging my head as I licked and sucked, doing my best to shatter him.

For a second, I thought I'd won.

He sucked in a wobbly breath, his body swelling in my mouth.

But then that damn side of him that protected me at all costs resurfaced and, with a savage growl, he pushed me away. "Della...no." He staggered sideways, tripping to the centre of the bedroom, doing his best to hoist up and rearrange his jeans. "Are you trying to kill me, woman?"

His anger and denial hurt, but not the same as before.

I kind of understood now.

I sort of finally saw.

This wasn't about me at all.

This was about this room.

*This place.*

I thought I'd had it hard here.

That lying in bed jealous and petty was painful.

But really...I hadn't.

Yes, Ren had always been forbidden, but at least, he hadn't been a mortal sin.

Me...on the other hand.

If Ren had felt the *slightest* tug toward me—a tug that overstepped even the smallest of margins...then I could understand why this room wasn't just a room.

Because I hadn't just been a girl he wanted; I had been a child.

A child who meant more to him than anything else in the world.

A living, breathing nightmare.

This room had become his judge and executioner, its very walls, furniture, and windows condemning him for every dream he might have had, for every fanciful wish, for every fleeting thought.

*God, I'm sorry.*

Pushing off my knees, I let go of my anger. I drowned in apology. I moved toward him as gently and as carefully as I could because he was spooked and hurting, and I'd been the one to do it.

"You truly did love me, didn't you?" I whispered.

His gorgeous coffee eyes widened, his chest rising and falling. "Of course, I love you."

"That wasn't what I said." Pressing my fingers to his heart, I hated that he flinched. That his sun-bronzed hair shivered as he stayed tight and wound as if he'd bolt at any moment. "You loved me more than you should, even before I kissed you."

His face contorted. "I-I loved you as a brother."

"No, you loved me as something more." Tears trickled down my face at the truth—the exquisite, agonising truth. I wrapped my arms around his waist, not caring he still had his jeans bunched in one hand, hiding his decency. "I'm sorry, Ren."

He rippled with stress, not hugging me back. "Della, I—"

Those two words were an arrow, shooting from the bow of his mouth, ricocheting around the room until they punctured us through the heart.

In their simplicity, they admitted everything.

His head came down and his lips sought mine with a level of devotion and need that transcended time and logic. His arms banded around me, fierce and possessive. And the ice in his muscles cracked, melted, and cascaded away in a waterfall of released tension.

"I didn't realise until we'd left." Burying his face in my hair, his entire body quaked as if this was his true confession. "I didn't know. You have to believe me. I was a kid. You were mine. There was no other future I could think of that you weren't there beside me."

"It's okay." I stroked his back, being the rock he'd always been for me.

How had I not seen it? It wasn't me or my kiss that made him realise there was something more.

There had *always* been something more.

Our love hadn't honoured boundaries fashioned by age or circumstance. Our love had thrown us together and told us the truth way too early.

It had laughed in our face and said, *This is the person you will adore forever. This is the person designed, crafted, and perfected for you. But you can't touch them. Not yet. Not for decades. Not until you're worthy of the gift I've given you.*

Time, it seemed, had a nasty sense of humour.

Time had hurt Ren far worse than it had me.

"Being back here makes me wonder if I ever overstepped," Ren murmured. "It makes me second-guess *everything*. Every time I touched you, what was I thinking? Every time I kissed you, what did it mean? Every time I saw you naked, was I averting my eyes like I thought, or was I watching you when I shouldn't?"

He exhaled with a ragged groan. "I don't know anymore. I don't know if I did right by you, or if all along I was some perverted—"

"Stop."

He sucked in a breath, his chest heaving as if he'd run miles.

"Trust me when I say this, Ren Wild, you were and are the most honourable man I've ever known. I understand how you could second-guess. I know how time can play tricks and make you remember different things. But I need you to listen now because not *once* did you make me feel awkward around you. Your touches were strictly brotherly. Your kisses perfectly pure. I grew up so safe and happy because I knew you adored me. I knew we were special. I knew we had something that no one else could ever steal or share. So please, Ren. Please don't let the past damage what we have or make you fear you did anything wrong. Because you didn't. Not a single moment was wrong. Not a single—"

He kissed me.

He clutched me close and kissed me deep, shutting me up, telling me he trusted me, assuring me he was okay.

I crumpled in his arms, submitting entirely to his hot mouth and skilful tongue.

His fingers slid into my hair, cradling me as he bowed over me, tucking me into him, doing his best to join us together in all the right ways.

On and on, we kissed.

Heads dancing.

Tongues licking.

Hearts racing.

Ren had always been a masterful kisser, but something was different about this one. Something new and honest and true.

He held nothing back.

He tasted me and let me taste him.

He commanded possession and let me possess in return.

And the entire time we kissed, I didn't tell him what else I remembered.

How, when he was eighteen, I knew he dreamed of someone he wanted because he'd cry out in his sleep, waking me to see his young face straining with want and misery.

How, when he was nineteen, I knew he pleasured himself in the dark once our beds were separated and we could no longer touch, and I'd hear his soft groan as he came—the same groan I now recognised as a woman.

Ren had kept everything he was going through a secret from me, but it didn't mean I wasn't aware.

He was a boy.

He was human.

He was perfect.

My lips tingled from his as I reached for his undone waistband.

He shook his head, rubbing our lips together. "No—"

"Yes."

His heart pounded harder as I pushed the material down. His face drained of colour as I broke our kiss and looked between us. There, on the bare flesh of his hipbone, with his boxers and jeans pushed low enough to reveal the splattering of hair but not enough to reveal his cock, was his brand.

The same brand I'd kissed before, licked before, pressed my cheek to and cursed my parents for what they'd done to him, all while thanking them because, in a way, they'd bought him for me.

Time had used them, too.

Time had ensured they brought us together.

The oval brand with its *Mc97* glinted cruelly in the light. Running my fingertip over the scar tissue, I whispered, "This room is nothing more than a room. The only thing that means anything is you and me." My fingers drifted to the dark warmth of his underwear, ducking down and fisting his hard length. "You *can* touch me, Ren. You *can* kiss me. There's nothing stopping us. I *want* you to touch me. I need it…and I think you need it, too."

He shuddered again, his breath short and fast, eyes wild and black. "You're pushing me too far, Della Ribbon. I don't know how much longer I can keep saying no."

"Good because I want you to say yes."

"But it's not right."

"It is."

"I can't stop thinking, ah—"

I squeezed him, making his head tip back, revealing a long, powerful throat with its five o'clock shadow and Adam's apple bobbing as he swallowed. With his eyes closed, he strangled, "But I nursed you when you had chicken pox in that very bed. I sat in that chair as you learned about sex, and I hid just how much I didn't know. I watched you sleep when you were still a kid. I had dreams that—"

"None of that matters now." Pushing firmly, I backed him toward the single bed that used to be his. The one with black sheets and no colour. The one I'd curled into, when he wasn't looking, to smell his pillow.

He tripped backward, his jeans slipping to half-thigh. Landing on his ass, he snapped out of whatever trance I'd put him in and shook his head. "No." Standing up again, he begged, "Let's go rent a room somewhere. Or pitch the tent. Somewhere it's just us. I want you, Della. And you're right, I need you. But...this place is too much."

"Please, Ren." Colliding with him, I dug my fingers into his hair and wrenched his mouth back down to mine. "Please." I kept my fingers lashed in the soft copper strands, piercing my tongue into his mouth.

And finally...he snapped.

His hands clamped on my ass, hoisting me up with impressive strength and encouraging my legs to wrap around his hips.

The moment I latched on, he moved until he slammed me against the wall. My spine bruised as he wedged me tight, rocking into me, his lips harsh and dominating as the kiss I'd given him turned into one of crushing need from him.

His hands trailed upward, squeezing my breasts before cupping my cheeks and holding me steady.

And then he kissed me.

Truly, deeply, *deliciously* kissed me.

His mouth opened wide, his tongue dancing with mine, our heads shifting and breaths hitching as he consumed my every thought.

"You just had to push, didn't you?" He nipped my lip, biting and licking his way down my jaw to my throat. There, he sank sharp incisors into my flesh, making me cry out and claw at his shoulders. "Had to make me do this. Had to make me accept."

My hands fell to his hips while he continued to rock into me, making me wet, ensuring my entire body throbbed for his.

Luckily, I wore a skirt. My one and only skirt with a grey sweater with silver thread.

His touch found my thighs again, swatting the material away, hooking his fingers into the cotton between my legs. "I can't stop. I doubt I'll ever be able to stop."

I expected him to put me down and wait until I'd removed my underwear, but I'd pushed him too far, and he merely yanked the fabric aside and drove two fingers deep, deep inside me.

"See, Della?" He withdrew and plunged inside me again. "This is what happens when you push me." He wasn't gentle. He wasn't kind. He was ruthless and merciless and I *loved* it.

His hand cupped me as his fingers pulsed, dragging heat from everywhere. "Is this what you want? Tell me this is what you want. Tell me this is okay. Goddammit, Della, tell me you need me as much as I need you because I'm going out of my goddamn mind."

I convulsed as he rocked his fingers so deep, a sliver of pain cut through me. Pain that only made my pleasure all that more intense. "Yes. God, yes."

"This is what you pushed me for? This is what you've broken me for?"

"*Yes!*"

His touch rocked up, pulsating in the perfect way he knew I loved. I moaned as my body responded with tingling, tangling bliss.

"You've always driven me wild." He kissed me again, his tongue lashing and cruel. "Always been too bold." His kiss turned deeper still, making me breathe him, ensuring my body wasn't just made up of my cells, but his too. A synergy of bodies. A blending of him and me and past and present and the lovely, lovely knowledge that whatever distance had been between us was no more. "Always been too much for me. So much braver than me."

"No," I cried out as he thrust his cock against my leg in time to the fierce drive of his fingers. "You've always been braver. I understand now how hard it would've been—"

"Hard?" His teeth found my neck again, biting, licking, consuming. A small cough nudged my fear. "Hard is nothing compared to how hard I am now. How fucking hard I am for you."

I had no reply, only a boneless sigh and a desperation that had a will of its own.

A desperation I'd always had.

A desperation that had always wanted Ren in any way it could have him.

This had always been our future.

There was no way we could fight an attraction like this. No way of denying a connection like this.

This was destiny.

---

Pure and simple.

Dragging my hips closer to his, Ren broke the kiss and stared down. His lips were red, skin flushed, hair a mess. He looked savage. Clothes were wrong on him when he seemed so primitive and free.

In a flash, I saw him naked in rippled resplendent glory, standing in his chosen home—the forest where we'd shared our childhood. With the trees we called friends, and the river we called parent, behind him.

That was where Ren belonged.

That was where a man so much more than human should be.

With fingers inside me, he cupped my cheek with his free hand, trembling even now, but this time with lust so vicious it tore pieces off our hearts.

We stared at each other.

Him and me.

Us.

And he said, "I told you I loved you, Della."

"I know."

"I told you I always have."

"I know."

Withdrawing his fingers, he grabbed his cock and lined up with my body. "Are you happy knowing I can't deny you? Are you pleased with yourself that I have you pinned against the wall and can't stop? Are you happy that after this, I'll never know if I loved you the way I should have? That I'll forever wonder? Forever think of fucking you here, in this room, and no longer care about any of it?"

"Yes. So many times yes."

"Good."

I smirked. "Fine."

He thrust, filling me with one quick impale. "This is what you make me become." He didn't wait for me to adjust, just rocked deeper again and again. "This is the power you've always had over me ever since I woke up and saw my soulmate and not just my friend."

My fingers clawed at him.

I gasped as he sought my lips and kissed me as ferociously as he took me against the wall. "This is what I was hiding from you as well as myself." He thrust. "This." He drove deeper. "Fuck." He roared as he tried to climb inside me. "This. It has *always* been this. Always been you." His forehead crashed on mine as his rhythm lost any melody. "Fuck, it's always been you, Della."

Tears sprang with the heartbreak in which he admitted such a thing.

Love melted my soul with the shock in his eyes that he'd finally seen.

"Ribbon…" His gaze glittered as he blinked in disbelief. Disbelief that it had taken him two years of being together to finally snap and admit to himself.

"I-I don't care anymore." He smiled with sharp teeth and sharper joy. "I don't care what people think. I don't care if they judge. I." *Thrust.* "Don't." *Thrust.* *"Care."*

"Finally." I laughed as he suckled my neck, driving into me again and again. His lips were poisonous and his tongue venomous, slowly killing me as I scratched him, marked him, begging him to treat me worse.

And he did.

We raged and fucked and claimed.

A battle.

A war.

Love at its rawest.

And it was right.

*Unbelievably* right.

Threading my fingers in his hair, I moaned, "It's always been you, Ren. It will *always* be you." My oath triggered the rest of his undoing, and whatever gates he kept locked blew wide apart.

"You're mine." He growled.

"I know."

"And I'm yours."

"I know."

"Fuck." His breathing turned to heavy grunts, a cough rattling just once as he rode me faster, climbing higher, driving and demanding.

Our kisses were messy and out of control.

Our hands heavy and greedy to touch.

His lips bruised mine, injecting need and desire into my blood until I shivered uncontrollably.

His body hardened inside me until he groaned in pleasure-pain.

He thrust faster.

On and on, affirmation after affirmation, love after love.

And when he pressed his fingers to my clit and rubbed in perfect rhythm to his thrusts, I was no longer fighting but sprinting toward the promise only he could give.

My body spun and spindled and shattered outward, rippling around his invasion, making tears prickle my eyes.

The second my orgasm finished, Ren buried his face in my hair, swallowed a howl, and drove so hard, so deep, I was sure we'd end up in the stables beyond.

"I can't stop. I'm-I'm..." His rumbling, hungry groan tore from his throat as his body quaked in mine. He went taut, dangerous. Then his body pulsed over and over, hot splashes marking me as his, finding his release as quickly as I'd found mine.

For a long moment, neither of us moved.

Our hearts clanged like church bells.

Our limbs throbbed like pounding drums.

And then a softness replaced the madness, and Ren scattered feather kisses all over my face as we clung to each other, coming down from our addictive high.

He coughed quietly, making yet more tears swell in my eyes.

Sweet, fuzzy feelings battled with scared, timid things, and I wanted to hug him close and fight every hour, every year and stay right there, together.

Accepting another kiss, I whispered, "Ren...will you do something for me?"

He smiled, dazed and satisfied. "Anything."

"I want you to see a doc—"

But a knock sounded on the door.

The unlocked door.

And it opened.

And Cassie walked in.

And she saw.

Everything.

# Chapter Forty-Four

## REN

## 2020

*"SHIT."* My hand flew up as if I could stop her mid-step. "Cassie. Out!"

She froze, drinking in the sight of me with my jeans around my thighs, Della sex-mauled and panting in my arms, and our semi-naked bodies joined in a way that needed no explanation.

"Holy shit." Cassie clamped a hand over her mouth, spinning around. "What the—"

With her back turned, I winced as I disengaged from Della. Stepping back, I dropped her gently to the floor. Once she was steady, I hoisted up my jeans and tucked my still hard flesh into my jeans.

The sound of my zipper and clink of my buckle sent my cheeks blazing, made worse by Della rearranging her underwear and smoothing down her skirt.

Clothes might cover us, but they didn't stop the raging heartbeats, tangled hair, or swollen lips of what we'd just been doing.

Of all the fucking times.

Of all the fucking places.

I felt as if I'd been skinned alive and every organ left on display. I felt butchered and broken and bruised, and it was all Della's fault. But I also felt awed and amazed and absolutely stupefied that I hadn't known what fears lurked inside my heart.

That I'd avoided coming to terms with what we'd done for two years, and it'd taken a stupid bedroom full of our youth to make me snap.

I hated that she'd pushed me.

But I loved her for it too, because I felt lighter than I had…in, well, *ever*.

I was centred and calm, and I didn't want a fight with Cassie messing up that special connection that had sprung between Della and me. I wanted to bask in it. I wanted to forget about everyone else for a while and just love her. I needed to reassure her that I was fine and the fear she'd been nursing was completely unfounded.

Dragging shaking hands through my hair, I did my best to put myself back together.

Giving me a guilty look, Della checked me over, found I was marginally suitable for company, then said softly, "You can turn around, Cassie."

Cassie peered over her shoulder warily, eyes narrowed. For a second, she stared at us, hurt and hating. Then she spun around, her mouth falling wide with shock. A few squeaks came out before she cleared her throat and snapped, "I mean…I suspected *something* was going on but…to actually know it's true?" She crossed her arms tight. "I-I don't know what to say."

I didn't want anything to do with this.

I was sorry she'd seen us together, but that was her fault for walking in unannounced.

I was sorry she had to face the truth that I was with Della, but it wasn't like I was hers. We were kids when we hooked up. It meant nothing.

I cleared my throat, hiding yet another cough. "Cassie, I think you better go— "

"Wait." Della held up her hand. "There isn't anything *to* say." She glanced at me before finishing, "We're together. It's that simple. I'm sorry I didn't tell you, Cas."

Cassie's eyes narrowed, flitting to me, then back to Della, then back to me. Her anger only increased. "You're *together*? Well, that just makes it all fine and dandy, doesn't it?" She rolled her eyes. "Don't you think it's a little…I dunno? *Disgusting* to do something like that in your old room? A room where you told me and my family you were brother and sister?"

"That's in the past." Della's face hardened, prepared to take on Cassie in a way that worried me. "It's none of your business what we do or don't do in whatever place we choose."

"It kinda is, seeing as this is my home!"

"It was ours, too!" Della shouted back.

"Yeah, and you were kids!"

"And now we're not, so get over it!"

Cassie sniffed. "It still doesn't make it right."

"I don't care. I'm not looking for your approval." Della crossed her arms. "This has nothing to do with you."

Cassie faced me, her temper zeroing in on me instead. "You promised me when I saw you guys that night in the stable that you hadn't kissed her before. That you'd never touched her. You stood before my parents and assured us all that there was nothing going on."

I wanted to leave. The walls were too close. The door too far. But this wasn't just Della's fight. It was mine too, and I'd always known we'd have to face it, sooner or later.

Standing taller, I wished I could shed the scent of sex from my skin. "I told the truth. Nothing was going on." I winced. "Then."

Cassie pursed her lips, eyes full of storms. "How long?"

Dangerous, dangerous question.

"Two years," I muttered.

"Two *years?*" Cassie's face blanched. "Della..." She looked at her as if her heart was broken.

Della's own heartbreak painted her features as she shrugged helplessly. "I-I couldn't tell you. I'm sorry."

Cassie put up a hand, blocking Della from view as she locked eyes on me. "You expect me to believe you've only been fucking her for two years? You guys suddenly vanished into the night. Who's to say you didn't do what I just witnessed the *minute* you were away from here? Who's to say you weren't fucking—"

"Don't you *dare* accuse me of something I haven't done." My jaw clenched with disgust. "What sort of person do you think I am?"

"One who was obviously lying to himself."

"If you think that low of me, then leave!" I pointed at the door. "Like Della said, this has nothing to do with—"

"He didn't touch me until I was eighteen." Della leapt to my defence, standing in front of me like a shield. "He left me, actually. For six months, he put distance between us, but it only showed we'd been running from the truth and couldn't anymore."

Cassie cocked her chin, not giving an inch. "The truth about what?"

"The truth that I was in love with her, and she was in love with me." I growled. "We didn't plan it. Believe me, I tried to fight it. But…she's mine. So, are we done here?"

Silence fell.

Tempers cooled a little, only for Cassie to turn her attention back on Della and fire up all over again. "It still doesn't change the fact that you didn't tell me."

"Well, we're telling you now." I did my best to keep my patience. "We're together and engaged and—"

"Wait. *What?*" Her skin whitened. "Oh, my God. You're *engaged?*" Cassie shook her head. "And you didn't think I deserved to know? You didn't think my friendship valued a heads up? You didn't think our past, Ren, gave me some sort of right to know?"

"Our past meant nothing. We fooled around, that's all."

Cassie pressed a fist to her heart. "Wow, Ren. Just wow."

Regret swamped me. "Look, I'm sorry, okay? I just meant, Della was always—"

"Yours." Her eyes glossed. "I get it. Can't say I'm even surprised. There was always something more between you two. Sleeping in the same bed? Joined at the hip all the time? It wasn't normal." She rolled her eyes. "Dad told me to let it go, that you'd both had a rough start to life, and it was understandable that you'd found family in each other and overcompensated…but I always had my suspicions."

"You never said anything." Della frowned.

"I didn't know how. I tried to joke about it a couple of times, but Dad overheard me and told me to give you a break. He said who cared if you loved each other so much that it was a little creepy? I should be happy you had each other." She laughed. "But you have to understand, I have two brothers, so I know what siblings are like and, I'm sorry, but you two? You were never siblings."

I froze.

All along, I'd believed my lie was ironclad and impenetrable.

Turned out, the only person believing it was me.

Everyone else was just waiting for us to wake up, grow up, and admit it.

"Fucking hell." I coughed.

She hugged herself tighter, giving me a helpless shrug. "It's done now. Secret's out."

"I can explain." Della stepped forward, her fingers twirling the cheap gemstone ring I'd bought her. The ring that promised a marriage, a life, a forever.

It was a testament to how distraught Cassie had been at her

mother's funeral and how grief-blind she'd been this past week that she hadn't noticed Della's tattoo, her ring, or my bracelet with its missing diamantes.

We hadn't taken them off—not that a tattoo *could* be taken off.

They screamed the truth even when Della didn't want to voice it.

Cassie's eyes tracked her, narrowing at the glint of fake sapphire. "When are you getting married?"

"We can't. Not yet," I said.

Before Cassie could ask any more questions, Della jumped in. "I know we hurt you, and I wanted to tell you...so many times. I just didn't know how without coming across as cruel or vindictive or proud."

Cassie softened a little. "I knew how you felt about him, Della."

"I know."

"Walking in and seeing you guys together is worse than being told point-blank."

"I know that, too." Della's shoulders fell. "We didn't plan it. It just...happened."

"Well, I'm never coming in here unannounced again." She gave a wry smile laced with hurt. "God, the images...I can't get them out of my head."

"I'm sorry," Della said softly. "Truly."

Cassie looked at the ceiling before shaking away her anger. "I just have one more thing to say and then I'll let it go."

"What?" Della asked.

"You didn't tell me the biggest thing in your life—when we'd all practically grown up together—but you acted miffed that I didn't tell you about my daughter. Kinda hypocritical and it made me feel terrible. I get that you're together—I even accept it and saw it coming, but I'm hurt that you hid it."

Della balled her hands. "I agree. It was my fault. Ren wanted to tell you, but I...I was nervous."

"Nervous. About me? Why?"

Della looked away.

"Ah, I get it." Cassie laughed sadly. "You thought I'd try to steal him from you, is that it?"

Della flinched, twirling her ring again as if it could invoke a spell and fix this mess. She looked as if she didn't trust that promise on her finger. The proposal I'd made. The conviction that one day I *would* marry her.

I stepped forward, taking the heat off Della. "I'm the one who's made a mess of this. Not her."

Cassie chuckled softly. "Same ole' Ren, taking the blame when it isn't his fault." She gave me a smile that wasn't cruel or sarcastic but honest and hurting. "You didn't make a mess of this; *we* did."

Moving toward Della, she stood before her awkwardly. "I guess I owe you an apology, too. I know what I was like in my youth, and I'm not proud of some of the choices I made. I hate that those choices made it seem like I would take Ren away from you."

I scowled, pissed off that they spoke as if I were some possession to be passed around. As if I had no say in the matter.

Della nodded slowly, looking younger but sterner and far more regal. "You don't owe me anything, Cas. So many times I wanted to tell you the truth. I'm sorry for not trusting you like I should have."

Cassie sighed. "I just wish I'd known sooner."

"I wish I'd told you sooner." Della gave her a tentative smile. "So...you're okay with this?"

Cassie nodded. "Of course. It's not like it's even a shock. We're family and I love you both."

Della wrapped her arms around Cassie, hugging her hard. "Thank you."

They clung to each other for the longest moment before Cassie pulled away. "I grew up the moment they put my daughter in my arms, and that's why I can honestly say I'm happy for you guys. I'm overjoyed that you figured it out and are together but...not everyone is."

"Wh-what do you mean?" Della threw me a worried look.

"I mean...I didn't come here to catch you guys doing, um—" She waved her hand. "I came to tell you something, and I've already taken too long." Casting a look over her shoulder, her entire body stiffened. "You don't have a lot of time."

My system leapt into high alert, adrenaline flooding me as she glanced at the open door again. "What do you mean?"

"I mean...Liam just called. He's doing work experience with the local police to see if he wants to join."

"Why is that a problem?" I clipped, doing my best not to let my mind run away with nasty conclusions.

"It isn't." Cassie rubbed her arm. "He'll do great at it. But it is a problem when he calls me in a panic because he overheard a conversation mentioning you."

"Mentioning Ren?" Della asked sharply. "What did they say?"

Pacing in front of us, Cassie twisted her loose hair into a rope until it draped over her shoulder. "God, I don't know how to fix this. Having you guys back has meant the world to Dad. He can grieve without worrying about the farm. And I know he wants you to stay on indefinitely. But...I don't know how that's going to happen."

"Why?" Striding toward her, I grabbed her shoulders and spun her to face me. "Spit it out, Cassie. What's going on?"

"They're on their way over here."

"Who?" I growled. "*Who* is on their way?"

"The police."

My insides turned to ice as Cassie gave me a terrified look. "The town's been talking, Ren. They know something's going on. There's been rumours for years about how fast you disappeared and theories about why."

Letting Cassie go, I stormed toward Della, staying close to her side, sensing a threat but unsure how to protect her from it. "Theories are pointless. Besides, it's none of their goddamn business."

"I agree, it's not. But Liam, bless his heart, overheard what you told Mom and Dad that night. He was hiding on the stairs."

*"What?"*

She winced. "He knew you'd been bought, and the people who kept you were called Mclary. He heard Della was theirs and how you ran away with her."

I tripped backward. "Oh, fuck."

"Oh, no." Della turned white.

"Goddammit!" Raking a hand through my hair, I glowered. "I only told John and Patricia, so I could prove she wasn't my sister—not for that information to become public knowledge!"

"I know. And he feels sick about it, but he was a kid, Ren." Cassie's face etched with apology. "All he heard was a story about cattle brands and fingers being cut off and you saying the police were probably after you for kidnapping Della. It was too juicy *not* to tell his friends."

"Shit." I hung my head. "I should never have said anything."

"But Ren never kidnapped me," Della said, strained and stressed. "He didn't know. And anyway, my parents weren't exactly the best people in the world. He did me a favour taking me from them."

"I know that." Cassie nodded. "And Liam knows he screwed up. I've yelled at him—many times. Only, the gossip he shared when he was in school has circulated enough for it to reach the ears of parents and teachers, and now…well; now you're back in town, and I guess it got them talking again."

Squeezing the back of my neck, I paced the small room. At the time, when I'd stood before Patricia and John and given them enough information to ruin my life, I'd been fully prepared to be waltzed out of there in handcuffs.

Back then, I didn't care as I would've sacrificed my freedom to ensure Della could stay with them.

But now…now, I had too much to lose.

My eyes met Della's. "We need to leave. Right now."

Della didn't speak, just nodded and immediately turned to the backpacks we'd unpacked by the dresser.

Cassie stood by the door, watching as we prepared to pack up any hope of staying here for winter.

John was right when he sent us away.

We shouldn't have come.

"You-you can't leave. Not again," Cassie murmured. "Dad needs you, Ren. We all want you to stay."

"We can't." I grabbed a bag from Della and wrenched open a drawer where we'd stuffed our clothes, fighting a cough. "I won't lose her. Not now. I didn't do anything wrong—"

"Stop."

Everything inside me slammed into a brick wall.

My head shot up, eyes locking onto the two shadows behind Cassie. They morphed from the stable gloom, two uniformed officers who I recognised from selling a couple of hay bales to on and off over the years.

Della froze, dropping her bag. "Wait. No."

"Sorry, ma'am." The older of the two with a greying moustache stepped closer, scanned all three of us, then said, "Ren Wild, you're under arrest for the kidnapping of Della Mclary and you're coming with us."

# Chapter Forty-Five

## REN

## 2020

I'D BEEN TRAPPED before.

It was so long ago now that time had healed me from a lot of it, but sitting in a brightly lit room with a locked door, two-way mirror, and handcuffs that had been removed from my wrists glinting silver on the table, shot me straight back to a different type of captivity.

Here, I wasn't expected to work until I passed out or eat scraps before the pigs could get them, but I *was* expected to give them something.

Something I didn't know how.

The door opened, depositing a visitor into my tiny prison. The officer with his greying moustache and skinny frame sighed wearily as if working through the night was about as fun for him as it was for me.

He scuttled into the spare chair on the opposite side of the table.

The manila folder in his hands slapped against the table, and he gave me an exasperated smile.

I didn't buy it, but I did buy his exhaustion and the fact that he was old, tired, and wasn't out for a witch hunt…just doing his job as an upholder of the law and protecting his town's citizens.

"So…" He cleared his throat and splayed his hands flat on the table on either side of the folder. "I know we asked you before, but you have to give us something."

I leaned back in the chair, stiff and slightly chilled from sitting there for so long. My lungs ached and the slight rattle in my chest pissed me off. "I'm not evading your questions. If I knew the answers, I would give them."

He frowned. "So, you still don't know where the Mclary's farm is? You don't know your mother's name? You can't prove anything of what you told me? That you were bought for labour and ran away when you were ten?"

"I have no evidence. I don't even know my real last name. All I know is I didn't cut my finger off—Willem Mclary did. I didn't brand my hip—Willem Mclary did. The only crime I'm agreeing to is I *did* take their daughter, but not by choice. I was a kid running for his life. The *last* thing I wanted was a baby."

I chuckled, remembering the juvenile hate I'd had for her when I'd first found her in my bag. "She'd squashed all my rations and drained me of all my strength. If I wasn't so sure they'd have killed me, I would've gone back and dropped her off."

"But you didn't."

"I didn't."

He tapped the table with a fingernail. "But that was nineteen years ago. You could've dropped her off at any other point. To any police station in any town."

"I tried."

He sat up taller. "Ah, yes. In the town you didn't know with a family you can't name."

"That's right."

"You left her for a couple of days?"

"Yes. Like I told you, I only went back because I saw her on TV. Some news reporter said she'd be put in foster care if no one claimed her. I might've hated her back then, but she didn't deserve to be lost."

My heart pinched a little with memories. Of her blistering joy when I'd gone back. Of my profound connection knowing I would never leave her again. That I would do anything it took to give her the life she deserved. That I was in love with her as deeply and as truly as anyone could love another—regardless of age.

Silence fell as the cop stared at me. His name was Martin Murray and he was a good man. Honest and hardworking and I wasn't afraid of him. I wasn't afraid of being coerced into confessing something I didn't do. I was only afraid of the repercussions that I legitimately deserved for taking something that wasn't mine.

I wasn't trying to deny that fact.

I was merely trying to make them see that I'd never hurt

Della. I'd done everything I could to raise her right. And just had to hope that that offered some leniency for my crime. And I also had to hope that Della forgave me if I ended up in jail and left her on her own.

At least she had the Wilsons again.

At least she was safe.

*Is she thinking about me?*

What sort of panic was she going through since I'd been marched from our bedroom and stuffed into the police cruiser?

I coughed, missing her so damn much.

Finally, Martin Murray laughed with a thread of frustration. "You know, I've seen you grow up. Not that often, but I walked the beat when you were busy picking up Cassie Wilson so she didn't drive home drunk. Wherever you were, Della was by your side. It was stranger seeing you two apart rather than together. I know you treated her well. And I know in your mind, it wasn't kidnapping. I'm not trying to throw you in jail, Mr. Wild. I'm only trying to solve this case."

"You know my name is Ren. Use it."

He nodded once. "You have to understand how difficult you're making this investigation."

"Not my intention." Sitting still, I waited for the next question—yet another thing I couldn't answer. But he sighed again and opened the file. "I have something to show you."

"Okay..." I shifted forward, leaning closer. My eyes locked on the typed front page of whatever document he had. A bunch of numbers decorated the top, along with the words *unsolved* and a date and then a name.

Della's name.

*Missing Case of Della Donna Mclary.*

She had a middle name.

I never knew.

My mouth went dry as he flicked over the page and slipped out a glossy photo of the place that haunted my nightmares. "Is this their farm?"

Words vanished down my throat, leaving me mute.

I nodded around a harsh cough.

The same dilapidated farmhouse with its rotten veranda and haphazard shutters. The same barn in the distance where I'd slept with other stinky, starving kids. The machinery and tractors and animal feed all scattered uncared for in the muddy yards.

I hadn't forgotten anything about it.

Not a single thing.

Not the sweat on my back or the pain in my muscles or the fever in my blood.

Not the soul-crushing feeling of abandonment and abuse.

Martin held up another image. "This them? Willem and Marion Mclary?"

Again, I hadn't forgotten a single thing.

From the dirty dungarees Willem wore to the faded sundress his wife preferred. Everything was grimy and unloved and held an aura of perpetual greed.

I nodded again.

"And this?" His third photo showed Della.

A rosy cheeked baby who didn't belong. A baby with inquisitive blue eyes and a ribbon twisted around her chubby fist. All she wore was a diaper and a food splattered purple bib.

She sat in her highchair in the same kitchen where I'd scurried like a cockroach and stolen crumbs from the floor when they weren't looking.

My voice returned, its volume restored thanks to the baby who taught me how to read and write. "That's her. Della Mclary."

"Why do you call each other Wild now?"

"Because she chose that for us to share."

"But it's not a legitimate name?"

"No."

His forehead furrowed. "How have you gone this long in life using a fake name with no documentation?"

I shrugged. "Luck?"

He chuckled. "I think you make your own luck, Ren."

"I make my own way, if that's what you mean."

We made eye contact and smiled.

I'd found an unlikely friend in this cop. This cop trying to persecute me for a nineteen-year-old unsolved crime.

Pulling a wad of papers out, Martin skimmed the text before giving me some information, for a change. "Della was reported missing by her father. When the local police went to their farm to write up the report, they made a note of lack of sanitation and signs of other inhabitants in the barn. You said that's where you slept with the others?"

"Yes."

"Why didn't the police see them when they went over?"

"There was a bunker." I flicked through the rolodex of things from that time. "Mclary was a doomsdayer. Had a bunker full of food and supplies. He'd stuff us all down there if he got whiff of a visitor coming." I laughed, not that it was a laughing matter. "It was a monthly occurrence, thanks to the pastor having a drink or two with Willem. He donated to the church, you see…keeping up his image."

"And how many children were there with you?" Martin picked up a pen, holding it above a blank piece of paper.

"Not sure." I frowned, doing my best to count when, back then, I didn't know how numbers worked. "Ten. Fifteen, perhaps?"

"And all boys?"

"No. Not all boys." My black look gave him all he needed to know. "The girls were Mclary's favourite."

Martin whitened, scribbling something down. "And you don't know where they went after they were burned out on the farm?"

"A few were killed, I know that much. And a man in a black suit came and took others away. Another sale. Another transaction. Don't know what happened after that."

The cop, whose entire career was probably based on writing up DUIs and sorting out domestic disputes, put down his pen and rubbed his eyes. Those sort of images weren't the kind you could rub away.

Slowly, he sifted through the file again and pulled out another document. "What I'm about to tell you may or may not have power over what your future holds, but after your arrest, we did our best to track down the Mclary's. To tell them the good news that we've found their missing daughter."

I kept my emotions hidden about that.

I would kill them all before they took Della away from me.

"They're dead. Both of them."

I jerked in my chair. "How long?"

Turned out…I didn't need to kill anyone.

"Six years."

"How?"

"Marion Mclary shot Willem point-blank with a shotgun, then turned it on herself."

My mouth fell open. "What?"

"Murder and suicide." Martin shrugged. "The case was open and shut. Their estate was placed into the hands of the bank that'd been threatening foreclosure for years, but it never sold."

"What does that mean?"

"It means the farm is untouched, and we might find evidence

of what you're saying."

"And if you do?"

"Then there is no crime as far as I'm concerned."

"Are you authorised to make that call?"

Martin stood. "This is my town, and you're my citizen. I've known you since you were a teen, and John has been ringing my phone every ten minutes, demanding you be released. He vouches for you. We can't hold you for longer than twenty-four hours without evidence, and hopefully whatever evidence we do find absolves any wrongdoing, and this will just be a minor inconvenience."

I looked up at him, towering like a praying mantis. "So...now what?"

"Now, you and me are taking a little road trip. And hopefully, when we come back, all this mess will be sorted out, once and for all."

# *Chapter Forty-Six*

## DELLA

## 2031

*INCIDENT NUMBER ONE.*
*The first of the five I warned you about.*
*Ren's arrest for my supposed kidnapping.*

I don't need to explain the level of panic I faced as the police took him away. How I sprinted after the cruiser, hammering on the window until I couldn't run fast enough. How I collapsed on the road with my knees bitten by gravel, and my tears tearing air from my lungs. How Cassie picked me up and dragged me into the house and how John got on the phone and made an absolute nuisance of himself demanding information on Ren.

It was the longest night of my life.

Three times, I tried to steal John's Land Rover keys and drive to where they'd taken Ren. And three times, John had taken them from me with a stern look and sterner wisdom that attacking a police officer and making threats wasn't the way to end this smoothly.

By the time dawn arrived, everyone was exhausted and still in yesterday's clothes waiting for news—any news.

And then, the phone call came that Ren was being taken out of town for a while, and I well and truly lost it.

I grabbed the phone from John and threw curse words down the line to whomever was unlucky enough to listen. I threatened and pleaded and cried, only for the stoic voice of authority to say it was a matter that needed to be concluded, and this was the fastest way.

I was hung up on.

I should've breathed deep and centred myself.

I should've allowed John to talk sense into me and calm down enough to understand that they couldn't really separate us.

---

*Could they?*

*I didn't know if they could. I didn't know how the law worked, or what they could charge him with, or how long they'd keep him from me.*

*All I knew was I'd lived the worst time of my life when Ren left me, and I couldn't do it again. I couldn't sit by and let them do this to us. I couldn't let them take his freedom.*

*So, I bolted across the driveway to the disarray of our room and dumped out Ren's backpack onto his bed.*

*The last thing to fall out was my manuscript, wrapped in plastic and bound with string, protected at all costs.*

*It was my only piece of evidence that Ren hadn't taken me maliciously or held me against my will. My only way of proving this was all a massive misunderstanding.*

*I despised my parents for what they did to him. As far as I was concerned, they were dead and always would be. They were despicable human beings, and Ren was a freaking saint in comparison.*

*I expected a fight when I slung on some clean clothes, tied my hair with my ribbon, and flew back across the drive. I anticipated having to run to the police station with no car to make my journey swifter.*

*But I shouldn't have doubted.*

*Cassie and John stood by the ancient Land Rover, keys jingling in anxious hands, a look of going to battle on their faces.*

*I didn't burst into tears again, but I did hug them fiercely and climbed into the back seat where Cassie kept flicking glances at my manuscript but didn't dare ask what it was.*

*And when we arrived at the police station, we were almost too late.*

*Ren had been given a clean black t-shirt and black coat that came to his thighs. With his scruffy jeans and weathered boots, he looked like a surly detective about to go study a corpse. He strode from the station with an officer beside him, face unreadable and hands balled.*

*"Della."*

*His look of shock unravelled me, and tears spilled down my face. All I wanted to do was leap into his arms and offer up anything to trade his life for mine. But I did the only thing I could.*

*Ignoring him, I locked my attention on the grey-haired officer beside him and ran at full speed with my manuscript in outstretched hands as if it held all the answers.*

*"He didn't kidnap me. He was a minor. He didn't know any better. Please—" Shoving the heavy paper into the policeman's arms, I demanded. "Read it. It has everything you need to know. The only way I can prove I was happy with Ren. Happier than I'd ever be with parents who bought and sold children for their own gain. Please, you have to believe me. Release him."*

Ren pulled me to the side. He wasn't wearing handcuffs, and his fingers were soft on my cheek. "It's okay, Della. I agreed to go with them. It's all right."

"What do you mean?"

"I mean…something has come to light, and this might be the fastest way to clear this up."

John stepped forward. "Wherever you're taking Ren, we're all coming."

The officer shook his head. "Sorry. It's over an eight-hour drive. Mr. Wild has agreed to accompany us, but no others."

Ren lashed an arm around me, kissing my temple as he turned to face the policeman. "Bring her."

"What?"

"Please," Ren said. "She has a right to see it."

"See what?" Cassie asked.

The officer ignored her, staring at Ren. "I don't think that would be wise."

Ren pointed at the manuscript weighing heavily in the cop's hands. "That is our tale. That is our truth. Della is my truth. And she deserves to know."

I couldn't stop shaking, cuddling into his side. My future hung in the balance, and the officer looked at John as a friend rather than a law enforcer. "I can't take you all. There isn't enough room."

John's chest puffed up. "We'll drive ourselves."

"No." Ren shook his head. "This is something Della and I need to do on our own."

"Do what?" Cassie asked, finally earning the attention of everyone.

The officer shot a look at Ren then me, before he admitted, "The Mclary's are dead. Their estate is still untouched, and Mr. Wild has agreed to help us with this investigation."

Dead?

I shuddered harder.

Parents who gave me life.

Parents I hated more than anything.

Gone.

"She's coming." Ren straightened. "Or I'm not."

How were they dead?

How long had they been dead?

All this time they'd been a dark, devilish stain chasing us across the country.

Before I could ask what any of this meant, the officer slowly nodded. "Okay. She comes."

Marching toward the cop car with my words in his hands, and the second *officer who'd arrested Ren last night sitting patiently behind the wheel, he added, "Let's go. We have a long drive ahead of us."*

*\* \* \* \* \**

*I can't explain the feeling of being chauffeured in the back of a police car for eight hours.*

*Every traffic light we stopped at, people peered inside, sneering at us, believing we were criminals. Every bathroom break and snack grab were met with leery stares and confused looks as to why we weren't handcuffed.*

*Six hours into the trip, we found a diner on a lonely stretch of road and shared an awkward dinner. As we ate our meals, the waitress couldn't take her eyes off Ren as if he were some infamous outlaw that only made him all the more attractive.*

*I don't want to mention how jealous that made me. How petty I was, even then, to be angry with women for finding Ren as handsome as I did. Little did they know I still had his kisses on my mouth and his orgasm inside me.*

*Those were my secrets, and I clung to the knowledge...doing my best not to fear what we were driving to, and what would happen when we got there.*

*Martin Murray, who introduced himself as we pulled away from the police station, was quiet in manner and talk, leaving his fellow officer, Steve Hopkins, to fill in the gaps.*

*Not that there were any gaps to fill as no one was in the mood for conversation.*

*Ren and I shared a few lingering looks, a few whispered sentences, but silence had infected us, too, our thoughts already in the past—the past we were driving across country to.*

*When we finally arrived in some quiet country town with a bedraggled Main Street, sparse unloved houses, and a church with a wonky cross, Officer Murray drove straight to the small satellite office of the local law enforcement, and together, we all sat down with Bob Colton and Remy Jones—two more officers who were the first to the scene of my parents' death—and chatted about tomorrow's adventures on no sleep, lots of coffee, and a long journey.*

*Bob Colton had already collected the keys for the Mclary farmstead from the bank who were looking at possibly demolishing the house and sub-dividing the land—seeing as no one was interested in buying such a big place that needed so much work.*

*Then again, we were there to enlighten everyone on what truly happened at that farm. And it would be yet another reason it wouldn't sell.*

*On the drive over, Martin had filled me in on what he'd told Ren.*

*About what my mother did to my father.*

*About the empty house where two corpses had lain rotting for weeks before someone reported the stench.*

*About how, when the forensic team combed the house for clues on why my mother had murdered my father, they hadn't found a single shred of missing children, malicious abuse, or a barn full of bought employees.*

*That worried Ren. I could tell.*

*The crease between his eyes never stopped frowning. His eyes dark and turbulent.*

*If they'd been alone when they'd died, where were the kids? Had they sold them or killed them?*

*Those questions squatted in my mind, making sleep impossible as we were put up for the night in some dingy motel with only cold water in the shower and a single towel to share.*

*At least, they'd given Ren and me the same room.*

*There was no talk of what we were to each other, or if it was illegal for us to stay together, or what the hell all of this meant. For now, everyone was focused on finding out where we'd truly come from and just what Ren had endured.*

*A policeman sitting outside our door was the only sign we weren't just guests on this little foray and Ren was still a suspect.*

*When Martin had surveyed our room and stepped outside to leave us to it, he pointed a finger at Ren and said, "I'm trusting you not to run, boy. You came here freely. Continue to be cooperative and this will be smoother for all of us."*

*Ren nodded as the door closed, and I whispered under my breath, "His name is Ren...not boy."*

# Chapter Forty-Seven

## REN

## 2020

THE FIRST STEP onto Mclary's property filled me with a complex recipe of emotions.

Hate.

Horror.

Rage.

It felt as if I'd only left yesterday, yet the house was smaller than I remembered, the tractors not as scary, the barn not as huge and hungry for tiny children.

With our entourage of two officers from home, two officers who'd overseen the murder/suicide, and another two for good measure, Della and I were as popular as we'd ever been.

We all moved down the muddy driveway past rotting bales of hay and around a pile of scrap iron to the front door where I'd bolted with a baby Della clinging unseen in my stolen backpack.

Della slipped her hand into mine as we crossed the threshold into the house, and just like that, I was a ten-year-old kid again.

My world narrowed to terror.

My throat constricted.

My body reacted.

Bruised and beaten, starving and sad. Ghost images of a screeching Della ripped my head toward the kitchen. Long ago echoes of a TV program showing what a real family was wrenched my head to the decrepit lounge.

Della felt my tension and squeezed my fingers, dragging me back to the present.

Coughing, I gave her a grateful look, forcing myself to stay in the now.

"How do you want to do this?" one of the officers asked. I didn't know which one, and I didn't care. I merely drifted forward, clutching Della's hand, taking comfort in the thud of my boots and the reminder that I wasn't ten anymore.

No one could hurt me again.

They were dead.

*Good fucking riddance.*

"Where's the box of evidence that you guys gathered in the murder/suicide investigation?" Martin Murray asked, leading the officers into the kitchen where notepads came out, and a box was brought in from a cruiser and placed on the well-used bench.

"This is all we took. Some bank statements. A few IOUs from a local feed store. An unpaid invoice for a tractor service, along with this." Remy Jones, a middle-aged pot-bellied man held up a red notepad that had been curled and rolled with an elastic band and a pen jabbed in the pages. "We figured she killed him and then herself because they were up to their eyeballs in debt, and it was only a matter of time before they lost everything. She blamed him for their lack of fortune; couldn't be bothered struggling anymore. *Bang, bang.*"

My eyes locked onto the notepad as he waved it around with his stupid conclusions. Mrs Mclary didn't shoot her husband for something as useless as money. She shot him because she'd had enough of him raping girls. Maybe in her twisted mind, she thought he cheated on her, or perhaps, she'd finally woken up to how fucking horrible they were and what they were doing to kids.

Either way, she'd killed pure evil and then done the world a favour by eradicating herself, too.

I tried to look away from the notebook as the officer flicked through its pages with a scowl. "This thing makes no sense, though. It's just a bunch of numbers with prices beside it. Four hundred here. Two hundred there. A thousand dollars a few times, but that's rare." He shrugged, tossing it back onto the counter with a slap. "Must be another IOU book, or maybe how much they paid for stock?"

No one seemed interested in answering him, but I couldn't tear my gaze off that damn red notebook.

Something familiar…something tugging me to tumble backward through time.

Red.

Pages.

Pen.

The farmhouse fell away, replaced with an older version—a version where Marion Mclary still lived, and she sat rocking on her rocker by the grimy window, her spindly hand scribbling.

I'd been tasked at lugging in firewood. Load after load until my arms shook and my shoulders threatened to pop from their sockets.

She hadn't cared.

On and on she rocked, writing in that little notebook before creaking her way toward the bookcase that lived in a shadowy part of the living room.

The past and present blended as I followed the tug of my feet, leading me toward the bookcase that still groaned under the weight of cookery books that were never used and auto mechanic magazines that were torn up as fire kindling.

"Ren?" Della asked softly, but I wasn't really there with her.

I was in an in-between world. A place where I was neither thirty nor ten. I was plasma, merely a figment as I reached for the book where I'd seen Mrs Mclary stuff cash that afternoon before swatting me around the head for spying.

Pulling the Bible free, a few coins tinkled inside as I released Della's hand and flopped open the Book of God. Inside, instead of silky pages of testament, someone had hacked away and created a box—a carved out section for secrets.

Martin Murray came up behind me, muttering something to his colleague as I gingerly reached in and held up a matching notebook to the red one he held, except this one was black, sinister, and dripping with filth.

Someone reached over and pinched it from my fingers, leaving me to stare at a few measly bucks and a chewed-on pencil in the Bible. Placing it back on the shelf, I shook my head clear from memories and re-settled into my current existence.

I expected the same hum of conversation from before. The same beat of footsteps as cops trawled the house. The same knowledge of safety that comes from hustle and bustle when you aren't the main attraction.

Only, I kind of was.

Bob Colton scanned the notebook pages then gave me a strange, almost scared look. Snapping his fingers, he commanded, "The red notebook. Now."

An officer scrambled into the kitchen, darting back with the matching notebook to the black one he held.

The moment Bob had it in his hands, he strode to the sideboard, shoved aside an old candelabra with decades' worth of dripped wax, and spread out both booklets, his finger trailing one line of text before matching it with another.

"Oh, my God." He flicked me another look. "Do you know what this is? How did you know where to look? You've been in this house five minutes and already found more than we did."

Della gave me a worried glance, staying silent beside me.

This was the house she was born in, yet it was as foreign to her as it was familiar to me. I shook my head, swallowing a cough. "I saw her one day. Writing something. She stored cash in the Bible."

"There are two hundred and seventeen names here." Bob's face turned to chalk.

"What do you mean?" Martin brushed up to him, skimming the same text.

I didn't understand why both men suddenly looked at me as if I was some unknown specimen. Some sort of thing that shouldn't be standing before them.

Martin swallowed hard, his face matching Bob's in chalkiness. "You said there were ten or fifteen."

"Ten or fifteen?" I questioned.

"Children. You said there were ten or fifteen children in captivity here."

"Yes. At any one time. I have no idea how many came and went on top of that."

"Holy fuck." Bob Colton clamped a hand over his mouth and spun to look at his team. "Call for help. Cadaver dogs. Diggers. As many hands on deck as you can."

Della asked nervously. "Wh-what's going on?"

Martin's grey eyes landed on hers, wide as full moons. "The two notebooks are a ledger."

My heart sank to my toes. My lungs stabbed with pain. "She kept records?"

He nodded, beckoning me forward to glance at the two spread apart notebooks. "See? The red one has the line number and price. The black one holds the name." His voice became unsteady with fury for all the children the Mclary's had bought and hurt. "Number eight in the red notebook correlates to a girl in the black one called Isabelle May." His uniform creaked as he murmured sickly, "They paid two hundred dollars for her."

Della sucked in a gasp, her eyes dancing over text faster than

I could, latching onto names, breathing them like a chant. "Duncan Scott, Ryan Jones, Jade Black, Monica Frost." Her blue eyes glittered with malice for her mother and father as she snatched the notebooks and flicked the pages faster and faster, skimming and skimming until she finally froze, face tight, body stiff, hands shaking. "Ren Shaw."

Icicles replaced my heart as my feet locked to the floor. "What?" My question was barely audible as Della read the number beside my name and tracked it to the number in the red notebook.

Tears spilled down her cheeks as the notebooks fell from her hands, and she threw herself into my arms. "Seven hundred and fifty dollars."

And the farmhouse vanished.

And all that mattered was holding Della as we trembled together.

Because I finally had answers to whom I was.

I was Ren Shaw.

And my mother had sold me for a measly seven hundred and fifty dollars.

\* \* \* \* \*

I suppose I had something to be thankful for.

For the past six hours, the Mclary farmhouse had become a hive of activity with cops buzzing and machinery humming and dogs sniffing.

I was no longer the suspect of a kidnapping investigation. I was the kid who should never have survived and, instead of side glances whenever I touched Della, I received thumbs-up for taking her away from this morgue.

Because it was a morgue.

In the past few hours, the cops who'd brought reinforcements from every county they could, who'd strung up police tape, and blocked off every way onto the property, had already found four tiny skeletons.

One beneath the veranda just tossed like one would a mouldy potato.

Three in the offal pit, boy bones with sheep bones and pig.

And one behind the house that had at least been partially buried with fingers sprouting through the grass like a new species of weed.

No one noticed us anymore.

No one commanded us to leave or get back.

We were invisible as I led Della out of the farmhouse and

toward the fields I'd toiled in for two years.

Funny, how two years had felt like an eternity back then but were nothing in the scheme of a life. Odd, how two years had scared me so spectacularly, leaving gorge marks in my soul and unfilled holes in my psyche.

We didn't speak as we walked hand in hand, ducking past digging cops, keeping a wide berth of dogs as they galloped from one side of the yard to the other, barking warnings that there were yet more bodies below the earth.

We bypassed two police who studied discarded building materials on the ground. One kicked a partial fallen wall with his foot, making it break into dust. "Shit, that's asbestos." Talking into a crackling walkie-talkie, he said, "Get a contractor here who's qualified in contaminated removal."

Spotting us, he pointed away, indicating to give the crumbling wall a wide berth. "Hazardous substance. Stay back."

We didn't speak, just merely drifted away, letting the farm guide us where it wanted to.

I didn't know where we were going.

I didn't care.

I just had to walk; otherwise, I'd explode with the tumbling, tearing feelings inside me.

I felt guilty.

So fucking guilty that I'd run and not tried to help the others.

I'd been selfish and afraid, and I should've done something.

But I hadn't.

And now, the hundreds of missing children files would be stamped deceased and their families notified. Whether it was parents who'd sold their kids, or an evil uncle or aunt, someone would have missed the lives that the Mclary's had bought, abused, and ultimately snuffed out.

At least, I hoped someone would because it was too sad to think otherwise.

Della's hand twitched hot and tight in mine. We didn't just hold hands; we held ourselves together as we traversed the fields and somehow, some reason, my feet turned toward the barn that had been my bedroom for so long.

Where fleas had made me itch and hessian sacks made scratchy blankets. Where nightmares had tormented me just as surely as life had.

"Ren..." Della said. "I don't think—"

I squeezed her fingers and marched onward, keeping my face

blank as a cop to our left shouted with dismay that he'd found another body.

How many did the ground contain? Was this still a farm or a cemetery?

The first touch of shadow from the large creaking barn was a physical scratch on my skin, making me prickle with goosebumps. The soaring ceilings and musty scent of hay cloying with memories.

I *hated* this place.

I hated it as fiercely as I'd hated Mclary.

I wanted to burn it to the goddamn ground, but I swallowed my pyro tendencies and weaved my way through stables, past pallets that had been beds, and into the metal crush where Mclary had drenched his stock.

And there...

*Shit.*

My jaw clenched, and a wave of bile scalded my throat.

Della cried out, planting herself in front of me and shaking her head. "Don't, Ren. Let's go."

"No." Pushing past her, I walked heavily until I reached the rack with Mclary's tools. The rack where I'd stolen a knife and let some other poor kid take the blame. The rack that most likely held the tool used to cut off my finger. The rack where a long metal brand waited for its next victim.

For once, my hand didn't shake as I pulled the heavy rod with its oval *Mc97* stamp off the wall and hefted its weight.

Today, it was dull, cold metal that could do no damage.

Back then, it had been a molten-glowing weapon that turned me into a possession.

Della crept to my side, resting her head on my arm. "He was a sick fuck, and I'm so sorry."

My lips twisted into a smile. "Language, Della Ribbon."

"Oh, I'm sorry. He was a *fucking* sick fuck, and I'm glad he's dead."

I sighed, shaking my head. "How can you make me smile at a time like this?"

"Same way you make me the luckiest girl alive even when we stand in a place like this." Her voice caught. "To know I came from these people..." A tear ran down her face. "I'm disgusted. I-I'm *appalled*. I feel like I'm going to be sick for what they—"

"Della." Turning to face her, I let the brand clatter to the concrete floor and gathered her in my arms. "Stop."

She clung to me, her fingernails digging into my back. "I'm so sorry, Ren." Her tears soaked into my t-shirt. "So sorry for what they did to you."

"I'm not." I kissed her brow, pushing her away with a quiet cough. "I would live it all over again because it gave me you."

Her face contorted with love and abhorrence and everything in between. "We shouldn't have come here."

"We didn't have a choice." Looking past her to the innocuous barn that had been the stage for so many vile things, I murmured, "I don't regret running that night, but I do regret not coming back and trying to help. For not going to the authorities and telling them what I escaped from. For not doing *something*. If I can do something now…even if it's too late, then I have to try."

Her slender frame wedged against mine again, gripping with a fury that made my heart leap with love and gratitude. "You saved two lives that night, Ren. Two lives that wouldn't have made it if you hadn't taken that chance."

"Is it enough? Is it enough to be grateful that we have each other when so many kids died here?"

"It has to be." She pressed a kiss to my chest, snuggling into the borrowed coat I wore. "I love you, Ren Wil—" Her head came up, forehead furrowed. "Shaw. Your real last name is Shaw."

I shook my head and kissed her nose. "No. It's not."

"Who are you then?"

"I'm Ren Wild, protector of Della Wild.

"A boy who survived."

\* \* \* \* \*

Night had fallen by the time the mayhem slowed down.

A building crew had arrived to remove the asbestos, a trailer was parked up to catalogue the corpses they'd found, and the farm crawled with trespassers.

Officers set up spotlights for the evening crew, while fellow workers handed out takeaway cups of coffee and store-bought sandwiches.

I was hungry, tired, and ready to leave this place.

My bones ached and my lungs throbbed. I couldn't get rid of the pressure inside me, the ever constant rattle these days.

I wanted nothing more than to sneak away in the dark and vanish with Della.

But I didn't know if we were allowed.

Was I still under arrest?

Was I free to go or bound to stay?

Another eleven bodies had been found throughout the farm, all in various states of decay and mutilation.

Della had refused to eat an offered muffin, and my stomach was a snarling mess of snakes.

When dusk crept over the overcast day, we'd sat on the steps of the veranda watching, always watching, as tarps covered freshly dug up bones and dogs panted with a job well done on their leashes.

Della stayed close, sharing body heat as the air chilled both of us. I opened my coat wide, welcoming her against me.

"Mr. Shaw?"

My eyes tracked a young detective as she stomped past in muddy boots with a clipboard.

"Mr. Shaw?"

I glanced at the beagle slurping up water in a stainless-steel dish that its handler had put down for him.

"Mr. Shaw?" Someone tapped my shoulder, wrenching my head to look behind me. Martin Murray bent over me, his eyebrow raised.

"You want something?" I asked, my voice gravel and soot from lack of rest.

"Yes. We found something you might want to see."

Standing on creaking legs, I helped Della up and shrugged out of my coat, so she could keep its warmth. I coughed as my heat dispersed.

She tried to refuse, but I merely bundled her tighter, did up the button, and kissed her forehead. Turning my attention to Martin, I ran a hand over my face, trying to wake myself up.

"Miss Mclary? Mr. Shaw?" A female officer with long black hair in a plait appeared from the house. "Can you come with us, please?"

Della padded toward her, but I stopped short. "That is not my name nor Della's. We're Wild. Use it."

Martin scowled. "But it is. You finally know your real name."

"It ceased to be my real name the day I was sold."

He studied me, finally nodding. "You know, all records and proceedings going forward are going to be under the name Ren Shaw and Della Mclary. You have to get used to it."

"What proceedings?"

He looked away, embarrassed. "Well, I still don't know what will happen with the kidnapping charge. Whether it will become a state crime now Willem and Marion Mclary are dead, or…or if it can just be ignored."

"When will you know?" I asked, following him and the female officer into the gloomy house with its feeble lighting in cobwebbed shades.

"Once this mess has been sorted out."

"They're dead children, Mr. Murray, not a mess," Della said sternly. "And if you bring a case against Ren, I'll contest it. I'm the only living Mclary left. And I say I wasn't kidnapped."

Martin squeezed the back of his neck, indicating his stress levels were as strained as ours. "Another topic for another day. For now, let's focus on what we found."

Together, we moved deeper into the house toward the narrow staircase leading upstairs.

The steps groaned and cracked as we trailed single file up and up, then followed obediently down the dingy corridor. I'd never been upstairs, and I guessed one of these rooms had been Della's nursery once upon a time. Now, they were just store rooms with junk and miscellaneous boxes with a master at the end with a stripped mattress and stained carpet.

The sweet smell of decay hinted that this was where Marion Mclary had decided to do the deed.

"We found this," the female detective said, marching to her colleague who was taking photos of a hidden panel in the wardrobe. "A cubby full of documents."

"What sort of documents?" Della asked as we moved deeper into the room, peering at the scattered paperwork all over the bed and yet more coming from the secret hole in the wall.

"Birth certificates."

I inhaled sharply, stalking toward the bed and fisting a few stained pages. Some were hand scribbled, and others were computer printed. Some girls. Some boys. Too many to count.

"They asked whoever sold their child to give them their birth certificate too?" Della stood next to me wrinkling her nose in disgust. "That's not just sick. That's…diabolical. It's as if they fully believed they were buying an animal and had the bill of sale to prove it."

Martin Murray nodded. "I agree. A case like this can't explain the rationale of the people who committed the crimes."

"How many?" I snapped, doing my best to rein in my hope that mine existed in the pile.

The female officer said, "We've counted. There's one hundred and sixty-seven. Compared to the two hundred and seventeen names, I'm guessing some kids were born and never registered, some didn't have their birth certificates, and a few were sold with the child, if what you say is true, Mr. Shaw, and they were moved on once they could no longer do the work required."

"Have you found mine?" I asked quietly, wishing I didn't have hope bubbling in my chest because I already tasted bitter disappointment.

But to finally have that piece of paper? To finally be free to marry Della? It would be a gift after such a grotesque day.

"No, I'm afraid not." The female officer scanned the pages in front of us. "I mean, there's always a chance we'll find more, but not at this stage. However—" She turned to a colleague and collected a page protected by cloudy cellophane. "We did find this one."

Della was the one to take it. Only right, seeing as it had her name on it.

In shaky calligraphy, her name, Della Donna Mclary, stated she was born on 27th of June to Willem and Marion Mclary.

She gave me a weak smile. "I'm going to scribble that out and make it Wild instead."

I chuckled softly. "Or I could just marry you and make it legally Wild."

Her face fell. "If you can somehow make Wild legally yours, first."

"I'm working on it."

She smiled sadly. "Work on making your birthday the same as mine, too. Can't break a lifelong tradition now, can we?"

I ran a finger over her birth certificate, stopping on the date. "I don't care when I was born. I'm sharing yours forever."

Martin looked away as I glanced at him, he'd been listening but pretended to give us privacy and another moment or two to study her birth certificate before holding up yet another document.

This one was dog-eared and had been written on something soft, so the pen had almost pressed through the page, leaving embossed letters and not just ink. "This was in the secret cubby, too." Passing it to me, he nodded for me to take it.

I did, gingerly.

I didn't want to touch what they'd touched. I didn't want to read what they'd written, but as my eyes fell to the top line, and I understood what it was, I passed it to Della.

I couldn't have it against my skin.

And besides, something this important should be read

correctly with no pauses or stumbles. Something this important should be burned and never read at all.

Della flinched as she took it from my hands. "A suicide note."

"Yes." Martin Murray nodded. "One that explains a little but not a lot. But one that I feel will mean more to you than to us."

With that cryptic comment, he left us to talk to the team by the wardrobe, and Della and I drifted to the window where torches and spotlights shone through the darkness, illuminating skeletons of those who weren't as lucky as us.

I coughed and swallowed, my hands balling. "Should we read it?"

Della skimmed it. "I don't know."

We stood there for a moment, soaking in the ramifications. Finally, I stood taller. "Read it."

"You sure?"

"I'm sure." Crossing my arms, I waited.

Slowly, she smoothed the page and began.

*"To whomever finds this.*

*"My name is Marion Mclary and I have ten minutes left to live. When my husband returns from the fields, I'm going to take the shotgun and shoot him in his heartless chest and then, I'm going to put myself out of my misery."*

Della glanced up, her face whitening before her eyes locked back on the page.

*"The kids are gone. Half of them sold at rock bottom price to Kyle Harold and half poisoned by the creek. At least none of them will escape and tell the world what we've done.*

*Then again, I don't care what happens after I've gone. I don't care that everything will come to light, and the church will turn on us, and our friends will know the truth.*

*I don't care because I stopped caring the day I married into this evil and went along with my husband's plans.*

*I'm not entirely to blame. After all, I did become the buyer and seller of our little worker bees. As far as I was concerned, we needed labour and labour ain't cheap…unless you buy it young.*

*I could've continued with what we were doing. This isn't the kind of letter where I confess to my crimes and beg for forgiveness.*

*There is nothing to forgive. We lived our life the way we wanted.*

*I don't care Willem raped those little girls. I don't care he mutilated those little boys. Everyone needs discipline in their lives. Even if those lives were short.*

*I know I have a one-way ticket to the devil, and I'm not going fill this page with lies.*

*But I am going to admit a secret that Willem never knew. The secret that's the reason why I'm pulling the trigger.*

*Della Donna Mclary.*

*My baby girl.*

*She wasn't supposed to be born. I tried to kill her. I tried to starve her out. But the church says thou shall not abort, so I let her come into our dark world.*

*And for a time, I didn't feel any different.*

*I didn't see her in the girls screaming as Willem molested them. I didn't see her in the kids starving in the barn.*

*She wasn't like them.*

*But then one day, I did see her like them. I saw her eyes flicker as Willem booted that boy from the kitchen. I saw her scream when Willem shot the kid for letting the sheep out.*

*And I knew she'd either end up in her father's bed, or worse, become like us.*

*Just because I'm not apologising for what we did, doesn't mean I didn't know it was against the Lord's teachings.*

*And for once, I wanted to do right by God rather than just sing pretty hymns in church.*

*I was going to do the world a favour.*

*I was going to kill her before she became me.*

*For weeks, I tried to do it.*

*Holding her under in the bath until she blew bubbles.*

*Clamping my hand over her nose and mouth until she kicked.*

*I could inspect a child from some white trash family and offer money for their offspring, yet I couldn't kill my own daughter.*

*Then I saw that skinny runt of a boy think about escaping. He snuck into the house one night, scurrying like a rat in the dark, stealing food and placing them in Willem's backpack by the door.*

*Normally, I would've told Willem to shoot him. To kill him dead before the sun rose.*

*But...he was my chance.*

*My one chance at killing my daughter without having her blood on my hands.*

*So...I let him believe he wasn't noticed.*

*I held my tongue when he looked at my Della, and I watched that scrawny toad make his move.*

*When he slipped from the locked barn the next night—revealing a security issue—I knew it was time and grabbed my sleeping daughter and stuffed her in the backpack where his rations were ready to escape.*

*She was a good girl. She didn't wake up as I zipped her in and hid her in the darkness.*

*That little rat poked his head into my house, sniffed around, then slung on the backpack with surprise in his eyes from the extra weight.*

*He looked as if he'd take it off again and check his supplies.*

*I couldn't have that.*

*So, I yelled for my sleeping husband. I told him we had a runaway and to get the shotgun.*

*And then, we had some sport as that little boy took off in the corn, bounding like the rat he was, carrying my daughter with him.*

*I hoped a bullet would take them both out.*

*I hoped two mistakes could be fixed with one.*

*But Willem missed.*

*And to this day, I don't know if the boy and my baby are dead.*

*I like to think they are because she was born to evil, and he was sold to the devil. Nothing good can come of them surviving.*

*But now, my secret is on paper, and I'm ready to kill my husband. I blame him for not knowing if she's dead or not. I blame him for this life of dirt and destitution. I blame him for everything, and I've had enough.*

*I've had enough of the raping, killing, and struggling. We have labour, yet the farm doesn't grow food anymore. We have stock, but they get sick and die.*

*Consider this my intent to cancel the missing person's report that Willem filed. Turned out, that man rather loved his daughter. He loved her enough to want her in all the wrong ways. I knew. I saw it before he could touch her.*

*At least I saved her from that fate.*

*I am Marion Mclary, and I don't apologise for what me and my husband are.*

*I only apologise for letting my spawn run away and not knowing if she'll grow up to be like us.*

*She deserves to die.*

*Just like that boy who took her."*

# Chapter Forty-Eight

## REN

## 2020

A WEEK PASSED where we returned to Cherry River, kept our heads down, and tried to move on. I wasn't arrested with the strict provision I stayed in town and didn't travel.

John hired a lawyer on my behalf—just in case the state decided to go ahead with prosecuting me for Della's disappearance, and I did my best to repay him by preparing the fields for a good rest over winter for a bumper crop come summer.

John and Cassie asked questions that first afternoon, but Della and I didn't know how to answer them.

Our minds were still messed up from what we'd seen. Images of dirt-smeared bones, time-tattered clothing, and the bay of cadaver dogs replayed on a loop inside my head.

What happened back at Mclary's had affected both of us.

Della more so than me.

She'd learned she hadn't, by some miracle, chosen to belong to me by crawling into the backpack, after all. She'd been placed there by her homicidal mother.

I finally had answers to my how and why of how I ended up with a baby.

And she'd learned she'd been unwanted in a sea of mistakes and, despite her rage when we were at the farm watching police exhume such horror, a heavy shame and thick depression cloaked her.

She withdrew into herself, and there was nothing I could do about it.

The day we travelled the eight hours back to Cherry River, we barely talked. The day after, she didn't want to discuss it. The day after that, she snapped at Cassie to leave it alone.

For a week, I let her stew and put up with her half-hearted smiles and weak assurances.

But she couldn't hide from me because I understood more than she knew.

I understood she was searching.

Searching deep inside herself for a hint that she might be what her mother said.

A devil.

A monster.

Just like them.

And how could she not after seeing what they'd done?

But I also knew she'd find no trace of evilness because she was as pure and as perfect as they were vile and villainous.

On the eighth day of her despondency, I packed up the tent and sleeping bags and told John we'd be back in a night or two. Cassie was staying in town with Chip and her daughter, and Della fought me a little on leaving John on his own, but we needed to reconnect, and I needed to remind her of something.

As we walked, just the two of us, over the fields toward the treeline we knew so well, I clutched her hand hard. The fake sapphire I'd bought her had gone smoky with age and chipped from wear, but she still wore it religiously, just like I wore my leather band with its metal letters with a single diamante remaining.

As we walked, I struggled not to cough.

I was fully aware how Della flinched whenever I did. It was an annoying sound, I agreed, but that was all it was—an annoyance.

I felt okay in myself. Nothing stopped me from living a life of physical activity and labour.

Her worry was a tad frustrating, but I could understand, just as I could understand her quietness now. They were circumstances outside her control, yet they affected her wholeheartedly.

Hopefully, I'd be able to reassure her on both accounts.

Once in the forest and far enough away from the farm, I pitched the tent, gathered her close, and made love to her like old times beneath the glittering stars.

At first, she resisted, claiming a headache. Then she lied and said she wasn't interested.

Her refusal didn't annoy me because yet again, I understood. "Della…"

She refused to meet my eyes, staring into the fire I'd built and coaxed into a warm blaze.

"Nothing has changed, Little Ribbon."

Tears she'd bottled up cascaded down her cheeks as I went to her and cuddled her close. "Let me help…please?" Kissing her, I guided her onto the sleeping bag I'd spread on the ground, slowly undressing her, not making any sudden movements in case she ran.

My voice didn't speak, but my body did.

It assured her that she was still who she believed and I was still who she knew. It convinced her, slowly, gently, that what we had outweighed any pain or terror from the past.

Hesitantly, she responded to my kisses, purred into my touch, and when she spread her legs and I slipped inside her, her gasp was full of sorrow.

We moved together, hands always touching, lips always kissing, our bodies thrusting in affirmation of life and love.

The cool air didn't stop us. The owl hoots didn't scare us. I didn't care it was late in the season and snow seasoned the air. I didn't care we shivered as we moved together, chasing an orgasm that wasn't just about pleasure, but a declaration that we might have been touched by evil, but it hadn't claimed us.

We'd chosen our own path, and we always would.

Afterward, with my body still in Della's, I smoothed back her hair and cupped her cheeks. Lying over her with her trapped beneath me, I murmured, "You have never been, nor will you ever be like them, Della Ribbon."

She flinched, the fire dancing in her eyes with golden spirals. For a second, a flash of ire said she wouldn't talk to me. Then torment drenched her voice. "But how do you know? How do you know I won't snap one day and—"

"I know because I raised you."

"What if that filth can't be changed? What if I'm lying to you and myself? What if I'm not a good person and could kill—"

"You *are* a good person."

"But how do you *know*? Truly know?" Her gaze searched mine, desperate for an answer. "I'm so afraid I have no control. That I am what they made—not what you guided. That I have no choice."

"You *do* have a choice. We all have a choice."

"But genetics—"

"Have nothing to do with it." I stared deep into her, needing her to believe me. "I know you are good and sweet and kind because I *know* you. I've known you your entire life."

She squirmed beneath me. "That's not an answer."

"It is. It's the best one. I've seen you grow, Della. I've seen you uncensored and undisciplined and uncivilized. I've seen you in every mood there is, and not once did you hurt anyone or anything. You weren't malicious. You weren't cruel. You were—"

"I was, though, don't you see? I was cruel to you."

I chuckled, hiding yet another cough. "You were never cruel to me."

"But—"

"No buts." Running a thumb over her pink lips, I whispered, "They had you for a year, Della. I've had you for almost twenty. Whatever they taught you or said to you is drowned out by the endless conversations and love we've shared."

She frowned, running her tongue over my thumb. "Did you ever look at me like she did? Did you ever think I could be like them?"

"Never."

"Not even when you didn't want me?"

"Not even then." Kissing her softly, I added, "And not wanting you lasted for a heartbeat before I became yours."

"I'm sorry, Ren."

"Nothing to apologise for."

"I know…but I need to. Seeing that place. Seeing those bodies. Seeing how *real* it all was."

I pushed those memories aside, just as I always shoved memories of that farmhouse away. "I accept your apology if it makes you feel better, but only if you accept mine."

She frowned. "Why are *you* apologising?"

"Because I always blamed you for making my running all that much harder. I cursed you for being in my bag when all along, I should've been thanking you." Pressing my forehead to hers, I hardened inside her, comforted by her body heat and already desperate for more. "Without you, I would've been shot before I ever crept back into the house to collect my supplies. My escape was all down to you being in that bag. You are the reason I'm alive, Della. Not the other way around."

Her eyes softened, and the shadows that had lurked inside her dissolved. "Kiss me, Ren Shaw. I'm sick of apologies."

I raised an eyebrow, my lips thinning in reproof. "Ask me again with the correct name."

She smiled. "Kiss me, Ren Wild. Make love to me. Promise me you'll never let me go."

So I did.

And I promised.

And I never let go.

* * * * *

Another week passed, slipping us back into routine.

Della spent more time with Cassie discussing horses and Cassie's future dream of one day opening an equine business, and I returned to my odd jobs around the farm.

The air was cooler now, making the frustrating ache in my chest three times worse.

Some days, I barely noticed it.

But then some days, like today, I felt as if lunch lodged in my throat and wouldn't swallow. I willingly coughed, trying to eradicate the obstruction, forcing deeper coughs and longer barks, begging for a reprieve from the pressure.

It was there, while I hung onto a stable door, bent over trying to clear the weight in my lungs, that John found me.

I thought I was on my own.

I refused to cough so badly in people's presence because I knew how annoying the noise could be.

But as John stomped toward me in his dirty overalls and a rusty tool kit to lend a hand, I'd destroyed any hope of stopping, thanks to willingly encouraging a coughing fit.

His eyes tightened as I held up my hand, swallowing back wracking heaves, clamping my other hand over my mouth and doing my best to stop.

"Ren?" John placed his tool kit on the cobblestones, coming to put a hand on my back as I rode out the final waves of affliction. "Take it easy." His gaze travelled to the hose in the corner, his body swaying in its direction. "Want some water? Choking on something?"

I shook my head, smothering yet another cough and standing up with a gasp. "I'm—" A couple more coughs caught me unaware, lashing my chest with pain. Finally, when I could breathe again, I said, "I'm fine." Smiling with watery eyes, I inhaled deep, fighting the tickle to cough again. "Just hay dust."

Turning, I reached for the nails that I'd been using to fix a loose hinge only for John to fist my wrist.

"What is that?" His fingers latched tight, cutting off my arteries.

"Don't touch me." I tugged, feeling a residual thread of panic from being held against my will. No matter how many years passed, I doubted I'd fully have control over my attacks.

"Goddammit, Ren. What the *hell* is this?" He held up my palm, shoving it under my nose.

Red.

Liquid.

Blood.

*My* blood.

*Fuck.*

I froze, running my tongue over my lip and tasting the nasty flavour of copper. My eyes met his, and I broke beneath the love there. The love he had for me. And the worry. Shit, the worry.

"It's okay, John." I yanked my hand free, wiping the blood on my jeans. "Don't—"

Fisting his keys from his overalls pocket, he grabbed my bicep, once again layering me with a fissure of fear. "We're leaving. Right now."

"Leaving? To go where?" He pulled me from the stable.

So many parts of me wanted to shove him to the ground for manhandling me, but I understood his violence came from panic just like my panic came from violence.

"Doctor." His eyes welled with fury and impatience. "You've been coughing ever since you got back home. I'm not putting up with it anymore."

"But what about Della?" I twisted my arm free, raising my eyebrow when he tried to hold on to me. "Let go, John. I won't ask again." My gritted teeth and feral tone hinted I wasn't coping.

He dropped his hand but didn't stop his fast pace to the barn doors. "She's with Cassie. They popped into town to see Chip at work. We have time."

"I-I can't make her worry."

He stopped, turning to face me. "And you can't make me worry, Ren. I'm not losing you like I lost Patricia. I love you like a son, but if you don't see a doctor, I will kick you out of my house, so help me God."

I smirked. "Winter is close. You wouldn't dare."

He didn't smile back. "Try me. Now get your ass in the truck."

\* \* \* \* \*

It was as if my lungs knew they had an audience because I hadn't been able to ignore the tickle and wheeze since John drove me above normal speed limits to his local practitioner.

There was no discussion over identifications or money.

No discussions period as his regular doctor called his name ten minutes after we arrived, and we were ushered into a small white office with posters of body parts and skeletons on the wall.

To start with, I resented John for dragging me down here.

I worried if Della was safe and what time she'd be home.

What would she do if she found scattered tools and no workmen to use them?

What the hell would I tell her about John's kidnapping and the blood stain on my jeans?

But then those questions switched to others that made my heart pound a little bit harder.

*What if I'm in trouble?*

*What if...it's serious?*

"How long have you been coughing, Ren?" The elderly doctor with jowls from losing weight clicked his pen, waiting for me to reply.

"Two and a bit years, give or take."

"And this is the first time you've coughed up blood?"

"Yes." I rubbed at the red stain on my clothes, then placed my hand over it as if I could stop it from being real. I didn't want to reveal my ever-growing fear, but I couldn't stop my question. "Is that bad?"

"Well..." The doctor stroked his jaw. "Sometimes, yes. Sometimes, no. If you were coughing a lot, you could've just irritated the lining of your throat and burst a few blood vessels. However, if the blood came from your lungs, it's a different matter."

"Oh." My heart skipped a beat.

"First, before we go down scary roads like that, let's just see how your health is in general, okay?" He narrowed his eyes. "Do you exercise? Eat well?"

"I'm active and try my best."

"Okay, have you ever been on medications or dealt with long-term illnesses?"

"No." I massaged the back of my neck. "Never."

"Any heart palpitations? Lack of appetite? Abdominal pain? Chest pain? Shortness of breath?"

Shit, I'd had all of those on and off over the past few years.

I glanced at John who sat beside me.

Just like there hadn't been any discussion about money or I.Ds, there'd been no discussion if he would accompany me into the appointment.

"Go on, Ren. Answer the man." He scowled, angry with me but also afraid. I understood his fear came from Patricia dying—that he'd leap onto anyone ill because he'd lost someone. But just because I understood didn't mean I liked being smothered or being told what to do.

The doctor probed me again. "How old are you?"

"Thirty-ish."

"You don't know your date of birth?"

"No."

"So you don't know your family history and if lung issues are common?"

"No." I crossed my arms. "Can't you just give me some antibiotics and clear it up? I probably should've had some a couple of years ago when I got the flu. It turned into a chest infection."

His eyes narrowed as if I'd given him a clue. "Do you often get chest infections?"

"He had pneumonia when he was a lad. Fifteen, I think," John said gruffly. "Occasionally, he'd get a cold, and they'd stick on his chest for a while, but he was healthy apart from that."

I threw him a look. "Didn't know you were keeping such close tabs on me."

He smiled sternly. "I notice when all my kids are ill."

I swallowed hard. I knew John loved me like his other sons. Hell, he'd often called me son and treated me no differently.

But to have his concern overflow, to have him bristle beside me and force me into this all because he was worried, made me feel warm and cared for—despite my temper.

Tapping his pen against his lips, the doctor re-read his notes, the wrinkles on his forehead growing deeper. His blue eyes met mine with an intensity I didn't like. "Have you ever been around asbestos?"

"The building stuff?"

"Correct. Sometimes it's blue, brown, green…white."

"Not that I recall." I snapped my fingers. "No, wait, that's not true. The police said there was asbestos at the farm I visited last week."

"Did you inhale any of it?"

I shook my head. "No, we weren't close enough."

John went dangerously still. "He lived there. When he was a boy."

"Ah." The doctor nodded, his face falling. "How long did you live there?"

My insides went cold and still. "Two years."

"How long ago?"

I bit my lip, begging my brain to do simple math. "Um, twenty years ago, I guess."

His pen scratched on paper, wrenching hope from my achy chest. For a moment, he didn't say anything, studying me as if he had X-ray vision and could see my lungs and the secrets they hid.

Finally, he glanced at John before asking me, "And in that time, did you play with any building supplies or have contact with such things?"

I laughed before I could stop myself. *Play?* There was no play. I'd been beaten with a piece of lumber, had wall debris smashed over my head, and a hot brand driven into my skin.

If that was play, I didn't want to know what abuse was.

The doctor, whose name hadn't been provided, pursed his lips. "Something funny?"

Swallowing a twisted chuckle, I said, "Sorry. No. I didn't play, but I did use the tractor to break apart an old shed that Mcla—the farmer didn't want. I buried it."

"And have you done any other work around suspect buildings?"

I went to shake my head, only a horrible thought appeared. "I did. In 2015 when I got a job as a menial labourer. I was paid cash to dismantle unwanted structures at night. It seemed...shady, and no one else wanted to do it."

*Fuck.*

I'd been so happy to take the extra cash.

I didn't have a clue back then about contaminations or that man-made materials could be so deadly.

My ignorance had given me extra pocket money, but at what price?

John put his head in his hands, elbows wedged on his knees.

I wanted to pat his back and assure him that whatever conclusions his doctor was cooking were wrong. I wanted to say I'd worn masks and gloves and knew what the hell I was dealing with.

But the lies solidified on my tongue and terror turned into stones inside me.

No one spoke.

All of us dealing with ramifications, deep in separate thought. Shakes infected me the more I fell into the pit of despair.

"Right then." The doctor shattered the taut silence, scribbling more notes. Spinning in his chair, he faced the computer and started typing with two fingers. "There are numerous explanations for your symptoms, so we're not going to worry just yet. You're young and fit, which is always a good thing." He threw me a look, stabbing his fingers on the keys. The process was laborious and not at all smooth like Della's typing.

"However, I've dealt with a lot of claimants over the years and learned that jumping to conclusions can sometimes be a good thing." His eyes burned into me. "Sometimes, they can save a life."

Hitting enter, a printer whirred into action.

Grabbing the document, he signed it then passed it to me. "You need to go to the hospital. I've referred you for blood tests, X-rays, and possibly a CT scan."

"What? Why?" The stones inside me manifested into rocks, weighing me down, pushing a painful cough from my lips.

"I'm not wasting time testing for bacterial infections or immune deficiencies. I've dealt with too many cases not to see the warning signs. Once I know the answer to this question, then we'll look at other possibilities."

"The answer to what question?" John asked, his voice tight, face harrowed.

"The warning signs of what?" I blurted at the same time.

Giving us both a grave look, the doctor answered us in one go, announcing the nature of my death. "Mesothelioma."

# Chapter Forty-Nine

## DELLA

## 2031

HE NEVER TOLD *me.*

*After decades together, unbreakable trust, and a never ending connection, he didn't tell me.*

*He*
*didn't*
*tell*
*me.*

*Just writing those words breaks my heart into smithereens.*

*It breaks me in so many ways. It makes me sob, rage, beg, curse, and scream.*

*For so long now, I've shown you how pedantically Ren protected me all my life. Revealed how he would do anything for me, in any circumstance, time, or place.*

*I've painted his picture over and over, showing you exactly what sort of man he was, and how his greatest quality was also his biggest flaw.*

*He was selfless and careful and kind.*

*And in this…he was no different.*

*He decided to carry the burden alone.*

*I hated him for that.*

*I cursed him every day for lying.*

*I never knew what he went through that night.*

*How John drove him straight to the hospital, signed with his insurance, and sat with Ren for hours, waiting for the tests.*

*All I knew at the time was Cassie received a phone call as we were on our way back from spending the afternoon with Chip and Nina, saying they'd gone into town for a beer and dinner.*

*It was a tad unusual, but John had treated Ren to a meal out—just the two of them— before, so I wasn't overly concerned.*

*I wasn't concerned when Ren came home later than normal and tossed his jeans into the wash straight away.*

*I wasn't concerned when he ran more 'errands' with John a few days later, leaving Cassie and me sketching out stables and arena concepts for her horse business.*

*I wasn't even concerned when the phone rang for Ren and he took it alone in the farmhouse, returning a little while later subdued and quiet but still willing to kiss and laugh when I poked him to liveliness.*

*All that time.*

*All those minutes and hours and days.*

*I didn't know.*

*How*

*did*

*I*

*not*

*know?*

*How did I not see?*

*I loved him past sanity.*

*I loved him more than anything else in the world, so…how?*

# Chapter Fifty

## REN

## 2021

I WAS SICK.

Sick of lying.

Of hiding.

Of holding Della late at night, listening to her soft breathing, all while fighting the terror that'd set up home inside me.

The lies I'd told the past few months.

*Fuck.*

The lies I'd told over and over again.

I wished I could take them all back.

I wished I could kill my mother for ever selling me to a place that had tried to kill me when I was young and didn't succeed until I was older.

I'd run with Della, so full of hope and boldness for life. I'd protected her by any means necessary. I'd sacrificed everything for her. I'd given her my heart and soul.

Yet...I couldn't protect her from this.

I'd believed I was just like any ten-year-old kid the day I'd escaped from hell.

I'd fallen in love and grown up and planned a future with the woman I wanted.

And the entire time we'd plotted course and travelled through time, I'd been a dead man walking.

I might have run from Mclary's. I might still live and breathe and exist, but I'd died there.

I was a ghost.

Della had fallen in love with someone who was already dead....He just didn't know it yet.

God, the pain.

The torment.

The undying *yearn* to somehow reverse the clock and forbid such tragedy from happening.

I thought I was prepared to die. I believed I would accept when my time came because I would've had an entire lifetime with Della by my side.

I wanted kids with her.

I wanted the privilege of growing old with her.

I wanted to marry her.

Now...that lifetime was no longer an option.

No one knew how long I had.

Statistics had been thrown around until I had to stop listening. I refused to let depression latch onto one answer while hope clung to another.

How fucking twisted that I got my wish?

I would die before her.

It was a guarantee now, not merely a possibility.

And I would die so much earlier than I wanted.

That was the worst part.

Lying in bed, warm and cocooned in the dark—that was when the aching, quaking grief found me. Tears would leak from my eyes as I squeezed them shut against the agony of what existed in our future.

I'd clutch a sleeping girl close, stifling my urge to cough, hating the curse in my lungs.

The tests had come back positive.

Stage one mesothelioma.

John had been there when I'd heard the news. When the phone fell from my hand and the doctor on the other end asked us to come see him for further information. When I'd heard words such as latency period, chemotherapy, radiation, and surgery, I'd shut down.

I couldn't help it.

I turned blank inside to prevent pure, undiluted rage from consuming me.

Rage at life.

Rage at injustice.

Rage at unfairness.

Rage at love itself.

Life, it seemed, had decided I'd loved too deeply and for long enough. I'd had Della for longer than most couples, and we were still so young.

But I was greedy.

I didn't want to die.

I wanted more and more and *more*.

I wanted everything I would never have and it fucking tore me up inside that I couldn't.

So, when doctors hemmed and hawed about my prognosis, I said nothing.

John cried.

I didn't.

When treatment plans were discussed, John demanded all of it, any of it, immediately.

And I'd stared into silence and wondered.

How?

How would I ever tell Della?

How would I ever break her heart the way my own heart was breaking?

How could I protect her from all of this while ensuring she would be safe once I'd gone?

Being given that diagnosis was the start of a war between John and me.

He wanted to pay for surgery straight away.

I wouldn't accept charity.

He wanted to hook me up to drips and lock me in the hospital.

I needed to be outside.

Both of us wanted a solution, but I refused to accept the money he had from Patricia's life insurance, and I had no intention of letting Della see me frail and weak post-surgery.

John was willing to condemn me to a life of sickness if it meant extending that life by a few years.

But I had no intention of being bedridden.

I was incurable.

We both heard that truth.

And now, it was the hardest decision of my life to gamble on what option would give me most of what I wanted.

Rushing into it wasn't going to happen.

I needed to think.

To plan.

To strategize.

For a month, we argued while I researched, and he rang every hospital in the country. Not having any money or insurance, my choices were slim.

But then, John's doctor referred me to an oncologist who dealt with mesothelioma and agreed to see me for free, considering I was one of the younger patients to show symptoms, and I wasn't on death's door just yet.

I had time.

I had the potential to be studied.

I lied to Della once again, claiming I was inspecting a guy's farm for new fence lines, and headed to the appointment on my own.

I didn't want John there. I needed to do this alone. I wanted the luxury of showing my fear to a doctor rather than acting brave around a friend.

And that was how I found out two things that didn't save my life but definitely gave me hope.

There were off-label trials for men like me. Two drugs that had shown success in later stages but had yet to have conclusive evidence in stage one.

Keytruda—an immunotherapy that was administered by intravenous injection for thirty minutes every three weeks, and a listeria-based vaccine called CRS-207 that had shown promise.

One was a passive immunotherapy and one was an active, meaning my already pre-loaded immune system that had adapted and grown with me would have help in fighting the cells that were slowly killing me and be taught to recognise those cells.

I liked the sound of that.

I enjoyed the thought of my body becoming its own weapon instead of its own enemy.

I nodded along as the doctor advised there were still side effects, but not nearly as many as chemo, and accepted the fine print. And besides, the side effects were almost identical to the symptoms I already had—coughing, breathlessness, and lack of appetite—that I didn't care anyway.

Every three weeks was doable, and I could lie to Della about an hour trip away from home—either to the lumber mill for barn supplies or some other made-up excuse.

The oncologist suggested I think about it, but I knew I wanted to fight and fight hard, so I signed hundreds of waivers, put my life in his hands, and started the first round of treatment three days later.

I'd never been good with sharp things.

And needles?

Fuck, it was a nightmare.

Sitting in a low-ceilinged ward with dying people while chemicals flowed through my veins made claustrophobia press on me until my breathing turned shallow and my coughing became worse.

By the time it was over, I already dreaded the next appointment—glad I had twenty-one days to grow some balls to face it.

But at least I'd done something to give myself a chance. I hadn't just curled up and accepted the inevitable like John believed I had. I wasn't being a martyr by refusing to worry Della with this shit. This was my problem, and I would fix it.

*Hopefully.*

When I went home that night, I felt a little nauseous but overall fine, and I took Della to a diner, making sure I joked and acted perfectly normal.

Her eyes were sharper and attention closer, suspecting things but not sure what. But by the end of the meal, after seducing her with rich food and making her drunk with kisses, she slipped back into our trust and her wariness floated away.

That night, I made love to her with a passion bordering painful.

I refused to turn on the light, hoping she could feel me bruise her, love her, consume her, and always remember me as strong and *alive.*

Turned out, life was a slippery thing, but I grasped onto it with all my strength.

There was no way I was dying.

Not yet, at least.

I couldn't—not until I had my ring on Della's finger and her last name forever stitched to mine. And that was how a wet day in spring brought at least some answers to my prayers, along with a threat to my time-restrained freedom.

Martin Murray knocked off slushy snow from his boots and strode into the kitchen with a red nose from icy breezes. John had invited him onto his property with the taut wariness of a soldier being drafted for battle.

Ever since I'd been told what lived inside me, John had been overly protective of me.

Della sometimes raised an eyebrow at the way he layered my plate with vegetables and filled my palm with vitamins. He'd overstepped a few times, but I didn't have the heart to tell the old man to back off.

He'd done so much for me.

The lawyer he'd arranged—in case I was still prosecuted for Della's kidnapping—had now been given other duties, including drawing up my Will and Testament—leaving everything I had to Della, even though I had nothing of value—and arranging my funeral so it wasn't yet another burden when I was gone.

Rain turned to snowflakes as we all sat at the well-used dining table in a fire-warmed house and prepared to find out what happened with the Mclary case.

Nerves danced down my spine. Worry that I might be thrown in jail filled my broken lungs, granting a rattling cough. What if the investigation had finished, and I'd still been found at fault?

Della sensed my tension, running a gentle hand over my lower back.

Never again would I take her touch for granted.

Never again would I be annoyed at her or be short-tempered or argue.

It was a struggle not to count each time she touched me, keeping tally of how many I could earn before I wasn't there to earn more.

Shaking my head, I banished those thoughts as Martin cupped his hands around a cup of steaming coffee and looked at John as he lowered his big bulk into the chair at the head of the table.

"Thank you for seeing me." Martin cleared his throat, his eyes catching mine, then Della's.

Long ago, Della and I had sat here and been interrogated in a different way. I'd been coughing with pneumonia, and a five-year-old Della had tried to fight my battles. That had ended in a happy conclusion.

Would this?

"Why are you here?" I asked, not impolitely but with a reminder that the sooner this was over with, the better.

"I have news." Martin reached to the briefcase by his chair leg and pulled out a file. "Here." Skidding it across to us, he waited until I'd opened it and pulled out a page. It looked like gibberish full of police terminology, dates, reference numbers, and findings.

"What is it?" I looked up, stifling a cough.

"It's a summary of the report finalising the case of Mclary versus Mclary."

"And am I still in trouble?"

The thought of dying in prison?

Of living my last ticking time without Della?

Fuck, it was more than I could bear.

Della stiffened beside me, ready to leap up and strangle the detective, just like I was ready to commit murder to ensure I stayed out of jail.

Screw treatment and houses and towns, I'd take her back to the forest and live for however long I could, happy and content, just her and me.

"You can't blame him," Della snapped. "He didn't do anything—"

"Ribbon." I placed a rough hand over her soft one, keeping her steady. "Quiet."

She flashed me a look, her gaze lingering on my mouth.

I had an insane urge to kiss her, to kiss her as much as I possibly could before...I couldn't.

Martin shook his head. "No. We've ruled Miss Mclary was placed in that backpack by her mother, and you were unaware. Under that proviso, we aren't calling it a kidnapping."

"What *are* you calling it?" I asked around a slight cough.

Della narrowed her eyes, her fingers flinching under mine.

"A rescue." He smiled gently. "A miracle that two kids survived against all odds."

"Wow." John cleared his throat, tears glittering in his big eyes. Ever since losing Patricia, and now my secret malady, he wore his emotions on his sleeve—a gruff, grizzly bear turned into a teddy.

He was against me not telling Della. He hated that I'd forbid him from informing anyone.

But that was my choice, and he had to honour it.

Otherwise, well—I'd promised he'd never see us again if he did.

It was my secret to tell...when I was ready.

John flicked me a glance before asking the officer, "So...what does that mean?"

Martin grinned. "It means he's free."

My shoulders sagged as if someone cut my strings. Della slouched too, a massive sigh exploding from her lips and making the pages dance.

"Now that there's a surviving heir to the Mclary estate, I advise you to get in touch with a lawyer to see what value you'll receive once the bank has claimed the outstanding debt. You'll have to undergo a DNA test to confirm you are their descendent, but that's just a formality."

I stiffened, recalling what poison existed on that farm and that I hadn't been the only one living there. "Should she undergo any other tests? To make sure she's healthy?"

John smothered a heavy sigh laced with sadness. "Shit, you don't think she has—"

"Quiet," I hissed.

"What's he talking about?" Della asked. "Ren?"

"Nothing." I clutched her hand in mine. "That house wasn't exactly sanitary. It might be best if you have some tests to ensure you're healthy and nothing infected you when you were a baby."

Things like asbestos...a killer that took ten to forty years to make itself known.

She could've been infected by me and second-hand contamination. Or by her father or mother or crawling around in silicate minerals and fibrous crystals in the dirt.

I'd researched.

I'd studied.

I knew my enemy intimately.

Della had taught me the power of education, and I knew enough to understand what risks she faced and what conclusions I'd have in my future.

How I would die.

How it would feel.

How I would look to Della as I slowly traded life for death.

That was the hardest part.

Knowing how much it would hurt her...seeing me that way.

Martin raised an eyebrow. "Um, I can ask. I know a few officers found asbestos onsite, so it might not be a bad thing to rule out."

I froze.

I hadn't meant for him to blare the damn word.

John tensed in his chair as we both looked at Della.

Pleading that in this, she wouldn't be too smart.

That in this awful, awful matter, she'd not see the truth.

Martin scribbled something down. "Heaven forbid anything comes back positive, but there are open litigations and settlements for anyone who may have been exposed."

*Please...don't let her know.*

Della studied the table, her mind racing before she bit her lip and asked something that made my heart gallop for different things. "What about the other kids? Are you tracking them down?

Have you found any of them who were sold to that Kyle Harold my mother's letter mentioned?"

Martin took a sip of his coffee. "We've sent the names to a larger police force and, as far as I'm aware, they're in the process of going through missing persons and wanted offenders. I'll ask for an update and get back to you."

"Okay." Della nodded. "Hopefully, a few can be found before it's too late."

Too late.

*Too late.*

The words echoed in my skull.

Despite my anger at my body's desire to kill me, I couldn't be greedy.

I'd had so much longer than those kids.

I was the lucky one.

Once again, the guilt that I never went back settled heavily.

"We're also looking for your mother, Ren."

"Don't." I balled my hands. "As far as I'm concerned, she's dead. I never want to hear about her again, got it?"

Martin looked taken aback but slowly nodded. "Fair enough." Clearing his throat, he said, "Oh, I almost forgot." Reaching into his briefcase again, he pulled out a thick bunch of papers. "This is yours." Sliding it to Della, he waited for her to read the title and glance up.

"Did you read it?" Her fingers traced the words *The Boy & His Ribbon by Della Wild.*

"Yes."

I winced. "Please don't tell me you're going to arrest me for falling in love with a minor or incest."

He chuckled. "No. As much as society thinks we're out to ruin lives, we know when we come across good people, and you are good people. In fact..." His hand disappeared a final time into that damn briefcase, coming out with a framed piece of parchment. A matte black frame and simple glass, but as he pushed it toward me, it became my most precious thing in the world.

Utterly priceless because it finally allowed me to do what I'd been wanting to do for years.

It gave me a wish before I could have no more.

"I-I don't understand." I didn't dare touch it.

I couldn't.

*Is it real?*

Della started to cry. John welled up again. And I just kept staring, afraid, ecstatic, disbelieving.

"It's not going to bite you, Ren." Martin laughed. "It's legitimate. You have my word. It also means you'll have to start paying taxes now we know you exist."

"I-I don't know what to say." My hand tentatively stroked the glass, the reflection of the lights above dancing over the letters below.

"Don't need to say anything. You deserve it. I'm sorry it took almost thirty-one years to have one." He cleared his throat when no one said anything, adding, "You guys love each other. It's obvious to anyone who meets you. I suggest you do something about making the name Mclary a thing of the past."

Standing, he picked up his briefcase and strode to the door. "Oh, I also took the liberty of doing something I overheard about birthdays. I hope you don't mind." Tapping his temple, he smiled. "I'll let myself out. But if you ever need anything, you know where I am."

I barely managed a goodbye before my attention locked back on the birth certificate in front of me.

*My* birth certificate.

The birth certificate registered and legal in the name Della gave me.

Ren Wild.

And his birthday?

27th of June.

The same day as Della's...just as it should be.

For a second, all I could do was stare.

I was legal.

I was *real.*

I never believed something so simple could be so damn bittersweet.

I had permission to marry, all while serving a death sentence.

Pressure wrapped around my lungs with black affliction, but then my heart drowned it out with red affection. I was still alive, here and now. I still had Della, today and tomorrow. I still had a future, shortened but valued.

Time was never on our side.

It didn't matter then, and it didn't matter now.

Nothing mattered but *us.*

In a rush of daring, reckless true love, I stood so fast my chair toppled to the floor.

Eyes widened at my explosive behaviour, then gasps fell as I sank to one knee before the ribbon-hearted girl I'd loved forever.

Her blue eyes became twin puddles of tears as I grabbed her hand, kissed her knuckles, and whispered, "Della Donna Mclary..."

She flinched in my hold, and John's hands curled on the table.

My voice caught as I couldn't hold back my desperate, *desperate* need to have her as my own. Selfish, yes. Sad, absolutely. I would make her a widow before long, but even that couldn't stop me.

She was mine.

It was written in the stars and scribed in the galaxies, and nothing on earth could change that.

This was true inevitability, utter undeniability.

I didn't even need to ask a question.

"Marry me."

# *Chapter Fifty-One*

## DELLA

## 2034

*DO YOU HATE me?*

*Do you hate me for taking you on this journey, making you fall in love with Ren, all while knowing how it ends?*

*Do you hate me for telling the truth?*

*Believe me, I've often wondered if I should change our ending. If I should lie and create the perfect happily ever after—just like Ren wanted me to.*

*But...whenever I type a chapter full of happy fakery, it seems so forgetful, so cliché, so counterfeit.*

*At least, I gave you a warning. If you read the words I chose and saw the message I shared, you'd know.*

*You'd know more than I ever did.*

*In fact, you know more than I did back then, and I sympathise with the pain you're going through.*

*Ren.*

My *Ren.*

*The answer to my puzzle, the conclusion to my journey, the man I was always meant to belong to.*

*He wasn't immortal, after all.*

*But...I have to be honest. I have to make you see.*

*This was never that sort of tale.*

*This wasn't a romance—I was blatant about that from the start.*

*This wasn't even a love story—even though love is the only thing that matters.*

*This is a* life *story.*

*And life includes good times and bad.*

*It includes birth and growth and...yes, even death.*

*This is a story of truth.*

*This is a story of my heart.*

*A story we all go through because eventually…we all die.*

*Some before others, some quick and fast, some in their sleep far from now.*

*But before you give in to those tears and believe you know our ending, stop.*

*Keep reading.*

*Keep enduring.*

*Because I can promise you, the ending…it's better than you think.*

# *Chapter Fifty-Two*

## DELLA

## 2021

I SHOULD HAVE been on cloud nine.

Ren had proposed.

Ren had a birth certificate.

Ren wasn't arrested.

Ren was also lying.

His eyes lied. His voice lied. His body lied.

And it hurt.

So much.

Funny, how hiding the truth could hurt more than a fist or cruel word. Funny, how a person you trusted above everything could suddenly become so dangerous.

He was *lying*.

I knew.

I knew the signs because I'd lied to him often enough while he still cared for me as a sister. I knew how a lie festered inside you. How it sunk its hooks in, dragging you deeper into its web, whispering in your ear that your lies came from a good place, a worthy place, a place of protection.

Ren was lying.

And because of that, my heart that was normally so open toward him fashioned a little gate—not a door blocking him out, but a small barrier that wasn't there before.

I hated it.

I hated him for making it happen.

I grew up faster in two months than I ever did in two years. I felt it happen. My rosy outlook on life, the childish belief that nothing could tear us apart, the idealistic notion of perfect happiness...they'd been threatened, questioned, and found wanting.

All those 'errands', those 'work' phone calls—they were poisonous barbs digging into my skin, layering me with pain, punishing me for loving someone so much when they were only hurting me.

At least I knew he wasn't cheating on me. At no point did such a ridiculous thought enter my mind. Ren was mine. He was *still* mine. Even if he was being a bastard lately.

Did he think I was stupid?

Did he think I was too weak to know?

I didn't need a degree to know his lies stemmed from his cough.

A cough that, to start with, I'd hoped was just bad allergies. Ren, after a lifetime of dealing in grass and animals, had built up an immune system that didn't often feel the tickle of hay fever, but occasionally, if the wind blew in a different direction or if the season had grown a different spore within the grass, he'd have a few days of watery eyes and a stuffy nose.

It never lasted long.

It left as quickly as it arrived.

But this...it hadn't.

It had gotten worse.

It'd morphed into a cough that woke me up at night and made me cry silent tears in the dark.

I supposed it was my fault that he believed he could get away with such fibs. I didn't push him to see a doctor even though terror chanted in my blood every second of every day. I didn't sit him down and stare him in the eye and ask point-blank what he was keeping secret.

It was my fault as much as his; he didn't tell me because he was protecting me. And I didn't hound him because in a way...I *wanted* protecting. I wanted to continue believing in the fantasy that he was invincible.

But I also wanted him to trust that I wouldn't break, that I wouldn't leave, that I was strong enough to carry whatever burden he dealt with.

Of course, I didn't share my worries with anyone, and, as I slipped from the farmhouse where Cassie and I had been calling contractors and arena surface companies for her equine set-up, my shoulders rolled with tiredness.

I hadn't been sleeping.

I was sick of pretending.

My smiles were fake, and my tears hidden when Ren held me close last night and whispered about making me a legally married woman. His murmurs of togetherness and forevers were full of hypocrisy, and I'd turned my back on him.

I was tired.

So, *so* tired and I couldn't pretend anymore.

I just wanted the truth, so my mind could stop conjuring nightmares.

Pushing open the barn doors, I strode into the comforting shadows where splinters of light danced with hay dust and horse hair.

I wanted to go for a ride to clear my head, but as I moved toward the tack room, a voice caught my ears.

A voice I knew better than my own.

"…and when will you know?" Slight pause. "Ah." Another pause. "Yeah, okay."

My steps turned to tiptoes as I crept toward the stables and ducked behind some stacked bales. Through the stalky, golden grass, I spotted Ren.

My heart kicked like it always did.

He was so handsome with jeans slung low on narrow hips, a grey and black plaid shirt rucked up to his elbows, and boots that had travelled miles covered in dirt. He had one thick glove on his left hand and the other tucked into his back pocket as he held his phone with his right.

He leaned on the stable door, his head bowed, handsome face grim. "Yeah, I've had two so far." He closed his eyes. "Actually, that might be true. I haven't been coughing as much lately."

My hands balled beside me. *Who the hell is he talking to?*

He listened to whomever was on the phone for a long moment, before kicking the stable door softly as if he wanted to rage but wasn't prepared to pick up the aftermath of ruin. "I have another treatment in two weeks or so." He shook his head, his dark, unruly hair tumbling. "No, no side effects."

I crumpled word by word, unable to tear my eyes off him.

This was worse than my nightmares.

This was real.

"Yeah, I know. A test would be good. I want to know if I'm responding, too." He raked a hand through his hair. "Okay, sure."

I pulled back into the shadows as he turned to face me, his eyes landing on the bales I hid behind. His chocolate gaze glittered, but his jaw was tense and strong. "If it works...how long do I have?"

My heart.

God, my *heart*.

It was no longer beating and pumping inside me.

It was bleeding and gasping by my feet.

I wanted to scoop it up. I wanted to stop it growing cold and discarded and covered in old manure, but I couldn't because Ren pinched his nose, then looked at the ceiling as if he stared at God and cursed him.

"That's not enough," he groaned. "I'm-I'm getting married—"

Whoever he spoke to cut him off, and his gaze fell to the ground. "I know. Yeah, stay positive, I'll try." Running a hand over his face, he murmured, "Thank you." He punched the disconnect button, threw his phone to the floor, and collapsed against the stable door.

With his knees up around his ears, he picked up a piece of hay and twirled it in the most dejected, terribly broken way that my heart crawled from its manure grave and hauled itself back into my chest, desperate to go to him even smeared and dirty and dying.

"Fuck," Ren whispered. *"Fuck."*

\* \* \* \* \*

Staring into my reflection, I let the tears fall.

A girl I didn't recognise stared back at me. A girl with eyes the colour of grief and hair the pigment of sorrow.

Ren was already in bed, watching something on TV, waiting for me to finish my shower so we could snuggle together and lose our troubles in a movie that would never have the power of forget.

I'd left Ren in the stable.

He didn't know I'd heard.

He didn't know I knew...

Knew that he was sick enough to no longer look at the seasons as four adventures but four wheels pushing him closer to the one thing I never thought would be our enemy.

Not until decades from now.

Not until we'd raised children and grown sick of each other and became cranky and grey.

*Death.*

My fingertips pressed against the glass, tracing the tears on my cheeks in the coolness of the mirror.

I was naked.

Hair drenched from my shower and water still dripping over me.

I was cold.

Nipples pebbled, and skin raised with goosebumps.

I was empty.

Silent on the outside, screaming on the inside.

The mirror lied when it painted a picture of a girl just standing there crying. It should show the truth—the reality that I was hair tugging, skin bleeding, nails scratching, voice yelling, fists flailing, and knees bruised from begging for salvation.

I was chaos not calm.

A sob caught in my throat as I reached into the medicine cabinet and pulled out my nightly ritual.

Face cream applied.

Teeth brushed.

Pill...

The tiny pill sat in my palm—no longer just a drug designed to keep me free from pregnancy but a small, ticking explosive.

Time had once again screwed us.

It had given me to Ren too young.

It had granted only a few wonderful years when we could touch and kiss and love.

And now...it'd taken away our future as cruelly as it had shoved us into one before we were ready.

The pill.

The magical little pill that stopped things from happening.

And time, the demonic power that sped up all things.

Ren had asked how long he had.

When you asked that question, the answer was never good.

We were on borrowed days now, on bartered minutes, and bargained seconds.

My palm tipped sideways, and the pill scattered down the plughole.

Our dreams were slashed...all but one.

We didn't have the luxury of waiting.

Catching my eye one last time in the mirror, I dressed in the boy shorts and cami I wore to sleep, turned out the light, and went to bed where, for now...my lover still waited for me.

# Chapter Fifty-Three

## REN

## 2021

"I DON'T THINK I can do this anymore."

Another week of lying, sneaking, and hiding.

Outwardly, Della still smiled at me, accepted my kisses, and talked to me, but inwardly...she'd gone.

I didn't know how to explain it.

The empty feeling whenever I touched her. The heartache whenever we kissed—she'd pulled away even while her body was still mine.

I'd hurt her enough to shut down, and that fucking tore me into shreds.

John raised his head, his big paws curling around his coffee cup.

We'd started at sunrise today, thanks to spring arriving overnight with warm air, bright sun, and grass sprouting from the ground at a visible rate.

The farm had woken up from hibernation, demanding to be tended.

"I told you from the start to tell her." He gnawed on his inner cheek, his wrinkles tightening around his eyes. "She knows something isn't right."

"I know." I sighed heavily.

She'd always been too aware of me. Too smart for her own good.

John smiled sadly. "I know you're trying to protect her, but you're only hurting both of you." His eyes drifted with memories. "I didn't know Patty was close to leaving me—none of us did. The suddenness was what made it so hard. The fact that we didn't have time to say goodbye or look for hope or tick off a bucket list. She was here, and then she wasn't." He gulped, his knuckles turning white around his coffee mug. "You aren't going anywhere, Ren. Not for a very long time—"

"You heard what the doctors said, I only have a few—"

"Stop. You didn't let me finish. I was going to say...you aren't going anywhere, but we're realistic to know you have a fight ahead of you, and you need her by your side. We *all* want to be by your side. Liam, Cassie..."

"I know." I slugged my coffee in one gulp.

*What the hell am I doing?*

The distance between me and Della wasn't worth any price.

I needed to fix this.

I needed to tell her.

*Somehow.*

I stood from the table. "You're the best boss in the world, John, but I'm gonna stand you up today." I coughed a little. "Gotta take a few days off."

"Told you you didn't need to work while you're—"

"I'm not an invalid," I snapped. "Not yet, anyway. I want to work...just not when I've fucked up and need to fix it."

He chuckled. "Well, I'm docking your pay."

I smiled at his joke. "Wouldn't have it any other way." Marching to the back door, my legs filled with nervous energy. I'd woken this morning with an itinerary of fertilizing and weed-killing the back pastures. Nothing on that agenda said I'd finally have the guts to tell the love of my life I was dying.

But I couldn't keep lying anymore.

I had another treatment next week. Depending on how well it went, I'd be tested to see if I'd responded. Either good news or bad...I wanted Della to be there.

"Before you go." John lugged his bulk from the chair and moved toward the shelf where Patricia had grabbed the sex education book for an eight-year-old Della all those years ago. Pulling an envelope free, he came toward me. "No arguments, Ren. None, you hear me?"

I eyed him. "Depends...what is it?"

"I know you've been lucky enough to enter an off-label trial for your age group. But we don't know how long that'll last." Shoving the envelope into my hands, he muttered, "This is for after. Just in case."

Tearing it open, I didn't find cash like I had on my first pay packet.

Instead, I found a contract.

A contract written up between Cherry River Farm and me, its employee.

John had found a way to pay for my treatment by legally making me his worker—someone who now paid tax with a notable salary. Someone who could receive healthcare.

My eyes met his. "How many times are you going to meddle in my future, John?"

He chuckled. "As many times as it takes." Patting my shoulder, he nudged his chin at the door. "Go. Find your girl. Make it right between you."

"This discussion isn't over." I shoved the contract into my back pocket. "I'm not putting you in debt. No matter how you word it in fine print."

"Yeah, yeah. Go."

I gave him a final look, amazed that in my short life I'd been victim to the worst of evil and son to the best of them.

Stepping outside, I squinted against the rays of fierce sunshine. Yesterday, it seemed as if winter would never leave, and this morning, spring had well and truly kicked its ass.

I hoped the nice weather stuck around for a while because where we were going, we'd have enough to deal with to worry about snow.

Jogging into the barn, I tried not to get my hopes up that my usual breathlessness was better today. That I hadn't coughed as much. That the ache had faded somewhat.

I'd had two treatments of Keytruda, and, so far, I was lucky.

Barely any side effects and if possible…already some signs that the experiential immunotherapy was working.

*Please, please, God, let it be working.*

Tossing the gear we'd need into one backpack, I ensured we had water and snares and my knives were sharp and ready. Slipping on a black jacket that had seen better days, I hoisted the backpack onto my shoulders and made my way over the cobblestones to our one bedroom.

The Wilson's guest bedroom was all well and good for now, but soon I'd need to figure out a way to give Della the house she deserved. A home of our own…before it was just hers.

Opening the door, I caught Della perched on the end of the bed dressed in her riding gear. Jodhpurs that clung to curves and a tweed coat that brushed her thighs.

Her hair was plaited down her back with her blue ribbon in a bow at the end. "Ren." Guilt echoed in her tone as she slammed the laptop closed and tossed it onto the unmade sheets beside her. "What are you doing back so soon?" Her eyes travelled over me, making my body harden. "And why do you look like you're going camping?"

"Because we are." Moving toward her, I grabbed her wrist and pulled her from the bed. "What were you looking at?"

"Nothing." Her eyes narrowed with her lie.

"Were you researching something?"

Her head tilted. "Should I be?"

"Depends."

"On what?"

"On how much you already know."

She gasped. "Are you going to tell me *what* I should know?"

My heart pounded. "I can't keep lying to you."

Tears welled in her gaze. "Does that mean I can stop hating you?"

I walked into her, slotting her body against mine. "I think it will only make you hate me more."

She flinched, burrowing her face in my chest.

Squeezing her tight, we shared a hug full of sadness before I coughed gently and ruined it.

Her eyes met mine as I pulled away, reaching for her hand. "We need to talk."

"I was afraid you were going to say that." Her tongue licked as a tear rolled past her lips. "What if…what if I'm not ready? For weeks, I thought I was. I've been so angry that you've lied…but now?" Her face drained of colour. "I don't know if I'm ready, Ren."

Kissing her sweetly, I stared into her, wishing I could protect her.

Wishing I could change our future.

Wishing I could stop this.

"Let's go home, Della Ribbon. And then…we'll talk."

\* \* \* \* \*

We set up the tent in silence.

The once familiar tasks a little rusty as we grabbed nylon and inserted poles.

Firewood had already been collected. A snare already set. Our camp as homey as I could make it.

The tent was the last thing, and the minute it was up and pegged securely to the ground, I spread out our yoga mats and made up a sleeping bag bed.

Della didn't enter the tent. She drifted around the camp with an aura of loss and fear, kicking at pine cones and tugging her braid.

I let her drift because I needed the camp to be as perfect as I could before I told her...because once I did? Nothing else would matter.

Time was no longer relative.

Some days dragged with hazards and peril—every second doing its best to remind me that I no longer had the privilege of old age. And some days flashed past with peace and positivity—every heartbeat doing its best to assure me that I could beat the timeline the doctors gave me.

I'd been in Keytruda forums.

I'd read miracles and tragedies.

I aimed to be a goddamn miracle because there was no way I could leave Della yet. She was still so young; so pure and perfect. I didn't want to be the reason she faded and found life anything less than extraordinary.

Once my chores were complete and I had nothing left to distract myself with, I looked up to where Della hovered.

It was as if she knew before I spoke a word. And I was stupid to think she didn't. So idiotic to believe she hadn't figured out something was wrong...seriously fucking wrong.

The forest became thick with everything we couldn't say. Birds quietened. Trees stilled. Time itself slowed so we stood in a nucleus where nothing could touch us.

Her gaze shouted, her body swaying a little in disbelief to whatever she saw on my face.

Finally, when the strain grew too much to bear, I spread my hands in surrender with a dismal shrug. "I'm so sorry, Della."

I expected a fight.

She was angry and hurting and, whenever those two emotions combined, she was vicious. But instead, she folded in on herself as if some beast crumpled her like a discarded piece of manuscript—erasing part of our story, deleting all the chapters that could have been.

With the softest, saddest cry, she broke into a run and slammed into my arms.

I stumbled backward, holding her, hugging her, stabilising

both of us as her heart pounded against mine.

"I don't know what I was thinking," I murmured into her hair. "How I thought I could protect you from this. Please...forgive me."

She shook her head, face wedging against my shoulder. "Don't. Please don't."

"Don't what?"

"Don't tell me. Don't make it real."

I sighed, pressure banding and pain throbbing. "It's real. Whether I tell you or not, it's real."

Her arms squeezed me harder. "But you're mine. You're *mine*."

"And I'll always stay yours." My lips feathered on her temple, gulping back my first taste of bitter honesty. "No matter where I go."

Another bone deep sound came from her, making me rock on my heels as she wriggled closer.

How the fuck could I do this?

How could I voice something so tragic when all I wanted to do was pretend I was fine?

But a cough reminded me I *wasn't* fine.

I was slowly dying.

I didn't know how long we stood there—both of us petrified, both of us understanding what this meant. Every touch from here on out would have a different flavour. Every smile would be treasured and counted. Every laugh would be hoarded and noted.

*Nothing* would be taken for granted.

That sort of connection and awareness could make life utterly exhausting—doing our best to scribble down memories and strive for more achievements.

But that was the thing, I didn't want to race the clock and fill our lives with empty meaning. I didn't need to complete a bucket list or travel or seek cheap thrills.

I had everything I ever wanted, needed, and valued right there in my arms.

There was only one thing I needed, and it would be the hardest thing I'd ever ask of her. "Della..." Pulling away so I could see her face, I cupped her cheeks. "I'll tell you anything you want to know—everything I know, at least. But before I do, I need to know something from you."

Her tears dribbled over my fingers, my thumb running softly over her lips. "Ask me."

I closed my eyes, hunting for strength. When I opened them again, her tears had stopped, but her sadness still glittered bright.

"I need…" I shook my head, jaw locking. I looked to the side, fighting the crush of despair.

"Ren." Her fingers dug into my waist. "Ren…look at me."

It took a monumental effort; her beautiful face danced as liquid dared fill my eyes.

She smiled joylessly before sweeping up and pressing her mouth to mine.

The second she kissed me, I threw myself into her.

I groaned and gathered her close, frenzied in my desire for connection.

We stumbled again, but this time in undiluted lust.

Yet another thing that would become so much more. So much more than just sex and kisses and thrusts. Even as my mind imprinted her subtle minty taste and inhaled her light melon fragrance, I did my best to stop.

To stop kissing her as if I were already gone.

To stop remembering her as something I'd lost when she was alive and willing in my arms.

Her teeth teased my bottom lip, making my thoughts scatter. Hunger for her coiled in my belly, and I latched onto the simplicity of desire.

I'd wanted to be honest and clear the air.

But Della had once again given me something I didn't know I needed.

I missed her so fucking much.

I'd hurt her and driven her away and deserved her coldness.

But standing there, surrounded by nature and no one, all that existed between us was heat and passion and devotion.

There would be time for talking.

After.

Scooping her into my arms, I somehow managed to traverse the campsite with its leaf litter and hazardous tripping and carried her into the tent.

Placing her onto her feet, we kicked off our boots in synchronization before slamming to our knees, praying to each other, sacrificing our hearts, offering up everything we had to be worthy of one more day.

Her fingers landed in my hair, pulling my head to hers.

I obeyed, kissing her hard and fast, deep and long.

How was I supposed to stay strong when I had a girl like

Della? How was I supposed to be okay with this?

I had so many things I needed to do before I went.

I needed to find a way to provide for her. To protect her future and know she was safe. I needed to have a family with her. To at least see one or two wrinkles on her flawless face.

Our tongues met, then retreated. Our lips connected, then paused.

Out of all the things I'd miss, kissing Della was the most.

"Ren?"

Her whisper physically hurt me. "Yeah?"

More tears scattered down her face while she kneeled before me. "Promise me we'll always be together." Her hands clutched mine with crazed urgency. "Promise me this isn't over. Promise me like you promised five-year-old me that you'll never let me go. Never, ever leave me."

*Jesus Christ.*

My heart squeezed, and I wrapped her in my arms, dragging her onto my lap.

I wanted so fucking much to be able to promise. I would've given anything to assure her we had forever. That there wasn't a guillotine already poised above my neck.

I should do what I'd always done and *protect* her.

*Fuck, I should protect her.*

But my lungs burned, my back ached, and my body prodded me to be brave. "I will always love you." My avoidance of her promises wrenched a sob from her lungs. Her legs squeezed around my waist, her breath hitching with sorrow.

"I'll never stop, Della Ribbon." Her curls stuck to my lips as I inhaled her sweet scent. "Not until life rips me from your arms. And even then...it's not goodbye."

A cough tumbled from my mouth. A cough that made her stiffen and arms tighten.

Kissing her, I murmured, "I promise that every breath I take is for you. I've never loved anyone else and I never will."

She crawled closer, kissing me with a fury that threatened to make me snap. "My heart has always belonged to you."

"I know." My voice broke, and I fisted her hair to kiss her hard.

My body tightened, my heart pounded, and by the time the kiss ended, I was lightheaded and out of breath, and I didn't know if it was from her or the disease inside me.

The doctors had warned me that as I progressed, my strength

would go. I'd lose weight. I'd struggle to breathe. I'd fade away piece by piece.

That was my utmost terror.

That Della would remember me that way.

"I need you to promise me something." I didn't tear my mouth from hers, speaking directly into her. "Promise me that you'll remember me like this. That you'll stay with me. That you won't hate me for dy—"

"Stop. I-I can't." Her lips twisted beneath mine.

"Can't promise you'll stay by me while I go through—"

"Can't hear you say the word dying. *Please*, Ren." Her eyes met mine, so close and somber.

The knowledge I was the one causing her so much pain crippled me. "I thought I could do this." My neck bowed, my forehead touching hers. "But I can't. Not yet."

"Me, too. I'm not ready."

"I need you, Della."

Her hands fumbled on my belt, ripping open the buckle and unzipping my fly. "You have me. Always."

I half-smiled, repeating what she said as if it were a vow. "Always." As if that one word linked us beneath the eyes of nature, binding us better than any wedding ceremony.

Her hand dove between us, slipping into my boxers and fisting me.

My breath caught at the sudden shot of pleasure, and all I wanted to do was give in. We needed to lose ourselves from reality for a while, but I placed my hand over hers.

"Wait." I coughed quietly.

Her eyes met mine, wincing. "Why?"

*Why?*

Because we had so little time.

Because I needed so much more than I already had.

I never looked away even though it was the most vulnerable I'd ever been around her. "I know it's soon, and we agreed to wait...but I'm ready to come second best."

Her lips parted.

I waited to see if she understood.

Of *course*, she understood.

She was my intelligent, beautiful Della.

She bit her lip, her chest heaving with tears. "A-are you going to leave me that fast?" Her fingers twitched around my erection. Her eyes closed tight as if barricading herself against my answer.

"I—" I groaned, fighting yet another cough. "I don't know how to do this, Della. Don't know how to hurt you when it's the last thing I ever wanted to do."

"Then don't." She looked up. "Lie to me. Tell me this is all a terrible mistake."

"You know I can't do that. I've tried. I can't hide from you. Not anymore."

"I know." Her face held no colour, blood sinking inside to protect her heart. "Just…after. Tell me after."

"Fuck, Ribbon." I kissed her, tasting salt and misery and an end we both weren't ready for.

As we kissed, my hands undid the buttons of her jacket and pushed it off her shoulders. Our lips disconnected as I fumbled for her jodhpur zipper. She hadn't changed before trekking with me. She hadn't done anything apart from follow me dazedly from the stables and over the fields to the forest.

Popping the button against her flat stomach, she watched my fingers undress her.

"I stopped taking my pill a week ago. I—" She gave me a guilty half-smile. "I didn't discuss it with you. I threw it down the drain. I'm sorry."

"Sorry?"

"For making that decision alone."

I kissed her, jerking her close. "You made the right one. You made the only one."

"I want your baby, Ren. But…I don't know if I'm ready to share you. Especially now."

My heart sank. "Then we'll wait. I'll respect that."

I'd respect it and hope to God I survived long enough to make a child with her. Hope to heaven the drugs that would extend my life wouldn't make me sterile before it was too late.

Her hand moved again, pulling me free from my jeans and boxers until I stabbed upright between us. "How long, Ren?"

"Della…" Using my knuckle, I nudged her chin upward. "Please, stop." I bent to press my lips to hers, expecting a refusal but earning a soul-blistering kiss instead. "After, remember?"

"After." She nodded, her fingers stroking hotly.

My body became corrupted by her touch. Part of me was no longer interested in sex after talking about such morbid things, but the larger part was ever more desperate.

Desperate to live.

Desperate to start a new life.

Desperate to tell the Grim Reaper to fuck the hell off.

Ignoring the unsaid things between us, hiding the secrets dripping with pain, I whispered, "I want a child with you. Even if it will drive me insane the entire time you're pregnant. Despite what happened with the ectopic scare, I want a daughter like you. I'm selfish to risk everything to have that."

She smiled sadly. "And I want a son like you."

"Guess we'll have to have both, then."

"Do we have time?"

I winced, swallowing on my shortened longevity.

*Do you want to know? Are you so eager for me to break your heart?*

I sucked in a breath. "I——"

"Wait. Don't." She pressed her lips to mine. "Just kiss me."

So I did.

I kissed her, undressed her, laid her on her back, and slid from my clothes. Snuggling into one sleeping bag, I pulled the other up and over us, trapping our body heat.

My hand disappeared between her legs.

She jerked as I touched her, feeling her silky flesh, hot with want. Her eyes glowed sapphire as I pressed a finger inside her.

I wanted to make this last. To touch her for hours and lick, taste, and worship, but a baser desire lived within me. The knowledge she wasn't on the pill. The idea that we could create something bigger than ourselves.

I wanted to leave her with a legacy that was more than just money or possessions. I wanted her to have a piece of me. A child with my blood in its veins and a shred of my soul in its heart.

I stupidly wanted to find some way to always be there…even when I wasn't.

Her hips arched up, welcoming me to touch her deeper. I inserted another finger, making her wet, encouraging her to forget her grief and only remember pleasure.

I found her lips again, kissing in time to my pressure, my tongue in rhythm to my finger, my body winding tighter the longer she fondled and stroked.

For so long, I'd known her body as intimately as anyone could. I'd seen her legs grow from chubby to elegant. Her chest from flat to full. And now, I knew exactly what pleased her and how to make her submit entirely.

As I thrust deeper, she gasped into my mouth. "If we're lucky enough to have children, I promise to love them." She cupped my cheek, holding me steady. "But I also promise I'll love you more. I won't be able to help it."

My fingers stopped, wedged tight inside her. "That's something I can't agree to." Sorrow balled in my heart. "Don't you see? I *need* you to love them more, Della. I need someone else to hold your heart when I can't."

Her breath caught, body flinched, the precipice we'd been dancing over yawning. "I hate you for this." The fierceness in which she said it broke me.

"I know."

"I hate you *so* much, Ren."

"Hate me if you must but love me, too. Please…"
Withdrawing my fingers, I climbed over her, slotting my body into hers. When I felt her damp warmth, I pushed, spreading her, filling her, invading every last piece she could give me.

Tears cascaded down her cheeks, soaking into the sleeping bag below.

I rubbed away the droplets I could and licked at the ones I missed, cradling her as I made love to her.

How many times would we have this?

How many more moments of connection?

We rocked together—gentle and almost apologetic. Our touches safe and kisses guarded. But slowly…the hurt dissolved, leaving only lust and our bodies burning with desire.

Our pace turned faster, tame blending into violence.

Carnal hunger ripped through my veins, kicking my heart, coating my skin with need.

Della writhed beneath me, meeting me thrust for thrust.

Her face wasn't soft or open but angry and revengeful. Without speaking, she ran her fingernails down my back, deep and deliberately mean.

I bowed, groaning in pleasure-pain, my cock hardening to excruciation.

A blackness encroached my mind, filling me with a mad kind of savagery.

She felt the change. She matched it with her own.

Our lovemaking turned to war, and my thrusts switched from rocking to fucking.

"Goddamn you, Della." Fisting her hair, I held her down as I bucked inside her. She moaned as I yanked on the strands—the same strands I'd washed and braided and brushed. The hair I'd seen wet and tangled and even blue. The hair I'd inhaled while sleeping beside her in the tent and fought a love that couldn't be fought.

"I hate you," she whispered as I pulled out and pushed her onto her stomach. Gripping the back of her neck, I thrust back inside her, keeping her pinned and imprisoned. "You. Already. Said. That." I growled, sweating and aching and forever fighting a cough.

"I hate you because I love you," she cried as I hit the button inside her that added mind-bending intensity.

"Ribbon—" I grunted as her back arched, forcing herself onto me, ramming herself down my length.

"I hate you because I won't survive."

My body was stiff and awkward, every neuron locked inside her. "You will. You have to."

"I don't want to." Her mouth opened wide as I yanked her hair back and kissed her. My chest pressed to her back, riding her, knees digging into sleeping bags, and tent shivering with our speed.

I grunted, "You have no choice."

"I *do* have a choice."

I drove harder, deeper, crueller. "You don't. I can't face this if I believe otherwise."

Her face twisted into anguish. "Fuck you."

"I'll fuck you instead." Thrusting faster, I nipped at her ear. "I'll always be inside you, Della."

I rippled with the need to release. The toxic blend of punishment and pleasure was a dangerous place to be. I couldn't treat her gently. I couldn't keep my touch soft. I couldn't be *nice* anymore.

She felt me losing control and tried to make me come, teeth snapping at my mouth, back hollowing as she speared herself deeper onto me.

I tried to kiss her, but she merely bit me, utter wretchedness tumbling from her soul. A second later, she moaned with joy as I gave her the fury she wanted.

I fucked her harder.

"Is this what you want?"

She moaned. "I want you forever. That's what I want."

"And you have me forever."

She wriggled beneath me, activating predator instincts that planted a fist in her lower back, keeping her prone and open.

She groaned, guttural and feral, just like me. Fighting me for no other purpose than to piss me off.

She looked over her shoulder. "If you loved me, you'd stay."

What a horrid thing to say.

What a *disgusting* slur to utter.

"Don't you think I'm trying?" My anger turned to rage, and I fucked her with contempt instead of everlasting love. "You've pushed me too far, Della."

She bucked and pleaded, and I lost myself to her.

*I'm sorry.*

*So goddamn sorry.*

She made me angry, so fucking angry. She made me sad, so eternally sad.

And I didn't want to be either of those things because I had to be strong for her.

She squirmed as my rough palms caressed her spine, massaging with possessive strokes.

Grabbing handfuls of her ass, I forced her legs to spread wider, her feet kicking, flashing me her ribbon tattoo, drowning me in memories; painful, shard-filled memories of our shared childhood, stabbing me over and over, craving, wanting, *begging.*

A cough caught me unaware.

Another cough followed that one.

And I bent over, clamping my teeth into her shoulder, stifling any more.

I *refused* to be ill.

I refused to be a faulty clock deciding how many minutes I could have with her.

"I love you, Della." My cock throbbed, hard as wood; my mind raced, a mess with desire. I looped an arm around her stomach, holding her tight as I thrust into her from behind. "Forever."

Rage drenched my blood. Anger at life and love and loss.

My hips pistoned faster, taking out my sadness on her— letting her taste a little of the fury inside me. The grief and yearning for more.

Her head snapped up as my fingers found her clit, rubbing fast and hard. "God—"

Her body tightened around me, preparing for a release.

I loved taking her like this. Loved dancing on the border of animal and human, right and wrong, sexy and sadistic.

There were so many things I wanted to do to her.

So many, *many* things.

Would time give them to me?

"You've broken me, Ribbon. And now, I have to break you." I reared up on my hands, driving my body into hers, unapologetic, untamed, unforgiving.

She wanted me rough.

She had me.

I was jerky and fierce.

I was lost and afraid.

I was in love and utterly in pieces.

I wanted to punish her for the life she'd have after me. I wanted to free her from the pain I was about to cause her.

I hated her.

I loved her.

I missed her so fucking much already.

"God, Ren." Her cry unravelled the final parts of me, and I lost the remaining pieces that made me hers.

I fucked and thrust and layered her with bruises upon bruises.

And still, she begged for more.

My teeth found her skin, and my body answered hers. And our hearts clanged and pounded to the same song, the melody giving way to a crescendo, the crescendo exploding to the finale, and we rode that song until sweat glistened and moans echoed, and our bodies found the same pleasure as our hearts.

We came together, fast and spent.

We loved each other, even though it hurt.

We were bonded, so there would be a forever.

And not even death could stop us.

# *Chapter Fifty-Four*

## DELLA

## 2021

"WHAT ABOUT JULIE?"

I cracked open my gaze, shaking my head on Ren's naked chest. "No."

"Holly?"

"Nah."

"Daphne?"

"Definitely not." I peeled my face from his skin and rolled my eyes. "You're bad at baby naming."

"Those are common, nice names."

"Yes, and they're all girls."

He smiled even though it didn't erase the melancholy in his eyes. "We're having a girl, Della." His gaze travelled down my exposed breasts to my flat belly. "We made one. Today."

Goosebumps sprouted over my arms. "Could it happen that quick?"

He pulled me back down onto him, our shared heat slightly sticky and too hot, but I had no intention of leaving his side.

We'd calmed from our orgasms and separated enough to lie side by side until Ren gathered me to spoon against him as if he needed me to touch him at all times.

"After the short straw I've been dealt, we better have made a baby today. I think I deserve that much." He narrowed his eyes at the tent roof. "Hear me? Whoever you are? Impregnate this girl if you feel a shred of guilt for what you've done to me."

Tears stung my eyes all over again.

I'd forgotten how much I'd cried in the past week, and I'd

only shed more because we'd been avoiding the monster in the room.

The monster we came into the forest to face.

*How long?*

But before we did, I wanted to exist in light-hearted baby planning a little longer. "Okay, say I'm pregnant. Say you have magical sperm, and *bam*, I'm knocked up—out of wedlock, no less." I tapped his chin, making him chuckle. "Say all of that happened? Well, I'm telling you, I'm having a boy."

"Why do you want a boy so badly?"

"Because I want another you."

He sucked in a breath.

The comment was meant to be blasé, but no truer words had been spoken. I wanted another Ren to replace the one who was dying. I wanted Ren to somehow clone himself, heal himself, and never die—not until he was one-hundred-and-two and ready.

Our joking bled away.

We sighed heavily with no small amount of misery.

Oppressive silence smothered us, and we made no move to lighten it.

Exhaustion spread over me even though it was still light outside. I felt as if I'd run every marathon there ever was and still had so many to go.

I suffered no anger anymore. No rage or fury.

Just heart-weary desolation.

I didn't know how much time passed, but Ren squeezed me, rousing me from a strange, stressful doze. "Jacob."

"Huh?"

"If you're pregnant with my son. I want to call him Jacob."

"Why?"

He shrugged. "I just like the name. It feels...right."

My heart splashed into my stomach, annihilated by acid and circumstance. "Okay, Ren. I can live with Jacob."

He gave me the sweetest kiss, his lungs inhaling and exhaling with a gentle cough.

A cough that couldn't be ignored anymore.

We tensed, once again on the same tattered wavelength.

"Della..."

"Ren..."

We spoke together and stopped together.

"You go," I whispered.

He flinched. "I don't know what to say. You've guessed the

hardest part."

"I didn't guess. I overhead you. On the phone in the stable." My voice wobbled. "You asked how long. I knew we didn't have a lot of time."

"Shit." He kissed my forehead. "And you dealt with this for a week on your own?"

I brushed his concern away. "It's nothing compared to you. When did you find out?"

His tone strained. "Does it matter?"

"No." I burrowed into him. "Nothing matters now."

"I'm so sorry, Della."

"Don't do that. Don't apologise for something that isn't your fault."

"But how can I not? How can I not hate myself for what—"

"Stop, Ren." Every muscle clenched. "Just tell me. Tell me what's wrong with you."

He froze, his heart racing against me. "I've had it for twenty years."

I squeezed my eyes as if that would protect me from goblins.

"At Mclary's. I was put at risk..."

I wanted to tell him to stop, to never tell me, to laugh this awfulness away. But I nodded and held on with all my strength.

"You'll need to be tested too—just in case. But I'm hoping you weren't exposed like I was."

"Exposed to what?" I wanted to go deaf, to never listen to what devil hurt my love, but instead, my ears rang...waiting for his answer. And even though I knew it was coming. Even though I'd heard it in my head and watched it happen over and over in my nightmares, it still had the power to change my world.

To change me as a person.

To strip aside my remaining youth and make me so much older than I ever wanted to be.

"Asbestos poisoning." He swallowed hard, his chest working. "I have stage one mesothelioma."

I tried to speak, to be brave and ask questions, but I left him totally alone to explain.

A foreign word I didn't know.

A title to a host of unrecognisable evil.

I was clueless.

I was shell-shocked.

I didn't know myself anymore.

I only knew a canyon of vast quaking emptiness with a river

of the roughest, churniest despair.

Ren swallowed again, chewing on tears. "I've had two treatments with a drug called Keytruda. It's been proven in other studies to be very successful. Some even call it the miracle drug, and it doesn't cause as many side effects as chemo."

He struggled to continue, before clearing his throat and saying matter-of-factly, "It's an active immunotherapy method that stimulates my own immune system to work harder. It gives it a new code...kind of like a computer update to seek out the cells that are bad and attack. I've read forums of people who had cancers reduce—positive responders, they're called. There are some people called total responders, who, after treatment, show no sign of having cancer at all."

He squished me close. "I'm hoping to be one of those."

My voice caught in my throat. I had so many questions, but I was weak; sobbing silently into his chest, feeling his heart pound, hating it and its limited beats.

"I go again soon and want you to come with me. I'll be re-tested...we'll know then if there's hope."

There were so many things I wanted to know, but I couldn't think of a single one. Only the worst thing. The thing I didn't want an answer to, but suddenly was desperate to know.

Inhaling his smoky, wild smell, I asked around my tears. "How long?"

Ren groaned, rubbing his hand up and down my arm. "I don't want you worrying, Della. I want you to focus on the fact that I'm going to outlive every prediction. You have my word I'll—"

"And I'll support you every step of the way. But...how long, Ren?" Looking up, I stared into his deep, sorrow-filled eyes.

And he stared back at the heartache in mine. "Twelve to twenty-four months."

I gasped.

One to two years?

That was *nothing!*

That was torture.

That couldn't be allowed.

"Finding it at stage one is rare, so I'm already ahead of the game. No one really knows how long I'll have. I'm unusual, and that's why I've been given access to this trial even though the drug has already been approved. I promise you I'll have longer than two—"

"Stop." I shook my head, my hair sticking to the sleeping bag and crackling with static electricity. Electricity that I'd feed into his blood if it meant it could eradicate every inch of whatever disease was inside him.

Three seconds ago, I'd been broken beyond repair, destroyed and drowning beneath the knowledge that I couldn't handle this— I wouldn't be able to watch Ren die and stay strong.

But now…now I had a timeline.

I had an enemy.

I had the name of the weapons we'd use to fight it.

Kissing him, I filled with resilience, tenacity, hope. "No."

"No?" he whispered into my mouth.

"No." I nuzzled close, already planning healthy food regimens, study, research, and second opinions. My mind no longer had time for tears. I had a lover to save and ensure he became one of those total responders because there was no other ending for us.

"Not so soon. I won't let you leave me so soon."

He grinned softly. "I'll do everything in my power to obey."

"You better, Ren Wild." Grabbing his hand, I planted it on my stomach and, with a conviction that came from somewhere else, somewhere all-knowing and elemental, I vowed, "I'm pregnant with your child. And I refuse to raise him or her alone. You got me into this mess, and together, we'll find a way for you to survive it."

# *Chapter Fifty-Five*

## DELLA

## 2032

THE SIGNS WERE obvious...now I knew where to look.

The hints that we'd been given too much happiness and now deserved a dose of despair.

I wish I could put your mind at rest.

I want to shout 'surprise' and announce a nasty, practical joke.

But it isn't a joke...it never was.

Life had banished us into the struggle of fighting to stay together, and even if we'd seen the signs earlier, we wouldn't have been able to change fate.

Just like it'd been fate that made us fall in love.

It was fate that would ultimately kill us.

We weren't miracle workers or immune to normality. Our love didn't make us safe from adversity...if anything, it made us more susceptible to catastrophe.

Our hearts were linked.

If one went, so would the other.

If one hurt, both felt it.

A ripple effect that wouldn't just end when Ren died but would continue to haunt me until the day I died, too.

As we lay together after Ren told me, I swung between bravery and cowardice.

I wanted to head to the doctor's straight away and demand every treatment, drug, and trial. I wanted to assure him that I would be strong, and he could lean on me—that he wouldn't face a single piece of this alone.

But I also wanted to stay in that forest and never leave. I wanted to hand my hope to the wind and beg it to rewind time to when Ren was eight and he was never sold to my parents.

I was willing to give up an entire lifetime with him—to prevent us ever *meeting, to stop true love from forming, to end all of it—if it meant he would never have been exposed to asbestos.*

*I would accept he'd love another, marry another...that was how frantic I was to heal him.*

*I was willing to exist and grow up in that hell-house with a murdering mother and raping father if it meant Ren survived. Because, at least that way...I would never have known what I was about to lose as I wouldn't have had him to start with.*

*Was that selfless or selfish?*

*Selfless to want him to live or selfish not to want to face the pain?*

*No matter what happened in the future, I would keep fighting. I would keep clearing the carnage and carrying a sword into battle.*

*There was no other way.*

*Because I was Ren's.*

*Yesterday, tomorrow, for always.*

*By the time night had fallen, casting us in moon glow and star shadows, Ren and I were steady enough to venture outside and cook a simple meal.*

*Watching him boil water for pasta and use his knife to whittle a stick into a stirrer, I made up a story of enchantment where he was part seraph and indomitable—where the inescapable power of age held zero sway.*

*And that was the moment that I knew, just* knew *that love would be the hardest thing I'd ever have to endure.*

*It wasn't my origins or the fact I was never meant to exist. It wasn't seeing what my parents did or the dead children they'd tortured.*

*It was something only a lucky few enjoyed.*

*Something that was said to be worth any pain or price.*

*Love.*

*I was no longer a silly girl who idolized her prince and saviour.*

*I was a woman born to darkness and now, I bargained with that darkness for hope. Hope for the boy I was created for.*

*A boy I wanted to marry.*

*A boy I* did *marry.*

*A simple, perfect marriage that was the third largest incident of our lives.*

*Three out of five moments.*

*Wonderful moments.*

*Horrible moments.*

*Moments that make up a life.*

*One, two, three, four, five.*

*One, Ren was arrested, which led to a domino river of birth certificates and closure.*

*Two, Ren told me he was dying and began a nightmare we would face together.*

*Three, Ren married me a week after and made me the happiest and saddest girl alive.*

*Four...?*

*Well, four arrived eight and a half months later, bringing joy and sorrow in equal measure.*

*And five?*

*Ugh, five...*

*Five will come last.*

*Once our story is over.*

# Chapter Fifty-Six

## REN

## 2021

THERE WERE MANY things I'd experienced in my thirty or so years.

Some mundane and some uncommon, but I'd never felt more aware of my fragility and timelessness than when I said, 'I do.'

When I joined the ranks of husbands.

When I entered the community of marriage and swore my life to serve, protect, and adore.

Up until the moment I'd heard the word 'incurable,' I'd been a patient man.

I didn't rush. I weighed up the pros and cons before I leapt. I enjoyed knowing every outcome before I committed.

But now...

Now, I was the opposite of patient.

I was thirsty and unrepentant and impetuous.

And I didn't wait for anything.

Not that Della wanted to. She was just as hasty as me to bind our souls together.

After a few days in the forest, both discussing and skirting the subject of my impending demise, we returned home as a united front and braved the storm of telling Cassie and Liam together.

John had helped.

Tissues had been used.

Curses had been uttered.

Hugs had been given.

John was right when he said this would be easier with people by my side, and I stood a little taller, a little braver for tomorrow.

It also meant things got done a hell of a lot faster.

Between all of us, we arranged a simple gazebo in the garden and a reverend to marry us. I gave up my concepts of marrying Della in a simple meadow, relinquishing planning to the grandiose ideals of Cassie and letting her invite Adam and his family.

While she plotted our wedding, Della and I visited oncology and the doctor who'd kindly put me on the off-label trial of Keytruda.

Rick Mackenzie was an old Scot who'd been away from home for decades but still had a burr of Scottish accent. He'd been gentle, explaining what I couldn't to Della, and answering her unsteady questions.

I'd held Della's hand, flinching when she flinched and soothing her when she cried.

I chose to have another treatment of Keytruda before my tests to see if I'd improved, and Della hissed between her teeth as the nurse pricked me with the needle and began the thirty-minute siphon of man-made magic into my body.

Once again, claustrophobia clawed, but it was thirty minutes of hell for hopefully a lifetime with my wife.

Afterward, with no side effects to speak of, Rick arranged for another CT scan, blood work, and X-ray, and also took samples from Della...just in case.

Our results were due any day now, and it'd been the hardest thing not to get my hopes up about my own prognosis and keep all fear away from Della's.

On our way back from the hospital—only a couple of days before our wedding—I pulled into town and parked, and just like that day in the junk store in a town I didn't remember, I had the undeniable urge to buy Della a ring.

A ring she would wear for the rest of her life.

"I need to go shopping." I turned to her, my hand on the steering wheel.

"I think I can guess what for." She smiled, opening the door. "No peeking?"

"No peeking." We climbed from the vehicle, and I locked up. "Meet back here in an hour?"

An hour had turned to two as I couldn't find the perfect ring.

My budget was tight and my wishes too lofty.

But at least, in the end, I got something that would hopefully trump her milky, fake sapphire.

I coughed a little, clearing my throat as Nina appeared at the top of the silver-carpeted aisle, scattering flower petals and dragging my mind to the present.

Wedding.

Marriage.

I was getting hitched today.

The fire-haired little girl Cassie had created with an equally fire-headed country boy. When we'd first been introduced, Nina had been shy and scuffed her sneaker into the dirt. That childish uncertainty reminded me so much of Della growing up that my heart had overflowed with echoes from my past.

Of Della smacking a kiss on my lips in the fields when she was nine.

Of Della squealing as I'd blown raspberries on her stomach when she was eight.

Of Della always there, always gorgeous, always mine.

It made standing at the top of the aisle beneath a flower coiled archway—a groom waiting for his bride in a new pair of jeans and white shirt—all the more poignant because finally, *finally* my dreams had come true.

I no longer had to fall asleep to find her. She was there in my every waking moment.

Raising Della had been my biggest challenge and my greatest honour and, as she appeared—blonde hair loose and simple white dress kissing her ankles, her tattoo blue with its ribboned R—I fell even more.

My heart no longer resided in my chest.

It made a home in her hand.

It settled content in her hold.

And it would stay there, even when the rest of me was gone.

My mouth went dry as she drifted toward me, looking ethereal and so damn young.

I never wanted to forget.

Not a single thing.

Not a fraction of a moment.

*I'm so sorry, Little Ribbon.*

*So sorry for marrying you with an ending already close.*

I should annul this marriage, never consummate it, and leave her untouched so she never knew the pain of being a widow.

But there were things I could do and things I couldn't…and this was one I couldn't.

I *had* to marry her.

I'd wanted to marry her since I'd found her.

John walked beside her—our joint father who'd adopted us heart and soul—while Cassie trailed behind her—a sister to us both.

Funny, how the two women who'd been in my life the longest had switched roles.

Once, Della had been my sister, while Cassie was my lover.

Now, Della was my almost-wife, and Cassie was my family.

And when Della arrived before me and John gave her to me with a smile and a look that cleaved my contaminated chest in two, I'd never been so happy or so sad.

All my dreams had come true and, because of that...my life was almost over.

I clutched her hand as we faced the reverend together. We shook equally, afraid and eager, nervous and sure.

The reverend smiled and nodded and spoke about the sanctity of our union.

I didn't listen.

I couldn't.

My entire attention locked on the stunning girl beside me, on the perfect way her hand fit in mine, and the knowledge that after this, she would no longer be a Mclary.

She'd be a Wild.

Her five-year-old suggestion no longer fake but so, so real.

With our eyes joined and love flowing, the reverend gave us state regulated verses and offered up church approved vows, waiting for us to parrot them after him.

Simple and uncomplicated.

No penned poems or scripted sonnets.

Just the bare essentials to bind us.

I couldn't tear my eyes off her as she repeated after him, "I, Della Mclary, choose you, Ren Wild, to be my lawfully wedded husband. For richer, for poorer, in sickness, and in health, for as long as we both shall live."

Sickness.

The worst one.

The one I was about to drag her through.

*I'm so sorry, Della.*

My voice shook as I struggled to hold myself together. "I, Ren Wild, take you, Della Mclary, to be my lawfully wedded wife. For richer, for poorer, in sickness, and in health, for as long as we both shall live."

Disguising the grief in my throat, I pressed a kiss to her ear, closing my eyes on the tears that threatened. "And long past that. Forever, Ribbon. Forever."

She shivered and laughed quietly as I pulled the ring I'd bought from my pocket. Her eyes widened at the solitaire diamond with an italic inscription inside:

*Wild forever and always. I love you.*

She shook her head, another emotional chuckle falling free. "I-I can't believe this."

I brushed aside a curl, imprinting the feel of her soft cheek. "What can't you believe?"

"That once again, we shared the same idea." Opening her palm, she revealed a glossy gold band with the same promise from my dinged-up leather bangle stamped inside.

## DW ♥ RW4EVA

I wanted to curse.

To swear.

Profanity seemed the only cure to release the overwhelming pressure and love inside me, but with God watching us become man and wife, I just drew her close and kissed her deep, all while John chuckled, and Cassie swooned, and the reverend cleared his throat with reprimand.

"You're supposed to wait until *after* you've said the words 'I do.'"

With Della's lips on mine, we smiled and laughed, teeth clacking as we both murmured, "I do."

"I do."

My fingers fumbled on hers, switching her chipped sapphire to her other hand and sliding the diamond over her wedding finger. Once I'd trapped her with vows and jewellery, she trapped me.

I never thought a piece of precious metal could transfix me, but as that ring settled cold then turned warm, I no longer felt alone.

I felt an overpowering sensation of home and heart and hearth.

"You may kiss the bride." The reverend clasped his hands and stepped back.

There would be many things I remembered on my death bed.

So many wonderful things.

But that kiss?

That first kiss where Della was my wife would always be the brightest.

That kiss was our beginning, middle, and end.

That kiss bound us past life and death, sickness and health.

That kiss was life itself, never ending, forever existing, two souls entwined...

...for eternity.

\* \* \* \* \*

"Are you sitting down?"

My fingers tightened around my phone, my eyes tracking Della as she packed a few clothes for us to return to the forest for a small honeymoon.

Only a couple of days, just enough to consummate—more than once—and to forget our future. If we could.

"No. Should I be?" My voice was gruff, belying the injection of panic.

Rick Mackenzie, my oncologist with his Scottish calmness, said, "Let's get the important stuff out of the way, shall we? Let's start with Della Mclary."

"Della Wild now. As of a few hours ago."

Della threw me a kiss, folding a t-shirt neatly.

"Congratulations."

"Thanks." My knees wobbled, depositing me onto the pushed together single beds of our youth. "Is she okay?" My eyes never left Della's as she plopped the t-shirt into the small pile we were taking with us and came toward me.

Slotting herself into the V of my spread legs, her fingers curled in my hair, and I held her waist to my nose.

I inhaled hard, smothering a cough as Rick said, "She's fine. No signs of any asbestos related diseases."

A cry that could only be described as tormented thanks fell from my lips, soaking into her belly button. "Oh, thank God."

Della hugged my head, trembling. "I love you, Ren."

Her whisper scattered around me as Rick continued, "As for you...I really should ask you to come into my office so we can go through any questions you might have, but...well, I can't wait. I wanted to tell you straight away."

Blackness slithered its way through me, blotting out my hope, tearing up the calendar pages of my heart, deleting the months I thought I had. His urgency created pure terror. "What is it?"

*You have one month to live.*

*Kiss your wife goodbye.*

*Hope you have your casket sorted.*

I planted a hand over my eyes, begging the depression to

stop.

Rick's voice cut through the medley. "You're a positive responder, Ren."

For a second, I had no idea what that was.

All my research and knowledge, gone.

*Poof.*

Then the words deconstructed and reassembled into a sentence I could understand. *You're not dying...yet.*

The phone slipped through my hand. It bounced on the carpet like an undetonated bomb.

Was it real?

Was it true?

Not only had I gotten one dream by marrying Della today, I'd earned an extension from leaving her too?

"Ren?" Della's worried voice cut through the buzzing in my head. "You okay?" Ducking, she collected the phone and held it to my ear. "He's still talking."

I cupped her hand with mine, ignoring the phone.

My lungs blazed with pain, but I didn't trust that pain anymore. It was trying to make me believe in a lie.

*I'm not dying...yet.*

Gripping her hard, I breathed fast. "It's-it's good news. Fuck, it's *excellent* news."

For all my positive thinking, I hadn't dared hope for this.

It would fucking break me if it turned out to be bad.

She nodded frantically, tears sparkling. "Thank God." Urging me to take the phone, she said, "Find out more. Talk to him."

Licking my lips, I obeyed, still shell-shocked and disbelieving but ready to listen. "Sorry. Minor accident. Wh-what did you say?"

"What happened? You drop the phone?" Rick chuckled. "You wouldn't be the first. But...be happy. You didn't mis-hear. I said you're showing signs of improvement. As you know, mesothelioma is aggressive, and the tumours are small and dispersed throughout your lungs and abdomen. However, the treatment has halted any from multiplying. In some areas, they've even decreased."

"Holy *shit.*"

Della whacked me on the shoulder. "Language."

I laughed, daring to grab a piece of lightness in all of this. "Sorry, Doctor Mackenzie."

"Bah, I've heard worse. And call me Rick. Think we're on first-name terms now that I'm healing ya."

Della bent and pressed her head against the phone, trying to hear. I pulled it away and put it on speaker so we both could listen.

Coughing just a little, I asked, "So...what now?"

"Now? We keep you on three weekly treatments and watch for more progress. If, in a few months' time, your lungs show significant improvement, you come off the drug and are announced in stable condition."

*Don't ask.*

*Don't ask.*

"And my prognosis?"

I asked.

*Shit.*

This was a happy time.

The best of times.

I shouldn't ruin it by asking for the new date of my death.

However, Rick laughed encouragingly, light-hearted even, infecting me with his optimism. "Screw one to two years, Ren. You've just bought yourself a few more. I don't know how many more, but you're young, only stage one, and prepared to do whatever it takes. That in itself puts you miles ahead. As far as I'm concerned, we'll keep you alive for however long you decide."

"Forever." Standing, I pressed a kiss to Della's lips, talking more to her than my doctor. "I choose forever."

She kissed me back, breathing, "Forever, Ren. A hundred forevers."

"On that note, I'm gonna leave you two newlyweds to enjoy the good news. See you soon, Ren." Rick hung up.

Tossing the phone onto the bed, I swooped my wife into my arms and spun her around. "I hope you didn't marry me thinking I'd be dead in a couple of years, *Mrs* Wild."

Her head tipped back, blonde hair flying, diamond ring glinting. "God, you calling me that does things to me."

"Things?"

Her lips crashed down on mine. "Bad things. Wet things."

I stumbled to the wall, wedging her beside our old dresser. "I mean it, Della. I'm going to fight. Every fucking day."

"And I'm going to love you, every fucking day." She plastered my face with kisses like she used to do when she was a kid and excitement overflowed.

"Language." I nipped at her lip.

"Kiss me, husband." Her lips kissed every part of me, from chin to throat to ear.

I loved she still retained that childish enthusiasm.

I loved that she was giddy with joy, celebrating the best news of all.

Her lips gave up their flurry of kisses, seeking my mouth with sweet desperation.

I matched her with a different kind of fury.

One of bittersweet relief and explosive gratefulness.

I'd sworn my life to this woman.

We no longer had to play pretend husband and wife.

We were *real*.

As real as any other couple and just as permitted to love unconditionally.

And yet, I would forever be more than just a husband to Della. And she would forever be more than just my wife.

Our relationship would always have a different depth to it.

A unique connection that had been formed thanks to so many facets of love.

Love that had already been tested in so many different ways.

Breaking the kiss, I grabbed her hand and twirled her wedding ring.

"Wild forever and always." I quoted the inscription. "Time means nothing when it comes to true love. Promise me you understand that."

She searched my eyes, finding nothing but my soul bare and hers for the taking.

Death would still come for me.

But for now...we were hiding.

Hiding out of its reach, creating a life that would be so infinitely precious and pure.

She blinked back tears. "I understand, Ren."

"Good."

She smiled softly. "Fine."

The familiarity of such a silly phrase meant we didn't end up camping that night.

We fell together and consummated our marriage in the very same beds where we'd denied such a future from existing.

From children to adults.

From friends to soulmates.

Forever.

Forever.

And always.

# Chapter Fifty-Seven

## REN

## 2021

"REN?"

John lugged his big body from the couch where he'd been nursing a beer. "Can I have a word?"

Liam sat on the floor with his very pregnant girlfriend, and Adam had his wife, Carly, on his lap while their two kids played on the carpet.

Since Della and I hadn't made it to the forest for our honeymoon, the Wilsons had improvised and hosted an all-day affair of just hanging out. And for once, I didn't mind being around people.

These weren't just people.

They were *our* people.

Family.

Cassie had hired a last-minute caterer to feed us, seeing as Patricia's culinary magic was no more, and the Wilson grandchildren did a good job at pegging up the hole left by her missing presence—even though nothing could replace such an amazing woman.

Della and I were planning on going away tonight. We'd have a few days to ourselves before I threw myself back into my farm chores, saved some cash, and planned where we would live.

The one bedroom in the stable was too cramped, and although I'd had such good news yesterday, I wouldn't take any bonus years for granted.

I needed to sort out our future...soon.

"Sure, what's up?" I asked, swigging the final mouthful of my own beer—just one to celebrate—and catching the ever watchful, always loving eye of my wife.

Della had been Mrs Wild for twenty-four hours, and I couldn't stop looking at her or my ring on her finger.

She gave me a smile from where she sat with Cassie and Nina on the floor doing a puzzle. Pieces were scattered everywhere with Nina giving directions to her mother and aunt.

Cassie looked up, grinned at me, then glanced at her father and nodded secretly.

*What the—*

I didn't like that.

I didn't like secrets.

My hackles rose.

"Come into the kitchen." John tipped his white head toward the scuffed, well-used table and chairs. "Bring Della. This concerns her, too."

Whenever we had conversations at that table, things happened.

Big things.

Life-changing things.

I wanted to groan. What had he done now, the meddling ass? I still had his Cherry River contract tucked in the dresser in our room. I'd read the fine print, and sure enough, he'd given full insurance to all my health-related incidents.

I'd made a mental note to call the lawyer who had my Will and Testament and ask him how much John would stand to lose by covering me. I'd heard horror stories of some drugs costing thousands per week, sometimes tens of thousands.

I didn't want to die, but I wouldn't put anyone into destitution to save my life, either.

John was worth a lot with his land. If he were to sell, he'd be a millionaire without a doubt. But all that equity was tied into his legacy, and I never wanted to be the reason he'd be forced to sell.

Della cast me a look, climbing to her feet.

"Go on," Cassie whispered. "You'll want to hear this."

My eyes skipped over the Wilson children and grandchildren before Della clutched my hand and tugged me toward where John had sat down. The entire vibe of the place had changed. Everyone was in on this, whatever it was.

I narrowed my eyes warily. "What's going on?"

"Sit." John pointed at the chairs beside him, waiting until Della and I obeyed.

We sat, and my tension wound even more. "Okay, we're

sitting. Now what?"

He smirked. "Always so suspicious."

"Always justified around you."

He chuckled, his large paws linking on the table top. "One of these days, you're going to learn to relax, Ren. Mark my words."

Phrases like that were double-edged swords. 'One of these days' implied a timeline that stretched into infinity. We both knew I didn't have infinity—not that anyone did. We all died...eventually.

But just because I'd had incredible news that I wouldn't be going anywhere for a while, it didn't stop the bitter-sweetness that it would be sooner than I liked.

"One of these days, you'll stop surprising me with your harebrained ideas." I smiled. "I mean, who gives a fifteen-year-old kid a place to stay and makes him family? Who hires a lawyer for a supposed kidnapper—"

"Yeah, okay. I'm a saint. I get the point."

Della laughed, making my heart wing as I reclined in my chair.

I chuckled under my breath. "Yeah, a saint who interferes."

He held up his hand. "Guilty."

"Once Ren has stopped giving you a hard time, John...what is it you wanted to talk to us about?" Della asked quietly, blonde hair scooped over her shoulder. Her ribbon around her throat today.

The same throat I'd squeezed from behind and pushed down while I took her.

Tearing my gaze away, I cleared my mind from inappropriate thoughts.

John grinned. "First, I want to say a very happy marriage to you two. It was an absolute honour to give you away, Della."

Della's cheeks pinked with affection. "The honour was mine, Uncle John."

My skin prickled with warning as John looked at me. "It's tradition, don't you think, that the father—or at least, pretend father of the bride, gives a gift on their wedding day?"

"John..." I warned. "What did you do?"

"What?" He blinked innocently.

He wasn't innocent.

Smiling, he raised his voice. "Cassie, darlin'? I forgot the file. Do you mind?"

"Not at all." Cassie leapt to her feet, earning a screech from

Nina for disrupting the puzzle, then practically skipped into the kitchen where she placed a blue folder in front of her dad, kissed his white hair, then winked at me.

My nervousness blew into all-out alert. "What exactly is going on?"

"You'll see." Cassie blew Della a kiss, then went to sit with her daughter.

"John?" My eyebrow rose as the big man opened the file and smoothed out the papers with a hairy hand.

"Hold your horses, Ren. Give me a moment to find the right words."

"What words?"

"The words to tell you what I did and make you somehow accept it, without getting all high and mighty."

"Oh, for God's sake." I crossed my arms. "If this gift is more than just a bottle of wine then I'm not accepting it."

"Wind your neck in, Ren." John pointed a finger in my face. "Just 'cause you're sick—" He cut himself off with a terrified wince. "God, I'm sorry. I didn't mean to—"

"It's fine." I forced myself to relax and take the blame. "My fault. I'm winding you up."

Della scooted forward, placing a dainty hand on John's massive wrist. "He's the one being an ass. Take all the time you want and don't worry about his reaction." Her blue eyes met mine with a sharp glare. "I'll deal with him."

"You'll *deal* with me?"

"Yep." She stuck her chin in the air.

"Just because I married you doesn't mean I obey you, *Mrs Wild*."

"Oh, yeah?" She tried to stop a smile. "Well, I'll just have to beat you until you do."

"I'd like to see you try."

Lust sprung hotly.

Della averted her eyes, cheeks pinked and skin flushed.

John groaned. "Ever since that phone call from your oncologist yesterday, you've been incorrigible, Ren."

I shrugged, no longer caring what he was about to do. "What can I say? I'm the happiest guy alive."

No one mentioned the part of that sentence that lingered in the dark.

*I'm the happiest guy alive...for now.*

I could joke and laugh and be truly happy that I'd bought

myself more time, but I also couldn't deny that the awful word still existed.

*Incurable.*

"Right, well, before you two disappear into the forest to do God knows what, I've done something." He laid his hand firmly on the folder like a judge would a gavel. "I've told you that I love you as much as I love my own kids. You *are* my kids. There is no difference. And because of that...I couldn't not do what I've done, if that makes sense."

"Your cryptic reply is not helping my ability to stay calm, John," I muttered, doing my best to read the papers his hand obscured. "What exactly is going on?"

"Having you guys back here, knowing the farm will be taken care of and that you're both happy and safe...that's a gift for me, do you understand? It's a gift because I saw where you guys came from, and I feel as if I played some small part in getting you this far."

"You did," I said fiercely. "Without you, I would've died of pneumonia."

"Without you, we wouldn't have trusted anyone or been fit to be around society," Della murmured.

"Well, I'm glad. But you're both stronger and braver than you give yourselves credit for, so I won't take all the praise." He looked down at the table, refusing to meet my eyes. "What I will do, though, is take your word that you'll accept this."

"Accept what?" My back stiffened, muscles locking.

"Give me your word." He narrowed his eyes. "Before I tell you."

"Not going to happen." I crossed my arms.

"Della?" John turned to her. "Give me your word, sweetie, seeing as that stubborn husband of yours won't."

"I won't risk his temper." She laughed. "Best spit it out. Otherwise, Ren will just snatch what you're hiding and find out anyway."

*She's right.*

I was seconds away from stopping this charade.

John chuckled. "You're probably right. Look at the man."

They both looked at me, twin expressions of affection and exasperation.

I scowled harder. "Ganging up on me won't make me take this any easier."

John laughed again, before slipping back into seriousness. "I changed my Will and Testament."

My heart stopped beating. The ruckus in the lounge quietened as the adults tuned in to listen. "Excuse me?" I leaned forward, ever so slowly. As methodical as a viper. "*What* did you say?"

John puffed out his barrel chest. "I asked Adam, Liam, and Cassie before I did it, and they're all on board. Don't think for a moment there is any bad blood about this, or that it can be taken away from you in the future. Because it can't."

"You're terrifying me." I swallowed hard. "What. Did. You. Do. John?" My teeth chopped every word.

His chin cocked, daring me to challenge him. "I split the farm five ways."

"*What?*" I shot to my feet. "What does that mean?"

"It means, Cassie has a fifth for her horse business, Adam has a fifth to do what he wants, Liam has a fifth for his interests, Della has a fifth, and you...well, you, Ren, you have a fifth, too. Just because Patty and I only gave birth to three kids doesn't mean we don't have five in our hearts. Our Will didn't include you guys, and now, it does. You each have fifty acres. It's a decision I needed to make. And it's a decision you have to accept because I'm not changing it."

Della started to cry beside me. "Y-you can't do that. It's too much."

"No, sweetheart." John reached across and wiped away a tear, his large hand almost smothering her entire cheek. "It's not nearly enough. I know you and Ren will protect this farm and work it the way it's meant to. If Adam and Liam want to sell out at some point, buy their shares and claim it for your own." He flicked a glance at Cassie. "I know my daughter won't be going anywhere, not now there's help on hand with her horses, and I love that Chip has entered the family business by running the books. I have no doubt between all of you, you'll make this land earn its keep ten times over."

I'd gone silent.

Words had vanished.

Anger twisted with guilt and fired into rage.

Della shook her head. "But it's not fair Ren and I get a piece each. Just give us one."

"No. You were two people before you became one. It's already drawn up." Sliding a stapled together document, he smiled. "See? You're listed as my inheritors, but the farm is officially yours now. I want to retire and enjoy my grandbabies. I don't want to be up at dawn anymore, but I also don't want to leave this place. You're allowing me to stay while doing all the hard yards for me."

I still hadn't said anything.

Didn't know how.

Didn't know if I wanted to yell, kill him, or burst into goddamn tears.

He'd not only given me land but a future I'd been desperate to give to Della. He'd provided for us when that was *my* job.

It felt like charity.

It felt like a slap in the fucking face.

Did he do this because I was dying?

Did he do this because he thought I couldn't give Della what she deserved?

My temper steadily grew until John looked up and made eye contact with me.

And he knew.

He knew what I struggled with because despite not being my true father, we were more alike than we thought.

"I'm not stupid, Ren. I know what you're thinking. You think I did this because of your diagnosis—"

"You don't know a thing about me—"

"Wrong." He stood, squaring off with me. "I know what it's like to love someone so much your only wish is to keep them safe. I know what it's like to fear their future if you're not in it. I know what it's like—" His voice broke, and his fists balled before he growled. "I know what it's like to face a future without the person you love, and it's so hard, Ren."

I vibrated with the urge to hit him.

He made me feel weak and wanting. Made me feel selfish for dying before I'd provided for Della—that I wouldn't be able to pave her future the best I could so she could walk safely ahead without me.

I was sad for him for losing Patricia.

Of *course*, I was.

But our situations were entirely different.

"I don't need your charity, John," I hissed. "I don't need you putting words in my mouth—"

"No, you need to accept that this isn't about you. It has nothing to do with you and has *everything* to do with love. I love you, Ren. And knowing what you're going through, it cuts me up inside. Out of anyone, you did not deserve this. You didn't deserve *any* of it. Not when you were a kid and not now."

My nostrils flared; my teeth grated together. "I'll survive. I always do."

"I know that. But I also know that love can be as much of a destroyer as it can be a gift. I didn't do this out of charity. I did it because you deserve it. You *and* Della. And I did it for me because I want you here. I don't want you to leave again. I want my farm looked after for years to come.

"But I'm also realistic that eventually, you won't be able to work the fields anymore. Your energy levels will mean you'll have to hire people. It's a responsibility and one that will be yours until your dying day. That isn't charity, Ren. That's reality, and I'm giving it to you, knowing you can cope with it."

His gaze fell on Della, who stood taut and stressed, watching us scream at each other. "I'll be beside you every step of this, Della. Ren has the hard part of battling this disease, but you have the hardest part by being left behind. I miss Patty every day. And I would never put that on anyone, especially someone so young."

Della broke into tears, running into his arms.

I couldn't move.

Glued to the floor.

Confused and lost and *howling*.

I would never be prepared to say goodbye to Della and leave her alone like Patty had left John. I wished I could take back my wish to die before her and man up and take that agony on her behalf.

She had the worst part of this.

Her pain wouldn't stop like mine on my dying day.

Her pain would continue, year after year, forever.

*Fucking hell.*

The urge to vomit prickled my skin with heat.

The diabolical, unchangeable, grief-stricken knowledge that I couldn't change any of this.

I couldn't stop it.

I couldn't refuse it.

None of this was new.

But, somehow, John had made it all so much more *real*.

I was trapped inside a body that had condemned me, and as much as I raged and begged for a solution—*any* solution—I wouldn't get free of my fate.

I clenched my jaw as caustic tears stung my eyes.

Yesterday, I'd married Della and felt as if my world was complete. Today, I wished she'd never met me so I could protect her—like I was born to protect her—and *never* break her heart this way.

I could call every specialist. I could research every study. I could try every drug, treatment, and experiment, hoping, always hoping, praying, threatening, bribing, selling my soul for a chance...*one chance*...but eventually...

Eventually, Della would be on her own.

And I'd be screaming in the void, yelling in perpetuity, pounding on the veil of this world and the next, desperate for Della to hear me. For her to know I might have gone, but I would *never* leave her. I would haunt her. I would be beside her when she slept and next to her when she moved on.

I would be there always because I couldn't accept anything less.

John looked over Della's head, his arms tight around her.

He followed where my thoughts had spiraled and gave me the saddest smile. A smile that said he understood. That he'd hold my wife when I was gone. That he would protect her when I couldn't.

He nodded. He vowed. He made me grateful as well as furious.

Then John's face slipped from understanding into the authoritative I-don't-take-any-shit farmer I knew. His voice was harsh and hard and almost cold in its delivery. "You *will* accept this, Ren. You will be happy about this."

I didn't know if he spoke about his oath to protect what was mine, the inevitability of my death, or the land he tried to stuff into my hands.

"This is merely a gift from one man to his son and daughter." John's temper simmered. "I'm not stepping on your toes or doubting that you can make a fortune for yourself. I'm not stopping you from living the life you want. If you don't want it? Fine, sell it. I don't care. Because it's *yours*. You earned it fair and square every day you broke sweat toiling in those meadows. You earned it the day you proved what a great kid you are. So don't you *dare* argue with me on this. Don't you motherfucking dare."

His voice broke again before he let Della go and grabbed another piece of paper. With a huff, he threw the document across the table to me. "Oh, and before you say anything, this is also for you."

I caught the fluttering piece of paper mid-air. My hands shook as I scanned the form and the rage, despair, and absolute dread at facing a future I didn't want disappeared.

My temper exploded in a bomb of gratitude.

Gratitude I didn't know how to stop, show, or share.

"Fuck," I grunted as I stroked the headline from the local building authority, approving a residential dwelling to be erected on the newly subdivided land of Cherry River Farm.

A home with planning permission on the two sections belonging to Mr. and Mrs Wild.

I could hate John.

I could hate myself.

But I couldn't hate true goodness and generosity.

Lurching around the table, I stood before his large bulk.

A cough fell from my lips.

A cough followed by another, thanks to the stress in my blood and the harsh breathing in my lungs.

And John let me cough.

He didn't flinch or look away as if I were a walking corpse already.

He merely waited.

Father Time himself, giving me every second I needed.

And once I finished coughing, his eyes widened in surprise as I pulled him into a hug. A hug full of violence and fists and curses. But a hug, nevertheless. "Goddamn you, John," I muttered into his ear. "Goddamn you for everything."

He merely patted my back and said, "You're welcome."

# Chapter Fifty-Eight

## DELLA

## 2022

THE NIGHT REN told me he was sick, my world fell apart. But...I also fell into something else too.

They said love had the power to make you become someone better than you were, but adversity and hardship revealed the truth about who you were at heart.

Nothing was truer than that.

I learned I had the power to say no to my tears whenever Ren coughed. I had the ability to laugh and stay light, even knowing my husband was on borrowed time.

Sadness was a part of everything we did, but we didn't let it consume us.

We lived life like we had before—throwing ourselves into work and play and tackling everything we could.

And...there was something else.

Something I'd tripped into, thanks to Ren.

Something I didn't figure out for an embarrassingly long time. Something that could be classed as unbelievable or just pure coincidental.

I liked to think it was the first one.

A marvel, a wonder, a phenomenon.

The fact that before Ren destroyed me, he'd made love to me, growling at the gods to impregnate me if they felt a shred of guilt for what they'd done to him.

I'd been off the pill for a week.

We'd had sex once before the forest and then multiple times afterward—thanks to getting married and ensuring we consummated the hell out of our union.

But...it didn't change facts.

My world had fallen apart...

And, I'd fallen pregnant.

I was *pregnant.*

And for months, I didn't know.

My body was used to not bleeding—thanks to being on a mini-pill which shut my cycle down. And Ren was the single most important thing on my mind; nothing else mattered.

If I wasn't with him during the day, I was reading about trials and diet supplements at night.

If we weren't working every hour the sun gave us in the fields, we were making love or sleeping under the stars.

I felt the same as always. I had no morning sickness, no nausea, stomach pains, breast tenderness, or food cravings.

There were no signs from before.

No hint that I was pregnant—ectopic or otherwise.

And then, John went ahead and gifted us a future that was solid and unbelievably safe, and we had even more on our minds.

One hundred acres of land.

Land with our names on it.

Land that Ren would turn into a fortune.

When I'd stood watching them argue about such a gift, I'd been pregnant.

When Ren took me to bed that night and made love to me roughly, dominantly, I'd been pregnant.

When I went with him to his next treatment and check-up with his oncologist, I'd been pregnant.

Son or daughter?

Boy or girl?

I didn't know.

Because I didn't even know I was knocked-up.

The news stayed secret for three and a half months.

There were no missing periods to count. No calendar days to circle. No nudges to perhaps take a test.

As the months went on, Ren and I carved out an hour here and there during the busy season to visit the bank.

The novelty of having drivers licenses—after sitting the tests—and marriage certificates never failed to bring a smile to our faces.

We weren't illegal or unknown.

We were hard working, trust-worthy, and had assets, thanks

to John.

The bank approved us for a loan to build a modest three bed, two bath house on the land John had so kindly given us.

Signing the documents—agreeing to a debt named 'mortgage' which literally translated to death pledge in French—we didn't waste any time. We'd gone from forest children to mortgaged adults, and somehow, we were no longer afraid of ties or roots. We'd found our corner of the world and were perfectly content.

A week later, we'd signed with a building company that promised a full house finished and delivered in six months and broke ground a few days later.

Life sped ahead as if in apology.

The winds blew in our favour, sailing us through smooth waters after being in a storm for so long.

Even Ren's health wasn't as terrifying as before. Another three treatments of Keytruda, and Rick Mackenzie decided he'd reached stable condition.

Ren was taken off the three weekly appointments but kept regular check-ups.

He no longer coughed as badly, and his slight rattle was quieter at night. His body was strong and toned, his appetite big and demanding, his smile bright and pain-free.

He didn't slow down for a moment—despite the nasty secret squatting in his lungs.

If anything, he became more physical, glowing with life and longevity.

I schooled my heart not to get too hopeful.

I begged my ears not to take the good news from doctors and twist it to believe he was cured.

Ren would *never* be cured.

But we had bought some time.

And we spent every second wisely.

When the diggers churned meadow to mud for the house's foundation, Ren and I kissed with our boots in the freshly tilled dirt beneath the moon.

When we weren't overseeing the builders creating our house, we were helping Cassie with her own construction. She'd taken her land and run with it—designing a larger barn, stables, arena, and round pen for her new equine venture.

As I'd been part of the conception and brain storming phase, Cassie asked if I'd help manage it with her. To become her partner, if I wanted, or an employee, if I preferred.

Her eyes gave another offer, too. An offer that said I'd forever have work and a way to support myself…even when Ren wasn't there with me.

We'd hugged with tears streaming and broke apart when Ren appeared with a heavy sack of horse feed over his shoulder.

He constantly worked.

He never stopped.

He made me nervous.

Yes, his body was stable.

But, surely, he shouldn't over-do it?

By the time I noticed what was cooking inside me, the foundations of our house were poured, the framework was up, and Ren was site foreman as well as farm overseer, cracking the whip every day to ensure things ran smoothly.

Watching him stride across pastures in faded, scuffed jeans and a white t-shirt stained with toil and tractor grease, I'd never been more in love with him. When he showered away sweat and grime from a long day working, I'd never been more in lust with him.

Just because I knew an end was coming, didn't mean I could stop loving him. And I fell even deeper when our first income poured in from a smaller paddock that we'd sold as free-standing hay—not having the time to cut and bale ourselves.

The money was more than enough to pay our mortgage payment for the next four months.

Holding that income, Ren had gone quiet, pensive, his thoughts going to that dark place where I couldn't follow.

The place of urgency to create a world for me before it was too late.

I'd left him to his thoughts, and he'd found me as I finished riding Cassie's warmblood Mighty Mo, then merely took my hand, and guided me to find John dozing on the deck of his farmhouse.

Ren didn't wake him up, just merely tucked an envelope of cash into his plaid shirt pocket and smiled at me.

Ren was a proud man as well as selfless and kind-hearted.

And that pride would always be a little bruised at accepting two-fifths of Cherry River Farm.

Thanks to earning money from that gifted land, his principals meant he had to pay John his dues—a rent, a tax…a thank you.

* * * * *

"We'll put the crib here. And we'll paint the walls a light green, don't you think? So he feels at home in the greenness of the forest before we take him there?" Ren spun to face me. "Good idea?"

His health.

His happiness.

His wonderment.

I laughed gently. "*Great* idea."

His gaze fell on my belly that had finally shown what was camping inside it.

Six months pregnant and everything was perfect.

Finally, after seventeen weeks of being utterly oblivious to what we'd created together, I'd stood naked before Ren after a shared shower, and he'd frowned at my lower belly. Dripping wet with a towel wrapped around narrow hips, he'd prodded me gently, his eyebrows knitting together at the firmness.

I'd winced as something sharp responded. Something that didn't feel like me.

I shifted backward from his touch, only for him to fall to his knees. He ran his hands over the area of my stomach that had hardened almost overnight. "Della, a-are you pregnant?"

Funny that he was the one to question first.

We'd made an appointment to see a family doctor the next day, and—thanks to identification and insurance—it was the easiest thing in the world to be seen, have an ultra sound, and be checked over.

According to the doctor, it wasn't unusual for first time mothers not to show for a while. I was physically active with strong stomach muscles and good posture. I already ate healthy and had a vivacious appetite.

I'd been giving my body exactly what it needed with no need for any natural nudges for better.

That had been two and a half months ago. My stomach had stayed flat for as long as it could, but now, it could no longer contain the steadily growing baby bump.

Ren came toward me, running his fingertips around my belly button. "How is he today?"

"Active." I rolled my eyes. "Your son thinks he's a footballer."

He chuckled. "I've never played sport in my life."

"Yes, but you do have a habit of kicking things."

"I also have a habit of loving you. For the past two decades."

"And you better not stop anytime soon, seeing as it's your spawn I'm carrying."

"Never, Ribbon. It's physically impossible to stop loving you." His lips spread into a smile as he bent to kiss me.

I leaned in to him, allowing his tongue to enter my mouth and flatten against mine in a sensual dance of hello and welcome.

I loved this man with every part of my heart.

He was my luck.

My wishing star.

My ever after.

I was pregnant with his child.

His son.

We'd blended ourselves.

We'd beat time at its own game, and instead of death, we'd claimed life.

And we'd keep claiming it.

Again.

And again.

For as long as possible.

\* \* \* \* \*

Amazing how fast time could skip ahead.

Incredible how easy routine became when you were doing something you loved with the person you belonged to.

My life before—with its stress of loving Ren in secret, going to school, and pretending student friendships—was no longer on my radar.

At eight and a half months pregnant, life had never been so good.

Ren pampered me every night—even though he still worked every hour of sunlight and beyond. He rubbed my back, kissed my belly, brushed my hair, and slipped on my boots, seeing as I could no longer see past my fat stomach.

Jacob wasn't even in the world yet, but his father absolutely adored him.

Ren read articles online on how babies could hear in the womb, and often stayed up late talking to him.

On those nights, when Ren fell asleep whispering stories and telling tales, I'd listen to him in the dark.

For as long as I could remember, Ren was a bad sleeper. He'd toss and turn, pace in the night, and get up before dawn, just to avoid struggling with sleep that wouldn't come.

I was used to it.

It had always been that way.

Yet now, Ren had overtaken me in the sleep awards.

When his head hit the pillow, he was out.

His eyes flickering with dreams, his breath rattling with memory of what lived inside him, his body overly warm with circulation that ran just a little too hot.

Normally, I'd believe it was thanks to his long day at work.

But...I'd read up on his condition, and I knew the symptoms in and out.

Night sweats and fatigue.

Those were the ones I and only I knew that Ren had.

In everyday life, he was the poster boy of good health.

But when it was just us in bed, a scary little beast would sit on my pillow and whisper falsities about what Ren projected.

I didn't trust that he wasn't hiding how he truly felt.

I didn't believe he was as pain free as he made us think.

Instead of suffering silently, I should have spoken up—and I did, *of course I did*; it wasn't a matter to brush aside. I told Rick Mackenzie at Ren's last check-up, even as Ren glared at me as if I'd betrayed his confidence.

But the oncologist had just smiled and nodded and, in a bedside manner that I didn't appreciate—either stress or pregnancy snappiness—said unfortunately, it was to be expected.

Ren was stable, but he was still sick.

His body was fighting the good fight, so of course, he would sleep soundly.

His system was hoarding rest like a starving man hoarded food.

And I got that...but it didn't make it any easier.

The past eight and a bit months had made me believe in a fairy-tale.

The knowledge of what existed in our future was muted somehow beneath summer sun and lazy Sundays around the pond.

I'd stupidly allowed time to fuzz the urgency inside me, and I cursed myself to the depths of hell when, a few days later, my worries were vindicated in the worst possible way.

I stood in our kitchen in our new house.

It wasn't entirely finished—the walls were yet to be painted, curtains put up, and fireplace installed, but we'd moved in a week ago to a night of seduction in a bare bedroom with just a king mattress that we'd bought.

We kissed in every room to christen the place. And eventually, we would have sex in every room, but for now, I was too heavily pregnant for Ren to touch in any other manner than with tenderness.

I'd burst into tears as Ren carried me over the threshold the first time and paraded me around the first home we'd ever owned.

Our home.

No one else's.

*Ours.*

It wasn't overly large but had a cosy reading nook, cute living room, and country kitchen. Our bedroom was a simple square with large glass doors that led to a wraparound deck that welcomed the outside in.

The whole design was like a large tent with the main dwellings in the middle and sleeping quarters on either side.

We were twenty-three and thirty-three, both so young, so happy, so blessed.

And as I looked up from where I stood in the kitchen, the view of rolling meadows and untouched perfection better than any dream—I melted at how incredible it all was.

I rubbed my bulging belly, poking at the tiny foot making itself known in my side.

I sighed contentedly as I kept one eye on the view and one on cutting the crusts off Ren's turkey and mayo sandwiches.

Height of summer and he was working late.

The field had been cut three days ago and allowed to air dry in the heat. He'd turned it this morning and raked it into long rows, and now, as the sun hung low in the sky teasing with dusk, he was about to bale.

No rest for the farmer in summer.

Packing the sandwich into a bag with an apple, bottle of water, and a couple of Hershey's Kisses, I left the sun-drenched house we'd built and waddled my way down the garden with its flagstone pavers, through the yet-to-be-painted gate, and to the meadow beyond.

The sound of the tractor churned and coughed, the motor of the baler whirring in rhythm and clunking with age as loose grass went in one end and spat out the other as a rectangle bound by string.

Halfway across the large field, the crunch of metal and the abrupt sound of an engine ceasing wrenched my head up.

*Oh, dear.*

The first cut of the season was always the thickest, and the old equipment sometimes didn't cope.

Peering into the setting sun, I caught sight of Ren as he leapt from the tractor and went to investigate the attached baler.

He staggered a little from jumping from a height.

He stumbled forward as if gathering his momentum.

I thought nothing of it.

I'd seen him trip from the tractor a thousand times.

He might not be the most agile, but he was springy.

My eyes stayed on him, expecting him to solve the puzzle of his legs and stay upright.

Only...this time, he didn't find his feet.

His arms didn't spread out for balance. His body didn't twist for purchase. His spine rolled, his head flopped, and he tumbled forward, vanishing into the rowed grass.

For a second, I couldn't compute what had happened.

My retinas still burned with a picture of him standing.

But he was gone.

Disappeared.

*No, no, no, no.*

"*Ren!*" My screech sent a cloud of sparrows and starlings feeding on bugs in the grass into the skies. "Ren!" I dropped his dinner and forgot I was pregnant.

I broke into an ungainly sprint. "*Ren!*"

He didn't get up.

He didn't appear.

*Please, please, please.*

I ran and ran.

Waddled and waddled.

Galloped and galloped.

The field was big, and I was slow.

It took an eternity to reach him, and by the time I did, my belly sliced with an agonising blade.

Grimacing, I ignored it, skidding to my knees beside Ren.

"Come on. You're okay," I gasped, telling Ren he was okay, but maybe telling myself more. "Wake up." Face first in the grass, I brushed aside his sun-bronzed hair and found a closed eye.

Slack lips.

Smooth forehead.

Shallow breath.

Another slice cut right around my middle, wrenching a grunt and groan-scream from my lips.

Once again, I ignored it, and with all my strength, pushed Ren's shoulder until he rolled and flopped onto his back.

His hands stayed unmoving.

His arms bent.

Legs crossed over each other from being rolled.

Grass stuck to his hair and face, and my hands shook as I tried to brush it aside.

He didn't move.

Didn't flinch.

Didn't speak.

Another lacerating pain rippled through my abdomen as I bent over him, tapping his cheeks. "Ren." Tapping turned to slapping the more unresponsive he became. "Ren! Don't you dare do this to me, Ren."

Tears cascaded.

More pain pulverised my belly.

No one was around to help.

Pulling his head close, I had no lap to cradle him, thanks to my pregnant belly. I had to settle with an awkward hug.

I rocked him.

I cried for him.

I did the only thing I could.

I screamed.

And something answered that scream, deep in my belly, twisting and tearing, desperate to get out.

Once again, I ignored it.

"No, no, *no*." I hugged Ren, another blood-curdling cry tumbling from my lips.

I didn't know what I screamed, only that I did.

I screamed again and again.

And still, he didn't wake up.

And then, in a flash of sunset, something winging caught my eye.

Cassie.

*Thank God, Cassie.*

She bolted fast on Mighty Mo. Bare back and just a halter, as if she'd snatched the horse from his stable and kicked him into a run. His hooves ploughed through grass rows, jumping others. "Della!"

I groaned, tipping forward into the grass as my own pain overcame me. Planting a hand over the worst pressure I'd ever felt, my palm nudged the small hardness of my pocket-stored cell-phone.

Stupid.

*So stupid.*

Wrenching it out, I shook and grunted as yet another knife punctured my insides. Crawling closer to Ren, I blinked back tears and punched the numbers for help.

The call connected quickly.

An operator urgent and brisk. "What's your emergency?"

My breath tore and laced with misery and woe. Another vicious band of agony worked through my belly, my hips naturally spreading, my thighs growing warm.

"A man. He's unconscious. He has stage one mesothelioma. *Please*—" Pain cut me off. "Send an ambulance. Cherry River—"

I hissed as yet another wave hit me, this one stronger than the last. I moaned into the phone, buckling over, holding the baby in my belly. The baby who'd chosen this exact moment to arrive. "—Farm. Please hurry."

"Okay, ma'am, we're sending someone right now."

A gush of wetness drenched my underwear, and I laughed.

*Laughed* with sick disbelief and incredulous timing.

"Oh, *Goooddd*," I groaned, not able to hold my belly and my husband at the same time.

Death had visited.

Life wouldn't be ignored.

Both battled to kill me.

"You okay, Ma'am?" the operator asked.

I shook my head, my lips spread wide.

I couldn't speak.

But I didn't need to.

Cassie arrived in a flurry of horse and hooves, leaping off to slam to her knees beside me. Mighty Mo snorted like a dragon, wired and amped, feeding on stress.

Cassie ignored him, took one look at Ren, then focused entirely on me. "Shit, Della." Snatching my phone, she barked. "Ambulance. Two of the damn things. One for a man with asbestos cancer and another who's just gone into labour."

She nodded to whatever the woman said on the other end. "Yes. Back meadow. John Wilson will help you."

I screamed as yet another deeper, demanding fury filled me. A fury tangled with bone and blood and bruises.

"You need to hurry," Cassie snapped.

Throwing my phone into the grass, she gathered me close, placed her hand on Ren's shallow breathing chest, and kissed my cheek. "It's okay, Della. You'll both be fine. You'll see."

I was glad she was there.

Grateful for help.

Only problem was...I didn't believe her.

# Chapter Fifty-Nine

## REN

## 2022

*FLASH.*
The field with grass at optimum dryness to bale.
*Flash.*
A clunk and crunch as the baler wrapped up in stalks.
*Flash.*
Red and blue lights around me. Sirens loud inside me.
*Flash.*
Intruders, questions, the swish and sway of reckless driving.
*Flash.*
Wheels screeching, oxygen flowing, a sharp prick in my arm.
*Flash.*
Della's screaming, strangers shouting, a world in utter disarray.

Something dragged me down, something heavy and warm and thick. I wanted to go with it, to give in, but the awful, awful sound of the one person I'd promised to protect every day of my goddamn life wrenched me through the fog.

I clung to her voice, clawing to her, crawling to her, fighting mud and sludge and pain.

My eyes opened.

I was no longer in the field.

I was no longer dressed from the waist up.

I was no longer a farmer but a patient.

"Oh, thank God!" Della grabbed my hand, her fingernails digging in. "Ren. I thought…" She shook her head. "You wouldn't wake up."

The outside world had been replaced with the insides of a hospital.

An emergency room with traffic and trauma and triage.

My throat was raw and lungs seared.

I'd been in pain lately.

The backache.

The chest ache.

But I had things to do.

Life to conquer.

A future to pave.

Della bowed over me, pressing her forehead to my cheek. "Please, please don't scare me like that again."

My arm came up from where I lay on a narrow bed, hugging her head, kissing her hard. "I'm sorry, Ribbon." I coughed, and she flinched.

Her eyes widened, then she buckled over me, digging her face into the crutch of my shoulder, her lips spread in a guttural scream.

My weakness?

My confusion?

None of it fucking mattered.

Jack-knifing upward, I tore at wires stuck to my chest and ripped an oxygen tube from my nose. "Della."

"Hey, Mr. Wild. You need—"

"*Stop!*" I roared, clutching onto Della as she stumbled by my bedside. "What the hell is wrong with my wife?"

"She refused to leave," a skinny nurse with mousy blonde hair snipped. "She's in labour. Apart from physically manhandling her, we couldn't do anything about it."

"Goddammit." I swung my legs off the narrow bed, dislodging yet more medical equipment. My lungs burned. Chest throbbed. Heart palpitated in an uneven rhythm.

But I didn't care about any of it.

"Get back into bed, sir," someone commanded.

I grimaced as my world flipped upside down. My feet found a ground that rocked. My mind found a world that sloshed and greyed. I swam in light-headedness, scooping Della into my arms, and laying her pregnant weight on the very same bed I'd just vacated.

"Sir, she needs to be in maternity."

"She's in pain, can't you see? Help her instead of spouting bullshit!"

Della screamed as yet another contraction worked through her. Her legs spread wide and dirty shoes dug into sterilized white. "Oh, *fuucckk*. God, it hurts." Her hand found mine, squeezing me to the point of metacarpals crunching.

"Someone get her something!" I yelled. "What the hell good are you, huh? Do your goddamn jobs and *help* her!"

My lungs wheezed, and a ribcage-splintering cough found me, bending me in half.

"Sir, you need to calm down."

Coughing, coughing, always fucking coughing, my anger spilled like magma. When I could breathe, I roared, "And you need to fucking help her! *Now!*"

Della groaned, adding another layer to the mayhem.

"Sir—"

"What the *hell* is going on here?!" A doctor with a shaved head and goatee marched forward, waving his arms as if he could part the sea of medical staff like the messiah.

Grabbing a clipboard that hung on the end of the bed, he scanned the notes, then pointed in my face. "You. Seeing as you're awake. Oncology. Now. You need some tests." Spinning to face the skinny nurse loitering around Della, he ordered, "You, go get the midwife assigned to Mrs Wild."

His eyes fell on another staff member. "You, go tell those people demanding answers that he's woken up and she's about to have a baby. We need silence, not anarchy."

When his bossy gaze met mine again and found I hadn't left Della's side, he bared his teeth. "*Get.* Oncology. Now."

"I'm not leaving." I stepped closer to the bed, partly to touch Della's face and partly because I needed to lean against something. Coughs rattled and wheezed, not appreciating I fought their desire to make me bend over again.

I *refused* to cough.

I wasn't the one in need of treatment, Della was.

"My wife is having a baby. If someone doesn't look after her—"

"Threats now?" The doctor rolled his eyes. "Leave before I have you committed."

"I'm not leaving until I know my wife is okay."

"Oh, for Pete's sake," the doctor grumbled. "If you collapse, you'll be strapped in the psych ward just to teach you a lesson."

"I'm not going to collapse." My needs faded every time in lieu of Della's. I could be on death's door and tell the devil to wait until I knew Della was safe.

My jaw locked together as I fought another wave of coughing. "So, are you going to do something?"

"You're in a hospital, Mr Wild. Of course, we're going to do something."

Della moaned and writhed as another nurse dashed toward us. With efficient jerks, she pulled a curtain around us, cutting us off from the emergency room mania.

Once private, she pushed Della's dress up her legs, pulled her underwear down, and laid a green cloth over her lap. With calm hands, she manhandled Della's feet, placing them as close to the side of the bed as possible.

No one mentioned she wasn't in a hospital gown or tried to remove her shoes.

It was too late for any of that.

"The midwife is on the way," the nurse said. "We don't have anywhere else for you to go on such short notice, and you're too far along to be moved. You'll deliver here and then be transferred to maternity."

Della grimaced, her skin blotchy with pain. "Okay."

It wasn't okay.

*None* of this was okay.

I'd woken to the worst kind of horror.

The goatee, bald-headed doctor nodded brusquely. "Glad order has been restored. They'll look after you from here. Now, if you'll excuse me." Sweeping out from the curtain-created room, his voice barked more commands outside.

I coughed again, fighting it from turning into a fit. "You all right?" I asked Della, pressing my fist into her pillow for stability.

She bit her lip, nodding in agony. Her face shone with sweat, scrunched and red.

*I'd* done this to her.

I was the monster responsible for such torture.

"I'm so sorry, Della."

For five months—since we found out she was pregnant—I'd been fucking petrified of losing her.

I wasn't a happy, expectant father.

I was surly and snappy and scared shitless of losing her.

So many things tore me into knots, and as the days marched onward, and she grew fatter and more cumbersome, I'd had nightmares of losing her.

At least she hadn't struggled with this pregnancy as she had with her first.

But that didn't make me worry any less.

And now, my wife had gone into premature labour. Only by a couple of weeks but enough to make her every grunt and groan rip my broken lungs into ribbons.

I was so selfish to want a kid with her.

So self-centred to expect her to go through this purgatory.

I didn't know how much time passed.

I didn't know how long the gates of Hell could stay open.

I felt weak and useless and begged time to hurry.

All I could offer was my hand as she bore down and started to push.

The midwife arrived and spoke soothing and calm.

The noise from outside our curtain faded.

The fear that Della would die in childbirth continued to terrorize me.

On and on Della struggled, until finally, she gave one last scream, and something tiny with the wail of something huge arrived.

He sounded pissed off, insulted, and angry.

Once again, my breath rattled and lungs struggled to convert air into oxygen.

My vision danced with greyness as a flurry of activity happened between Della's legs, and something bloody and raisin-like was burrito-wrapped and placed on her heaving chest.

For a second, I hated it.

I despised it for hurting the creature I loved most in the world.

But then, its ugly, pinched face turned to me, and my knees almost gave out.

Because what I'd told Della was true.

My love for her would never change.

It would never diminish.

Never fade or struggle to choose.

Staring into that bloody, new-born face, love grew.

And grew.

And *grew*.

It grew until it spilled into every nook and cranny inside me, a sticky syrup there to stay.

The heart was a miraculous thing—I'd always known it was. And now, it fabricated a new chamber, building a home for Jacob inside the castle where Della had always lived.

My heart was no longer just an organ…it was a city ruled by my wife and son.

My son…Jacob.

The tiny noisy human.

The baby that carried my blood, my breath, my bone.

The child who would protect my wife long after I had gone.

# *Chapter Sixty*

## DELLA

## 2032

THE FOURTH INCIDENT.

*Ren's collapse and Jacob's birth.*

*A date that would forever herald happy and horrified memories.*

*When they put my baby in my arms and Ren kissed my brow with a look of utter awe and besotted wonderment, I knew it had all been worth it.*

*The stress of his collapse.*

*The pain of Jacob's delivery.*

*I would do it all over again because we held life in our arms.*

*However, I must warn you.*

*I must advise you that you have a choice from here, dear reader.*

*A choice that I never had, but a choice, regardless.*

*Up until now, life was perfect.*

*And it can remain perfect...for you.*

*You've read a story that pens as a fairy-tale with its troubled beginning, love conquering all, happy marriage, and perfect baby.*

*After all, I did start this book with the words 'Once Upon A Time...' which requisites a happily ever after.*

*And I can give you that.*

*You can stop here and bask in our marriage, new home, good fortune, and baby in his baby carriage.*

*But if you don't...be brave.*

*Be brave, just like I am, because our tale is based on fact, not fantasy.*

*It is based on life. A life that everyone must endure.*

*Life that some would rather not read about because it's too close to the truth.*

*Why cry for a story when there are so many hardships in your own world?*

*And I get that.*
*I really do.*
*So…I tell you again.*
*You can stop.*
*I won't think any less of you.*
*I won't be sad you didn't stay with me until the end.*
*But, please know, from here on out, I can't lie to you.*
*I will give you happiness.*
*I will give you hope.*
*But I will also give you pain.*
*But you already know that.*
*You know what's coming.*
*We all know time is never on our side.*
*This is your final warning.*
*Stop.*
*Close the book.*
*Move on.*

*But if you're like me and understand that nothing perfect lasts forever, if you're strong enough to accept what life ultimately gives, it taketh away, then thank you.*

*Thank you for being there beside me.*
*Thank you for not leaving me alone.*

# Chapter Sixty-One

## REN

## 2022

"THE TESTS show your mesothelioma has spread."

Any happy feelings I had from watching my son come into the world popped like a shitty balloon.

I balled my hands. "It's not mine. It's never *been* mine. I didn't fucking want it in the first place."

"Sorry. Bad phrasing." Rick had the decency to look apologetic, his white lab coat bright on my over-stretched senses. "But it doesn't change facts. The tumours have increased. You're no longer stage one."

Shit.

Shit.

*Shit.*

The entire time I'd been subjected to yet more tests, I'd refused to sit down, but now, I tumbled into a chair in front of Rick Mackenzie's desk. He'd come in especially to oversee my results, seeking an answer to why I'd fallen unconscious in the pasture.

All I could remember was struggling to breathe.

And then…nothing.

"Did you hear me, Ren?" he asked gently.

I nodded, leaning forward and wedging my elbows on my knees. "Yes, I heard you." My voice was barely audible, not prepared to accept such things.

How could a single day hold the highest of highs and lowest of lows?

After Della had given birth and Jacob had been cleaned,

---

weighed, and returned, the hospital staff had ensured Della was comfortable, helped dress her in a clean gown, and wheeled her to maternity where she'd earned a much-needed rest.

I'd ignored the annoyingly persistent doctors about heading to oncology while Jacob underwent his own tests—seeing as he was premature. He was carefully checked, just to make sure he was in working order.

And thank God, everything functioned as it should.

He was a robust little thing.

Only once Jacob and Della were asleep, and wouldn't know any better, did I take the lift to the level where permanent sickness slinked down the corridors and death slithered on the air, trawling the wards for its next victim.

I *despised* this place.

I despised it even more after coming from maternity where the flapping of cranes could still be heard from dropping off new-borns, bringing new life to every corner.

My chest ached as I coughed.

Rick's forehead furrowed. "Cough up any blood lately?"

"No." I sat taller, straightening my torso for a better breath. "Not since that first time. Think I'd just irritated my throat."

Rick nodded, studying my file that had grown rather comprehensive. He slouched, running a hand through his salt and pepper hair. "As a doctor, I know these things happen and this was an inevitability, but as your friend, I can't help feeling like I let you down."

I narrowed my eyes. "Why do you say that?"

"You were responding so well to Keytruda. We should've just kept you on it."

"Yeah, but I'd gone stable." I didn't know why I was arguing or trying to make him feel better. I guessed I didn't want him feeling as wretched about this as I did.

How the hell would I tell Della?

How would I admit that the past year—running full tilt into our future with houses and businesses and babies might be one of our last? I'd worked my damnedest to get things sorted. I'd arranged my funeral and paid for it behind Della's back. I'd taken out life insurance on myself in Della's name to cover the cost of our mortgage with enough left to send Jacob to school. The fine print had been exhausting with my diagnosis but as long as I lived seven years, they'd pay out. If I didn't...I'd have to look at alternatives.

I'd covered my bases the best I could.

I'd crossed my t's and dotted my i's or whatever that saying was.

I had the worst parts of my death covered.

But just because we'd finally earned everything we wanted, and I'd protected Della as much as I could, it didn't mean I was ready to fucking die.

We had so much to look forward to, yet I might be leaving her with a brand-new baby and a broken heart.

"Christ." I clamped a hand over my mouth as a rush of horror filled me. My fingers dug into my cheeks as my heart slammed.

Rick looked up. "You okay?"

Dropping my hand, I groaned, "No, I'm not fucking okay. Della just had our child. How the hell can I leave her with that on her own?"

"You're not dying straight away, Ren."

My vision greyed as my heart turned arrhythmic. "How long?"

He shrugged. "There's still plenty of time. You're stage two. Yes, it sucks, but it's better than stage four. We'll put you back on Keytruda and supplement immunotherapy with a few sessions of chemo."

I froze. "Chemo?"

"We'll give you drugs to combat the side effects. They've proven to help with nausea and hair loss. We won't keep you on it long. Just enough to zap those bastards."

I looked away, my eyes dancing over the room, desperate to find something that wasn't a medical sketch or graphic image. I wanted trees and grass and sunlight. I needed to get out of this godforsaken place.

"We should discuss what happened in the field," Rick said. "What made you pass out? Pain? Breathlessness?"

I shrugged, dropping my gaze to the floor. At least that was boringly safe with its grey-yellow linoleum. "I couldn't breathe. I don't remember, really. Just...air that refused to come."

"Okay. Have you been overdoing it?"

I chuckled under my breath. "Define overdoing it."

"Working from sun-up to sun-down, not resting, not stopping to eat a decent meal?"

"Ah." I grinned morosely. "Based on that, then yes. I might have been overdoing it."

Rick scowled, his Scottish accent thickening. "This isn't a joking matter."

"Don't you think I don't know that?"

"I know you're trying to get your life in order...before you can't. But you also have to give yourself the best possible chance—"

"No. I have to give *her* the best possible chance. My pain ends when I die. Hers doesn't."

Rick stilled. "*Are* you in pain?"

I clenched my jaw. I hadn't meant to reveal that. I'd done a good job of hiding that even from Della. It wasn't often. It wasn't all the time. But the discomfort was starting to weigh on me.

"If you need painkillers—"

"I can handle it."

Rick clicked his pen with sharp stabs. "It's not about handling it, Ren. It's about taking that uncomfortableness away, so your body can focus on other things."

"So your answer is yet more drugs? Drugs on top of drugs." I rolled my eyes. "I'm surprised I don't bleed chemicals at this point."

Rick sighed, frustrated. "What other option do you have? Be a walking infusion of pharmaceuticals or die sooner? It's not really something that can be debated."

My hands curled. None of this was fair.

I knew I was being a prick. I knew my surly temper wasn't helping. And I knew that I'd deliberately done this to myself because I shouldn't have worked so damn hard.

I *knew* all of that.

And yet...Della.

I couldn't leave her in a one bedroom stable at the generosity of the Wilsons. Of course, they'd never turn her out, but it wasn't just her anymore.

My allegiance had grown to incorporate my wife *and* my son.

And they both needed protecting the best way I could.

John had overstepped and given us land that we could never afford, and that ate away at me every goddamn day. But at least, by working the fields and making it earn its keep, I had an income to pay him back. A little at a time, a dollar here, a hundred there, until I'd repaid him at market value of what the hundred acres were worth.

I wouldn't finish that duty before my dying day, but I could whittle out a large chunk. Then the land would *truly* belong to

Della and Jacob because I'd bought it for them with blood, sweat, and the occasional tear in the dark.

A tear for everything I would miss.

A tear for everything I loved.

"Wh-what about surgery?" My voice was small, hunching in on itself.

I didn't want to be cut open, but I would if it gave me more time.

I would do anything for another year, another day, another hour.

Rick inhaled. "Surgery is an option. However, as with everything, it comes with risks."

"What sort of risks?"

"Well, there are a few procedures. EPP, Extra Pleural Pneumonectomy, is the most radical as it removes an entire lung, the lining around the lung, and the diaphragm. Needless to say, recovery after surgery can be long, and you'd have to change your lifestyle to accommodate living with a single lung, as well as be prepared for other complications down the line." He clasped his hands together, discarding the clicking of his pen. "I have thought about it, I won't lie. But with your tumours being so small and in both your lungs, it's not something I'd recommend."

I swallowed hard. "And the other options?"

"Pleurectomy/Decortication, also known as lung-sparing surgery. It's more detailed than EPP but leaves the lung intact and only removes the pleura lining. Again, I wouldn't recommend it. The only one I might consider is Thoracentesis, which can be done under local anaesthetic where a long, thin needle is used to drain fluid in the pleural space, or Pleurodesis, where talc is injected into the layers of the pleura and then suctioned out."

I winced. "Sounds painful."

"It's actually a fairly straightforward procedure that requires minimal healing, and ninety percent of patients claim it gives them relief from pain and breathlessness. The lungs create scar tissue, effectively sealing the pleura and preventing any more fluid build-up."

I nodded, doing my best to drink in long words and scary explanations.

Rick picked up his infernal pen again, clicking. "With multimodal treatment, you can still have years left, Ren. Don't give up just because you've progressed. We all knew that would happen. Don't let it get you down, okay?"

I forced a smile. "I'm not giving up, if that's what you're thinking."

"I wouldn't dare think that. Out of any case I've seen, you have something unique tying you here that will prove to be better than any surgery or drug."

"Oh?" I raised my eyebrow, coughing softly. "What's that?"

"Love." He smiled. "True love has its claws in you, and I doubt it will ever let go. Fight for that. *Live* for that. And we'll make sure to buy you enough time to watch your son grow."

# Chapter Sixty-Two

## DELLA

## 2023

THAT FIRST YEAR with a new-born and a husband fighting the worst kind of unfairness, I couldn't lie...it was the hardest year I'd ever endured.

After the initial wash of endorphins in the hospital with Ren and me kissing, watching baby Jacob as if he was the most fascinating thing we'd ever seen, and living in a cocoon of delight, life interrupted and sped up far too fast.

There was no time to tell Ren how shit-terrified I'd been when he'd collapsed.

No space to yell at him and tell him to take it slow.

He already knew he'd screwed up, and I didn't need to drag yet more sadness into our tentative world.

So, we buckled down and fought.

God, we fought.

We fought so hard I don't remember anything else.

All I remembered was the exhaustion from a baby thrust into a world of sad instability and eyes that were permanently swollen from all the tears I refused to shed.

While I nursed a grizzly baby, Ren had treatments every other week. One week, he'd be subjected to Keytruda—a drug I was fond of as it had helped him before. And one with chemo—a drug I was not fond of as it made him sick.

Even with the pills that Rick Mackenzie gave him to counteract the side effects, Ren had a rash where the chemicals entered his skin and complained of bone aches so bad, he submitted to taking painkillers on top of all the rest.

By the fourth session of chemo, his cheekbones were more defined and his body more sinew than muscle. He hadn't lost weight exactly but tightened, somehow. The parts of him that made him so dependable and capable sucking deep within to fight.

By the second month of Jacob being home and the builders kindly racing to finish our house, even while we lived there, Ren became allergic to sunlight.

His eyes couldn't handle the brightness, even with sunglasses. His skin burned instantly, even with sun cream. Whatever the doctors had injected into him had done something to his biological makeup, and it was hard not to smash apart everything in our newly finished house.

It was hard to stay strong for him when I was so helpless.

It was hard to keep Jacob happy when I didn't know the meaning of the word myself anymore.

It was in those moments—those life-sucking, abyssal moments—that I carried my child to the willow grotto and sat amongst their fronds.

I'd allow myself to be sad, only for a moment.

I'd allow myself to talk to Jacob about things no baby should know about their terminally-ill father, piecing myself back together again to be brave.

Even dealing with so much, Ren never let me down.

We took turns bathing Jacob and putting him to bed. We'd tell stories together, finding laughter amongst so many heartaches when we relived our own tales of childhood.

John hired an out of town contractor to finish the baling and, on the days when the chemo hit Ren bad, Cassie became a godsend by babysitting Jacob while I held Ren on the bathroom floor as he shivered and vomited and apologised for ever letting me see him that way.

Like I said, that first year was the hardest I'd ever endured.

But even though our life was a sequence of tough and tougher moments, I never regretted for a moment having Jacob.

As he grew from toothless babe to inquisitive bright-eyed creature, I could see why Ren had both hated and loved me when I was young.

I hated not knowing what I was doing. Hated the lack of rest, the loud crying, the struggle to learn a language I didn't know. But I loved, *loved* watching him develop a personality. I loved being responsible for his learning, growth, and the fact that he blossomed in weight, happiness, and joy even while his parents lost those things.

We'd been given the gift of life with our son, and the payment seemed to be the cost of his father's soul. And as much as I loved Jacob, I honestly didn't know if I could afford the price.

My heart broke on a minutely basis.

That was until Jacob's fourth month and Ren's oncologist announced he was happy with his results and took him off chemo.

The tumours hadn't shrunk like last time, but they had stabilised, and he was given a positive outlook again.

It was all agreed that Ren would stay on Keytruda…for the rest of his life. And slowly, as the chemo side effects left his body, he put back the weight he'd lost and ventured outside again where the sun was no longer his enemy.

We'd walk together over the meadows with Jacob in his arms, and we'd soak in the beauty of a sunset, imprinting the memory, clutching it tight for the day when they'd be no more.

Luckily, by the time Christmas arrived, no one would guess Ren was sick.

His smile was broad, strength impressive, and attitude toward life still as vicious and possessive as before.

When summer returned, there was no argument about who would work the fields, and Ren took his place on his beloved tractor, sucking hay, tipping his hat, his skin tanned and glowing.

On our son's first birthday, he made love to me with such passion and power, he convinced me what we'd lived through was just a nightmare.

A nightmare we'd woken from.

A nightmare we wouldn't have again.

As his body thrust into mine and his lips cast a spell over my mind and heart, I threw myself into a better dream.

One where Ren would be around to watch his son have his own sons and daughters.

A dream where we grew old together.

And for a while…it came true.

\* \* \* \* \*

# 2024

Jacob turned two, and we spent the day with the Wilsons in the old farmhouse.

Cassie helped me bake a cake with two *Spiderman* candles, and

John bounced his honorary grandson on his knee while Ren shared a drink with Liam and Chip on the couch.

So far, 2024 had been the opposite of 2023.

Ren was healthy—in relative terms—and happy.

Jacob was walking and into everything.

And Cassie's horse business—that she'd named Cherry Equestrian—had been running for six months. So far, she'd broken in three horses and entered one local show-jumping contest where she came second. The prize money was enough to buy more tack and a new saddle.

After an afternoon of birthday presents and eating cake, Jacob passed out as Ren carried him across the field to our house.

Occasionally, he'd cough, but thanks to Keytruda and painkillers, Ren was almost as content as the year when I'd been pregnant and he'd made the impossible possible by building a house, marrying me, and becoming a true Wild.

"By the way, I did what Rick suggested."

Ren's voice settled around our feet as the moon cast him in quicksilver shadows.

I looked up, my heart skipping a beat at the sharp lines of his jaw, slight stubble, and perfect lips. His brow was drawn and eyes dark, but his hair danced to its own beat with the slight breeze over the paddock.

"Oh?" I reached out and squeezed Jacob's tiny foot. It was too irresistible, dangling from his father's embrace, encased in a miniature sneaker. It constantly amazed me that manufacturers could make adult apparel in toddler sizes.

"About the lawsuit."

"Ah, right." I nodded.

Rick had mentioned it to me, too. He'd told me alone, actually. Mentioning the god-awful subject of *after*.

*After* Ren was gone.

*After.*

I hated, *hated* that word.

Apparently, due to having his life cut short by unnatural means, Ren was fully within his right to claim compensation. There were claimants and lawsuits toward the asbestos company numbering in the thousands, but the successful pay outs were either while the victim was still alive or the person left behind filed within one to two years.

After that, it was too late.

Letting Jacob's foot go, I shuddered. "I don't like the thought of benefiting from your…" I swallowed, cursing the familiar sting in my eyes.

Ren shuffled Jacob to one arm, then reached for my hand. His grip was warm and dry and strong. "If it wasn't for them, I wouldn't be going anywhere for a very long time." His voice hardened. "You know I hate charity, but this…it isn't like that. This is *justice*. They killed me when I was ten years old, Della. The least they can do is compensate you and Jacob."

"I'm not taking money from those monsters."

"But I will." He squeezed my fingers. "I'd do anything for you. Rick's already filed my case with a lawyer who has a few active claimants. He said there's better success in numbers, so he'll wait for a couple more to come forward and then take it to trial."

I sighed heavily, kicking at weeds and pulling up the roots out of habit. "When will you know if you win a settlement?"

"Not sure." He kissed Jacob's downy blond head. "But hopefully not too long."

He didn't say it, but he didn't need to.

These days, there were conversations flying around all the time that weren't said.

*Hopefully not too long.*

*Hopefully before I'm dead.*

\* \* \* \* \*

# 2025

Christmas was whiter than usual with a blizzard that meant the tractor was used as a plough, fashioning a pathway between our house and the Wilsons.

Ice laced window frames, and trees were sacrificed to burn to keep the chill at bay.

This year, with Jacob three and Nina eleven, we opted to have Christmas at our place where the sparse amount of furniture meant opening presents and reaping season carnage wasn't nearly as destructive as in John's house with its over-packed bookcases and rooms that held more than just mementoes; it held entire lifetimes.

Ren and I had yet to create that amount of clutter, and the main point of decoration was a small pine tree Ren had cut down, potted, and taken me shopping to buy as many gaudy baubles as I wanted.

I had to admit, I'd gone a bit overboard with the tinsel.

But watching our son laugh and rip into brightly printed paper, revealing a remote-control car, books that could be read in the bath, and a set of miniature diggers to play in the dirt, it was worth it.

"I still remember our first Christmas," Ren murmured, slotting himself beside me as I leaned against the kitchen bench after serving warm apple and cinnamon muffins. We'd had a big lunch of roasted veggies, turkey, and all the trimmings, so appetites weren't all that hungry.

I wrapped my arms around his waist. "I remember it, too."

I remembered how Cassie had come into our room and made fun of me for sleeping in the same bed as Ren. How her tone had been weird, and I didn't like it whenever she looked at the boy who was mine.

"You kissed me under the mistletoe." He chuckled as Jacob fell over the plush rug by the fireplace, chasing his remote-control car as Nina careened it into things, kamikaze style. "Remember?"

I didn't actually.

My five-year-old brain had been obsessing about Cassie and the strangers I didn't like, rather than the comforting presence of my beloved brother. I scrunched up my nose, pretending I did. "I think it was *you* who kissed *me*, not the other way around."

He pursed his lips, his excellent memory that would've made him worthy of any scholar or doctor or any profession he chose whisking through time to a different Christmas and snowy night.

"You know...you're right." He turned me to face him, planting possessive hands on my hips. "I scooped you up and asked you to kiss me." His face glowed with fondness. "I gave you my cheek, but you smacked my lips instead."

"Like this?" I stood on tiptoes, pressing my mouth to his.

But this time, I didn't smack like a child.

I kissed like a wife.

And there was nothing innocent about it.

He groaned, his body tensing for more. "*Exactly* like that."

We laughed together, enjoying our inside joke of five-year-olds kissing fifteen-year-olds—both totally unaware what existed in their future.

Our lips parted, tongues touched, and later, once everyone had left and Jacob was asleep in his bed, Ren took me in all the ways he could.

It was the best Christmas present even though he'd bought me a new laptop and I'd bought him a new oil skin jacket.

Every touch was precious.

Every thrust was infinite.

Every year more treasured than the last.

\* \* \* \* \*

# 2026

We hadn't celebrated our shared birthday in a while, thanks to parenthood, hospital visits, farm running, horse businesses, and all the other things that made up a hectic life, but on 27th of June— our official date of creation (even if Ren had borrowed it from me)—we asked Cassie to babysit our monster four-year-old and headed to a local diner for our tradition.

The meal of greasy food and naughty but oh-so-delicious burgers was a flashback to a lifetime of togetherness.

Halfway through the meal, Ren tugged at the ribbon holding my braid together, unravelling it with a look of intensity.

I gulped, burning up in the coffee fire of his gaze, then tears welled as he pulled a fresh string of blue from his pocket. "I'm afraid I've been rather slack on replacing your ribbon the past few years. This one is looking a little faded." With swift fingers—used to tying bows from my childhood—he retied my braid with new, bright cobalt, then went back to eating as if nothing had happened.

I'd wanted to pounce on him there and then, but it was almost a game to him. A game to see how much he could seduce me by not even touching me.

By the time we'd polished off a chocolate brownie for dessert, I was ready to fool around in the back of the second-hand pick-up truck we'd bought two years ago.

However, Ren took my hand and guided me down Main Street.

My skin itched for his touch. My lips watered for his kiss. My patience was stretched with need.

"Are we ambling aimlessly, or do we have a plan?" I asked. "Because I need you and a bed and alone time, stat."

He chuckled. "Stat, huh?"

"Immediately."

"Well, you'll have to be patient. I'm looking for something."

Ren smiled, the street lights casting his handsome face in shadows and illumination. I was seriously the luckiest woman in the world to love someone so beautiful inside and out.

I wanted to leap into his arms and force him to take me, but I ordered myself to be a grown-up. "Looking for what?"

He grinned wider, tugging me down a side street with a single glowing sign still on at this time of night. "That."

"Jill's Quill?"

"Yup." He nodded. "For your seventeenth birthday present, I bought you ink that teases me every day you slide out of bed and every moment you walk barefoot toward me. I don't think I ever told you how much that ribboned R means to me. Didn't really know how. So…I figured, why bother telling you when I could show you?"

Coughing once, he dragged me toward the tattoo parlour and through the glass door.

"Ah, you must be my nine o'clock." A spritely woman looked up with colourful tatted sleeves and a stretched hoop in her ear. "Sit. Let's get started."

Ren didn't give me time to ask what the hell was going on before he pushed me toward the black pleather couch and took a seat on the plastic wrapped recliner in front of the artist. "You got the design I emailed?"

"Yup." The artist, who I assumed was Jill, snapped on a pair of gloves and grabbed a stencil already printed and ready to go from the table beside her. "Where do you want it?"

Ren pointed to his forearm. "There."

"Alrighty."

I had no idea what it was or how this had happened so suddenly.

Nerves bubbled in my belly the entire time the tattoo gun buzzed.

Afterward, Ren ordered, "Pay the woman, Della Ribbon. This is, after all, your birthday present to me."

Laughing under my breath, I rolled my eyes at the craziness of my husband. I slipped cash from my purse, waited until Jill rung me up, then turned to face him with a hand on my hip. "Okay, enough of the secrets. Show me."

With a soul-stealing look, he came toward me, holding out his arm. "It's not a secret that I love you."

My eyes locked on his fresh ink.

Blue, the same colour as mine.

A ribbon wrapping around his arm instead of my foot.

A ribbon that looped into a J before finishing in a D, just like mine finished in an R.

He was right.

Telling me how much my tattoo meant to him would've been useless.

Because nothing could describe the tidal wave of lust, love, and loss that filled me.

He'd marked himself forever.

He'd take me and Jacob wherever he went.

He was mine, not death's or pain's or time's.

*Mine.*

The permanent ink said so.

\* \* \* \* \*

# 2027

"I can't believe you're making me do this." Ren laughed, hoisting five-year-old Jacob onto his hip.

The past few years had been a whirlwind of Ren teaching his son everything he could. From camping trips in summer, to tractor snow ploughing in winter, and even sitting with him and doing 'homework' like I'd done even though Jacob only attended preschool.

Ren was besotted with his son, just like I knew he would be.

And I was besotted with both of them, often drifting into a dreamy trance while watching Ren interact with Jacob—laughing with him, joking, arguing, and even scolding.

Each day, I fell helplessly in love with him.

Which only added another layer to my hurt.

And each month I hoped I'd fall pregnant again, desperate to give Ren the daughter he wanted.

But each year, it never came true.

"Don't blame me. Blame Cassie." I stuck out my tongue as Jacob squirmed in Ren's arms.

"Down. Down." Jacob pointed at the ground. "Nina has chocolate. I want some."

"After." Kissing my unruly child on the nose, I made sure his string tie was neat, his black shirt was buttoned, and tiny Wranglers were hay free. Once he was presentable, I tackled my husband, rubbing at a dirt smudge on his cheek, lamenting over the soil beneath his nails, and tucking his matching black shirt into his waistband to reveal the silver belt buckle I'd bought him last Christmas.

He'd rolled his sleeves up to reveal his ribbon tattoo with our initials in it, his hair obscured by a cowboy hat.

He was a quintessential country boy and had some god-like power that made me find him ever more handsome as the years went by.

However, nothing could hide the fact he was lankier than filled out these days.

That was the reason for the photo-shoot.

To permanently etch us in place, where time and sickness couldn't touch us. It'd been Cassie's idea when I'd had a weak moment and sobbed in her arms.

It wasn't often I buckled beneath the always impending knowledge of our future, but when I broke, I broke big.

Luckily, she was always there to pick up my pieces, drown me with wine, and send me back to my family with a patched up heart and paper bravery.

The past few months had been hard.

Ren had gone downhill again.

At the start of the year, his coughing came back with a vengeance, and, whenever he lay down or bent over, he struggled to stop. His throat became raw, his energy levels depleted.

The more he tried to hide his discomfort, the worse it got, and Jacob flinched just as much as I did when he had a coughing fit.

Rick said Ren's tumours hadn't spread, but he was suffering pleural effusion and suggested surgery. If he didn't, Ren would continue to drown in his own lungs, thanks to fluid constantly building.

For a week, Ren and I tossed up the pros and cons.

Pros—if the surgery went well with no hiccups, it would mean he'd have a better quality of life, wouldn't cough or be out of breath so badly, and be back to being active and strong. If the Keytruda kept his immune system supported and attacking his mesothelioma, there was no reason he couldn't have many more years.

Cons—if the surgery ran into complications, he might be hospitalised for a while, running the risk of becoming ill with pneumonia or worse...putting his body under such strain it suffered respiratory distress or cardiovascular problems.

In the end, it was Jacob who helped us decide.

He ran into our bedroom one morning and slammed to a stop as Ren came out of the bathroom, dripping wet and wrapped in a towel.

His adorable little face scrunched up as he pointed across the room. "You're skinny." Running over to his father, he poked Ren in the side—or as high as he could reach—saying, "One, two, three ribs, Daddy. Eat more, 'kay?"

Ren had looked at me, another awful cough tumbling from his lips.

He just nodded, and I knew.

The next week, Rick organised the Pleurodesis surgery, and Ren had a night in the hospital after the procedure, just to make sure there were no issues. Rick told us to be kind to ourselves and not panic about the results for a few days. However, by the fourth day at home, Ren's colour was already better, his appetite improved, and his coughing nowhere near as wracking.

It had been a gamble, but it'd paid off, and yet again, we had a future with sunshine rather than shadows.

For so long now, we'd existed in the middle of a seesaw. Sometimes sliding one way, only to scramble back to the middle before slamming to the ground.

Ren never missed a treatment of Keytruda, and for now, he remained stable with no side effects. We were optimistic but also realistic.

Hence the photo-shoot to capture Ren fit and smiley…just in case.

"Okay? You ready?" The purple-haired photographer popped her bubble-gum, smiling. "Arrange yourself on the hay bale. The light is good against the barn, so we'll start there, then make our way around the farm and any other places you want, okay?"

I nodded. "Sounds great."

Cassie stood to the side with Chip and Nina, ready for her own photo-shoot once ours was done. John lingered, overseeing with encouragement and wisecracks, occasionally agreeing to photo bomb and be forever immortalized.

As Ren gathered me in his arms, smoothing my white dress, and Jacob stood obediently in front of us with my hand on his shoulder, my heart fluttered for more.

More of this.

More of everything.

Just *more*.

# Chapter Sixty-Three

## REN

## 2028

"YOU TRULY ARE a miracle, Ren Wild."

I smirked at my oncologist who'd become a firm friend over the years.

Rick Mackenzie was a rare type of human who I didn't just tolerate but genuinely liked his company. He was calming, encouraging, and made me fight just that little bit harder because to let him down was unthinkable.

"I have too much to live for." I put my t-shirt back on after yet another chest X-ray. If my lungs didn't kill me, the radiation from all the X-rays would.

"I told you love would turn out to be your biggest ally."

I glanced at my tattoo, familiar crests of affection rising in my heart. "Love is worth fighting for."

"I think you just stole that from a Hallmark card." Rick chuckled, typing into his computer the results of today's check-up. I let him finish before he suddenly said, "Oh, almost forgot!" Wrenching open his desk drawer, he pulled out a folder with a flourish. "After waiting so long, the trial went well."

"Oh, yeah?" I sat down, recalling the affidavit I had to give, the tests I'd submitted to from doctors trying to prove I was lying, right through to agreeing to be shadowed for a few weeks seeing as I was one of the younger patients but also one who'd survived the longest.

Lawyers had taken every bill and invoice I'd incurred in the years, along with tallying up the free healthcare I'd received, thanks to the off-label trial.

The asbestos trust did not want to pay out.

But my evidence was conclusive.

"They were found guilty on six counts of negligence and undue personal injury. The trust fund will pay out in three months."

My jaw fell open. "A-are you serious?"

"Deadly."

I flinched. I'd become rather sensitive to that word.

"Sorry." He laughed. "But this is good news, Ren. *Really* good news."

"How good?" I leaned forward.

When Rick suggested suing the asbestos manufacturer, I hadn't held out hope. Pay outs ranged from nothing to mega bucks, but I'd never done this for the money.

It had been my only avenue of revenge—to hurt them in their pocket while they stole my life. In a way, I still didn't feel right about it. I'd gotten sick while at Mclary's. In my mind, I blamed him. It had been a struggle separating the two.

"Two and a half million good." Rick grinned, clicking his pen like an addict.

"Wait. *What?*" My ears rang. "I must have heard you wrong."

"You didn't."

"*What* did you say?" My skin slicked with cold sweat. "*How* much?"

"Two and a half *million* dollars. You've done what you wanted."

My life slowed, saying no to death and thank you to all my wishes coming true.

I couldn't believe it, even as the fears I'd always carried fell away.

Never again would we be destitute or homeless.

*Della is safe.*

"I've protected her," I breathed, still in shock.

With or without me.

Della and Jacob would always be safe.

It didn't make any of this easier, but the shackles of panic fell away.

I'd beaten the clock at its own game.

"You have." Rick smiled. "In sickness and in health."

"For richer and for poorer." I met his eyes.

My hands shook as I curled them into fists.

Yet another small victory over death.

I smiled, grateful, vindicated, hopeful. "She and Jacob will want for nothing."

\* \* \* \* \*

# 2029

"Dad! *Daaad!*"

"In here, kiddo." I tossed back a painkiller, chasing it with orange juice. Morning sunshine streamed into the kitchen, painting everything in summer softness.

Jacob appeared at breakneck speed, his cargo shorts full to the brim with Legos. His blond hair was shaggy and in need of a cut. His eyes mischievous and far too smart for his seven-year age. "I need your help building the tower on my castle."

Reaching down, I grabbed him from the floor and plopped up onto the kitchen bench just as Della padded barefoot from the bedroom wing.

She caught my eye, smiling sexily.

I'd had her this morning. I'd had her on her stomach with my hand fisted in her hair. But that didn't stop my body from reacting.

"Hi." She kissed me, pouring herself a glass of juice before kissing Jacob. "Hey, Wild One."

Jacob wrinkled his nose. "Ugh, kissing is for girls."

"Oh, really?" Della attacked his face with kisses while I held him prisoner.

He squirmed and squealed while I laughed and Della blew raspberries on his neck. "Wrong, mister. Kisses are for little boys who I love."

Wiping his face on my shirt, he stuck out his tongue. "Eww, you suck." A smile twisted his lips, though, reminding me so much of Della that age. The defiance, the independence, the urge to grow up too fast.

God, I loved this family.

Scooting Jacob off the bench, I put him back on his feet. "I'll come help you in a minute, okay? Just need to talk to Mom real quick."

Jacob gave me a stern look. "You better. I'm timing you." He took off, and I let loose the cough that had been tickling my chest, turning away from Della and clamping a hand over my mouth.

She rested her palm on my back, rubbing gently as I rode out the worst of it. Once I could breathe again, I turned to face her.

"Had some news today."

"More news like last year when you came home and told me we were millionaires?"

I chuckled. "No, not quite."

The asbestos trust fund had paid out, depositing an unbelievable sum into our bank account. We'd paid off the mortgage, given some to John for the remaining balance of the land—which led to an explosive argument—and set up the rest into an account that would earn good interest while being a safety net for Della and Jacob.

My life insurance was just a cherry on top now, and the relief that gave me—to know they would always have a home—was indescribable.

"Our lawyer contacted us. The bank finally managed to sell the Mclary place." Not once did I ever tie Della to those monsters. It was never *her* parents' farm. It was purely a nightmare where we'd both lived for a time.

"Oh?" Her eyebrow rose. "What does that mean?"

"It means, after the debt was paid, there wasn't much left. Fifty thousand, give or take."

Della wrinkled her nose, looking all the more beautiful. "I don't want it. I won't take anything from them."

Smoothing the tiny wrinkle by her eye, I kissed her softly.

At least I'd earned my final wish—I'd lived long enough to see age change her, just a little—a wrinkle that only appeared when she smiled or scowled.

"Thought you might say that." Letting her go, I placed our empty glasses in the sink. "That's why I asked him to set up a charity for any of the kids found who the Mclary's hurt."

Della froze. "You did?"

"You'll need to sign the forms, seeing as you're the main trustee, but I knew you wouldn't want their money, and at least, this way, it can be put to righting some of their wrongs."

Over the years, the police had found one or two children who'd been sold. The man who'd purchased has-been workers still hadn't been captured, but newspapers had kept track of the story, spreading composite sketches and even a photo that one of the kids—now in his thirties—had of him.

No one mentioned if my mother had been found—just as I requested. And the case was only shared when good news could be given.

Their evil might never be fully erased, but at least some souls had been saved.

"You're the best, husband of mine."

"I'm only what you made me, wife of mine."

"Wrong. You're Ren Wild. The boy who survived and is still surviving."

Kissing her, I murmured, "And I'll keep surviving...for as long as I can."

* * * * *

# 2030

"Jacob, come here. I found a clue."

My voice vibrated with love as the lanky eight-year-old charged over the field toward me, his face alight and blond hair glowing.

He was the perfect blend of Della and me. Slightly wary of people but entirely fearless in nature. Blond hair from her and dark eyes from me. Quiet seriousness mixed with effortless charm.

Della had turned thirty, and I'd knocked on forty—time extending the dream I didn't think I'd have, watching my son change from kid to boy, and my wife grow in wisdom and kindness every day.

The blue overalls Jacob had dressed in—that were usually reserved for helping me grease and oil the tractor—had paint splashes down the front and a bunny sticker stuck to his chest. His nose had a green spot, and his hands had red and yellow streaks from decorating Easter eggs earlier today.

The entire Wilson crew had come together to enjoy a holiday we hadn't celebrated before.

It had been Della's idea.

Our kitchen had become a warzone of glitter, stickers, and gemstones as the kids decorated eggs in whatever fashion they chose.

Once the novelty of covering themselves and everything else in paint faded, Della and I ushered everyone outside and gave each group of kids a clue to start a chocolate treasure hunt, then set them loose on Cherry River, searching barns, stables, tack rooms, rivers, and grottos.

"Where's the clue?" Jacob asked, his wicker basket knocking against his legs as he slammed to a stop.

I pointed at the chicken coop ahead. Chocolate eggs were

mixed with real eggs and the key to collecting them was to scatter a handful of feed for the protective mother hens. "In there. Better go fast; otherwise, Nina is gonna pinch all the good stuff."

"Oh, no she won't." He took off with a whoosh of wildflowers, tripping a little in his haste.

Della laughed softly. "You really know how to wind him up."

"Only because I remember how easy it was to wind you up when you were that age."

She took my hand, linking our fingers. "I was never that competitive."

"Bah!" I laughed, cursing my lungs when it turned into a coughing fit. "I just had to mention something you shouldn't do, and you just had to do it."

Sunshine dappled her beside me. Her hair was longer—almost down to her ass. Her jeans scuffed and weathered. Her grey jacket torn on the wrist and grass-stained on the elbow.

A typical wardrobe for us.

A normal acceptance that we were part of the wilderness, and a little dirt never hurt anybody.

Seeing her so simple and innocent and gorgeous, I no longer cared about trailing after the chocolate hunting kids.

I wanted to stand still for a moment with the girl of my heart.

Tugging her hand, I waited until she faced me, then looped my arms around her hips. "Hi." I nuzzled her, inhaling her scent and growing instantly hard.

There was something about this woman that I would never get sick of.

No matter how many years we spent together.

No matter how many miracles I burned through to stay by her side.

I would never stop wanting her, loving her, needing her.

Della tipped her head up, her blue eyes begging for a kiss.

I obliged, lowering my mouth to hers, granting a soft hello before slipping into a sinful command. Pressing her against me, I swayed with her in the meadow, allowing the breeze to shift us this way and that, tuning out the world until it was just us again.

Us as children.

Us as newlyweds.

Us with our entire world spread at our feet.

When we broke apart, we both breathed heavier, and my eyes lingered on our house in the distance, wondering if it would be rude to drag her back to bed.

"Don't even think about it." She grinned, clutching my hand and tugging me toward the kids. They fought with high-pitched voices, arguing over who deserved the most chocolate and who would read the next clue.

"What? I wasn't doing anything."

"You were thinking it." She brought our linked hands up and kissed my knuckles. "I love you, Ren Wild."

I smiled softly, my eyes tracking the blue satin in her hair that was always nearby. Last year, the ribbon wheel had run out, and I couldn't replace the fading piece of blue anymore.

I'd ensured her favourite possession never tore since I was fourteen. I had no intention of letting her down now, and had it on my list to find another cardboard circle that would last for the rest of her lifetime.

I might not be there in the future to cut it for her, but at least she'd never go without.

As we walked side by side, like any other happily married couple, I winced at the ever-growing pain in my chest. I'd been hiding it rather well. I'd been lying rather successfully.

I didn't need to hurt her anymore by telling her my stage two had become stage three, and the Keytruda was slowly failing.

My body still fought a hard battle.

And I wasn't going anywhere just yet.

But...I had to be honest.

I was getting...tired.

My body no longer felt as healthy, and there would come a time that the meat on my bones would be sacrificed to keep me alive just a little longer.

I already feared that day.

I already mourned the inevitable.

I already struggled with how to say goodbye.

# Chapter Sixty-Four

## REN

## 2032

"YOU CAN'T GIVE him a knife for his birthday, Ren."

I looked up from wrapping the Swiss Army tool that I'd bought from the local hunting and fishing store. I'd also bought a kid's size backpack, collapsible pots, mugs, water containers, a cosy sleeping bag, and everything else I wished I'd had when I was Jacob's age.

"He's ten, Little Ribbon. He's not a kid."

"Ten is *exactly* a kid." Della sat beside me, snapping the scissors I'd used to cut the sticky tape to keep the *Star Wars* wrapping paper in place. "I love you, you know this. And I love that you never let having nine fingers slow you down, but, Ren, I rather like our son with ten."

She laughed quietly as I dragged her chair closer to mine, obscuring my face as I coughed. Once I had my breath back, I smirked. "He's not going to cut a finger off."

"How do you know? He's a menace to himself. He needed stitches last year from falling off Cassie's pony. He broke his wrist a few weeks after that from back flipping into the pond and hitting dirt instead." She clucked her tongue. "I worry about him."

"Don't. He's only testing his boundaries and capabilities."

Just like I'd tested mine and knew the god-awful conclusion.

My battle was slowly coming to an end.

Della knew.

I knew.

John, Cassie, Liam, and Jacob knew.

I'd had a check-up and treatment last week, and the look Rick Mackenzie gave me was as grave as the image in the mirror.

Keytruda had been hailed as the miracle drug. It had given me an extra eight years than the normal prognosis.

But sometimes, it just stopped working.

No one knew why, and no doctor could explain it.

And as much as I would never admit it, my body didn't feel right anymore.

There was no denying that I had a cancerous passenger inside me and it was finally winning. My hair no longer shone; my eyes no longer sparkled. My skin was stretched over bones that ached more by the day, and the breathlessness that had been cured for so long, thanks to surgery, was back in full force.

I was a ticking clock, and Della hadn't left my side for longer than an hour or two, both of us so terribly aware that we didn't have many hours left to waste.

We'd done our best to protect my disease from Jacob, but he was just as smart as Della, and the kids at school had done their best to tell him what was wrong with me—just like they'd tried to explain to Della about sex when she was young.

Their explanations did more harm than good with terminology that was terrifying. They'd given Jacob nightmares of me being buried and eaten alive by worms because that's what their dad said happened to great-grandma. Another had promised I'd die but would come back as a zombie and eat him in his sleep.

Turned out, keeping facts from loved ones—no matter how young they were—was never a good idea.

It'd taken a few dinners with Della holding his hand and me talking to him, man to man, for him to calm down and not flinch when I hugged him.

He knew that I wouldn't be around for as long as other dads.

He knew he couldn't beg or argue to make that change.

And he also knew he could be angry with me but never at Della because none of this was her fault.

It'd been a depressing week, but finally, either his brain numbed him to the reality of our future, or his upcoming birthday had pushed his worries aside because he was the same happy kid as before.

He had the choice of a party with all his friends for his birthday or a camping trip just him, me, and Della. He'd chosen camping, and that was exactly what I was going to do. Regardless if the thought of hiking miles into the forest no longer filled me with excitement but worry on how I'd do it without passing out.

Della watched my nine fingers as I finished wrapping the

boxed knife and smoothed the neat package.

"He doesn't even realise that that will be his greatest treasure when he's older." Tears glossed her eyes, overflowing as she kept staring at my hands. "His first knife from his dad. A dad I hope to God he remembers."

"Hey…" Pulling her into my arms, I kissed her hair. "Don't do that. Please. I can't stand it."

She clutched me tight, her arms squeezing until I coughed again. She allowed a couple of sobs before shutting the hatch and smiling with salt-wet cheeks. "Sorry. Moment of weakness, that's all."

I kept holding her, not letting go.

She thought I didn't know, but a few times a year, she'd unload her broken heart to Cassie, talk about me, miss me, then bottle it all back up again to be strong for me.

I never asked what Cassie said to her.

I never pried and begged to know what fears Della shared.

I knew enough not to need to.

Living with a dying man was not easy.

Especially when that dying man had loved you since you were born.

I hated that making love to my wife made me pant as if I'd run two lengths of the paddock at full tilt.

I hated that I couldn't stop the light-headedness and abhorrent sensation of having no control over my body.

I hated everything about this.

Letting Della go, I kissed the soft skin beside her mouth. "It's important he knows I don't think of him as a kid. I was eight when I first used tools and farming equipment—"

"I know he idolizes you, but he's not you, Ren. He hasn't been thrust into survival mode and forced to grow up far before his time. He doesn't know hardship like you do." Her fingers landed on my cheek, tracing the sharper cheekbone and stroking a more angled jaw. "You were never ten years old when you ran with me. You were fifty in a kid's body. You were never a typical child."

"And Jacob is not a typical son."

She grinned sadly. "You're right. He's your son."

"No. He's *our* son." I coughed again, cursing the ever-tightening curse in my chest. "And our son is smart and brave and wise, and he *will* remember me. Just like you will. You'll both remember how much I love you and that I'll never be truly gone."

Della nodded, unable to speak.

For a moment, I let us sit in the puddle of sadness, then I stood, coughed, and tapped her on the butt. "Go get the backpack and the child. It's time to camp."

# Chapter Sixty-Five

# DELLA

# 2032

WE SET UP camp as a family.

Erecting the tent, we put our sleeping bags in one wing and Jacob's in the other.

Our journey hadn't been as easy as previous excursions. We hadn't gone as far, but it had taken twice as long. I'd carried the backpack—against Ren's wishes—but I couldn't allow him to lug more weight when he already struggled with his own.

Ren's cough crucified him, bending him over a few times, spitting up blood toward the end.

I'd told Jacob to run ahead as Ren clutched my hand through one attack, stumbling for breath, his hand on his heart as it palpitated to an uneven rhythm.

I'd murmured calm nothings, rubbed his back, cursing the noticeable nodules of his spine.

I'd been strong for him and kept my panic hidden.

But it didn't mean it didn't grow with every little reminder that things were coming to an end. That our life together was almost over.

My heart was held together with sticky tape and bandages.

My eyes were made of tears and terror.

I couldn't explain the toll loving Ren took on me when he faded day by day from this world to the next.

Some days, I wished I could stop loving him.

I wished I could pack up my feelings in neatly labelled boxes, and store them in the attic of my mind for a time when dust and time had made them less painful.

But that only made me feel like a weak, wicked woman, and I'd throw myself into loving him even more.

*Here, take my heart. Take my soul. Take every second I have left because I don't want them without you.*

By the time we made it to the camp, I was sick with loathing at life and love, utterly unable to talk.

My heart was in knots; my stomach tied up with rotten string.

I missed the man who used to run wild amongst the trees.

I missed the boy who made me believe in fairy-tales.

As we finished the tent, Ren's coughing couldn't be ignored and, after a while, he gave me a tear-invoking smile and went to sit by the log we'd chosen as a bench.

He understood that he wasn't the only one struggling with this.

Jacob hated hearing him cough.

And my nerves were frayed and burning.

As I pottered about doing final tasks, I couldn't keep my eyes off Ren as he sat whittling a stick with his ever-trusty knife. His face pensive and calm.

My heart swelled with injustice and rage. My motions jerky and harsh.

The backpack was my worst enemy.

The twigs and wilderness my greatest foe.

I wanted everything to hurt as much as I did and stomped around, snapping things and kicking others.

Ren caught me as I moved around him, pulling out the small cooler box with our meat for breakfast and dinner, placing it where the fire would go.

"Ribbon." He smiled kindly, his face still so damn handsome but so much more defined than before. A definition that came from sickness. A definition that no one could agree was right.

I tried to pull away, biting my lip from saying hurtful things, painful things, things that I never normally let spill.

I was so *angry*.

So furious.

So *hurt*.

When I didn't bow to his touch like normal, Ren's eyes narrowed. "I know this is hard. But please…don't be angry with me."

For a second, I wanted to slap him.

I wanted to pummel his broken chest and kick him in the shins.

It made no sense.

My violence was confused and smarting.

I *hated* seeing him so skinny.

I despised hugging his once solid, comforting frame only to find bone instead of muscle.

I hated my tears and fears and the fact that as the final day crept closer, my strength grew non-existent.

I didn't like the seething mass inside my belly.

I didn't enjoy having to control my temper toward my husband and son because it wasn't them who made me angry.

*God* made me angry.

*Life* made me angry.

Love made me so *fucking* angry.

And I needed to shout at someone, fight something, attack anything to get rid of the tight fury inside me.

My nostrils flared as I continued to look down at him.

He looked so gorgeous and regal. So wise and perceptive and everlasting.

And I wanted to hit him and hit him and *hit him* because he'd achieved the impossible. He'd run from evil, endured horrors, saved me, guided me, loved me, married me, and now...now he was leaving me.

He didn't have that right.

He didn't have that luxury.

He *owed* me.

He owed me to stay because why else had we been given this life together?

"Ah, Della." Ren stood, smothering a cough. With hands that still had strength and dominance, he squeezed my biceps. "Yell at me. Scream at me. Tell me what you're feeling."

I shook my head, short and jerky. "You know I can't."

"Why not?"

"Because Jacob is somewhere close by, and...and it's not your fault."

"None of this is anyone's fault, but I'm just as angry as you. I'm fucking furious that I can't hold you forever and be beside you as you grow old." His voice darkened. "Don't you think I've punched things, kicked things? Tried to somehow relieve that filthy pressure inside?"

"I know you have. I've patched up your bruised knuckles." I smiled, doing my best to make a tense moment into a light-hearted one, but Ren didn't let it go.

"You have to let it out, Della. You can't allow it to fester." His eyes cast into the twilight-shrouded forest, a bird twirl whistling from his lips.

A call he'd taught Jacob to recognise and repeat—a way of keeping tabs on him when he tarried off without us.

An answering tune came from the distance, faint but close enough not to panic.

"He's out of hearing distance—for the most part." Ren cupped my cheek. "Tell me. Hit me if you need."

For a second, I considered it.

I honestly contemplated hitting the love of my life.

The love who was dying.

But then, my rage vanished as quickly as it had built, and I melted into his embrace. "I'm just so afraid, Ren. So afraid I won't be able to do this. That nothing will make sense or be worthwhile anymore. How can I look after Jacob when you're not here to look after me? How am I supposed to care about anything when the only thing I've ever cared about is gone?"

Even though tears didn't fall, sadness vibrated in my voice, cloying as smoke.

"I don't know. I honestly don't know." He hugged me tight, the rattle in his lungs a constant song. "All I know is, out of the two of us, you're the bravest one. You'll get through it. Somehow."

Tearing myself out of his arms, I glowered at him. "Don't call me brave, Ren. You know nothing of bravery."

He scowled. "Know nothing? Are you sure?"

"Yes, because for decades *you've* been the braver one, but you've never seen it. You've never once blamed me for what happened to you. You've never once cried for what life has given you. You've never broken down or—"

"Only because I have you."

"Yes, and soon, I won't have you at all."

Jacob came bounding from the trees, his arms chock-a-block with twigs and kindling. "Found some." He pranced to the cleared circle to make a blaze, utterly oblivious to the sort-of-fight he'd interrupted.

And I was glad.

Because I honestly didn't have the strength.

The way I was feeling, I was weak enough to consider a Romeo and Juliet ending and bequeath Jacob to Cassie.

I would be that terrible.

I would be that monstrous to leave my child an orphan because I didn't have the courage to be a widow.

"Who's hungry?" I asked brightly. Too brightly. Tearing myself from Ren's hold, I grabbed the grill plate from the backpack. Ducking to my haunches, I helped Jacob build a fire.

"Me! I'm starving." Jacob rubbed his tummy. "And then, after dinner, please tell me there's cake."

Ren chuckled, sitting back down, forever watching us. "In a diner, a long time ago, a waitress once told me there was always time for cake." His dark coffee eyes met mine. "Your mom was five and blew spit all over the cupcakes instead of blowing out a single flame."

Jacob laughed. "Eww. I'll take care of the blowing. Thanks, Mom."

I couldn't move, entranced by Ren's gaze, enchanted by him.

He whispered, "You made a wish that night, Della Ribbon. A wish I've always tried to honour. Please understand, I'll still be keeping that promise even after I'm—"

"Enough." Tearing my eyes from his, I snatched a lighter from the backpack and let fire chew its way through the carefully stacked sticks.

Ren stayed quiet as the fire grew and, once the blaze was big enough, I placed the grill plate on top—balanced by a few rocks—and slapped three juicy steaks into the flames. I'd made a potato salad back at home with mayo, along with some spinach wrapped rice rolls.

The birthday cake for Jacob's tenth celebration was carefully tucked in Tupperware—a vanilla sponge in the shape of the little white pony, Binky, that he'd been learning to ride.

Organising this trip had given my mind something to hook onto, and I'd slipped back into my role as mother.

Once the steaks were cooked, I divided up the potato salad and rice rolls onto the collapsible plates Ren had bought for Jacob's birthday and did my best to act normal with conversation.

Partway through the meal, I subtly handed Ren a high-strength painkiller as his skin flushed with sweat and his forehead never smoothed.

I'd long since become acquainted with his tolerance levels and pain.

He gave me a look before sighing and holding out his palm.

I dropped the pill into it before Jacob noticed, nodding like a satisfied nurse as he swallowed.

Afterward, I headed to the river, taking a torch to wash up quickly, leaving my two beloved boys to talk about whatever boys do.

And there, in the ether of silence and starlight, I fell to my knees and drove my fists into the leaf-littered dirt.

I let my rage break free.

I punched the earth. I kicked the sky. I ripped time itself apart.

*"Why?"* I screamed quietly.

*"How could you?"* I asked painfully.

*"Not yet,"* I begged brokenly.

But no one answered.

No owl hooted.

No shooting star offered salvation.

And yet, howling at the moon and spreading my fears in the dark was cathartic enough to piece myself back together again, wipe away my tears, pick up the clean plates, and head back to the fire and my boys.

\* \* \* \* \*

"Wow, Dad. Thanks!" Jacob hurled himself into Ren's arms.

*Star Wars* wrapping paper scattered on the forest floor, forgotten as the Swiss Army knife became his prized possession.

"Don't hurt yourself with that, you hear?" I laughed as he kissed Ren's cheek.

Ren patted his back. "You're welcome. I can show you what each thing does if you want?"

"Nah, it's okay. I've played with one of yours before."

"Oh, you have, have you?" Ren raised an eyebrow in my direction, smirking. "Told you, Della. Our son isn't a kid anymore."

I stood, brushing leaves off my ass. A few floated into the fire with a quick whoosh of fuel. I laughed again, forcing happiness. "Fine. What do I know? Ten seems to be the new adult these days."

Ren chuckled.

"Don't move. I'll be right back." Leaving them to discuss blade points and miniature saw skills, I secretly pulled the Tupperware container out of the backpack and went to hide by the tent to stab ten candles into the poor vanilla pony.

With my pocketed lighter, I lit them all then headed back carrying the birthday dessert singing, "Happy birthday to you. Happy birthday to you. Happy birthday to, Jacob! Happy birthday to you."

Jacob groaned, burying his head in his hands. "Ugh, no singing, Mom. That's just embarrassing."

Ren ruffled his blond head, tugging his son's small ear. "Never take these moments for granted, Wild One. It's these that you'll remember forever." His dark eyes met mine and once again, the fracturing brokenness inside threatened to overwhelm me.

Tearing my gaze away, I cleared my throat and dropped to my haunches, delivering the cake to Jacob. "Make a wish and blow them out."

Squeezing his eyes tight, Jacob paused for a moment, then, as serious as if he sat an exam, he blew all ten out in one breath.

Ren grabbed the knife that was forever wedged in his boot, placed the blade in the fire for a few seconds to sterilize it, then cut off the pony's head and gave it to Jacob. "Birthday boy gets first bite."

"Thanks." Jacob shoved it in his face, icing going everywhere.

Ren and I laughed, sharing another heart-warming, heart-breaking look as he passed me a leg and he had the tail.

We ate quietly for a bit, enjoying the sugar, remembering our first birthday together where cupcakes had been our first taste of refined goodness instead of the fructose found in fruit.

So much had happened since then, yet it felt as if nothing had happened at all.

Ren was still a forest dweller, and I was still madly in love with him.

I'd been in love with him for thirty-two years, and it wasn't enough.

It would *never* be enough.

Sucking in a shaky breath, I scooted closer to Ren. He smiled sadly, coughing a little before putting his arm around me.

I kissed his throat, inhaling the heady wild flavour of the man who'd raised me and the man I'd married.

I'd loved him in every way someone could love another—platonically, sisterly, wifely. And now, I loved him in a way that couldn't be explained. A way that transcended everything. A way that had no name because the way we loved existed past language and law. An astral kind of love that made its home in the stars and vacationed on Jupiter.

"You know..." Jacob looked up, his boyish, beautiful face softening with affection rather than acting annoyed at seeing us cuddle. "I made my wish for you guys." His dark eyes, so similar to Ren's, welled up. "I wished that you were better, Dad. I wished you weren't gonna have to go someplace."

Instantly, Ren reached across and dragged Jacob into a three-way hug. Jacob on his knees between us, his tiny frame so slight but so strong.

Tears trickled down my face as Ren shuddered with emotion.

When we could talk without sobbing, Ren said softly, "I wish that too, Wild One, but you have to understand. A wish is something that you want to come true, no matter how impossible it is. Some do come true. And some...don't. But it doesn't mean I'm not still here. Not still inside you. You'll hear me if you listen hard enough because I have no intention of missing you grow into a man."

Jacob grinned, bucking up and proving just how brave he was. Braver than me by far. "Fine. Just don't yell at me when I screw up, 'kay?"

Ren chuckled. "No promises. Depends how badly you screw up." Letting us both go, Ren placed a hand over his mouth and coughed. Once he'd gotten his breath again, he said, "Now, I know you're old, and it's not cool anymore, but how about a story? I can do a horror, so you won't sleep. I can do a romance, so you gag. I have a lot of stories these days tucked inside this skull." He tapped his temple. "What's it gonna be?"

Jacob pursed his lips, thinking. "Is the horror about why you have that brand on your hip?"

I stiffened, but Ren merely nodded, sagely, calmly. "Yeah, but you've already heard that story before."

"Meh, tell it again. But do the voices of that nasty farmer and everything."

Ren glanced at me, his head cocked in question.

I smiled and nodded.

We had no secrets from our son. We'd been honest about everything once the kids at school terrified him about Ren's illness. If he had a question, we did our best to answer it. Better our tale came from us than a township who still sometimes thought our last name Wild was brother and sister and looked at Jacob in disgust.

It wasn't many.

But enough to ensure Jacob should be forearmed about our unusual love story.

Throwing more sticks onto the fire, I passed Ren a water from the cooler beside me.

"Thanks, Ribbon." He smiled, sharing a galaxy of things in his stare.

"Always." Dropping off the log, I settled myself between his legs and rested my head on his thigh. *"Always."*

His hand landed in my hair, playing with the strands as his deep, provocative voice filled the forest. "Once upon a time, there was a boy whose mother didn't want him..."

# Chapter Sixty-Six

## REN

## 2032

MAKING LOVE TO Della was still my favourite thing to do.

It didn't matter that I had to stay sitting upright so I didn't have a coughing fit.

It didn't matter that my breath came short and my heart went wild.

Nothing else mattered when I slid into my wife and felt that epic sensation of connection. Her heat, her body, her welcome.

She was better than any painkiller and more potent than any cure.

Sex with Della always reminded me to keep fighting, no matter how bad some days became.

With our lips locked, we stayed as quiet as we could.

The tent was large enough to give us privacy from Jacob—with us zipped behind our partition and Jacob zipped behind his—but we had to be careful.

Had to be secret.

We touched in the dark, hands trailing over naked skin that was as familiar to each other as our own. Her fingers found me, squeezing hard. My fingers found her, sinking deep.

We kissed slow and passionate and hungry.

Our bodies quickened for more, thirsty.

I wanted her, but I also wanted to delay and enjoy every moment because there was no denying now, no pretending that we'd have forever.

I was tired.

Exhausted.

It wasn't just about the constant pain or struggle to breathe; it was the agony in my wife's and son's eyes. The hidden tears and smothered flinches as they saw me skinny and coughing.

I didn't want them to remember me like that.

I wanted them to remember me as a man who could protect them from everything, including death itself.

Clutching my last few bursts of energy, I dragged Della up my lap until she straddled me.

She gasped into our kiss as I knocked her hand from my erection, and my fingers slid from her. She positioned herself over me, and I groaned as she slid ever so slowly down.

She took me, claimed me, made me hers all over again until her thighs touched mine and my body fully seated within hers.

Once sheathed, we didn't move.

The darkness was absolute and I couldn't see her face, but we stared at each other as if we could. Because, really, we could see every glitter and glimmer of emotion. We could read each other's breaths, feel each other's souls, understand how bittersweet every day had been.

And when we moved, we did it together. Della arching on my lap before sinking back down. Me rocking upward and filling her.

I held her close with one hand on her hip and one arm around her back.

Her breasts warmed my aching chest as we clutched each other so damn hard.

There was no space between us.

No air.

No crack for sadness to wriggle in.

We were plastered together, concreted, mortared, riding slowly, sensually, ignoring everything but this.

There was no her or me, just us.

An us who rode faster, deeper, stronger.

An us who would never be separated because nothing could ever wedge us apart.

As we moved quicker, chasing pleasure and satisfaction, we didn't speak a word.

We kissed, we licked, we bit and groaned, but we didn't speak.

Speaking would ruin this.

Would ruin the rawness between us.

Because in that tent, we forgot we were human. We didn't communicate in letters and sentences, we communicated in the forgotten tongue amongst soulmates.

We sat in nothingness and made promises webbed from everything.

We re-married in the power of so much more than this world. We pledged and vowed in the eyes of the cosmos that recognised we weren't whole unless we were together.

It accepted our promise that we would wait.

We would be patient.

We would find each other again and be given the gift of ever after once we'd shed mortal shells and accepted that holding onto physical creation was never the answer.

That letting go was.

That threading yourself together with a cord that transcended time and space was the only way to be happy.

To be free.

Goosebumps scattered down my arms as our kisses and thrusts became tangled with the strings we'd just knotted, growing tighter and tighter, never to break apart.

And when we came together, our bliss was also silent. A mere echo of heartbeats as we shared mirroring, quaking pleasure.

It would forever be a regret that I wasn't able to have a daughter with Della. That no matter how many times we went to bed together, we never got pregnant again.

I would never know if it was the drugs that made me infertile or if the universe decided I'd had my happily ever after with my son.

Either way, I would be leaving soon, and Della would have to lean on Jacob.

A ten-year-old boy.

A twisted full circle of life.

I hadn't meant to hold on until Jacob's tenth birthday.

I'd meant to hold on until his twentieth, thirtieth, but ten?

It was almost too cruel.

I'd been his age when I'd first taken Della.

His age when my life changed, and I'd fought to keep us alive and happy.

And through all odds and obstacles, I'd done it.

A runty kid with an abusive past had somehow created a world anyone would envy.

I needed Della to see that—to trust our son wasn't just a kid but had a man inside him. He would be there for her, just like I'd been there for her. He would be brave, just like I'd been brave. He would cope, and together, they would survive.

Della's hands cupped my cheeks tenderly, kissing me in the dark.

I submitted to her, stroking her tongue with mine, tilting my head to deepen.

When my heart was once again skipping and kicking out of sync, she disengaged from me then fell to her side, waiting for me to spoon her.

I knew what would happen if I lay down.

I knew how bad the coughing would get.

My lungs were on borrowed time, and I had no intention of dying tonight.

Reclining just a little, I rolled her over until her head landed on my belly and her arm slung over my hips.

We stayed that way for an eternity. A sleeping bag thrown over us to stay warm, the night crickets and scurrying creatures our symphony.

And then, in the infinite dark, Della started to cry.

Her tears ran over my skin.

Her grief bathed me in salt.

I clutched her close, shuddering against helplessness, my own tears spilling over.

I hadn't fully let myself grieve.

I'd shared a tear or two but never let the torrent go.

But now, where no one could see me, with the dark blinding us, hiding us, I allowed the silent sobs to break me.

My sorrow only made Della's worse, and she cried harder.

I didn't try to comfort her.

I didn't seek comfort for myself.

This was a purging.

This was necessary.

This was goodbye.

We clung to each other as we spent every tear.

We didn't worry about clocks or dawns, only about trying to find peace to our pain.

And when my eyes dried and my heart settled, I stroked her hair softly. "I've loved you every second of my life."

Her body flinched against mine, her head burrowing into my belly. "Don't. Don't do this."

"You're the reason I've been blessed with so much."

"Stop, please stop."

"You've been more than just a wife to me; you've been my entire reason of existence."

"God...Ren." Her tears came fresh. Her hold bound tight.

I knew I was hurting her, but she had to know.

Had to hear me repeat all the things she already knew, so she'd understand that *none* of it would change. My love for her would go on and on. She had to accept that. Had to accept that my physical love was almost done, but my spiritual love would never end.

"Without you, I would've died many years ago, and for that, I want to thank you. Thank you for giving me you, Della. Thank you for giving me a son. Thank you for giving me *us*."

Her fingernails dug deep as if she could latch onto me forever.

"I love you." I coughed quietly. "But those words aren't enough. They don't do justice to how much I care."

A sob broke free. "I love you, Ren. I love you more than I can bear." Her nails turned to lips, kissing my stomach with desperation. "Please, you're still here. Don't talk as if you're not."

I ignored her, telling her a story like I used to when she was a little girl and couldn't sleep. "The moment you took your first breath in that monster's den, you stole mine and have held it in your palm ever since.

"On the days I'd see you with your mother, I'd curse you. On the evenings where I'd slink past, I'd study you. I was forever aware of you, wishing I could share your food, your innocence, your touch.

"My thoughts were that of a starving kid but now, as a man, I look back on those fuzzy childhood memories and wish I could live it all over again. I wish I could go back with the wisdom I have now and understand what you'd mean to me.

"I'd never get angry with you. Never yell or leave. I wish I could relive every touch, every smile, first word, and first kiss. I wish you could feel how grateful I was every time you kissed me, laughed with me, gave me the honour of calling you mine.

"I'm grateful, Della. For all of it.

"Without your selflessness and the unconditional way you made me fall for you, I doubt I'd be whole now. I wouldn't be able to lie here with you in my arms, knowing what is about to happen, and be calm enough to love you until that last fucking second."

"Stop." Her sobs drenched my naked skin, but I didn't stop.

I couldn't.

The story wasn't over.

"I know it wasn't easy for you, waiting until I opened my

eyes. Hiding the fact you were in love with me when I was so stupidly blind. But you need to know I was in love with you for far longer than I ever let on. I'd wanted you for years.

"You truly are my other half, Della." My voice broke, cracked, shattered. "And now...now I'm leaving you again. But this time, it's not by choice."

My arm latched her closer, smothering her against me. "It's not fair. I know I should say I'm okay with it, but, Ribbon...I'm fucking terrified." A cough exploded from my lips.

"Ren." Della crawled up my body, curling into me with her knees bent and face tucked in the crook of my shoulder, her tears loud in my ear.

I hugged her closer as my own tears came again, and honesty that I'd promised myself would stay trapped inside overflowed. "For the first time, you won't be there. I won't have you by my side. I don't want to go anywhere without you. I can't do it. I-I—" I coughed again, working myself up, causing my lungs to falter.

"Ren...stop."

"No, I-I have to get this out. I'm so sorry, Della. So eternally sorry that I'm leaving against our wishes. I wish I never got sick. I wish I could continue holding you—"

"I know. Me too."

"I don't want to leave you. I don't want to hurt you. I can't believe I have the audacity to complain about dying while you...you have the harder path. I never wanted to do this to you, Della. Never wanted to cause you so much pain."

"I know you didn't."

"And I'm sorry for being weak now. For ruining this even more."

"You're not—"

"You were my biggest joy, and now, you're my greatest sadness." I swiped my face free from tears, glowering at the blackness. "Fuck, I'm not being fair. I'm being so selfish. So cruel. I should tell you I'm not afraid. That I'm okay saying goodbye—"

A cough ripped my voice apart, tearing through the night.

It took a while before I could breathe well enough to continue. "I should accept that this is just life. But I *don't* accept it. I rage against it. Because fate's plan was *you*. You and me. *Together.* And now..."

I coughed again, shaking both of us.

"Shush, Ren. I know. I know more than you think." Her touch feathered over my wet cheeks, her hand shaking. "I'm just as angry as you. Just as twisted with hate at how unfair all of this is. I'm not ready to say goodbye, either." She kissed me, her sadness mixing with mine. "I never will be."

I held her close, kissing her violently, wanting to drink her soul and take her with me. "Without you, what am I? *Who* am I?" My teeth nipped at her lip. "Almost every memory I have, you're in. Almost every recollection, you're there. And I know I'm the same for you. Our lives are so entwined, there is no *before*. No time where we were separate. Therefore, there can be no ending. Right?"

I kissed her again and again. "We're tied together for life a- and we'll just have to hold onto that. This isn't the end. It can't be. It just can't."

Della nodded, kissing me as furiously as I kissed her. "I'm tied to you just as surely as you're tied to me, Ren Wild. We'll never lose each other. *Ever.*"

Our breathing was haggard as our foreheads pressed together, and Della climbed back onto my lap.

Somehow, I was hard even though I was distraught, and she slid me inside her, connecting us even while we said our goodbyes.

As we rocked together, I allowed myself to be spiteful. To speak the truth. To ease some of the burden I'd been carrying. "You'll have a lifetime without me. I'm fucking heartbroken that it won't be us anymore."

Her sobs came hard. "Me too."

"I'm jealous of your future, Little Ribbon."

"Don't be. I will always belong to you."

"I'm livid at my inability to stop this. I want to bargain with the devil for one more year. I'd sell my soul for just one more day with you."

"I'd sell mine, too."

We grinded against each other, roughly, meanly. My hands guided her hips, clamping her down harder, forcing her to take all of me.

Talking ceased as we fought each other and our grief.

My coughing mixed with our groans, and hands slapped over our mouths to stay silent and not wake Jacob.

Before, we'd made love.

Now, we fucked.

And it was messy, wet, and nasty.

It was our version of the war inside our hearts, the physical need to hurt each other when none of this was our fault.

Finally, when my thrusts went deep and Della came around me, and my body released the sick cocktail of rage and relief, we clung to each other, sweaty and sad, our tempers no longer as hot.

My lungs were in agony.

My heart no longer rhythmical but failing hour by hour.

Kissing her cheek, I breathed, "I need you to move on, Della. I want you to be happy. I need you to live even when I'm no longer here."

She shook her head. "No."

"Yes. Live for Jacob. Live for me."

"I can't."

"You can." Hugging her close, I promised, "You can. Because this isn't the end. We will never end because that isn't what true love is. True love is constant. It has no beginning, middle, or end. Life might end, but love…that's immortal."

"I love you so much, Ren."

"I know."

"I'll always be yours."

I nodded, accepting her vow even when I shouldn't. "I'll wait for you, Della. I'll watch you and Jacob…somehow."

"Promise me you'll always be near."

"I promise."

She kissed me sweet, a single word on her breath. "Good."

And I knew what I needed to say in return.

A phrase that meant so much.

Four little letters that held such history and hope.

Tangling my fingers in her hair, I touched my lips to hers.

And all I whispered was, "Fine."

# Chapter Sixty-Seven

## DELLA

## 2032

REN DIED ONE week after Jacob turned ten.

It was as if he'd been holding on until that special age.

Clinging to life to see his son turn the same age he'd been when he'd saved me.

The symbolism in that tore out my heart, injecting exquisite sorrow that I'd never overcome.

I'd been rescued from a life of murder and hell by a ten-year-old boy who'd fallen in love with me. And I'd been left in the hands of another ten-year-old boy who was just as destroyed as I was now that his father was gone.

The fifth and final incident.

The one I'd hoped so badly wouldn't come true.

My tears hadn't stopped since I'd woken in the night, six days ago, and knew.

I *knew*.

I couldn't explain it.

After we'd returned from Jacob's birthday in the forest, neither of us mentioned our goodbyes in the tented dark. We continued as normal, with Ren slowly fading, and his refusals about going to the hospital coming often.

Rick Mackenzie had taken to visiting us, instead of Ren going to him, and the last house call...we'd all known would be the final one.

He'd wanted Ren to be admitted. To be put on Fentanyl and a steady dose of whatever drugs could extend his final moments.

But Ren refused.

His life belonged to the land and sky, and his death wouldn't be spent in a building with concrete and glass.

I honoured that choice even if I hated watching him dim before me. How his body slowly gave up, piece by piece. How his energy levels diminished, breath by breath.

To start with, I trawled the internet for a last-minute miracle. I studied the use of goji berries and apricot kernels and every supposed super food out there.

But in the end, Ren stole my phone.

He turned off the internet, returning us to a world where it was just us and no one else, and we lived in our memories because that was all that was left.

The Wilsons visited often, all of us tasting what lingered in the air.

Liam and Chip and John shared a drink with Ren while they watched some nonsense on TV. Cassie and Nina curled up against him, saying their own goodbyes. And Jacob and me...we were his constant shadow. Part of him. Part of us. So damn aware that he'd be gone soon, and the house would be so empty without him.

And then six days ago, that terrible night arrived.

Ren coughed, but no more than often.

He had a fever, but not hotter than before.

We cleaned our teeth together, read a bit before turning out the light, and kissed each other goodnight like we did every evening.

A simple, domestic night.

The epitome of intimacy and marriage.

I lay beside him, listening to that god-awful wheeze—the wheeze that I hated for stealing what was mine.

And I kissed him again. And again. Never fully satisfied.

Finally, he drifted off with our hands touching and bodies moulded into one.

I had dreams about boys and backpacks and kisses.

Midnight ticked onward, creeping us into a new tomorrow.

But somewhere between two and three, while the moon seduced the stars, I woke up.

Something prickled my awareness.

Something triggered the trip line of my instincts.

I sat up in bed and looked around.

There was something there.

Something unseen.

My breath turned shaky as something cool rippled over my

skin.

And I knew.

Just *knew*.

Tears flowed before I even turned to Ren.

He lay on his back instead of propped up, but he wasn't coughing.

He looked more at peace than he had in years—no pain, no torment, no struggle.

Lying down, I pressed against his side, looped my arm around his waist, and hooked my leg over his.

He smiled in his sleep, his nose nuzzling my hair.

I squeezed him hard. So hard.

And then, the rattle and wheeze that had become so familiar hitched and halted.

And tears streamed unbidden down my face.

There was no time to call for help. No seconds to waste screaming for him to wake up or begging him to fight for just one more day.

He'd protected me.

Provided for me.

Given me everything he had to give.

And in that darkness between the hours of two and three, the boy who would forever hold my heart took his last breath.

His body was still beside me...but his spirit...

It'd gone.

And I'd felt him.

I'd woken to his kiss; I'd shivered in his goodbye.

Swallowing silent sobs, I laid a hand on his chest, begging for a heartbeat.

His skin was still warm.

But there was no heartbeat.

For a second, I was repulsed.

The animalistic part of me blaring with warning to stay away from the dead.

But this was Ren.

This was the other piece of my soul.

I was not afraid of him.

And so, I hugged my husband, telling him he was not alone.

And even though it ripped my heart apart, I told him to go and be happy.

To be free.

For the first time in my entire life, I was no longer part of a pair.

He'd gone to a place I could not go.

And as dawn crested and his skin grew steadily colder, life intruded on our bedroom tomb.

Jacob.

He'd be awake soon.

He couldn't see.

And so, I'd done what any mother would do.

I left my dead soulmate and climbed out of bed to lock the door. I picked up the phone and ordered an ambulance. I called Cassie and John and told them.

I dressed in a fugue and went to my son's bedroom to hold him, tell him, break him.

And we cried together.

God, we cried so much.

We cried when Ren was taken away.

We cried when he didn't come back.

We cried when two days passed, then three and four and five.

Without Cassie and John, my son and I would've starved that week.

It was nothing but a blur of black, perpetual despair.

Ren's body was cremated as per his wishes, the funeral already arranged, his Will and Testament activated seamlessly as everything was choreographed from the grave.

I didn't remember sleeping or eating or even living…just existing…just *surviving*.

I'd died with Ren, but on the outside, I still played my part.

I consoled our—*my*—son.

I held him close as he sobbed.

I whispered stories when he couldn't sleep.

I did my best to do what Ren would have done and that was to protect him from the pain.

But now…I couldn't protect him, because today, it was the last time we'd hold Ren in our arms.

The silver urn was heavy and gleamed in the sun.

The trees around us swaying and sad.

The funeral had been announced in the local paper, and I'd expected a quiet affair of the Wilsons and the doctor Ren had grown close to over the years.

I wasn't prepared for the entire town to attend.

Deep in the heart of the forest with no strict address or location, teachers and parents, friends and policemen had all gathered to say farewell.

There were no chairs or service.

No priest or hymns.

Just me holding Ren's ashes.

Standing at the altar of his church.

I didn't think I could speak.

I knew I couldn't do Ren justice, but as Jacob came to stand beside me, a breeze whisked through the trees, kicking up leaves in a wind-devil.

And once again that prickle, that *knowledge* overwhelmed me, and the tears that were in constant supply erupted.

I cried in front of strangers.

I sobbed in front of family.

And when I'd finished hugging Ren for the last time, I stood taller, braver, older, and opened the single printed page from the manuscript I'd been writing on and off for years. When Ren had bought me a new laptop, and I'd tasted the first signs of him leaving me, I'd turned to the salvation of the keys.

I'd done my best to write all the happy moments and try to forget the sad.

I focused on our fairy-tale, never knowing the words I'd chosen for my prologue would be part of the eulogy at Ren's goodbye.

He was forty-two and gone.

A life cut far too short.

Jacob nudged me, holding out his arms for his father. "I'll hold him, Mom. While you—" Tears strangled his boyish voice, but beneath the childhood pitch lurked the rasp of a man.

He'd aged overnight, and I finally understood why it was so important to Ren to never treat him as a kid. To forever nurture that wisdom that was already ingrained in his soul.

Ren needed Jacob to accept his place before he was no longer there to guide him, giving him knives and truths and chores normally withheld for a more mature age.

And he'd known he could handle it.

Because he'd handled it himself.

My vision blurred with yet more tears as I ducked to Jacob's height and held out my arms. Without a word, I transferred my loved one into his son's arms and brushed the skirts of my simple black dress.

Today, I wore no ribbon.

No usual flair of blue.

Today, that ribbon fluttered around the lid of the silver urn, hugging Ren one last time.

Jacob squeezed the urn, pressing his cheek to the coolness, breaking my heart all over again. "I love you, Dad. No matter that you're just ash now."

A sob grabbled with my voice as I forced myself to turn from the touching, breaking moment and face the tear-streaked members of our town.

John cried silently. Cassie hugged Nina while Chip hugged her. Liam hugged his wife and son while Adam and his family hovered close by. Behind them, the town stood poised and waiting for whatever words I could deliver that might stop the pain.

But I didn't have that power. No one did.

And even if such a magic existed, I wouldn't want it.

I wouldn't want my smarting, bleeding grief to be erased because that was the price of love, and I'd loved dearly.

Reading from my printed page, even though the words were typed on my heart, I took lines from the prologue and shared them, all while keeping others just for me.

*"First, I want to say thank you. Thank you for falling in love with Ren just as much as me. Thank you for understanding that love spans decades, infects souls, and turns you immortal because, when you love that deeply, nothing can ever die."*

I looked up, meeting the eyes of John.

He nodded, biting his trembling lip, his mind awash with Patricia and Ren.

I spoke for me and for everyone with lost loved ones.

I hoped they'd see what Ren and I had seen…that love truly was mystical and miraculous.

My voice threaded tears with truth.

*"Love transcends time, space, distance, universes.*

*"Love can't be confined to pages or photos or memories—it's forever alive and wild and free. Romance comes and goes, lust flickers and smoulders, trials appear and test, life gets in the way and educates, pain can derail happiness, joy can delete sadness, togetherness is more than just a fairy-tale…it's a choice.*

*"A choice to love and cherish and honour and trust and adore.*

*"A choice to choose love, all the while knowing it has the power to break you.*

*"A choice, dear friends, to give someone your entire heart.*

*"But in the end, love is what life is about.*
*"And love is the purpose of everything."*

John broke from the ranks, striding in leaf-crunching boots to bear hug me. Cassie joined him, her subtle perfume clouding around us.

"We're here. You and Jakey are not alone." John let me go, blowing his nose on a handkerchief.

"I love you, Della." Cassie kissed my cheek and squeezed my arm before guiding her father back to their places.

With their kind support, I stood braver in the face of heartbreak and tucked my page away.

I smiled at the crowd, wobbly and watery. "Ren died knowing how loved he was. And we're still here, knowing he'll always love us in return. Some might say our romance is over. That his death ruins our story. And I'd agree, but only because romance can be killed, but love...it can't. It lives on, and I'm patient enough to wait for our happily ever after."

Townsfolk nodded, some sharing looks, others glassy-eyed with their own memories.

But I'd said what I needed to.

I'd done what was expected for a grieving widow to honour her dead lover.

Now, we had something else much more important to do.

Turning to Jacob, I held out my hand. "Ready?"

He hugged the silver urn tighter. "No."

I kissed his soft hair. "He'll always love you, Jacob."

"I don't want to say goodbye."

"But we're not."

"I don't want to let him go."

Bending closer, I whispered, "We're not letting him go. We're setting him free. The wind will guide him to visit us; the forest will keep him safe. He'll be all around us, Wild One."

His face shone with tears. "But who will I talk to?" He stroked the urn. "At least he's still here."

A tear rolled down my cheek. "He's not in there, Jacob. His spirit is already listening. He hears you when you talk to him, even without his ashes."

"You sure?" He hiccupped. "Promise?"

I opened my arms.

Jacob launched into them, wedging the urn between us. "I promise. He's watching us right now, and he'd want us to be brave, okay?"

Pulling back, he wiped his cheeks with his black-suited forearm. "Okay. I'll be brave. For him."

Standing, I didn't look back at the crowd, merely waited for my son to take my hand.

When he did, we moved farther away, deeper into the green-shrouded forest.

Once we found a perfect sun-lit spot, we stopped.

"Ready?"

"'kay."

Together, with shaking hands and slippery grip, we unscrewed the lid.

Another flute of a breeze found its way through the boughs and leaves to lick around us.

My skin prickled. My heart answered. I felt him near.

*I love you, Ren.*

As we started to tip, I whispered, "Don't say farewell, Wild One. Don't say the words goodbye because it isn't. If you must say something, say I love you. Because he'll hear it and know he's not forgotten."

"I'll never forget him," Jacob vowed.

"Neither will I."

Together, we tipped the silver jar and let my husband and his father free.

The grey of Ren's mortal body swirled and clouded, giving wings to his immortal soul, becoming one with the trees and skies he loved so much.

Even though I knew this wasn't goodbye.

Even though I knew I'd see him again, it was the hardest thing I'd ever done to watch him vanish before us.

The faraway murmur of people leaving hinted we should probably head back, but Jacob stalked toward a tree, holding the Swiss Army knife Ren had given him.

Studiously, firmly, he scratched something into the bark, stabbing and carving.

I let him.

I didn't try to stop him or interfere.

And once he'd finished and his face was once again wet with tears, I moved closer to see what he'd done.

And just like the father had wounded me, so did the son.

My heart was no longer intact but a lake of mourning.

"Do you like it, Mom?" He sniffed back sadness.

I shook my head as my fingers traced the wonky lines of Ren's tattoo.

A swirl of ribbon with the initials J and D with an extra kick in its tail with an R.

All three of us.

Always together as the tree grew higher and our family soared closer toward the heavens.

"I don't like it. I love it."

A small smile tilted his lips. "Good."

My eyes shot wide as I spun to study him. The phrase Ren and I had used. The one word that meant so much.

I had to finish it.

To acknowledge that there would always be so much of Ren in this child. That every day he would surprise me, remind me, heal and hurt me.

On a shaky breath, I said, "Fine."

And together, we walked out of the forest, toward the house Ren and I had built together, and crossed the threshold alone.

Ren wasn't in the fields, or on the tractor, or in the barn.

He wasn't in the forest, or baling hay, or dozing in the meadow.

He was gone...*gone*.

And I had to put one foot in front of the other and accept it.

But I also accepted that this new reality was only temporary.

Life had so many paths and different journeys, but eventually, we all ended up in the same place.

I'd been lucky to share my life with Ren.

I was still lucky to share the rest of it with Jacob.

I wouldn't give up, even on the blackest of days.

I wouldn't stop living, even on the saddest of moments.

I would keep trying, learning, surviving, because I owed Ren that.

I owed him my life.

Jacob grabbed my hand, bringing me back from my thoughts and into our living room where we stood.

"You okay?" his innocent voice asked.

I smiled sadly. "Are you?"

"Not yet." He sniffed. "But we will be...right?"

His dark eyes, so similar to Ren's, blazed for an answer—a promise of healing.

Ducking to my knee, I hugged him tight, pressing his lanky body into mine, asking for healing for both of us. He kneeled with me, and I kissed his hair, inhaling deep, smelling the scents of my son mixed with the smells of my husband. A familiar wild intoxication that no soap or time could steal.

Hay and hope and happiness.

"We'll be okay, Wild One. I promise."

And we would be.

Because there was no expiration on love.

Ren was still mine.

Forever.

* * * * *

That night, I went to bed in sheets I hadn't washed and still smelled of Ren.

I crawled from my side into the middle and grabbed his pillow for mine.

And there, hidden beneath the place where Ren rested his head—glaring up as if impatient for me to find it—was a gift from beyond.

With air trapped in my lungs, I sat up and snatched it from where it had been hiding. My fingers shook as I unwrapped the blue paper, revealing something that made tears explode in a flurry.

A new ribbon wheel.

Full to the brim of cobalt satin, tucked in place with a pin.

The cardboard was pristine and untouched, ready to cut off lengths of ribbon to replace the faded old.

I stroked the wheel, feeling Ren all around me as a note fell from the package.

A note that would break me all over again.

Biting my lip to stem my sobs, I unfolded it and read.

*Dear Della Ribbon,*
*I miss you already.*
*I miss your voice and touch and kisses.*
*But please, don't miss me.*
*Because I'm right there beside you. I feel your sadness. I hear your tears.*
*I know it will take time, but eventually, I need you to be happy because I'm always there.*
*When you cut off a piece of this ribbon, my hand is enveloping yours.*
*When you replace old with new, my fingers are on yours tying it in your hair.*
*Everything you do, I'm there with you.*
*And hopefully, this cardboard wheel will last until you come find me.*
*And there, I'll be able to touch you once more.*

*Until that day.*
*I love you.*
*Forever and ever.*
*For always.*
*Ren.*

# *Epilogue*

# DELLA

# 2033

ANNIVERSARIES CAME IN so many different forms.
Happy and hard and horribly sad.
Today was an anniversary.
The day I lost the air in my lungs and the life in my heart.
The day I lost my Ren.
Three-hundred-and-sixty-five days without him.
Three-hundred-and-sixty-five days of soul-deep sorrow.
But I wasn't a girl left behind with the luxury of grief. I was
mother to the best son in the world, and for him, I woke in the
morning even when the darkness was acute. I kept living even
while my sadness was constant. I helped Cassie with her horse
business. I rode often for mental and spiritual health. I learned
how to run our acreage and hire help when required.
And John was true to his vow to Ren, always there for me
when the loneliness of missing a soulmate became too much.
Life had been gentle even after being so cruel.
And through it all, I had a contract with love.
A contract I did my best to uphold.
I never dared pity myself or begrudge my grief.
I was never angry that I'd loved the best man in the world
and lost him.
Ren had given me his legacy, and together, me and Jacob
would be okay.
Every day, I spoke to Ren as if he were there beside me.
He was in the sun, the sky, the meadow, the forest.
He was in everything. Waiting. Loving. Watching. And I lived

every day for him because I knew a time would come when we would find each other again, and I'd have the honour of regaling a lifetime of tales.

I accepted each new sunrise without Ren. I endured each new sunset without Ren.

I chose to continue because that was what he wanted and that was what I owed.

After a lifetime of sacrifice, it was now my turn.

My turn to keep moving, keep fighting, keep living.

And I did.

I accepted I'd had my epic love story.

I was one of the lucky ones.

And I didn't want another.

My heart was Ren's—no matter where he was—and it would stay his until we met again.

At least, my family understood that.

No one dared murmur I would get over him.

No one dared encourage me to put my past behind me and open my heart for another.

No one dared because they knew the truth.

The truth that a love like Ren and I had…it was once in a lifetime.

And it wasn't over yet.

The five stages of grief didn't matter.

There were no five stages for me.

And I didn't want there to be.

I didn't want the wound to heal because I never wanted to be anything less than Ren's. I still touched him in my dreams, kissed him in my thoughts, and accepted that I might endure in a world without him, but I *would* see him again.

I knew that.

And I could be patient.

"Mom!" Jacob's voice rang through the sun-dappled house. *"Moomm!"*

"What is it?" I pressed a hand to my forehead, pushing aside my melancholy thoughts, tucking them into the pocket of my heart where yearning was a regular friend.

"Package for you. Need you to sign!"

Abandoning my laundry folding, I cut through the living room to the front door where a deliveryman stood on the veranda and held out an e-tablet. "You Mrs Wild?"

I'd long stopped scolding myself at the sharp intake of breath whenever anyone called me that. I both loved and despised that name. "Yes. I am."

"Sign here, please."

I took his tablet, scribbled on the scratched screen, and passed it back to him. "What is it?"

"Dunno, but it's heavy. Need help carting it inside?" He raised an eyebrow beneath his red cap.

Jacob ducked to his haunches, testing the large box. "She doesn't need help. She has me."

I chuckled under my breath, running my fingertips over his dirty-blond head as he stood and huffed. "Ugh, it's too heavy."

"We'll do it together," I said.

"Leave you guys to it." The delivery guy tapped his cap in farewell and bounded off the veranda. My eyes tracked him as the sun glinted off the windscreen of his van, obscuring him just enough to show a tall man running through the garden, giving me a millisecond fantasy that it was Ren.

Tears welled.

Pain manifested.

And I closed the door on the illusion.

"Wait. The package." Jacob rolled his dark chocolate eyes at me, so much like Ren's I sometimes forgot he was part of me and merely saw the boy who'd saved my life.

In a way, he *had* saved my life...just like his father.

Without him, I wouldn't have continued trying.

Ren had saved me when I was a baby.

And his son had saved me when I was a woman.

Two boys of ten years old.

Two boys of my heart.

Charging toward the kitchen, he came skidding back with a pair of scissors.

My hands clamped on my hips. "What have I told you, Jacob Wild? No running with sharp implements." Just like his father, he always had a knife on his person for slicing through ropes and other farm necessities. I was surprised he'd chosen scissors instead of the Swiss Army blade in his pocket.

The blade I was constantly fishing out before washing.

"Yeah, yeah." He rolled his eyes again before falling to his knees and cutting the tape on the box.

Uncle John sometimes did this—delivered boxes of goodies from things he'd ordered online for Jacob and me.

Care packages, I called them.

Love reminders, he called them.

Either way, this wasn't one of those as Jacob tore out brown paper packaging and yanked out a book nestled with countless other books.

A book that my eyes skimmed, discarded, then shot back to with a cry.

A book that took the strength in my legs and crashed me to the floor.

"I-I don't understand." Tears streamed down my face, obscuring the blue cover with a lonely boy walking in a blizzard. A boy almost hidden by the title and wrapped up in a blue satin ribbon.

"*The Boy and His Ribbon by Della and Ren Wild*," Jacob muttered, reading eloquently and smoothly. His eyes flashed to mine. "Mom? Did you and Dad write this?"

My head shook blindly as I held out my hand.

Hardback.

Freshly printed.

Heavy as a gravestone.

It tingled in my hands, warm and alive and filled with ghosts. *What has he done?*

"Mom?" Jacob asked again, but for once, I couldn't put him first. I couldn't assure him. I couldn't push aside my own selfish pain. Jacob missed his father as much as I did...but he'd had Ren for ten years. I'd had him for thirty-two.

In this...my heart was cruel.

Standing on shaking legs, I couldn't tear my eyes off the cover, desperate to open it, petrified to read it.

"I...I'm going for a walk, Wild One. Okay?" My voice broke and patched together, thicker and rougher than before. "I...I won't go far."

"Mom?" His voice rose with worry. "Are you all right?"

"I'm fine." I drifted forward as if my legs were no longer made of sinew and bone but air and storm cloud. "I-I'm fine." I repeated, desperate to believe it.

I left my son.

I was a bad mother.

I abandoned my role and slipped back into a girl who missed her boy with every frisson of her soul.

I didn't know how long I walked, but finally, when the shadow strings of willow leaves enveloped me and the grotto where so many things had happened whispered it would keep me safe, I sank to the earth and opened the book.

The first page was copyright jargon.

The second, print information.

The third, the title.

The fourth... the dedication.

*For Della and Jacob.*

I keeled over, rocking the book to my chest, sobs wrenched from my very toes.

*No.*

I hadn't cried this badly... well, since the funeral.

I never let myself go.

Never could.

Never allowed.

I had to be strong for Jacob.

But that strength was now shattered and in pieces on the ground.

Four simple words.

Four words that broke me.

They *broke* me.

Ren.

His voice danced on the breeze as if he'd never gone. His wild scent of smoke and freedom swirled in my lungs. And the gentle, delicious pressure of his hand on my cheek forced me to look down at the pages, tear smudged and turning translucent.

*Read*, the breeze murmured.

*Listen*, the willow whispered.

*Heal*, the forest begged.

With another sob, I flipped the page.

A letter to the reader.

A letter from beyond.

*Dear Reader,*
*First, let me explain the nature of this book before I can explain it to my wife.*
*Once upon a time, a wonderful girl fell in love with an unworthy boy, and she decided to write their tale.*
*Her tale opened that stupid boy's eyes.*
*It made true love leap over rules and boundaries.*
*It survived years wrapped in plastic and protected at all costs in a well-travelled backpack.*
*It was the best tale the boy had ever read.*

*But it was also missing something.*
*It was missing the side of the story from the boy who fell in love with the girl,*
*but he wasn't as eloquent as she.*
*So he had to improvise.*
*He enlisted the help of a ghost writer to turn messy dictated thoughts into*
*words worthy of being beside hers, and he didn't have a lot of time to do it.*
*It was my hardest secret.*
*And even now, I'm unsure I did the right thing.*
*But it's too late to change my mind. Too late to approve or deny the finished*
*copy.*
*I just have to hope our story is enjoyed.*
*And I have to trust that every word I chose proves the same thing her words*
*do.*
*That I loved her.*
*Painfully so.*

The words danced and bounced as my hands shook and shook.

Sobs and heaving quakes took hold of me as I turned the page and found yet another letter.

I wasn't ready.

I wasn't prepared.

I would never be ready to say goodbye because that was what this was.

A goodbye.

A final farewell organised in secrecy.

*My Dear Beloved Ribbon,*
*I hope you can forgive me for taking our privacy and making it public.*
*I hope you can understand why I had to do it and why it had to be this way.*
*And I hope you can still love me for not being there to hold you.*
*For not being able to stop the pain.*
*This wasn't an easy thing to do—I almost stopped countless times.*
*But after years of watching over your shoulder as you typed, reading the*
*paragraphs you chose, and feeling the love you had for me, it was finally my*
*turn.*
*My turn to write you a love story.*
*And, God, what a love story it is.*
*You were the air I breathed and the life in my heart, Della.*
*You are the sole reason I existed and always will be.*
*Without you, I would never have been a father, brother, or husband.*
*Without you, I would never have known exquisite joy and utter heartbreak.*

*Without you, I would have been nothing.*
*And because of you...I am something.*
*I am loved.*
*I am missed.*
*I am wanted.*
*I was sold to the McClary's for one purpose and one purpose only.*
*To find you.*
*And I'll find you again...soon.*
*This isn't the end...we both know that.*
*I'll be waiting...somewhere.*
*I'll be watching...somehow.*
*And when the time comes for you to join me, I'll gather you in my arms and hold you tight.*
*Come find me.*
*Come find me on the meadow where the sun always shines, the river always flows, and the forest always welcomes.*
*Come find me, Little Ribbon, and there we'll live for eternity.*
*And now, because I can't stand to leave this tale so unfinished, please read the end.*
*The end I wrote for you.*
*Until we meet again...*
*I love you.*

I closed the book.

Unable to read more.

Not prepared to endure more pain.

One day, I would read it.

But not today.

Today, I needed to grieve...*truly* grieve.

To weep and wail and admit that there would always be a piece of me forever broken. A piece of me that would always be lost until my dying breath delivered me back to my loved one.

But even in my grief, I had responsibilities. I had a son who missed his father, and I had a world that needed to continue.

So, as I clawed my way to my feet, hugged Ren's book to my chest, and stepped from the willow's comforting fronds, I made a promise to keep going.

To do what Ren had said.

To let go...if only for a second.

My eyes fell on Jacob.

He sat in the middle of the hay field, golden all around him, gold sun above him, gold future ahead of him, and my heart did what it hadn't been able to do. What I never believed I was capable of.

It healed…just a little.

It accepted…just a little.

Our love story wasn't over.

It was just…paused.

With my white dress fluttering around my legs, I strode into the sunlight, carrying truth and heartache and everlasting love.

I was lucky.

Eternally lucky to have loved and cherished and adored.

And when that day came when this life was over, I would find that love again.

I would go home to him.

Because our story had never been about a fleeting romance or fairy-tale. It had always been about life.

It was about love.

It was about the journey from nothing to something.

The travels from individual to pair.

The adventure from empty to whole.

And that was what transformed mortal into magic.

It was what songs were made of.

What hearts were formed of.

What humans were born to become.

The sun shone brighter, drenching buttery light everywhere it touched.

The paddock was almost ready for baling.

The land providing routine and clockwork timing.

And as my son looked up from feeling my eyes upon him, he waved just like Ren used to. His hand switched into a come-hither, and I went.

I held my head tall. I let my tears fall. I allowed myself the freedom to love in all its painful, exquisite heartache.

And when I reached him, I sat in the wildflowers and hugged him.

He hugged me back, fiercely, healingly. "Did you read the end like he said?"

I shook my head. "I can't."

"You should." He kissed my cheek as we pulled apart, so wise, so brave, so pure. "If he told you to, you should."

I laughed gently. "Just like I did everything he told me, huh?"

"Yep." He smirked, growing serious again. "There's a whole box of books there. You should at least read one of them."

"Maybe."

"But what if it's good?"

"Then it will be good when I'm ready."

"But what if it makes you happy?"

I swallowed another wash of tears. "*You* make me happy. I don't need anything else."

He looked down, running his small hand through the blades of grass. "I miss him."

"Yeah, me too."

He picked a purple flower and held it to me. "Would you read me the story? If Dad wrote it, and you haven't read it either, it's kinda like him coming back, right?"

My chest squeezed as I took his gift and twirled the pretty petals. "Just because there are pages with his words on them doesn't mean he's alive, Wild One."

"I know. But..." He looked up earnest and imploring and hopeful. "I think he would want you to read it."

"I know."

"Can I read it?"

"Not until I know what he's written." I tapped his nose, so similar to mine. "Not sure if it's suitable for eleven-year-old nosy parkers."

He grinned. "I think he'd let me read it."

"I think you're getting too bossy."

"I think you're afraid."

I sucked in a breath, jerking back a little.

He noticed, crawling closer and hugging me tight. "I'm sorry, Mom."

It took a moment for me to swallow my sobs. "You're right, Jacob. I *am* afraid."

We sat huddled together for a while, letting the sun warm us even when the hollowness in my heart was always cold.

Finally, Jacob pulled away. "Read it, 'kay? Don't leave him in the box."

A tear escaped. "Okay."

"You will?"

"I will. I'll be brave. I owe him that much."

He nodded. "Yep and then you can read it to me."

I smiled, doing my best not to let my mind run away with questions. What had Ren done? What ending had he written? "We'll see."

Standing, I took his hand in mine and headed toward the

house.

Jacob squeezed my fingers with yet another question. "Even though he's gone...he would want us to be happy, right, Mom?"

I nodded. "Yes."

"Do you think he's watching us right now?"

"Undoubtedly."

"Do you think he's happy watching us?"

I pictured Ren somewhere free in the forest, peering through leaves and fantasy to protect us from afar. "Yes, I do."

"Well, that settles it then." His hand slipped from mine as he ran toward the house shouting, "Read it tonight. And maybe you'll be happy, too."

# *Epilogue Cont*

## DELLA

## 2033

THAT NIGHT, ONCE I'd cooked for Jacob and we'd watched some movie of his choosing, I curled up in bed and reached for the book.

I didn't want to.

I wasn't ready.

But I'd made a promise to my son, and I couldn't let my husband down.

The thought of Ren's voice locked in a cardboard box, ready to share his secrets, prepared to shed light on shared circumstances was too sad to refuse.

It would be the hardest thing I'd done since scattering his ashes, but I owed him this.

I owed him my strength to listen.

Tears fell again as I cracked open the pages and re-read Ren's letters.

I cried.

And cried.

And when my tears finally slowed, I sucked in a wobbly breath, gathered my courage, and pushed the heavy, sweet-smelling papers to the end.

One day, I would read the entire thing.

I would break my heart all over again all while being privileged enough to read the innermost thoughts of my husband. But for now, this book would sleep on his pillow beside me, something to hug when it all got too painful, something to stroke when I whispered to him in the dark.

One day, I would be ready.

But not today.

Today, I was barely clinging to sanity, shoved into the awkward admittance of wishing time away so I could find Ren sooner, all while begging the minutes to slow so I could have longer with Jacob.

Ren was a natural storyteller—his skills honed from years of telling me bedtime tales and indulging my every whim.

And tonight, just like old times, he was about to tell me a story.

*Our* story.

The only one I ever cared about.

The pages fell to the final chapter and I stroked the letters as I breathed, "Chapter Fifty-Nine. Ren, 2018."

My mind skipped back to that time.

A time when emotions were daggers and youth diesel on the fiery burn of desire. Everything was sharper then, more urgent then, more desperate.

Countless memories unravelled, reminding me of what I'd done.

How I'd been so hurt I'd lost my virginity to another.

How I'd been so tangled in my unrequited agony that I'd broken Ren and myself.

Only...as my eyes skimmed Ren's side of the tale, learning how much he loved me, how distraught he was as he left me that note and walked out the door, a strange smile twisted my tear-glossed lips.

The book didn't end there.

It didn't stop in a standalone of tragedy but led into a heart-happy duet.

And I understood what my brilliant husband had done.

And I was braver.

And I was thankful.

And my fractured heart glued a tiny piece back into place.

My fingers itched for my keyboard to finish the magic he'd begun.

A final letter was waiting for me.

*This is where you come in, Della Ribbon.*
*You'll get another box soon.*
*A box of chapters from the moment I admitted I was in love with you and*
*kissed you for the first time to the second we got married, held our son, and*

*grew as a family.*
*I've been honest. I've shared everything.*
*Now, it's your turn.*
*Finish our story, Della.*
*But this one, blend fact with a tiny piece of fiction.*
*Call the book* The Girl and Her Ren—*because that is what I am.*
*I am yours.*
*But fashion our story where we found that miracle.*
*A story where I was healed, grew old, and lived.*
*And at the end, insert this final paragraph:*

**"And there, as the sun set on the summer meadow, Della Ribbon turned to her Ren, and said, 'I'm pregnant with your daughter. I suppose you get to choose a girl's name now.' Her husband turned to her, happy, overjoyed, madly in love and kissed her.**
**They kissed for days because they knew no time could stop them.**
**And when they broke apart, he said, "I love you, Della, forever and for always."**
**And they had that daughter.**
**They had a family.**
**They were forever bound through marriage and true love. Together."**

*And then, if our story is ever made into a film, the credits will roll.*
*And the music will play.*
*And the audience will know...*
*That Della Ribbon and her Ren lived*
*happily*
*ever*
*after.*

*The End*

Thank you for trusting me and coming on this journey.
I hope you enjoyed Ren and Della's tale...despite the pain.

# Note to the Reader

**WHY DID YOU KILL OFF THE MAIN HERO?**

Ever since the moment Ren and Della popped into my head, I knew how it would end. Ren was rather adamant that his tale would be based firmly in reality. And, unfortunately, reality isn't kind.

It was honestly the hardest thing I've ever had to write. On a daily basis, I worried if I was doing the right thing. I'd wake up with panic attacks wondering if I'd upset my readers. And if it would be career suicide to do such an ending. But, each time I tried to prevent Ren from dying, he'd just throw it back in my face, and I knew I had to be **BRAVE**. That I had to accept this book wouldn't be for everyone. And hope that, despite its bittersweet ending, the story of Ren and Della Wild would find the audience it's meant to find.

I hope, regardless of the tears, you were able to see the story for what it was.

Brutal, heart-breaking, but somehow uplifting, knowing love never dies.

I'm extremely grateful you read to this point and accepted that this story is firmly based in *life*. We all have different versions of happily ever after. Some last for ever, some last for a while, and some don't last at all. But in the end, true love carries on and I am a *firm* believer that once bound together, we will find each other again. Either through reincarnation, heaven, or some other divine intervention.

**WHY DIDN'T REN AND DELLA HAVE ANY MORE CHILDREN?**

The Ribbon Duet is the first story I've told where I've taken no liberties or added some 'slightly fantastical' element that perhaps wouldn't happen in real life. I didn't want to do that with this. I needed it to be fully realistic, and the reality is, by the time Della had Jacob, Ren was severely ill again, and then submitted to an extensive course of Chemo. I didn't feel it would be realistic for him to be able to make her pregnant a second time.

Obviously, miracles happen, but he'd already been given a miracle by far outlasting the usual prognosis for his disease.

### WHY ARE THERE ENGLISH PHRASES & SPELLING IN A BOOK BASED IN THE USA?

First, I am fully aware that there is English Spelling and English Terminology in this book (because I'm English and also live in an English spelling country). It wasn't a typo or laziness on my part. I wrote it that way because those are the phrases I use and with *The Boy & His Ribbon* and *The Girl & Her Ren*, I turned off all thoughts and just WROTE.

Once the stories were on paper, I went over and changed all the spelling to US, started to remove phrases and words that aren't common in the USA and began 'Americanising it.'

However, a friend suggested that instead of trying to set it in America, why not leave it as a story that is transient of time and place. Not once did I ever mention a town name or city or country. Partly because Ren himself wouldn't know or care as child, but also because I wanted the reader to place Ren and Della wherever they were or even imagine a fictional world of their choosing.

It could be set in Canada, England, Scotland, USA or New Zealand. It could fit anywhere and I liked that.

However, the amazing Will Watt and Hayden Bishop (fully within their creative license) decided—when they started narration for *The Boy & His Ribbon*—that the characters could possibly be from South USA and gave them accents to match. As we hadn't discussed my concept of it being a very 'country neutral' book, once I heard the audio, I realised I'd have to explain why there are some English Phrases spoken in an American accent.

As the Audio was already recorded for *The Boy & His Ribbon*, it's not possible to go back and edit certain English colloquialisms without disrupting the Whispersync capability.

So, I decided to leave *The Girl & Her Ren* in the same manner so the 'voice' doesn't sound different.

I hope you can excuse the blend of two worlds and enjoy the story regardless.

### WHAT RESEARCH DID YOU DO FOR THIS STORY?

A lot on Asbestos related illnesses and forced child labour.

For anyone dealing with mesothelioma or know someone who is, I did my best to research and include realistic treatment options and terminology. As all things, there is only so much information available and I apologise if I incorrectly quoted facts.

A few links that were used are:

https://www.asbestos.com/cancer/
https://www.asbestos.com/treatment/
https://www.pleuralmesothelioma.com/cancer/progno
sis/
https://www.keytruda.com/
https://www.rxwiki.com/keytruda

Ren's purchase to work a farm isn't that far-fetched and there have been many documented issues of child labour around the globe, in both first world and third world countries.

These are just a few:

http://www.fao.org/childlabouragriculture/en/
https://www.hrw.org/news/2011/11/17/child-
farmworkers-united-states-worst-form-child-labor
https://www.huffingtonpost.ca/craig-and-marc-
kielburger/child-labour-is-canadas-i_b_1087892.html

# Upcoming Books

The Body Painter
The Argument

**For more up to date announcements and releases please
visit:**
www.pepperwinters.com

# *Playlist*

John Legend – Love Me Now
Selena Gomez & Marshmello – Wolves
Pink – What About Us
Selena Gomez - Back To You
Imagine Dragons - Nothing Left To Say
Imagine Dragons - Not Today
All of the Stars - Ed Sheeran
Charlie Puth - Kiss Me
Lana Del Rey – I still love him
Nothing Like Us - Justin Beiber
Calum Scott - If Our Love Is Wrong
Tom Odell - Grow Old with Me
I Found You - Kina Grannis & Imaginary Future
Calum Scott, Leona Lewis - You Are The Reason
Behind Blue Eyes – Limp Bizkit
Photograph – Ed Sheeran

# Acknowledgements

*The Boy & His Ribbon* was the easiest book I've ever written. *The Girl & Her Ren* was the hardest.

As mentioned in the 'Note to the Reader,' I always knew Ren's fate the moment he popped into my head and first told me his story, but it didn't mean I was comfortable with it, or brave enough to go through with it.

Almost daily, I'd message beta readers asking if I was doing the right thing. And every night, I'd wake in a panic wondering how this duet would be received.

However, I had no choice to do the ending Ren intended.

This was never a romance.

It was a life story, and with life comes death—just like Della said.

Saying that, I leaned on beta readers very heavily in this book. I think I wrote close to 210,000 words and ended up deleting 55,000 of them.

Entire scenes were axed. Entire plot points erased. It wasn't easy, but I hope it's made a better book for being ruthless.

I want to thank my husband for allowing me to sit on my butt for twelve hours a day to finish this—it's been two months of relying on him to feed the horses, cook, and clean. He's a rock star.

I want to thank Heather Pollock for being invaluable with her advice and being online at all hours of the day to read chapters and keep me from jumping off the cliff.

I want to thank Melissa Crump for being so diligent, kind, and helpful and incredibly fast in her feedback.

I want to think Tamicka Birch for giving me her honest opinion when I ruined the book and told her the ending and made her read the epilogue first.

I want to thank Melissa Staley, Vickie Leaf, Rochelle Kroesen, Yaya, Julie Lis, Heather Peiffer, Nicole Hartney, and Chanpreet Singh for their invaluable, kind critique.

I want to thank Jenny Sims and Tiffany Landers for their editing / proofreading, and for turning it around so fast.

I want to thank Will Watt and Hayden Bishop for narrating such excellent audio and making me fall in love with my characters even more.

I want to thank Nina Grinstead and the girls at Social Butterfly for helping with promo.

And finally, but most importantly, I want to thank you, the reader, for allowing me to hurt you with this story.

I hope you enjoyed it, despite the pain.

Xx00xx
*Pepper*